DISTRICT OF COLUMBIA

DISTRICT OF COLUMBIA

JEFFERSON FLANDERS

Munroe Hill Press
Lexington, Massachusetts

Cover design by Mick Wieland Design

ISBN-13: 978-0-9908675-5-5
eBook ISBN: 978-0-9908675-7-9

Munroe Hill Press
Lexington, Massachusetts

In memory of those who walked point...

"When power leads man towards arrogance, poetry reminds him of his limitations. When power narrows the areas of man's concern, poetry reminds him of the richness and diversity of his existence. When power corrupts, poetry cleanses..."

– John F. Kennedy, speech at Amherst College honoring Robert Frost, October, 1963

PART ONE

PROLOGUE

Washington, D.C.
November 1966

He stands alone, resolute and determined, at the edge of the roof.

The sun has almost set, and the lights of the city are coming on in the buildings around him. To his right, he can see the illuminated dome of the Capitol. In the near distance, he catches a glimpse of the Potomac, a glimmer in the growing dark.

A Chrysler sedan drives slowly up the street four stories below, its headlights illuminating its route. After it has passed, the street remains empty.

Knox remembers the first time he jumped off the north cliff of the Quarry, just after turning twelve years old, in response to the challenge of older friends. He had looked down at the gray-green water, the May sun shimmering on its placid surface, and then up at the sky, the wisps of clouds against an electric blue, a hawk circling above, serenely. The Lawrence twins, already treading water after their jumps, hooted and yelled at him to join them below. He backed up, giving himself some room, feeling the sun on his back and fighting his anxiety, before he ran at top speed toward the edge of the cliff. He hurled himself forward, feet first. Floating through the air, he plunged a hundred feet toward the waiting water in a glorious moment of flight.

As he entered the water, it felt no different than any other jump he'd made into a swimming pool. He didn't worry about touching bottom—the Quarry ran several hundred feet deep—and within seconds his descent naturally slowed and then stopped. He rose quickly to the light above. When his head broke the surface, Knox felt a mixture of pride and exhilaration. He had done it. He felt a glow of pleasure.

His first static-line jump from a C-130 Hercules had been different; it was part of a regimented process where he didn't have control. Standing in line with his fellow soldiers, Knox had chafed at waiting for the instructions of the jumpmaster. Once he stepped out of the aircraft, following the man in front of him, he felt the sudden tug of the ripcord and heard the "whoosh" of the parachute canopy deploying above, and he felt the strain on his harness digging into his chest and back. A thousand feet below, verdant Georgia farmland. As he descended, he could make out more and more details below, the cars and trucks moving on the highway, a tractor at work in a nearby field, the sun glinting off an irrigation pond. He focused during the last sixty seconds of the descent, intent on cushioning the impact of landing. He steered toward an open spot in the Jump Zone and as the ground rushed up at him, felt his boots hit. He rolled onto his side, transferring the force from his legs to his buttocks. He rose to his feet and quickly pulled his collapsed chute close to him before the wind could catch it.

He remembers the day clearly; the details still sharp. Despite the hard years in between then and now, there is nothing wrong with his memory. That is the problem, isn't it? The memories he couldn't lose, the ones seared in his mind, the ones he can't escape.

Knox removes his overcoat, and then his suit jacket, feeling the wind knife through his cotton shirt. He places the clothing on the ground next to him, taking care. He braces himself against the cold.

"There is no other way," he whispers to himself.

Could he set the past right? If he could not find redemption in this life, perhaps there could be some measure of atonement in the next.

He accepts his guilt, shared with his superiors, with the chain of command. No exceptions. He will not shirk from it. Carved in granite on the wall in Langley: *And ye shall know the truth and the truth shall make you free.* The truth, then. Like a stone tossed into a pond, the ripples had spread. What happened in Dallas had been simple physics. Newton's Third Law: every action has an equal and opposite reaction. The Cuban Project. Operation Mongoose. What they had engineered in Saigon, prompted by Cable 243, the message from Washington that gave Ambassador Lodge and the generals the green light to arrange the murder of Diem and his brother. Who knew what else had been done in the name of national security? Then, the reaction. Did they think that their targets wouldn't respond? Did they not expect turnabout being fair play?

Years ago, he had researched the history of assassination. Assassination—not an English or Latin word, but one borrowed from the Arabic, from the secretive cult led by the Old Man of the Mountain, a cult feared by Crusaders and Sunni caliphs and sultans alike. Assassination, a time-honored tactic but a very dangerous method to employ as a matter of official state policy, one that could quickly spiral out of control. "Will no one rid me of this troublesome priest?" There would always be someone eager to fulfill that request.

Then, there was another problem. Once you have crossed the line, can any leader rest secure? The Roman Emperor Domitian, who had poisoned his brother, Titus, to seize the throne, had lined the corridors of his palace in reflective mica so that he could spot possible assassins. He was properly paranoid. In the end, Domitian died at the hands of his servants.

They said that the young President had expressed concerns about the trip to Texas, that he didn't want to go. A premonition? Action and reaction? When Knox had heard the sickening news from Dallas, he wondered immediately if the Cubans had been behind it—Fidel Castro and Cuban state security, the Dirección General de Inteligencia, responding in kind. Turnabout? Then, again, it might have been the dark men from Chicago, already primed to kill. Or perhaps, one crazed loser. Was it the Universe's balancing act? What Cora and her hippie friends would call karma, the wheel turning.

Palmer Knox knew about the wheel. It had turned for him, hadn't it? He had become the tool of others. He had lost control, become the instrument of the President and his brother and the eager young men from Harvard and Yale and Princeton around him. They called the tune. They drafted the Presidential orders. He and others like him existed in the shadows, ready to do their bidding, to do the dirty work, to do what they wouldn't dream of doing themselves. No, the gentlemen of the Georgetown salons didn't get blood splattered on their tennis whites. Someone else did the deed. Someone else, blue-collar sons of the working class, men like him, from Southern or Midwestern small towns.

The envelope in his right pants pocket would start things. The note inside read, simply: *Dillon, The weight is too much. Set it right. Palmer.* And a business card of his spur-of-the-moment attorney, Samuel X. Scully, a greedy piece of work in his own right.

Is it fair to involve Dillon? To drag him in? Perhaps not. But where else could Knox turn? He trusts his friend. And Dillon is a member of the club, one of the young men on the rise, an Establishment favorite. He would have credibility. If anyone could expose the wrongdoing, bring it to an end, Dillon could.

Knox moves to stand closer to the cornice of the wall at the edge of the flat roof. So this is how it ends, he thinks. He smiles. After all the firefights, all the tight and dangerous corners, this is the uncomplicated way his life will end. Who would have ever imagined that? Who indeed? Palmer Knox, tough guy, paratrooper, expert marksman, cool head and steady hands in combat, veteran of ambushes and battles, a man who has seen too much, done too much. This is the way it ends. So quietly. So quickly.

He shivers as the wind cuts into his shirt. He feels no fear. He is ready. For a moment, he looks above to the first visible stars and sighs at their emerging night-sky beauty. The last time. He closes his eyes and extends his arms to his sides and then steps forward into the cool darkness that awaits.

ONE

Charlottesville
December 1960

The long table had been set for twenty-five. The best silverware shone brightly in the reflected glow of the already-lit candles, and from the ornate crystal chandelier overhead. Evergreen sprigs of white pine, cedar, and noble fir decorated the table. Copies of *The Island City* had been placed by every seat. All was ready for their guests.

Dillon looked around, taking in the scene. There was a warmth, and understated elegance, to the Randolph dining room that night. It made for an appealing and inviting picture.

From the kitchen, he could hear the clatter of pots and pans and the voices of the catering staff, laughing and talking as they went about preparing the food for the evening. That no doubt was annoying Lucy Johnson, his father's aged cook and housekeeper, who had grudgingly conceded that she couldn't handle the dinner party by herself and allowed outsiders to help out for the event. She would be glad when the night was over.

Through the French doors at the entrance to the dining room, Dillon could see the colored lights of the Randolphs' Christmas tree, the tinsel shimmering. Decorated with ornaments and ribbons, the tree reached almost to the ceiling of the living room. At its very tip, a golden angel spread her wings. He knew that when their guests reached the front circular driveway, past the recently-repainted sign for FAR RIDGE FARM, they would be impressed by the sight of the Randolph house, with its classical red-brick facade and Palladian lines meant to evoke Mr. Jefferson's nearby Monticello. From each of its tall windows, candles would twinkle, and the lights of the Christmas tree on the first floor would be visible.

The dinner, a celebration of the publication of *The Island City*, had been his Uncle Leigh's idea. Dillon had resisted the scheme—it seemed overly self-promotional—but Leigh had convinced him to agree to the party in a series of telephone calls to Washington.

"We're quite proud of you," he said. "Your family and friends want to honor you. For once, don't be so modest. It's a great poem. And when I raised the idea with your father, he loved it."

"Isn't the Christmas party the following week? Doesn't he want to save his energy for that?"

For as long as Dillon could remember, the Randolphs had held their holiday party at Far Ridge on the Saturday night two weeks before Christmas. It was a chance for John Custis to touch base with his supporters, donors, and friends, and for Leigh to connect with current and prospective clients of McFarlin & Randolph.

"We've decided to cancel the party this year," Leigh said. "John doesn't want all those people to see him in his current state."

"That's bad, Uncle Leigh." Dillon was dismayed at the news.

John Custis would never have agreed to cancel the party unless his health had significantly deteriorated since Dillon had last seen him. His father had been diagnosed with lung cancer shortly after returning from the Democratic National Convention in July. His recurring cough hadn't been worsened by the air-conditioning in his Los Angeles hotel as John Custis initially thought; the chest X-rays had told a different story. In late August, the surgeons at the University Hospital had removed his right lung. They had informed Leigh and Dillon after the operation that they were hopeful that the malignancy hadn't spread. Dillon knew that there had been worrying signs just before Thanksgiving, but he had held out hope that his father might rally. It was becoming clear that his health was failing, that he was living on borrowed time.

It had been hard for John Custis to accept the sudden grim diagnosis—it had come at the worst possible time. He had hoped for a Cabinet post in the new Administration or an ambassadorship in Europe, a reward for his years of faithful service to the Democratic Party, and his sickness had abruptly ended that dream. He had told his contacts in Washington that his health wouldn't allow him to serve in the government. John Custis wanted his illness kept quiet, and so only his family and closest friends knew that he had cancer.

"If the Christmas party is canceled, are you sure that holding a book party makes sense?" Dillon asked his uncle. "I appreciate the gesture on my behalf, but if he's not up to it…"

"This is a chance for him to honor his son," Leigh said. "He wants to have the party. He's looking forward to it greatly. He wants you there, and he gave me a list of who to invite. We'll keep it to twenty-five guests or so. To be blunt about it, he also wants a chance to say goodbye to his friends."

"Has it come to that?"

"It's not good. John doesn't believe he can beat this, Dillon. He told me last week that he could feel his body slipping away. And he hates taking the drugs, the morphine, for the pain."

"If he's taken a turn for the worse, should I come home now? Take a leave of absence? I can arrange for that quickly. Be at Far Ridge in a day."

"Absolutely not," Leigh said. "Your father would never want that. He wants you doing your duty at State. You'll see him at this party, and then you're back for the holidays."

And so it was that Dillon drove out from Washington to Charlottesville on the second Friday of December. He was aware that it might be the last time friends and family would gather at Far Ridge while John Custis was there to host them. If this was the way his father wanted to bid farewell, Dillon was willing to play his part.

* * *

At fifteen minutes before the appointed hour for the start of the party—at six o'clock—Dillon and Leigh began greeting the arriving guests at the front door. Dillon's father waited for them in the dining room, sitting in a wheelchair, conserving his strength for the dinner ahead.

There were no unfamiliar faces. Most of the guests were older, party loyalists who had known John Custis for decades. The women wore cocktail dresses, their hair in bouffants or the flipped bob cut made popular by Jackie Kennedy; the men were in suits, some with bright red and green Christmas ties.

After he had ushered the last guest into the dining room, Dillon took his place next to his father. John Custis sat at the head of the table, his face drawn and gaunt, his shirt and jacket now too large for him. He retained his leonine good looks, but he had aged dramatically since the summer. It was clear that he was sick.

Dillon surveyed the guests near him. His best friend from college, Charlie Woods, and his wife Molly, pregnant with their second child, near the middle of the table. Further down, the chairman of the University's English Department, Dr. Fredericks, and two of Dillon's favorite professors, Steve Burroughs and John LeVine. Then there were close family friends like Ted and Elizabeth Warrington, and Leigh's long-time law partner, Ford McFarlin, and his wife, Kitty.

There were no strangers at the Randolph table that night. The mood was light and festive; the guests happy and relaxed. After a brief grace led by Leigh, they ate heartily, enjoying the dinner (buttermilk rolls, beef tenderloin in a burgundy mushroom sauce, country ham, home-style butter beans, mashed potatoes, and bread pudding for dessert). The wine flowed freely, and the guests were soon immersed in table talk, gossiping, telling jokes, trading stories.

Kitty McFarlin, seated to Dillon's left, wanted to talk about the new president. "Isn't Jack *marvelous*?" She fiddled with a stray lock of hair. "So vigorous. And Jackie is so chic. Washington must be such an exciting place."

Dillon smiled. "He's not in office yet. The inauguration is not for another month. But it's true that there's a sea change coming, a generational change."

He turned to Leigh, who was sitting across from him at John Custis' right. "Kitty was just telling me how wonderful Jack Kennedy is." Dillon enjoyed teasing his uncle about the outcome of the election. Leigh had favored Stuart Symington, the Senator from Missouri, for the Democratic presidential nomination, and had been disappointed when Kennedy won the prize. He detested Joseph Kennedy, the patriarch of the family, for his pro-German stance while ambassador to Great Britain, and his friendship with Senator Joe McCarthy. In the end, Leigh had come around to back Jack Kennedy, but Dillon knew that he wouldn't have been completely crestfallen if Richard Nixon had won.

"We'll see if he's up to the job," Leigh said tartly. "From what they say, he's more of a swordsman than a statesman."

"That sounds an awful lot like jealousy to me, Leigh," Kitty said. "He can't help it if he's as handsome as a movie star. I heard a joke about it the other day. They say Pat Nixon told Jackie just before the election that 'I slept with the future President of the United States last night.' And then Jackie said, 'That Jack'll do anything for a vote.'"

Dillon and Leigh laughed. "Jack likes women," Dillon said. "It's no secret. And they love him—you saw that during the campaign with the young girls fawning over him at the rallies. It's that energy, that charisma, which will make him a great President."

Dillon felt that he understood Jack Kennedy better than most. Like Dillon, Jack was a second son, overshadowed in his childhood by an older brother. Like Dillon, he was a writer, an observer, someone who sought detachment, a certain distance. Dillon knew what it was like to try to live up to the memory of a heroic brother killed in action, although the commander of PT 109 was a hero in his own right. Dillon had relished Jack's witty response on achieving that honored status: "It was involuntary. They sunk my boat."

Leigh frowned. "Sounds like you've been seduced like the rest of them, Dillon. I'd rather have a work horse than a show horse."

"Spoken like a man," Kitty said. "I'll take the show horse any day."

"I think it's time we were stirred out of our complacency," Dillon said. "Time for some vigorous leadership. New blood."

"We're going to test that hypothesis," Leigh replied. "For the people have spoken. Although those phantom Kennedy voters in Chicago graveyards wouldn't be able to speak under any circumstances."

John Custis had remained silent during the exchange. Dillon wondered what he was thinking. His father typically joined any political discussion. It was strange for him to stay silent, particularly during a conversation involving the new Administration. He had been more supportive of Jack Kennedy's ambition than his brother.

As they were finishing their dessert, two waitresses appeared and began pouring champagne for the guests. When everyone at the table had their glass full, Leigh rose to his feet.

"We have a lot to celebrate tonight," he said. "A new president who Kitty McFarlin assures me will bring vigor to Washington. And a new book of poetry by my nephew Dillon, Charlottesville's own rising young poet." He raised his glass. "To Dillon Randolph, to the holidays, and to a fresh start for us all. As another poet once wrote: 'Come, my friends, 'Tis not too late to seek a newer world.'"

There were cries of "Hear, Hear" as the guests joined in the toast, clinking glasses together and drinking from their flutes. Leigh smiled at the applause that followed and paused until it petered out.

"Quite right," he said. "Now we should hear from the man of the hour. If you would, Dillon, can I prevail upon you to read from the opening of your poem?"

Dillon nodded and stood up. He looked down the table, making eye contact with Charlie and Leigh, before opening his copy of *The Island City*. He explained that he would read from the opening of the poem, and took a slow breath before he began.

> *Dawn light touches the Spree*
> *Caresses Tiergarten lindens and oaks*
> *Alone in bed, Charlotte stirs and sighs*
> *Watches as morning's glow kisses the windows*
> *A new day in the Island City*
> *May Day in the Island City*
>
> *Berliners drink their morning coffee*
> *Workers, East and West, march toward city center*
> *Dueling rallies and parades await*
> *Speeches and slogans to divide them*

Holiday in the Island City
May Day in the Island City

He closed the book and looked around the table, waiting until the guests had finished their polite applause to speak again. "Thank you. I'm touched that you are all here. Friends. Family." He paused for a moment and held up his copy of *The Island City*. "As to my little book of verse. The French poet Paul Valery once claimed that a poem is never finished, only abandoned. If he's correct, I can only hope that I didn't abandon this one too soon."

"You didn't," Leigh said. "And there's a copy for each of our guests. Your homework is to read it! Even our friends from the University faculty." The guests laughed.

John Custis rose to his feet. He held up his champagne flute, his hand visibly trembling. "To my son," he said. "Poet and diplomat."

After the guests had finished drinking the toast, Dillon stood next to his father and raised his glass. "To my father, John Custis Randolph," he said. "Who has served the people of Virginia, and his country, with integrity and honor."

Tears rolled down John Custis' cheeks as their guests stood and applauded him. He ducked his head, embarrassed by his public display of emotion. Dillon kept his hand on his father's shoulder, disturbed by how thin his frame had become.

Leigh thanked all for coming, and wished their guests a Merry Christmas and Happy New Year.

Dillon stood at the front door, his father next to him in a wheelchair, shaking hands with the guests as they departed.

"A night to remember," Leigh said after the last stragglers had made their exit.

"I'm tired," John Custis said. He turned to Dillon. "How are they treating you in Washington?"

"They keep me busy. The situation in Berlin is still tense. Rumors are that they will create a Task Force when Secretary Rusk takes over. I'm hoping they'll pick me for it."

His father nodded in approval. "I do wonder how Rusk will work out at State. The President needs a solid man with experience. A man tough enough to take on the Russians. Thank God it won't be Adlai. Senator Fulbright would have been my choice, but they say his civil rights record ruled him out. Hell, he's from Arkansas. Did they expect he'd be leading the charge for the Negroes? You can't get too far out in front of your own people."

"I see you still have your inside sources in Washington," Dillon said.

"I hear things. A few friends call now and then."

"I could come home early this year," Dillon began. "It's quiet at work. We're waiting for the new Administration. We could spend more time together."

His father shook his head. "I don't want you disrupting your life. Christmas is soon enough." He coughed. "Don't worry yourself too much. I'll hang on for a while. I fully intend to last long enough to see a Democrat move into the White House again."

* * *

He dreams of her.

He dreams of Christa, the long-gone Christa, the unattainable Christa.

Christa, naked, waiting for him in the oversized bed in the suite at the Savoy Hotel, her smooth skin, the beautiful hollow of her throat, her small, rounded breasts.

Christa, her eyes locked on his, straddling him, moving her body up-and-down in a slow rhythm, a serene smile on her face.

Outside, the sounds of Charlottenburg at midday, of traffic, people walking by on the street, a distant whistle from a traffic cop. Diffused light streams into the room through the gauzy curtains. They are alone, behind locked doors.

Christa leans forward to kiss him, her nipples first brushing across his chest and then the weight of her breasts pressing against him, as their lips meet. She smiles at him and finds his mouth with hers.

"Do you like this, Dillon?" she asks.

He gasps an answer: "I do. And you?"

"Herrliche," she says. "Delightful."

She rides him, now faster, gasping in pleasure, until she climaxes, her face transformed by passion.

Then, it is his turn. He mounts her, driving deep into her, pushing her down into the soft mattress. Her hands are on his hips, pulling him closer.

"You're mine," he tells her. "I won't let you go."

She says nothing, her smile unwavering.

And then he feels the sharp pleasure of his own surge, and she grabs him and digs her fingernails into his back as he comes in a sudden rush.

She wiggles out from under him, and finds her clothes and starts to dress. She has her underwear and slip on before he can say anything.

He realizes that something has gone wrong. Has she somehow taken offense? Her face is a mask, closed off to him.

"What is wrong?" he asks, as she pulls on her skirt and buttons her blouse.

When she turns to answer him, he realizes that they are outside, standing face-to-face in the sunny backyard of a suburban villa. Somehow he knows it is one of the CIA's Berlin safe houses. She has donned dark glasses, and he can't see her eyes. "You want me to leave, don't you?" she says.

"I don't." He is bewildered by the change in her mood. She is cold, dismissive.

"Oh, yes you do. You do."

"You have it wrong," he says, pleading. "I made a mistake. I want you to stay." He takes her hand and holds it, only to have her snatch it away.

"Too late, Dillon. Too, too late. You had your chance."

Then he is back in the hotel room, alone, and church bells are ringing insistently in the distance.

* * *

Dillon woke up, then, to the sound of the grandfather clock downstairs chiming. He counted five bells. He looked over at the window, illuminated by moonlight. He realized that he was far from Berlin and Christa, instead lying in his own bed at Far Ridge.

He tried to collect his thoughts. He knew that reading from *The Island City* in public had stirred up unwelcome memories and had triggered his dream. He had first met Christa after a poetry reading in Berlin. The unresolved past. He sighed. The dream had seemed so real, the sense of loss so acute.

He knew that there was nothing he could do. Christa was lost to him. She had been unlike any woman he had ever known. He found her alluring, mysterious, and, at times, disturbingly aloof. Could it have ended differently? She would never have come back to the States with him, but what if he had offered to stay in Germany? If he had sacrificed his career, moved in with her? Would it have worked? What kind of life would they have shared?

He found himself shrugging. It was a fantasy, one divorced from the reality of the here and now. He rose from his bed and put on his bathrobe. Outside his window, a half-moon shone. He heard the wind coursing through the oak trees in the backyard, near the formal garden his father had spent the last few years cultivating.

He left his room and walked down the darkened corridor to the main stairs, holding onto the polished banister as he made his way to the first floor. In the foyer, he passed by the tall grandfather clock—an antique crafted by the Clark brothers of Philadelphia in 1826—and continued through the dark and vacant dining room until he reached his father's study. He turned on the desk lamp and looked around. To his surprise, the plaques and awards and grouped photos chronicling John Custis' years in Congress, including "grip-and-grins" with the famous and near-famous, had been cleared from the wall. The bookshelves were untouched, still crammed with his father's law books and volumes of Virginia history.

Dillon moved over to the mahogany desk and picked up the silver-framed photograph of Dillon and Wash that was one of John Custis' favorites, the two brothers posing for the picture at Wash's Quantico graduation ceremony, smiling broadly for the camera. There was a new photo on the desk, a snapshot of Dillon taken in front of the Brandenburg Gate in Berlin. He knew why his father liked the image: Dillon the heroic diplomat, Dillon in action on the frontline of the Cold War.

It hadn't worked out the way it was supposed to—Wash had been his father's heir apparent, and his death in Korea had been a sharp blow. John Custis had always dreamed of Washington Custis Randolph replacing him in Congress, and perhaps rising even further—the Senate? A Cabinet position in a Democratic Administration?

And why not? Wash had been a natural leader. Tapped to live on the Lawn in his fourth year at the University; first in his class at Quantico, killed in action during the Chosin Reservoir battle as the Marines fought to escape the trap sprung by the Chinese Red Army. At Wash's memorial service at Christ Church, there had been a wreath of black magnolias in the shape of a "7"—signifying that he had been a member of the University's secret Seven Society, a fact revealed only after death.

Dillon had looked up to his older brother, admired him, and he had been hit hard by his death. When Dillon had decided to join the Foreign Service, it was in part because he wanted, like Wash, to serve his country. He also knew that his father expected it—such service was a tradition for the Randolphs.

Dillon had been closer to his Uncle Leigh than to his father growing up. He had found his father distant, always consumed by his job. The summer after Dillon's mother died, John Custis had immersed himself in work, and Leigh had stepped in and looked after Dillon. He had taught Dillon how to play tennis, and he had introduced him to poetry, encouraging him to memorize Wordsworth and Keats and some of the American poets, Stephen Vincent Benet and Robert Frost. Later, after Dillon had encountered Eliot and Pound and Auden as a student, and began seriously writing his own verse, Leigh had applauded his initial efforts.

It would have been a different childhood if Dillon hadn't lost his mother when he did. He didn't think about her if he could help it—the memories were too painful. She had been sick for quite some time, in and out of the hospital before she died. Dillon had grown to hate the smell of disinfectant and the austere setting of a hospital room. Before her illness, she had not been overly affectionate. She was a year older than her husband, and she had very clear ideas about what counted as proper behavior.

That part of his life seemed very remote, now. His father had removed anything that could remind them of Victoria Randolph, wife and mother, from the house. He never spoke of her to Wash and Dillon. The message was unmistakable—no dwelling on the past. Move on. Put the loss behind you.

Dillon went over to the bookcase and found the third volume of *Lee's Lieutenants* and sat down at his father's desk to read. He browsed through the book until he came to the section on the Shenandoah Valley campaign of 1864. It was easy to lose himself in Douglas Southall Freeman's description of the battle of Cedar Creek.

He welcomed the escape from the reality of his father's illness, from his loneliness, and from the evening's evocation of the memories of Christa and Berlin. He would read for an hour or so until he heard Lucy in the kitchen, and then he'd asked her to cook him an early breakfast—scrambled eggs, ham, and grits. He'd sit down at the kitchen table and eat his breakfast and compliment Lucy on her cooking, and he'd feel like he was home again and they could pretend that nothing had changed, would ever change.

TWO

John Custis Randolph died three days into the New Year, a month shy of his sixty-sixth birthday. He had promised Dillon that he would live to see the inauguration of Jack Kennedy, when John Custis could celebrate having a Democrat back in the White House after eight years in the political wilderness, but it was not to be. After he caught a cold in the last week of December, his health quickly deteriorated. His physician, Dr. French, hospitalized him two days after Christmas.

There was not much the doctors could do at that point. John Custis fought against the infection, struggling, gasping for air, for a long week, but at the end, his immune system failed. The day that his father's heart stopped, Dillon had arrived at the hospital for a visit and learned that he had missed the end by twenty minutes. He stayed by the bedside until Leigh arrived, and they said a prayer together.

"Go home," Leigh told him. "I've made the preliminary arrangements. I have a few more phone calls to make. He made me promise that I'd make sure the *Washington Post* had a flattering obituary. He took it for granted that the *Richmond Times-Dispatch* would say nice things."

"If there's anything I can do…"

Leigh shook his head. He embraced Dillon and then held him at arm's length.

"I've spent forty years handling the details for my brother. I'm not about to stop now."

Dillon drove home, feeling numb, and found himself drawn to his father's study. He sat in the desk chair and thought about his often-distant and awkward relationship with his father. He studied the photograph of his brother in his Marine officer's uniform, and the newer photo of Dillon at the Brandenburg Gate. Being John Custis Randolph's second son, living up to his expectations, spoken and unspoken, hadn't been easy for Dillon.

They held the service at Christ Church on Saturday, and the pews were filled. John Custis Randolph was respected, if not loved, and friends and political foes alike had turned out to honor him, the women in their Sunday best, the men in dark suits. The President-elect sent a telegram and a large arrangement of flowers, which Leigh had placed in a prominent spot in the church foyer.

Dillon sat in the first pew with Leigh, finding comfort in the familiar hymns ("O God Our Help in Ages Past," "A Mighty Fortress is Our God") and the poetic cadences of the Book of Common Prayer funeral service. The eulogy was brief. The minister, the Rev. Cullen, focused on John Custis' service to the country and danced around the fact that the former Congressman rarely attended services. In less than an hour, Dillon and Leigh were in a limousine en route to the cemetery, and once there, his father's burial took only a few minutes.

The reception they held at Far Ridge after the service was disorienting for Dillon. The house was deeply connected to John Custis, and it was hard to accept that he was no longer there. Dillon kept expecting his father to suddenly appear in his favorite tweed jacket and begin working the room. But that wasn't going to happen.

Dillon knew his father's death would be hardest on Leigh and Lucy. For his entire adult life, Leigh had been his older brother's confidante and political adviser. He had built the law firm into a prosperous and respected local institution, and it had financed John Custis' campaigns, even though he had faced only token Republican opposition in the general election. Lucy and her husband had worked at Far Ridge for decades, and when Mr. Johnson had died the year before, it was John Custis and Leigh who had consoled her.

The day after the funeral, they sat down with Lucy. Her eyes were swollen from crying, and her grief had deeply touched Dillon. He told Lucy that she didn't have to worry about the future, that there would be a place for her at Far Ridge for as long as she wanted one.

"If you would prefer to retire, you'll be taken care of," Leigh said. "Financially, I mean. We've established a pension of sorts for you."

"I want to keep on working," she said. "Will you be living here, Mr. Leigh?"

Leigh looked over at Dillon. "That's up to Dillon. Whatever he wants."

"You have a key, don't you?" Dillon asked.

"I'll split time between my house in town and here," Leigh said. "I'll stay at Far Ridge on the weekends when Dillon comes back from Washington."

Dillon realized that he was alone, now, except for Leigh, his only close relative. His parents, and his brother, gone. Uncle Leigh had been briefly married, with no children, and Dillon had no cousins.

Later that day, Dillon and Charlie Woods met for a beer at the Virginian. They had been friends since childhood, and had, for a time, been roommates at the University. Charlie had stayed in Charlottesville for law school and had joined McFarlin & Randolph after graduation. Leigh thought the world of him, and Dillon was sure that Charlie would be made a partner in due course.

On the jukebox, Paul Anka was singing "Put Your Head on My Shoulder," and the place was full of students, talking and laughing and enjoying themselves.

"A hard time for your family," Charlie said.

"My father would have been pleased with the turn-out at his funeral," Dillon said. "Not only Charlottesville's finest but also some regular people. John Custis always counted votes. He would have liked the eulogy. John Custis Randolph the statesman, seeking God's justice in the world. The truth is that he didn't have much use for the church, not like Leigh does. What do they say about the Episcopalians, the ruling class at prayer?"

"The Baptists call you folks the Whiskeypalians," Charlie said.

"And we know Baptists are just like us, except they keep the curtains closed."

"I'm a Presbyterian, as you know," Charlie said. "We don't drink as much as you High Church types, and we keep our curtains open. Best of both worlds. Come to think of it, I've got a joke about that."

"You're kidding."

"Johnny and Ralph are good ole boys, but not too bright. Ralph tells Johnny, 'I drove by your house Thursday night, and I saw the curtains in your bedroom were open, and you and Sadie Mae were naked and goin' at it.' Johnny shakes his head. 'That just cain't be. No way, no how. I wasn't home Thursday night.'" Charlie laughed at his own joke, pounding the table, and Dillon found himself joining in.

"That's a terrible joke," Dillon said.

"But you laughed. And it's good to laugh on a day like today."

"True enough."

"I know that it wasn't always easy between you and your father," Charlie said. "But he was damn proud of you. Even more proud after your posting in Berlin."

Dillon nodded. He knew that one of John Custis' highly-placed friends in the State Department had passed along the official version of Dillon's stay in Berlin. Dillon had been commended for his assistance—described in deliberately vague terms—in a successful British-American counterespionage operation. Dillon had never discussed the episode with his father and had managed to avoid talking about his time in Berlin at any length.

Charlie put his beer mug down on the table and leaned forward. "Am I ever going to get the full story on Berlin?"

"You have the full story," Dillon said. "The State Department in its infinite wisdom thought I should return to Washington and help out on the German Desk."

"After less than six months?"

"A shorter assignment than I expected, but sometimes that's the way it happens. The truth is that there's not much happening there. The action is in Bonn and Washington. And it's not like I had a wife and kids that had been relocated to Germany. I just packed my stuff in one suitcase and caught a flight back."

"So now what? I figure you're going to hold on to Far Ridge?"

Dillon nodded. "For now. Lucy will stay on and look after the housekeeping. I'll come back sometimes on the weekends, and on the holidays. I talked with Leigh about taking care of her retirement. He's setting up an annuity for her so she can stop working whenever she wants. Knowing Lucy, that isn't going to happen anytime soon."

"Any chance you'll come back home for good?" Charlie asked. "It'd be great if you did. Like old times."

"Maybe someday," Dillon said.

"Well, no one can say you don't live an exciting life," Charlie said. "Part of me envies you, but the other part of me doesn't. Guess I'm a small-town boy at heart. I think eventually you'll realize what you're missing."

"Not now. Not with a new President who wants to get the country moving again, who wants to make things happen. I think Washington's the place to be."

THREE

Washington, D.C.
January 1961

It was bitterly cold in the morning. A freak snowstorm the night before had dumped an unexpected eight inches of snow on the streets of the District of Columbia, blanketing the city. The temperature barely reached twenty degrees, and snow banks and drifts covered the capital. John Fitzgerald Kennedy's inauguration was going to take place in a winter setting, a fitting backdrop for a president from chilly New England.

Dillon and Jan Nowak, a colleague from State, had stationed themselves in the crowd gathered for the ceremony in front of the East Portico of the Capitol. The spectators had dressed for the cold—hats, gloves, scarves, heavy winter coats. Some in the crowd had wrapped themselves in blankets, and Dillon spotted a few people in bulky ski parkas. One of the red-faced men next to them was drinking from a metal thermos, the smell of coffee mingling with that of alcohol.

Dillon stamped his feet and slapped his gloved hands together against the cold, trying to stay warm. A sudden burst of wind cut into his cheeks. At least there were no clouds, and the bright sun provided some warmth, but it wasn't a day anyone would choose for a public outdoor event.

Dillon was tall enough to see over the people in the crowd in front of him. The ceremonies began with an invocation by Cardinal Cushing of Boston. They listened to Marian Anderson sing the national anthem, and then Robert Frost, silver hair glinting in the sunlight, struggling with the wind and the glare, reciting a poem from heart when he couldn't make out his prepared text. After he finished, Jack Kennedy and President Eisenhower each congratulated him, shaking his hand.

Kennedy had arrived wearing a formal morning suit and top hat, but he had abandoned his overcoat and hat.

The crowd waited patiently through Lyndon Johnson taking the oath of office as vice president, administered by the Speaker of the House of Representatives, Sam Rayburn, a fellow Texan.

There was a buzz of anticipation as Chief Justice Earl Warren, facing the bareheaded Kennedy, began the swearing-in ceremony. When Kennedy finished reciting his oath of office, the crowd roared. Richard Nixon stepped forward to shake Kennedy's hand. Some of the people around Dillon were not only clapping, but also hooting and yelling.

"He's so damn young," Jan said. "Eisenhower looks like an old man. Like Jack's grandfather."

Dillon glanced over at the platform—Eisenhower wore a heavy wool coat and a light-colored scarf tucked in around his collar against the cold. He did look old. The contrast between the men couldn't have been starker.

"The young prince becomes King," Dillon said. "History in the making."

"You think they've fixed the marks that Ike's golf spikes made in the White House floors?" Jan grinned. "This Administration isn't going to waste time playing eighteen holes. We're going to do things."

When Kennedy took to the rostrum, Dillon was surprised at the eloquence of the speech that followed, its poetic use of imagery and alliteration, and its deft use of comparisons. The rhetoric was soaring ("The torch has been passed to a new generation of Americans") but also cautionary when the new President warned about "the dark powers of destruction unleashed by science." The speech was an extended call to action, a call to "bear the burden of a long twilight struggle," and while it wasn't novel, Kennedy's use of classical rhetorical devices like antimetabole ("...ask not what your country can do for you — ask what you can do for your country") made it particularly striking.

Dillon greatly admired the young President's cool style and wit, his charm and his ambition. He knew Leigh had thought that Kennedy was too young for the Presidency, that he should have waited his turn, but Dillon disagreed. Gray in your hair didn't make you any wiser. Jack's energy and curiosity, his desire for action, were what the country needed in its leadership. Dillon didn't think that Eisenhower had failed as President—he thought Ike's foreign policy had been sound, particularly on Germany and Berlin—but there had been a complacency in his approach, a reluctance to challenge the status quo. What was good for General Motors wasn't necessarily good for America.

The crowd cheered and clapped at the end of Kennedy's speech. Dillon was impressed; it was a smashing start to the Kennedy years. He couldn't imagine any other politician giving this speech, challenging the country the way Jack Kennedy had. Certainly not Dick Nixon or any other Republican. The Grand Old Party had become the party of business as usual, and the sort of national sacrifice Jack was calling for would shake things up.

"Now we have to make it come true," Jan said. "It's up to all of us to make it happen."

"That's all well and good, but I need to thaw out before we start making history," Dillon said.

Jan laughed. "In Chicago, this would count as a warm spell."

"We're not in Chicago, thank God. Let's get warmed up before we start changing the world. Grab a cup of hot coffee."

"As long as there's some whiskey in it," Jan said.

* * *

They formed the Group of Five in the winter of 1961 within weeks of the new Administration taking office.

At the beginning, they had called themselves the New Frontiersmen. It seemed a clever name for the group. They considered themselves Kennedy loyalists, moved by the young President's stirring rhetoric and call for a new generation of leadership. After a month or so, they abandoned the name, largely because Alex Landauer argued that it sounded too much like a pop music group (the Kingsmen or the Jazz

Crusaders). They settled on the Group of Five, and most of the time they just referred to themselves as The Group.

During that first year, they met to play low-stakes poker—Five Card Stud—twice a month, on Thursday nights, rotating the location. Each member hosted the game in the alphabetical order of their surname: Palmer Knox, followed by Alex Landauer, Jan Nowak, Dillon, and finishing the rotation with Grayson Talbott.

They joked about how they represented a Shadow Government for the future, primed for the passing of the generational torch that Jack had announced in his Inaugural Address. Two from the State Department—Jan and Dillon—one from the White House, Grayson; one from Defense, Alex; and Palmer, who, when asked by outsiders, claimed to be part of the Treasury Department, but worked at the recently-opened CIA headquarters in Langley, Virginia.

Dillon had the most experience in government, having entered the Foreign Service during the Eisenhower years. He had been posted to Sydney, Canberra, and Berlin before returning to Washington to join the German Desk.

Palmer, the oldest of the five, had served in the Army as a paratrooper before being recruited by the Agency. Dillon gravitated to him. They had seen more of the world than the others. Neither had any illusions about the nature of the country's adversaries. The Cold War wasn't an abstraction. Dillon had observed firsthand in Berlin what life under Communism entailed, and he had lost a brother in Korea during the battle of the Chosin Reservoir. Palmer had also served in Korea, and had gone ashore with Army Task Force 201 when Eisenhower sent U.S. forces to Beirut to support Lebanese President Camille Chamoun, who was facing a restive Muslim population.

Jan Nowak, Dillon's State Department colleague, was a soft-spoken, slim young man from Chicago with dark horn-rimmed glasses and an unruly cowlick. He had been a Rhodes Scholar, which had given him extra credibility with Dean Rusk, the Secretary of State, who had also won the prestigious scholarship. Assigned to the Policy and Planning Staff, Jan had access to the seventh floor of State's Main Building where the Department's leaders had their offices. Jan chain-smoked Winston cigarettes—smoking was a coping mechanism for the stress of his job.

Grayson Talbott had paid his political dues on the Kennedy campaign as an advance man. He had left his job at a New York ad agency to come to Washington and join the White House staff. While Grayson wasn't in the inner circle, he was close to some of the political types around the President. He proudly wore his gold tone PT 109 tie clasp that proclaimed KENNEDY 60. He was a true believer: above his desk, he had framed a phrase from Jack Kennedy's Inaugural Address: *"The energy, the faith, and the devotion which we bring to this endeavor will light our country and all who serve it—and the glow from that fire can truly light the world."*

In contrast, Alex Landauer, one of McNamara's Whiz Kids, was no romantic. His connection came through Harvard—he was considered the most brilliant of the junior faculty in the Government Department, and had come to the notice of Dean McGeorge Bundy. His thesis on the challenges of imperium had been published as a book, *The Cost of Empire*, which considered how the Roman, Ottoman, Austro-Hungarian, and British empires had won and lost power. The book didn't make the *New York Times* bestseller list, but Alex gained a reputation as an original thinker. He had joined the other Cambridge academics who sought to put theory into practice with the new Administration.

Landauer came from a prominent Jewish family in New York, and he was used to getting his way. There was no questioning his intelligence or his scholarship. By all accounts, he was one of McNamara's leading thinkers in the Defense Department. Dillon respected Landauer, but he didn't like him—Alex could be arrogant and dismissive.

"As goes the Group of Five, so goes the Administration," Jan Nowak once proclaimed after one too many beers. "As goes the Administration, so goes the country. So we have to play the hand we're dealt the best that we can."

* * *

It quickly did not go as planned. There were jarring setbacks in the first few months of the new Administration. The Soviets scored a major propaganda victory in April by placing the first man in space, cosmonaut

Yuri Gagarin, who orbited the earth in Vostok 1, shocking Americans with this unexpected mastery of technology. Nikita Khrushchev called Gagarin the Russian Christopher Columbus.

Five days after Gagarin captured the world's imagination, on April 17th, there was a further embarrassment for the new President. The abortive Bay of Pigs invasion proved to be a fiasco that ended with a total defeat of the Cuban exiles who had hoped to overthrow Fidel Castro. More than a thousand of the insurgents had been taken prisoner by the regime's troops, and Castro loudly rejoiced at the defeat of the hated Yanquis who had backed the invaders.

The Bay of Pigs came as a shock to Dillon and the other members of the Group. It raised uncomfortable questions about the competency of those in charge at the White House and the CIA. The leading newspapers in New York, Chicago, and Washington had been sharply critical of the performance of the President and his advisers.

On the third Thursday of April, they had finished their poker game early and sat around the table in Dillon's apartment drinking beer and debating the events of the past few weeks. Not surprisingly, Grayson Talbott offered the most vigorous defense of the Administration's approach. "You can't expect it would go smoothly from Day One," he said. "We're getting the country moving. You have to expect that action carries some risk."

"The criticism of the President that I'm hearing is that he didn't go far enough," Alex Landauer said. He fixed his dark eyes on Talbott. "That he should have intervened. Air support. Naval bombardment. At the least, evacuate the Cubans stranded on the beach."

Grayson grimaced. "He made it clear from the start that there wouldn't be overt American involvement in this."

"That's sort of like being half-pregnant." It was Jan Nowak, a cigarette in his nicotine-stained fingers. He took a quick puff. "No one was fooled. It's clear that Palmer's buddies at CIA ran the entire show. Far from a Cuban operation. The President was smart in not sending in the Marines. What would Khrushchev have done in Berlin? It would have given him a pretext for a power play there. Tit for tat. The President made the right call in keeping us out. From what I can tell, the CIA figured he would salvage the operation when it went wrong, and they miscalculated badly."

They all turned to look at Palmer, but he shrugged and remained silent.

"Hindsight is always twenty-twenty," Grayson said. "A lot of misjudgments by many people. The Joint Chiefs. Mac Bundy. Dulles and the spooks didn't serve us well." He glanced over at Palmer. "Present company excluded."

"By us, you mean the White House?" Dillon asked.

"No, I mean the United States of America," Grayson said. "The failure hurts the country, not just this President."

"Look on the bright side," Alex said. "Jack campaigned on getting tougher with Cuba. He's proved that he's not afraid to act, even if he wasn't muscular enough for some of my colleagues."

"What do you think?" Grayson asked, turning to Dillon.

"The President and the people around him are privy to intelligence that shaped what they did," Dillon said. "They wouldn't have given the Agency the go-ahead if they didn't think the attack had a high probability of success. Somebody must have screwed up on the intel, and I blame them more than I do the White House."

"Exactly right," Grayson said. "The intelligence was lousy. There's going to be a house-cleaning." He looked over at Palmer. "I would think it may be quite unpleasant for some of the people in your shop."

Palmer shrugged. "Someone has to take the fall. The President got it right—victory has a hundred fathers and defeat is an orphan."

"A lot of people didn't like the idea from the start," Jan said. "Secretary Rusk was against it. So was Chester Bowles. State was skeptical."

Dillon didn't challenge Jan, but he had heard that Rusk had been noncommittal at a meeting the President held in early April reviewing the invasion plans. Senator Fulbright had argued against the idea on both practical and moral grounds. In the end, only Fulbright had opposed the idea when Kennedy "called the question" and asked for a vote.

"What do you think, Palmer?" Alex asked.

Palmer looked at him for a long moment. "Whether to support the invasion was a political decision. I try to steer clear of politics. As to the tactics, from what I can tell, it was as fucked up as you can get. A half-assed scheme. A beach landing without air cover."

"That's as good a summary of the Bay of Pigs as you'll ever get in the newspapers," Dillon said.

"Except Palmer ducked the question," Alex said.

"I didn't duck it," he replied. "I just didn't give you the answer you wanted—I gave you the answer you'd get from anyone who'd been through the Army War College. As to whether we should have done more? The Soviets gave Castro planes and tanks and bullets. That's foreign intervention in my book, so I think we would have been justified in whatever we decided to do."

* * *

Later, after the others had left, Dillon and Palmer remained at the table and talked. Palmer switched from beer to whiskey, and he cradled a glass in his large hands, gently swirling the dark liquid around, studying it as if he could learn something from the ripples and whorls.

"You kept quiet tonight," Dillon said. "Except for when Alex was questioning you."

"It's a touchy subject for everyone at the Agency," Palmer said. "I didn't want him or Grayson running back to their bosses with tales of how the CIA was whining about it and blaming others."

"Don't you trust them?"

"Not in the way I trust you. I'd only say this to you. Here's what I think. What really happened? The White House mismanaged the invasion from the very start. Ike would never have approved a full-scale amphibious assault with a so-called brigade of amateur soldiers, for Christ's sake.

Kennedy got talked into an invasion instead of an infiltration. Then he got cold feet. Moved the landing from Trinidad to the Bay of Pigs. Cut back the air support."

"So it was entirely the President's fault?" Dillon shook his head. "I don't buy that. His advisers failed him."

"I agree. The Agency screwed up. Big time. Dulles should have pulled the plug on the operation, but I think he wanted Kennedy to view us as the can-do people. Remember the Inauguration. Kennedy talked about defending freedom in its hour of maximum danger. Bearing any burden. Paying any price."

"You heard Grayson. Hindsight is twenty-twenty."

"There were a few at headquarters who thought that because they pulled off a coup in Iran and Guatemala that the same playbook would work in Cuba. Except, if you keep running off right tackle, sooner or later the bad guys figure out how to stop you. Castro's secret police spent three months rounding up anyone they suspected of being sympathetic to a counter-revolution. He had the Army do a sweep through the Escambay Mountains and kill or capture the guerrillas hiding there."

"But the invasion went ahead."

Palmer frowned. "Ten days before the invasion the two Agency guys in charge of the operation threatened to resign. They felt the changes that the White House demanded made success unlikely. Deputy Director Bissell talked them out of quitting. Then the night before, Bissell and General Cabell tried to get Rusk to support air strikes at dawn to protect the flotilla and the landing. Rusk wouldn't budge."

Dillon shook his head. "It's hard to find anyone at State who believed it was going to work, even with the original plan."

"What's the old saying? If you're going to strike at the king, make sure you kill him? The President kept scaling back the operation to the point where it was bound to fail. He changed the landing spot, reduced the number of bombing runs, wouldn't budge on trying to save the men on the beach with U.S. sorties. We had Navy aircraft in striking range." Palmer shrugged. "No air cover. Castro's T-33 jet trainers made mincemeat out of the Brigade's B-26s."

"The President is new to this."

"I'll say."

"What's done is done," Dillon said. "Jack Kennedy is smart. The people around him are smart. He'll learn from this. They say he's a quick study. He won't make the same mistake twice."

FOUR

Feliks Hawes turned up in Washington on a particularly humid July day. Dillon was far from enthused about the Englishman's impromptu visit. His presence summoned up difficult memories for Dillon, ones he would rather forget. He had last seen Hawes in Berlin, in May of 1959, when Operation West Wind had come to its abrupt, and violent, end.

Dillon met Hawes in the lobby of the State Department building. After they shook hands, Hawes mopped his forehead with his handkerchief and complained about the humidity. "It's like being trapped in a bloody sauna."

"It takes some time to get used to it during the summer," Dillon said. "Lots of people abandon Washington on the weekend, head for Chesapeake Bay. I go home to Charlottesville, to the mountains, as often as I can."

"Lucky you."

Dillon suggested that they walk over to a nearby park to talk, where it would be cooler in the shade. Hawes, sweating profusely, agreed immediately.

On their way to the park, Dillon thought about their first meeting in Berlin. He had finished a set of tennis at the Rot-Weiss Club with a friend, a British diplomat, when he found Hawes waiting courtside. Dillon had been in Germany only a few months. It had been an awkward encounter. Hawes, who worked for MI6's counterintelligence arm, hadn't wasted time with small talk. He warned Dillon that his girlfriend, a young actress from East Berlin, Christa Schiller, was being controlled by the Stasi, the East German security service. She had most likely been instructed to seduce Dillon.

Dillon had been angry; he had refused to believe that Christa, who had seemed to be doggedly apolitical, would betray him. But when she tried to manipulate him into smuggling goods into East Berlin—a move calculated to set up Dillon for blackmail, something Hawes had predicted—Dillon realized that the Englishman was right. Rather than urging him to end the affair, Hawes had encouraged Dillon to play along, to discover why he had been targeted. He never told Dillon the truth, that he planned to "turn" Christa and use her to expose a British intelligence officer working for the KGB in MI6's Berlin Station.

Hawes hadn't hesitated to put the lovers in harm's way, taking a calculated risk with their lives. His gamble had worked, disrupting a Soviet scheme to murder Christa and frame Dillon for her death, in the hopes of precipitating an international incident—a move that would strengthen the hand of hardliners in Moscow. In the end, it was a senior KGB officer who died. At the close of Operation West Wind, Dillon had been ordered to return to Washington, and Christa was resettled in Hamburg.

"It is cooler here," Hawes said, interrupting Dillon's memories. They had reached the park, and Dillon led the way to a bench where several mature elm and linden trees provided shade.

Hawes asked him about his current role at State, and Dillon explained how after his return from Germany, he had been assigned to the Bureau of European Affairs, German Desk. In the spring of 1961, he had been tapped for the Berlin Task Force, an ad hoc group developing policy options for the President.

"So you landed on your feet," Hawes said.

"You could say that."

Dillon couldn't complain, in one sense. His superiors had commended him for his contribution to the success of Operation West Wind. Hawes had made sure that Dillon was portrayed in a heroic light in the after-action reports, and that the depth of his relationship with Christa had been minimized. There were good reasons for downplaying their connection, to protect Christa against any retaliation from the East Germans or Soviets. If there were leaks about the operation, it was best that she be characterized in all the reports as a minor player in the episode.

When he had returned to the U.S., Dillon had been debriefed by State Department counterintelligence officers. He had stuck to the story he and Hawes had agreed upon, and the interview went well. Afterward, he felt drained and took a week off and retreated to Far Ridge. He kept to himself, taking long walks, and catching up on his reading. He wasn't quite sure what to do. Dillon thought about leaving the government and pursuing an academic life, but he had found purpose during his time in Berlin. He felt he had more to contribute.

Hawes must have sensed that Dillon was distracted because he cleared his throat. "Have you been back to Germany?" he asked.

"A few times. Frankfurt and Bonn. Berlin's been off-limits." Dillon had made no attempt to contact Christa when he was in the country. What was the point? They had ended their relationship, and he thought it was best to keep his distance. "How is Christa?" he asked Hawes.

"She's adapting," he said. Hawes explained that Christa had appeared in several plays with a local theater group. A few boyfriends, but nothing serious. She had kept a low profile. "She asked about you when we last talked," Hawes said. "She thought you'd be teaching at a small college by now."

"Perhaps one day I will."

"I read your book on the flight over," Hawes said. "Bought the last copy they had in Foyles. *The Island City*. A striking title."

Dillon didn't respond.

Hawes shifted in his seat and cleared his throat. "In Berlin, I did what was necessary. No apologies for that. But I wanted you to know that I'm not oblivious to the consequences. I wish it had ended differently."

"But it didn't."

"It didn't."

"Just one of those things," Dillon said. "Some bruised feelings, but no permanent damage. And I have quite a tale to tell, some day. Quite a tale." Dillon wasn't about to reveal the full extent of his feelings to Hawes or that at times he still dreamed of Christa.

"And you did your part. Like I told you in Berlin. In the end that counts for something. Perhaps everything."

After Hawes left to return to his hotel, Dillon didn't feel like sitting in a stuffy office and dealing with any more paperwork that day. He walked down to the Mall and made his way to the far western section, past the reflecting pool, where he climbed the steps of the Lincoln Memorial. He always found the statue of America's martyred president somehow comforting. The granite Lincoln seemed at ease, perched in his massive chair, gazing out with a calm, gentle look on his face. Dillon appreciated the irony that the place had become his favorite spot for reflection. As a son of Virginia, he should have gravitated to the Jefferson Memorial.

Hawes' visit had made him think about the past, and about his life since Berlin. Writing *The Island City* had offered a release for his disappointment and pain, his sadness, and his recurring sense of emotional emptiness. It helped him make better sense of what had happened in Berlin. His publisher had been delighted with his choice of topic, sure that its currency—Berlin was in the headlines and on the television news nearly every night—would help in promoting the book and selling more copies. Dillon thought that was absurd, but kept his thoughts to himself.

There were times when he felt alone, particularly when he'd see a slim young woman with chestnut hair on the street and be reminded of Christa. He told himself that loneliness was part and parcel of the human condition. He did his best to forget Christa. He had been out on a few dates in Washington, most arranged by friends, but they had not gone well. It was his fault, he knew. When he had compared the pretty young women he took out to dinner or a movie to Christa, he had found them wanting. He knew that he was being unfair. These daughters of prosperous families were pleasant enough. Conventional. Predictable. Most eager to find a husband and start a family. They didn't stir anything in him. Once, on a trip to New York, he picked up a woman in the Oak Bar of the Plaza Hotel, and he rationalized their slightly-tipsy sex as his consolation prize.

He settled into a routine. He kept himself busy. Long hours at the office, tennis once a week, poker nights with the Group, occasional weekend getaways to Far Ridge. In Charlottesville, he spent time with Charlie and Molly and their son Hillyer, and with his circle of friends from his college days.

He had unburdened himself to Leigh, careful not to reveal too much.

"You had a love affair go wrong," Leigh said. "One where you weren't calling the shots. You've never had that before, have you?"

Dillon nodded. "Nothing like this."

"And this German girl got to you. So now you know how it feels. It's going to hurt for some time, but you'll recover. There will be another girl, maybe the one you'll want to marry. You'll be a bit more cautious, which isn't a bad thing."

Dillon knew very little about Leigh's brief marriage. It had ended badly, with his wife leaving him for another man two years into the marriage. Leigh had quietly divorced her, and he never directly mentioned that time in his life. It was not a topic of discussion within the Randolph family. When he was in high school, Dillon had once asked Leigh if he ever thought about marrying again, and Leigh had laughed and said he would rather not be an old fool.

"My advice is to keep your head down," Leigh said. "Keep working. Give it six months or so. Trust me, things will look different." He paused. "Have you thought of coming back to Charlottesville?"

"To what end?"

"Settling down here. The Randolph name carries considerable weight."

"Politics? Is that what you're suggesting?"

"You know the people here. You know Washington. You know foreign policy. There's the legacy of your father. You'd start with a huge advantage."

"Congress? There's an incumbent, who's a member of our party."

"He might be willing to step aside. He'll never be a national figure—to his credit, he knows that. You could. I can see you in the Senate."

Dillon laughed. "I'm flattered by the thought, but it's not realistic. Uncle Leigh, even if it was something I wanted, I don't want to be a politician. And I'm probably too liberal for this district. Especially on the race question. If I moved back, it wouldn't be to run for office. You know I've thought about teaching. Writing poetry. Writing about poetry."

"Would that be enough? After what you've been exposed to, now? Wouldn't you like to leave a more substantial mark?"

"That was supposed to be Wash's life, not mine."

"Promise me that you'll think about it. You belong here, Dillon. And it's a great place to raise a family."

"I'll think about it, Leigh."

FIVE

At midnight on August 12th, just weeks after Feliks Hawes' visit to Washington, the situation in Berlin changed dramatically. The East German military and police suddenly threw up a makeshift wall of barbed wire and barricades to block off the Russian-controlled sector of the city. The Anti-Fascist Protection Rampart—the name for the structure used by the East German authorities—was hastily erected to stem the flow of refugees to the West.

The Berlin Task Force was caught by surprise. Word didn't reach Washington until the early evening on Saturday, when Dillon and his colleagues were home for the weekend. There had been no warning, not from the Embassy in Bonn or the Berlin Mission, nor from the American intelligence agencies (of which there were some twelve active with offices in the city). There had been few signs that the East Germans would move so quickly; their leader, Walter Ulbricht, had told the international press in June that he had no intention of erecting *eine Mauer*, a wall.

Early Sunday morning, Dillon had been called in for an emergency meeting at Main State. His former colleagues at the Berlin Mission had been scrambling to gather as much information as possible about the surprise closure of the sector border and the ongoing construction of a barrier. There had been no immediate response by the Allied military in Berlin. It soon became clear that there was no appetite at the highest levels to force a confrontation with the Soviets and East Germans.

"We're not going to war over this," Harold Braun, one of Dillon's colleagues on the German Desk, said. "I doubt the Berlin Garrison could hold out for more than a day or two, and once the shooting starts, the city would be completely cut off. No rescue column barreling up the autobahn."

"That could escalate into a full-scale war," Dillon said. "Why would Ulbricht and the Russians risk this?"

"Have you looked at the numbers of arrivals at Marienfelde?" Braun asked. "In August roughly fifteen-hundred refugees were crossing over each and every day. Educated young people. Professionals—doctors, engineers. For the East, it's a terrible brain drain. Can't blame Ulbricht, in a way. If he didn't close the border, they wouldn't have a functioning society. They say there's a joke going around in East Berlin. Ulbricht dies and is met at the pearly gates by St. Peter, and Peter insists he's in the wrong place, that Ulbricht has to go to hell. A few weeks later, a large group of minor demons turns up at the gates to heaven, and St. Peter tells them that they must be lost—they can't enter. The demons answer: 'We're not lost. Please help us. We're refugees.' If that's what the average East Germans think of Ulbricht, it's no wonder that he needs a wall."

"A huge risk, nonetheless."

"Is it? Possession is nine-tenths of the law. They built the wall entirely on their side of the sector border. The rest of the city remains free. You've read the same cables I have: we've told Khrushchev that we won't sit still if he tries anything further. That's why the President sent General Clay to Berlin and had the Army dispatch a convoy to Berlin."

"Symbolic moves." Dillon knew that it represented the prudent course, but he didn't like passively accepting the cordoning off of East Berlin.

"They are. But, if you step back for a moment, both sides got what they wanted. Khrushchev and Ulbricht can stop the outflow of refugees, which was an embarrassment and made them look weak. The Berlin Wall is a decisive move. And from our perspective, it cements the status quo in place. Khrushchev is less likely to insist on East Germany swallowing up the Allied sectors. We can point to the Wall as a failure of their system, and they can point to it as a rampart against fascism."

"That's quite cynical, you know."

Braun shrugged. He had cultivated a reputation as a cynic. "It's the reality on the ground. This is the modus vivendi for Berlin."

"What about the people of East Berlin? They're no better than prisoners, now."

"I suppose so. They're hostages to fortune, in a sense. Better they stay in place than we risk a thermonuclear war. Not such a sacrifice, when you see it that way."

* * *

It took a month before things quieted down, and Dillon could return to his settled routine. He had worked every weekend since the Wall went up, and when his colleague Eliot Garrison and his wife Gloria invited him for a late Sunday brunch at Martin's Carriage House in Georgetown, he had eagerly accepted. Dillon and Eliot had met in Dillon's first weeks at State, and they had been doubles partners a few times.

They were halfway through their meal when an attractive young blonde woman approached their table. Gloria greeted her warmly—introducing her as Jill Fairchild—and invited her to join them for coffee. With a quick glance at Dillon, Gloria explained that Jill had recently arrived in Washington from the West Coast, and was getting her master's in art history at George Washington University.

"We met at a gallery show," Gloria said. "And now we're fast friends!"

"Dillon is a colleague," Eliot said as a way of introduction. "An expert on Germany. He's been incommunicado for a month, dealing with the crisis in Berlin. Burning the midnight oil."

"That must be fascinating," Jill said.

"It's been a tad bit tense," Dillon said. "It's finally settled down, and I've been able to come up for air."

Dillon had been immediately taken by her. She looked like she had just come from the beach in California: tanned, blonde hair, blue eyes, a willowy body. She would have been a classic beauty if not for her slightly curved nose and the faded scar on her chin. Those imperfections made her more approachable, and all the more desirable, as did her

44

understated way of dressing, her single strand of pearls and the modest shift that hinted at her shapely body.

After the waiter brought Jill a cup of coffee, Dillon asked her about her graduate program.

"I'm researching American realist painters for my master's thesis," she said, looking directly at Dillon. "The Ashcan School. The Eight. The Fourteenth Street School."

Dillon shook his head. "I don't know much about modern art, to be truthful. I know a little bit about the French. Renoir and Monet. *The Houses of Parliament.*"

"The Impressionists, yes. The painters I'm studying found their approach too academic. They wanted to show the world as it is. Everyone knows Edward Hopper, but the rest have been forgotten. Robert Henri. John French Sloan. George Bellows. The National Gallery has a few of their paintings."

"You ought to give Dillon a tour some time," Gloria said. "Eliot tells me that he works too hard. He needs a break, now and then."

"I'd like that," Dillon said. "Would love to learn more. I spent an afternoon in the Louvre a few years ago, when I was a student. And when I was posted to Berlin, I visited the Dahlem Museum—the Gemäldegalerie. Got a chance to see the Dutch Masters, and that marvelous bust of Queen Nefertiti."

He remembered the rainy day he had visited the museum with Christa. They had strolled through the galleries, admiring the art, before a light lunch. Then they had gone to her top-floor flat in Wilmersdorf and slept together for the first time, the sound of the rain beating down on the roof above them. It was a day he would always remember. How could he forget?

"I envy you," Jill said. "That must have been wonderful."

"It was."

"You should know that Dillon is also an artist, of a different sort," Eliot said. "A poet. Two books of poetry." He grinned at Dillon. "I read the Berlin one. Enjoyed it. Some vivid descriptions of the city and its people."

"You've joined a very select group, then," Dillon said. "People who admit to reading my poetry. Small in number."

"I'll have something to look forward to, then," Jill said. "Joining that select group."

"I'd like to learn more about these painters of yours," Dillon said. "Perhaps you'll give me the tour?"

She nodded. "And in the meantime, I'll read some of your poetry."

They visited the Corcoran Gallery on their first date. Jill showed Dillon several paintings by George Bellows and Edward Hopper. Standing in front of a painting, she was transformed, a different woman. There was an energy to her, a passion, that Dillon found appealing, and he couldn't help wondering whether she would bring the same intensity to bed with her. At the same time, she had a reserve, a distance, that Dillon wanted to overcome. He wanted to possess her, to see her naked beneath him, her breathing ragged and sudden, her face transformed by pleasure.

They stopped for coffee at a nearby cafe. In the background, Dillon could hear the distinctive voice of Elvis Presley, singing "It's Now or Never." He sat across from her, studying her face.

"I was surprised by *The Island City*," Jill said. "I didn't expect a love story, even if it didn't quite work out in the end."

"It's a work of imagination," Dillon said lightly.

"Not all imagination, I suspect." She took a sip of her coffee.

He nodded. "True. There was a woman. It didn't work out. For different reasons than in the poem. A clean break. As my Uncle Leigh preaches, no point in looking back. It only slows you down."

"And you listen to your uncle?"

"Very much. He has very good instincts. We've always been very close. After we lost my mother, and my brother, Leigh held things together, even more so than my father."

"I'm sorry about your losses," she said. "I'm an only child. So no brothers or sisters."

"I miss my brother even after ten years. You don't forget."

"Is there anything more important than family?" she asked. "If the right man came along, I'd like to make a home, have children. I don't see why I couldn't continue to study art on the side. After all, they don't bar mothers from museums."

"And what's your idea of the right man?" Dillon asked.

"Is that a leading question?"

"It is." He took her hand; she had long, graceful fingers. "I always thought I'd be married by now. It never seemed to work out. I haven't given up on the idea. If you're looking for the right man, I'm looking for the right woman."

"And what's your idea of the right woman?"

He took her other hand in his. "Isn't she sitting here with me?"

"I'm very flattered. But you don't know me very well."

"That's something that we can fix," he said.

A week later, in Dillon's apartment, on their third date, they sat on his couch, drinking red wine and talking. When Dillon leaned in, she met his lips with a tentative kiss, and he pulled her closer. They kissed again, and she sighed when he gently touched her on her breast. When Dillon moved his hand onto her thigh, she stiffened immediately and pulled away from him.

"This may seem foolish to you," she said. "But I don't. I mean, I haven't…" She didn't finish her sentence.

"It's not foolish," he said.

"I want my first time to be with my husband," she said. "Does that seem terribly old fashioned?"

Dillon wasn't completely surprised; he knew that, depending on their upbringing, some women waited until marriage before having sex. He hadn't expected that from Jill—the art scene could be somewhat bohemian, but he was content to wait.

"It's old fashioned in a nice way," he said. "And whoever marries you will be a very lucky man."

He proposed to her a week later after a romantic, candle-lit dinner at the Occidental Grill. When he took the engagement ring out of his jacket pocket and motioned for her left hand, she let him slide the ring onto her finger as he asked her to marry him. She smiled and told him that he had made her the happiest girl in Washington.

She didn't seem surprised by his proposal, even though they had only known each other for less than a month. He had made his intentions clear enough, and she had encouraged him. While he could have waited longer, he didn't see the point in delay. He wanted her as his wife. Dillon knew that it wasn't a marriage of equals. He liked that she looked up to him, turned to him to explain the world and its mysteries. She was young and beautiful and intelligent, and he thought she would make a fine wife and mother.

* * *

Uncle Leigh made a rare trip to Washington after Dillon called him about Jill, their engagement, and how they were eager to get married. Dillon arranged for a six o'clock dinner with Jill and his uncle at the Willard Hotel, where Leigh was staying.

Dillon arrived fifteen minutes late, and he found Leigh and Jill already seated at the table, talking. They greeted him with smiles.

"Jill has been telling me about her research into Childe Hassam and the Ten," Leigh said. "It turns out that one of my friends in Charlottesville owns a Hassam. I've promised her that when she comes to Far Ridge, we'll make sure she gets to see it."

"I'd like that very much," Jill said.

Dillon took his seat across from Leigh, with Jill on his left.

"Leigh made a very interesting suggestion," Jill said. "He wondered if we might consider having the wedding in Charlottesville. A reception at Far Ridge."

"That's up to you," Dillon said. "We can marry here in Washington, or fly out to the West Coast, or have the ceremony in Charlottesville. I want a happy bride."

"I'd like the wedding in Charlottesville," she said.

"Bravo," Leigh said. "You'll be welcomed with open arms."

They had a pleasant dinner. Leigh told stories about Dillon's childhood, and got Jill to talk about her upbringing in Southern California. They all had too much to drink, and Dillon and Jill took a cab back to her apartment afterward. He kissed her goodnight there because he had an early meeting the following morning.

Dillon had a quick lunch with Leigh at noon. His uncle didn't wait long to come to the point.

"You make a handsome couple," he said. "She's a lovely girl, I'll grant you that. A bit of an intellectual, as well, and that suits you. An only child. She has exquisite manners. She was raised to be a lady."

"Her mother is from London. A war bride."

"And the father? Have you met him?"

"He died ten years ago, when she was eleven. Something Jill and I have in common, losing a parent at a young age. I've talked to her mother on the phone once."

"What was she like?"

"A plummy accent. Very curious. I think she wants to make sure that my intentions are honorable."

Leigh arched his eyebrows, and Dillon was reminded of his father, who was known for making the same expression.

"What about Jill's politics? No Birchers in the family? You know how those Southern Californians can be."

"Jill's a Democrat. She greatly admires Jackie. Not that she's particularly political."

"One thing we can count on these days. The Kennedys offer us exquisite style. Style over substance." He looked at Dillon for a long moment, weighing his words. "You're moving rather quickly. You feel you know her well enough?"

"I do. And I have the advantage of experience."

"No one disputes that." Leigh laughed. "Too much experience, perhaps. Are you prepared for the restrictions of marriage?" He paused. "Some men love the chase. They're bored unless there's a new conquest on the horizon."

"I'm ready to settle down. Start a family. All the things you've been pestering me about for years. Jill wants that, too."

"The girl in Germany. The actress. You're sure that you're over her?"

"It's been three years. Time enough. I'm ready to move on. Besides, it would never have lasted. We both could see that."

Leigh leaned back in his chair. "Lord knows, you don't need my blessing for your marriage, but you have it. She's lovely, and she'll be a credit to you in whatever direction your career heads."

When Dillon saw Jill that night, she was uncharacteristically direct about their dinner with Leigh.

"Did I pass muster?" she asked. "Did your uncle approve?"

"Don't be ridiculous. The only muster anyone had to pass was yours, and you said yes to me. Leigh thinks you're wonderful. A catch. Smart and beautiful. He's been bugging me for years to find the right girl and settle down. So he's happy."

"I'm no Southern belle."

"Thank God."

"You say that now, but you may feel differently later."

"Trust me, Jill, you're the woman that I want."

* * *

They were married in Charlottesville at Christ Episcopal Church, with the reception at Far Ridge, just as Leigh had suggested.

Charlie Wood was Dillon's best man; Jill's closest friend from college, Beth Peters, was her maid of honor. Dillon arranged for Jill's mother to fly from California for the ceremony. All of the members of the Group of Five attended; Grayson Talbott and Alex Landauer came stag, Jan Nowak with a date, and Palmer with his wife, Cora.

Jill wore an ivory wedding gown that showed off her slender figure, and she was, all agreed, a radiant bride. Leigh escorted her down the aisle to give her away to Dillon, and she flashed a smile as Dillon took her hand. They said their vows, and when Dillon kissed the bride they were rewarded with applause.

After the ceremony, they piled into cars and drove to Far Ridge. There was a large tent in the backyard, with a wooden floor for dancing, and the weather had cooperated—it was a cool, sunny September day. The guests attacked the buffet lunch with gusto, and the caterers made sure to keep refilling their champagne flutes.

Jill's mother, Evonne Fairchild, was a thin, nervous woman with a clipped British accent. Dillon found it a challenge to carry on a conversation with her of any length. She proclaimed herself delighted with the marriage. He watched her take in Far Ridge, the high ceilings, dark furniture, deep rugs.

"She's been sizing up the Randolphs," Leigh told Dillon in private. "A million questions, all very polite. She's desperate to know if you own the house free and clear since we lost your father. She's making calculations. How much we're worth."

"I've married Jill. Not her mother."

"And you're a lucky man," Leigh said. "From what I've seen, the mother is quite mercenary."

Dillon nodded. "I think that it's understandable. After Jill's father died, Mrs. Fairchild had to carry the load. I imagine financial matters have been a constant worry. You can't blame her for being concerned about money."

"And Jill? How did it impact her?"

"She's frugal, but she likes nice things. What woman doesn't?"

"Well, you'll always be able to keep her in style," Leigh said. "Your father has made sure of that."

"I'm earning my own keep," Dillon said. "Although I won't get rich off government pay."

"You're already rich. Ask Evonne Fairchild. She can probably give you an accurate estimate of your net worth down to the penny." He paused. "I suppose I'm being too hard on her. What mother doesn't want her daughter well married?"

Dillon didn't remember much of the reception. His college friends made sure that his glass was always full. He and Jill went table-to-table greeting guests and accepting compliments. At the appointed hour, Jill changed out of her wedding dress into evening wear.

Later, the guests waited in Far Ridge's circular driveway and cheered and threw rice at the couple as they made their way to a waiting limousine. They would spend the night at a hotel in Charlottesville, and leave in the morning for their honeymoon in Europe.

SIX

Dillon and Jill arrived in Europe two days after the wedding, on a Pan Am flight from Washington to Rome. Dillon had been in Italy some ten years before, when as a student at the University of Cologne he had traveled around Europe during school breaks.

Rome proved to be a disappointment—filled with too many American tourists and choking pollution from the small cars and motorbikes crowding the city. By the time they reached Venice, it was later in the month, and there were fewer visitors there. Jill had loved everything about the floating city—its canals and palaces and churches, its broad plazas, and its maze of narrow streets with small shops and restaurants.

She marveled at the Baroque jewel of Santa Maria della Salute and the ornate Rialto Bridge over the Grand Canal. They stayed in the Gritti Palace, near the Plaza San Marco. Dillon made sure they stopped by Harry's Bar, Hemingway's old haunt, at the end of the narrow Calle Vallaresso for a Bellini and a dry Montgomery martini. They spent hours in the Gallerie dell'Accademia, where Jill was delighted by the paintings of Hieronymus Bosch and Titian and the statues by Canova. For their dinners, they enjoyed the local favorites: fresh grilled sea bass, gnocchi with calamaretti, marinated mackerel, and seafood couscous.

Dillon felt relieved to be out of Washington, to put some distance between himself and work. When he read the Paris edition of the *Herald Tribune*, typically a few days late, over coffee in a cafe surrounded by happy Venetians, the current international disputes seemed far away. Particularly Vietnam. Back home the Yankees were once again winning the World Series, beating the Reds in five games. Dillon would finish his newspaper and watch the locals drinking coffee and talking and flirting and going about their lives and he would contrast that timelessness with the hyperactive routine he had left behind. But, he reminded himself, the day would come soon enough when he could return to the simple pleasures of civilian life.

* * *

It was a honeymoon, after all, when couples were meant to enjoy their private time alone, and Dillon took every opportunity to make love to his beautiful young wife.

Jill had been shy and passive on their wedding night in Charlottesville, but Dillon chalked it up to her inexperience and the stress of the day. On their honeymoon, they made love nearly every night. He quickly discovered that Jill wasn't particularly passionate. Her reserve in bed didn't bother him. Over time, she would warm up as she became more comfortable with him. He could be patient.

She had been sheltered; he could see that as she struggled with physical intimacy. She had one boyfriend before Dillon, and they hadn't progressed beyond kissing. Dillon tried to encourage her not to be so modest. Jill didn't like undressing in front of him, and she wanted the lights off whenever they made love. In the dim light, he could see that she often had her eyes tightly shut. When he would whisper to her that her body was beautiful and that he loved seeing it, she would just shake her head.

"I'm your husband," he said. "If anyone in the world should know what you're like naked, it's me."

"Please, Dillon, don't insist. It embarrasses me."

"You're so beautiful. Can you blame me for enjoying the view?"

"Please. It makes me uncomfortable."

He could see that she had tears in her eyes, so he agreed that they would keep the lights off.

They grew closer as the days passed. One night at dinner, a small jazz quartet began playing "Night and Day," and Dillon felt a surge of emotion that brought tears to his eyes. Jill looked at him with concern.

"Are you all right?"

"That was my father's favorite song," he explained. "Simply because my mother loved it. She thought the world of Fred Astaire."

"You haven't said much about her," Jill said. "Do you have any favorite memories of her?"

"I was quite young when she died. You know that."

"But you must have some memories."

"It was a long time ago. I don't like to dwell on it. It makes me sad, and it won't bring her back. Nothing will. So what's the point?"

"I don't know," she said. "I think of my father pushing me in a swing. I can remember that. We were both laughing. And one time when we went for ice cream. Those are good memories. There are others, too."

"We're different about that, then," Dillon said. "To each his own."

* * *

He had brought Robert Lowell's *Imitations* with him, and read aloud for Jill his translations of Rimbaud, Heine, Rilke, and Pasternak. Jill liked Rilke's poetry.

"It reminds me of your poem. *The Island City*. The sections about the girl, Charlotte."

"There are some similarities," he conceded.

"It's about the actress you dated, isn't it? You've called her Charlotte in the poem."

Dillon had told her about Christa, but he hadn't given her much in the way of detail, nor had he revealed the depth of his feelings.

"In part, it is about her," he said. "But there's imagination involved. You can't read it literally."

"Did you love her? Christa?"

Dillon frowned. He didn't want to talk about Christa Schiller. Certainly not on his honeymoon. What good could come from that? It was best to keep the memories at bay.

"I'm certainly not carrying a torch for her," he told her. "You're my wife. I love you."

"But did you love her? I just want to know."

"If you must. I fell in love with a woman who didn't exist, a fiction, an invention. I give Christa credit. She was a marvelous actress, and she had me fooled. That's reflected, in part, in the poem."

"Why would she do that?"

"Perhaps she thought I would make her an honest woman," he lied. "Bring her back to the States. A life of leisure. Or maybe a chance to break into Hollywood. I don't know. I broke it off before I found out."

"A German gold-digger," she said and giggled.

"Don't say that," he said, surprised at his own anger. "It wasn't like that."

He knew that he would never tell Jill the full story of his time in Berlin. It wasn't something he wanted to share. There were only a few people who knew what had happened. Christa, of course, knew most of it. Feliks Hawes and a few others were privy to aspects of his life in Berlin. Dillon preferred to keep it that way.

"I'm sorry," he said. "I don't mean to be short with you. You're naturally curious. But I told you before, I'm not wild about dwelling in the past. It's you and me, now. That's what matters to me."

"And I'm sorry, too, for what I said about Christa. I only want to know more about you. About what makes you tick."

"There will be plenty of time for that," he said. "Not just all at once."

* * *

They went house-hunting in Georgetown upon their return to Washington. They found a beautiful two-bedroom Federal period house built of ancient red brick. The house was three windows wide, with a fanlight over the front door and a wrought iron railing in the front. Jill was happy when Dillon made an immediate offer to buy it at the asking price. Since his father's death, Dillon had few financial concerns—he had not only inherited Far Ridge but also cash and securities that amounted to what he regarded as a small fortune.

Leigh encouraged the purchase. "You have the money, and you can't go wrong with Georgetown real estate. Last I looked, they weren't making any more. And having a second home there could prove handy."

A week before their visit to Far Ridge for Christmas, Jill complained about an upset stomach. She went to her doctor a few days later and upon her return, blushing deeply, told Dillon that she had been given a pregnancy test. A day later, they learned that she was pregnant. Dillon was delighted. He liked the idea of being a father, even if he hadn't expected it to happen so quickly.

"I'm so surprised," Jill said. She smiled, and suddenly looked very young. Dillon felt a wave of tenderness toward her. They had talked about having children, but not in the first year of their marriage.

"How do you feel about all this?" he asked.

"I'm scared. And excited."

"I think it's marvelous," he said.

"I'm going to get fat. Huge. I just know it. You'll think I'm ugly."

He shook his head. "You're so skinny. I can't imagine you'll ever be fat."

"I hope it's a boy," she said. "You want a son, don't you?"

Dillon laughed. "I love the idea of having a baby with you, boy or girl. And either way, I hope we'll have more than one."

He was surprised by her sudden tears. "Oh, Dillon, it's so overwhelming. I'm not really ready for this baby, let alone more."

Dillon pulled her to him and embraced her. "Don't worry. We'll make sure you have all the help you need. We can have your mother stay with us after the baby comes. And then a nanny. You won't have to do it all yourself."

"I'm sorry," she said. "I don't mean to complain. It's all so sudden."

"Sudden, but wonderful," he said.

SEVEN

Washington, D.C.
Winter 1962

Early in the New Year, Jan Nowak approached Dillon about a possible change in his role at State. He wanted to know if Dillon would be interested in transferring from the Berlin Task Force to the Bureau of Intelligence and Research, working for its new director, Roger Hilsman.

The Bureau, known as the INR within State, was the successor to the Research and Analysis Branch of the Office of Strategic Services, the legendary organization best known for operating behind enemy lines during the Second World War. As Jan explained it, the INR provided an independent analysis of events to State's policymakers on the sixth and seventh floors.

"They're looking for smart men with experience in the field," Jan explained. "Your name came up. You've impressed people with your work on the Task Force. And they like that you've had diplomatic postings. You're no desk jockey."

Dillon was flattered by being recruited for the INR. With the erection of the Wall, the action had shifted away from Berlin. He also didn't want to miss the chance to work with Hilsman, already a legendary figure at State. A West Pointer, Hilsman had fought with Merrill's Marauders and led guerrilla bands in Burma for the OSS. He had parachuted into Manchuria to free American prisoners in a Japanese POW camp in Mukden, including his father, a colonel in the Army who had been captured in the Philippines in 1942. His father supposedly asked Hilsman what had taken him so long.

Like nearly everyone in State, Dillon admired Hilsman, the perfect

Kennedyesque man of action, equal parts intellectual and warrior. In the decade or so after the war, Hilsman had earned a doctorate at Columbia, taught at Princeton, and ended up at the Library of Congress, where he was recruited for the State Department.

"I'm interested," Dillon said. "What's next?"

"An interview with Hilsman, but that's a formality."

Dillon found himself in Hilsman's office a week later. Hilsman looked more like a college professor than a former Army officer, with his button-down shirt, muted red tie, and horn-rimmed glasses.

"Read your file," he began. "Did some asking around. Apparently you helped out the Brits and the CIA on an operation in Berlin. Acquitted yourself well." He paused, waiting for Dillon to respond.

"I've never read my file, so you have me at a disadvantage," Dillon said. "As to Berlin, I did what needed to be done. Not something I asked for, but something I felt I had to do."

Hilsman seemed pleased with his answer. "We're looking for men who've been in the field, who understand that plans can only take you so far and then you have to improvise. Men who can figure out what is really going on. They also say that you're a quick study. That's what the Bureau does for the Department. Quick study, quick recommendations. We're here to cut through the bureaucratic red tape. How does that sound to you?"

"It's appealing. I want to contribute to getting things done. Moving the country forward."

"It comes with some risks," Hilsman said. "You won't always be popular. We're going to step on some toes. You may get the cold shoulder from some of the old-timers."

"You've read my file," Dillon said. "I know what it's like to not be popular."

Dillon's messy and indiscreet entanglement with the wife of a fellow diplomat, an affair which had ended badly, had no doubt been duly recorded in his personnel file. It had been almost five years since the episode, but he recognized that for some in the Department it represented a permanent blot on his record. Hilsman didn't strike him as the type who would care too much about a botched love affair.

Hilsman grinned. "That's true," he said. "And you've learned your lesson?"

"I'm married. We're expecting our first child."

"That's good. Any trouble you get into will be on account of policy, then, not from tomcatting around. And we'll have you take on something different, something important. Vietnam. The situation is heating up there, and we need to find options other than writing a blank check for Diem and his generals, a check they're likely to cash in a Swiss bank."

"I'd like that," Dillon said. "Something new."

* * *

Dillon quickly learned that traditionalists at Main State didn't care for the sudden prominence of the Bureau under Hilsman. His colleagues in the INR were cocky to a man (and there were no females in the Bureau other than a few secretaries), aware that their leader was respected at the Pentagon and the CIA, no paper-pusher, but a warrior, a man's man. As his staff, they basked in his glory. They had instant credibility. They were the can-do boys, eager to tackle the most difficult diplomatic challenges.

As a group, they were convinced that they were smart enough and dedicated enough to figure things out, to find the elegant solutions, to help fashion the policies that would be adopted by the new Administration. And why not? Couldn't they act as State's diplomatic equivalent of the Green Berets, a nimble, elite force leading the fight against world Communism?

After a few weeks on the job, however, Dillon discovered some of the limitations to the Bureau's approach. Take Vietnam. Not one of his colleagues could speak Vietnamese. A few spoke French, the language of the country's colonial masters. Even fewer had been to the country. Dillon never calculated how much time they had collectively spent on the ground, in-country, but it had to be only weeks. That didn't stop them from drawing conclusions. He worried that he and his colleagues might be too sure of themselves. Were they like those denizens of Plato's famous cave, trying to judge reality from the shadows on the wall? And what might be the consequences of their incomplete and limited knowledge?

* * *

It was a difficult pregnancy for Jill. She suffered from morning sickness and a troubling swelling of her hands and feet. Dillon had never imagined that carrying a baby would be so difficult for her—she had been so poised throughout the early months of their marriage. Now, she was anxious and moody, constantly worried. He tried his best to soothe her.

He had been surprised when she invited Palmer and Cora Knox to dinner. "I'm cooped up here all day," she said. "It's been incredibly boring."

Jill liked Cora, a fellow Californian. It surprised Dillon because they were so different. Cora was loud and opinionated, and she drank too much. She had adopted the new beehive hairstyle, which Dillon thought was quite unflattering on her.

The dinner proved to be a minor disaster from the very start. Dillon could smell the alcohol on Cora's breath when she and Palmer arrived, but that didn't stop her from finishing two glasses of wine before Jill had even served dinner, a pot roast with potatoes and green beans.

"Does Dillon talk to you about his work?" she asked Jill near the end of dinner.

"When it's something important," she said.

"Is that so, Dillon?" Cora asked, turning to him.

"I spare her all the boring office politics," he said, not sure where Cora was going with her questioning. "I tell her stories about my colorful colleagues, so when she meets them, she's prepared."

"Palmer doesn't introduce his colleagues to me, colorful or not. Not a single blessed one."

"We're here, aren't we?" Palmer asked. "Doesn't Dillon count?"

"Palmer won't say what it is he does on his trips," she said, slurring her words. "It's secret, secret, top secret. Hush hush."

"Cora," Palmer said. "Please."

"Please what? They must know that you're a spook. Who do you think you're fooling? Hush hush."

"For Christ's sake, why don't you just shut up for once?" Palmer flushed with anger.

There was an awkward silence. Dillon looked over at Jill, not sure what to say. She seemed frozen, taken aback at the situation.

"We should go," Palmer said to Dillon. He turned to Jill. "Thank you for dinner. It was delicious."

"Can't you stay for coffee?" Jill asked.

"I think it's best we go."

"Sorry," Cora said. "Sorry, sorry, sorry. I've ruined the evening."

"You haven't," Jill said. "We loved having you over. We must do this again, sometime soon. Before the baby."

"We should." Cora gave her a lopsided smile. "Let's count on it."

* * *

Two days after President Kennedy committed the country to putting a man on the moon during a speech at Rice Stadium, Dillon met Grayson Talbott for lunch at the Monocle. Grayson was all smiles. He thought the President's speech had been bold enough to command public attention.

"We're stressing that it's not enough to put a man on the moon's surface," he said. "You need to bring him back, kicking and screaming. That will keep the Russians from landing one of their cosmonauts on the moon, declaring victory, and leaving Ivan there as his oxygen runs out."

"Very funny," Dillon replied.

"I'll bet there were a lot of relieved Russian pilots after Jack laid down the challenge. They ducked having to volunteer for a suicide mission."

"There's some risk to setting an aggressive goal like that," Dillon said. "I assume that the scientists and NASA say it's something we can do."

"We can. Landing a man on the moon is about more than scientific breakthroughs. It's having a vision for the country. It's the next frontier. We can do this. It will prove our system is superior to theirs, and we could use the propaganda boost in Latin America, and Africa, and Southeast Asia."

"I read in the papers that Gallup says close to sixty percent of Americans don't think it's a great idea."

"Fifty-eight percent, to be precise," Grayson said. "They'll come around. Younger people love the idea. And there will be plenty of contracts for Boeing and McDonnell and Douglas. Well-paid jobs in lots of Congressional districts."

Dillon laughed. "That's not a particularly lofty reason for supporting the space program."

"Who said good policy couldn't also be good politics? Who said we couldn't keep an eye on 1964? We need some solid accomplishments to brag about, and space can be one of them. We won't need many votes in California or Florida to switch them over to Jack, and that would give us a clear mandate for the second term."

"What about Nixon? If he beats Pat Brown in November and becomes governor of California, it could set him up for another run in '64."

Grayson shook his head. "Brown's no pushover. It's tough to beat an incumbent. Nixon's been out of California for years. Sure, he carried the state in the presidential election, but local politics are different. Even if he wins, he looks like a job hopper if he runs for President. And if we continue to make progress, there will be no beating us. That's why we have to succeed. Think about how much better this country can be? With Jack and those he's brought to Washington—people like us—the sky's the limit."

"Things are looking up," Dillon said.

"How is Jill doing?" Grayson asked.

"Better, thank you. Can't say that it's been the happiest time. She's had a rough pregnancy. She's been moody. Emotional. I'm hoping that we can get back to normal once the baby comes. At least, we're in the home stretch. The due date is only ten days away."

"They say having a child changes you. Makes you think about the future more."

"I suppose that's true," Dillon replied. "I guess I'm going to find out. What about your love life, Grayson?"

"With my job? It's hard to find time to sleep, let alone to romance a girl. I figure that I'll get serious once I get off this merry-go-round. I won't waste any time, just like you. Meet a girl, marry her, start a family. One, two, three."

* * *

Jill went into labor a day after her due date of September 25th. She called Dillon at the office, and he rushed home and took her to the hospital. Then, he sat in the cramped waiting room with the other prospective fathers, drinking coffee and trying to distract himself by reading the newspaper.

Dr. Mancuso came to the waiting room three hours later to inform him that Jill had delivered a healthy baby girl. A nurse took Dillon to the nursery viewing area and pointed out through the glass his daughter, a bundled infant with a pink card: BABY GIRL RANDOLPH.

When Dillon was ushered into Jill's room, she was still groggy. He kissed her on the cheek and held her hand. "How is the baby?" she asked. "They only let me see her for a short time."

"She's fine," Dillon told her. "Adorable. A beautiful little girl."

"I don't know what I would have done without the spinal block," she said. "I was so sure that I was going to have a boy, I didn't really think about a girl's name. Not seriously."

"We don't have to name her this very moment."

"Can we call her Sandra? It was my grandmother's name. But only if you like it."

"I do," he said. "And you should rest, now. I called your mother, and she should be here tomorrow. She'll be there to help out when you and Sandra come out of the hospital."

"Thank you. If you don't mind, I'd like to sleep now."

"Of course. You deserve to sleep for as long as you like."

Dillon was delighted with her, and with the tiny pink face and swaddled bundle that was his daughter. Since his father's death, he had thought about what having a family meant. He hoped Sandra would soon have brothers and sisters, and that in the summer and on holidays Far Ridge would be filled with their laughter. Perhaps Leigh had it right—perhaps he should move back to Charlottesville after he was done with Washington, after he, and the Administration, had made their mark.

EIGHT

Washington, D.C.
October 1962

Thursday poker night with the Group of Five, this week's game at Grayson Talbott's place, an attractively decorated apartment within walking distance of the White House. Once again, Palmer was absent. He had telephoned Dillon on Monday to say that he had to leave town on a new work assignment, and wouldn't be able to make it.

After they had finished playing a few hands—with a chain-smoking Jan Nowak accumulating the most chips—Grayson raised the question of Cuba. They were willing to abandon their cards and talk. They all knew something about the emerging crisis. The White House had approved a U-2 reconnaissance overflight the previous Sunday after some intelligence reports suggested that the Soviets might be constructing missile sites in Cuba. On Monday, the CIA's National Photographic Interpretation Center reviewed the photos from the flight and identified objects that they interpreted as medium-range ballistic missiles. Dillon knew that Hilsman and McGeorge Bundy had conveyed the bad news to the President after the photographs had been analyzed.

"Is Khrushchev mad?" Grayson asked. "Placing nuclear-armed missiles so close to us, within range of Washington and New York, is incredibly reckless."

"He didn't expect to get caught during the construction phase," Alex said. "He wanted to present the President with a *fait accompli*."

Dillon shook his head. "Khrushchev must be trying to impress the hardliners in the Kremlin. I can't believe he wants to play chicken. Threatening us in our backyard is a mistake."

"It's been all hands on deck at the Pentagon," Alex said. "We've been asked to look at possible responses. Nikita may have bought himself an invasion of Cuba, and this time there will be plenty of air cover."

"It's best if we can find a way to defuse the situation," Jan said. "I hear that ExComm is considering diplomatic solutions. We don't want to give the Russians a ready-made excuse to move into Berlin."

The ExComm, an ad hoc committee of the President's closest advisers and aides, including Bobby Kennedy, Lyndon Johnson, General Maxwell Taylor, Dean Rusk, Robert McNamara, and the Joint Chiefs, had been meeting every day. Everyone at State and in the Pentagon desperately wanted the inside story on their deliberations. What options were on the table? What did the President think? Dillon had heard that bombing runs against the missile sites were under consideration. Alex's comments suggested there was truth to the rumors that the Pentagon was arguing for a full-scale invasion of Cuba. It was dismayingly easy to imagine how things might spiral out of control, how U.S. actions and Soviet counter-actions could lead to a broader conflict, perhaps even a nuclear exchange.

"One thing is very clear," Grayson said. "The President has to stand firm. He can't allow those missiles in Cuba. It's just a question of how to get them out."

"Trust me, we can take the missile sites out," Alex said. "Within minutes."

"That's what I'm worried about," Grayson replied. "Easy to start. Hard to finish."

* * *

On Monday evening, Dillon and Jill watched the President's televised speech where he outlined the grim situation for the American people. He revealed the existence of Soviet missiles in Cuba, ninety miles from Florida, and talked about how they constituted an explicit threat. Then Kennedy announced that he was imposing a strict quarantine on all offensive military equipment being shipped to Cuba. The U.S. Navy would stop and search all ships headed to Cuba and turn back any with weaponry aboard. Near the close of the speech, he encouraged Khrushchev to end what Kennedy called a reckless and provocative threat to world peace. He also made it clear that he was prepared to use military force, if necessary.

Dillon thought Kennedy appeared quite tense during the speech, ill-at-ease and stiff. He could only imagine the stress the man had to be under—the stakes were as high as they had ever been since the end of the Second World War.

"What does this mean, Dillon?" Jill asked. "Are we going to war?"

"I don't know," Dillon said. "But it's clear the President has drawn a line in the sand. No nuclear missiles in Cuba. He had to. Otherwise, we'd be at their mercy. They could launch against the East Coast in minutes."

"Why are the Russians doing this?"

"They're testing the President."

Jill shivered. "I pray we don't do anything impulsive."

"I think you and Sandy should go to Far Ridge. Just for the next few days."

"I want to stay here with you," she said.

Dillon shook his head. "It's much safer for you both in Charlottesville if something happens, which I don't think it will. But I don't want to take that chance."

"What about you? Is it safe for you to stay?"

"There's some risk, but it goes with the territory."

"What about Thea?"

"Of course she can go with you. If she is willing." They had interviewed several nannies before Jill chose Thea, a dour Scottish woman in her late forties. While Thea wasn't much of a conversationalist, she had proved quite helpful in caring for Sandy.

Later that night, Dillon telephoned Leigh and asked him to come to

Washington and drive Jill and Sandy back to Far Ridge. He wanted them to stay there until the crisis was safely over. Leigh immediately agreed and then fell silent for a long moment.

"Is the situation that bad?" he asked. "That dire?"

"Better safe than sorry. They've ordered the Army into position in Florida. Troop ships through the Panama Canal. That's all public. They want Moscow to realize that we're ready to act. Who knows whether it will escalate. I don't want Jill here in Washington. If there's a war, it's a logical target for the Soviets."

"My God, do you think it might come to that?"

"I pray not, but the President can't let them base missiles with nuclear warheads in Cuba. If the Russians don't back down, he'll have few options but to send the military in. Who can say what will happen then?"

On Tuesday morning, Leigh arrived in Georgetown around lunchtime. Dillon left work to meet him. After they had loaded Leigh's Chevrolet Parkwood station wagon with Jill and Thea's luggage, they stood by the car and talked while they waited for Jill and Thea to gather up Sandy's things and bring them to the vehicle.

"I'll make sure that Jill and the baby are comfortable," Leigh said. "How long do you think this situation will last?"

"It's coming to a head. A few days, at best."

Leigh shook his head. "Ike didn't have much in the way of charisma, but he knew what he was doing. When he was running Operation Overlord, young Jack couldn't get his PT boat out of the way of a Jap destroyer. The Russians would never have tried this with Ike. They wouldn't have dared."

"You sound like one of my friends, Palmer Knox. But you're both wrong. I agree that they're testing the President, but I think Jack can handle it."

"Pray to God that he can. The alternatives are unthinkable."

"We'll pull through. There are some wise men in the room, from what

I hear. Rusk, McGeorge Bundy, Adlai Stevenson, and they say Dean Acheson has been advising the President."

"I won't ask if you'll come to Far Ridge, because I know the answer."

"You know that I can't leave, Leigh. That would be the equivalent of desertion under fire. And like I said, I think we'll muddle through. Khrushchev is a bully, but he's not a madman. He's seeing how far he can push the new Administration, how it will react. I doubt that the Politburo will agree to start a war."

"I pray that you're correct. It's an incredibly dangerous game to play."

"Jack just has to stand fast," Dillon said. "He will, because he doesn't have much of a choice."

Jill appeared at the front door, Sandy in her arms. Thea carried two large bags.

"Time to go," Leigh said. "A lovely day for a drive."

Dillon took Sandy into his arms for a long moment. He handed her to Thea and embraced Jill, kissing her lightly on the lips.

"I'll drive out to bring you back as soon as it settles down," Dillon said. "That should be very soon."

* * *

They canceled their Thursday poker night until further notice. All of the members of the Group were consumed by the crisis. Dillon was loaned to the Berlin Task Force to develop contingency plans for any retaliatory Soviet moves against West Berlin. Alex was camped out at the Pentagon, and Grayson and the White House staff were dealing with an anxious Congress, to say nothing of the public.

Dillon tried to stay focused on work. He didn't sleep very much, and when he did, he tossed and turned. He phoned Jill every day after work. She and Thea had established a routine for Sandy that appeared to be working well. Jill had been able to go shopping in Charlottesville and had bought a few art books from a downtown bookstore. Dillon avoided talking about Cuba in any depth. He sensed that Jill didn't want any details. She and Sandy appeared to be comfortable at Far Ridge, and that was a relief.

Two days after the start of the quarantine, the Navy intercepted a Soviet cargo ship en route to Cuba and the vessel changed course. Then word came that some fourteen Russian ships heading to Cuba had turned back. That was followed by the chilling news that a U-2 had been shot down over Cuba by a SAM missile and the pilot killed. Grayson told Dillon in a brief phone call that the President had decided not to respond to the downing of the aircraft with force.

The following day, Grayson called and suggested that he, Dillon, and Jan meet for drinks at a bar near the White House. When Dillon arrived, Jan and Grayson already had half-empty cocktail glasses in front of them.

"Time to get gloriously drunk," Grayson said. "We've got a deal. Khrushchev is about to announce the removal of the missiles."

"A deal?" Dillon asked.

Grayson looked around to make sure he couldn't be overheard. "We traded some obsolete missiles in Turkey. Not officially, of course. But a small price to resolve this without blowing up the world."

"I'll drink to that," Jan said.

"So will I," Dillon said.

* * *

On the first day of November, three days after Khrushchev's declaration that he was abandoning the missile sites, when Dillon was sure the crisis had passed, he drove out to Far Ridge to collect Jill, Sandy, and Thea and bring them back to Washington.

He was pleased when Jill met him with a kiss on the lips and a long embrace.

"I couldn't bear watching the news," she said. "I didn't want to know. I figured that Leigh would tell me if it was war. Most days, I played with Sandy and took her in the baby carriage so she could get some fresh air. I'm so relieved that it's over. Thank God."

While Jill and Thea packed up for the return trip, Dillon and Leigh were left alone.

"Thea was quite the Stoic," Leigh said. "Her family went through the Blitz. She kept Jill focused on the baby."

"I hear Rusk is saying that we were eyeball to eyeball with the Russians and they blinked."

Leigh shook his head, displeased. "I thought we weren't practicing brinkmanship anymore. We came damn close to a thermonuclear war. It's Jack's fault, you know. He put us into this corner, and we're lucky as hell we got out without a catastrophe."

"That's not fair," Dillon said.

"He's in over his head. He fired Director Dulles and Richard Bissell over the Bay of Pigs. What's his excuse now? You heard what that bastard Nixon said about Kennedy being timid. 'Never has a man talked so big and acted so little.' Maybe Tricky Dick is on to something."

"Nixon is a sore loser," Dillon said. "It's very simple. Khrushchev misjudged the President. He should know better, now. Jack didn't blink and didn't overreact."

"If we have to have a Kennedy in the White House, I wish it was Joe, Jr., the one who died in the war. He was the one they were grooming for the job. Jack's the second stringer."

"You're wrong, Leigh. Jack's up to the task. He's proved that."

"Has he? His brother is a real piece of work. That's always the problem with short men. Bobby Kennedy thinks he has to prove how tough he is. That's damn dangerous."

Dillon nodded. It was common knowledge that half of the Cabinet couldn't stand Robert Kennedy, and that Lyndon Johnson loathed him. But the rumors were that Bobby had acted as a go-between with the Soviet ambassador in Washington, and that had been a key to resolving the crisis.

"The President trusts him, trusts his judgment. That's no small thing. I know it's not the normal chain of command, but Jack relies on him. He's family. You're not going to argue with that, are you?"

* * *

While most of the world watched the Cuban crisis with fear and dismay as events unfolded in Washington and Moscow, there was no letup in the dirty little war in Vietnam. In the weeks after the crisis was resolved, Dillon and his colleagues in the Bureau found the conflict in Indochina occupying more and more of their time and attention.

There was a flurry of activity in early December, when Mike Mansfield, the Senate Majority Leader, jolted the State Department with a warning about the progress of the war in Vietnam. The President had asked Mansfield to visit Vietnam and assess the situation. His report was grim. Outside of the cities, the countryside was insecure and the Viet Cong ruled at night. The rural population, the farmers and villagers, had yet to accept the Diem regime. "We are once again at the beginning of the beginning," Mansfield pronounced. While he lauded President Diem's patriotism, he questioned whether Diem could provide the leadership needed for the "immense job of social engineering" required to build a democratic nation.

Dillon wasn't surprised that Mansfield's report to the President was downbeat—there had been signs that Diem's generals were only half-heartedly pursuing the enemy. What caught Main State off guard was Mansfield's decision to go public with his critique. The Senator was an interesting character. He had served as a Marine in China, had studied Far Eastern history at the University of Montana, later becoming a professor there, and had visited Indochina on a fact-finding mission in

1953 near the end of the war between the French colonialists and the Viet Minh. He was no stranger to the region.

A day after Mansfield's report was made public, Hilsman forwarded to the seventh floor his own gloomy assessment of the political situation in South Vietnam, concluding the tide had not turned against the Viet Cong, despite assurances by the American military. Dillon had read Hilsman's memo in draft form and had been impressed by Hilsman's candor. At best, U.S. assistance had slowed down the rate of deterioration in the government's position, but it would be a challenge to maintain the status quo.

When he asked Jan Nowak about the Mansfield report, his friend frowned and hesitated before responding.

"You know the old trial attorney rule: never ask a witness a question where you don't know their answer beforehand. The President asked Mansfield his opinion. No one likes what he had to say. If you ask me, the White House sends too many of these oversight missions to Vietnam. Ros Gilpatric, General Taylor, and Walt Rostow last year. Hilsman and Forrestal this year. And now Mansfield. It's almost as if they're hoping somebody will discover a silver bullet over there that will win the war. But there's no magical fix. Who defeats an insurgency overnight?"

"Don't be too cynical," Dillon said. "We need differing points of view on what's going on. Mansfield's no newcomer to the issues. Maybe what he's saying can wake people up. See that Diem has to change course. If Vietnam falls to the Communists, the dominoes could start falling. Cambodia. Thailand. Indonesia. Much of Southeast Asia could turn Red before long."

"I'd bet on another fact-finding mission," Jan said. "Looking for that silver bullet."

"If it will convince people in the White House and State that we need a course correction, then it's a good thing. We shouldn't hide from the facts or the reality."

Jan smiled. "If the rumors I hear are true, you and your colleagues are next in line. I hope your passport is in order."

NINE

Saigon, Republic of Vietnam
January 1, 1963

Dillon began the New Year with drinks at the rooftop bar of the Hotel Caravelle in Saigon, thousands of miles from home. He felt exhausted and was battling jet lag. The New Year's festivities at the hotel were subdued, with only a few fireworks shot off the roof at midnight; a British diplomat explained that the Vietnamese saved their celebrating for Tet, the lunar New Year that was their most important holiday. Dillon drank too much—he downed more than his fair share of whiskey sours—and woke up the next day with a splitting headache.

Jan Nowak had been right about Dillon's need for an up-to-date passport. He had been included in yet another official fact-finding mission, this one led by his boss, Roger Hilsman, and Michael Forrestal, the staffer responsible for Southeast Asia on the National Security Council, and the son of the former Secretary of Defense, James Forrestal. They had ten days to assess the situation in Vietnam, which primarily involved interviewing in-country Americans, and a handful of South Vietnamese officials. Was progress being made? Was the Diem regime doing its part?

Dillon had suffered through the battery of shots required for a trip to Southeast Asia—malaria, hepatitis, cholera, and plague. With his arm still sore from the needle, he had shopped for tropical clothing. Even in the winter, Vietnam could be very hot.

While it was Dillon's first time in Asia, it was a repeat visit to Saigon for Hilsman. President Kennedy had sent him to Vietnam a year before, in late 1961, when Hilsman had interviewed Sir Robert Thompson, head of the British Advisory Mission to South Vietnam, and a counterinsurgency adviser to Diem. The two of them had hit it off, and Thompson had briefed Hilsman on the successful efforts of the British in holding off the Communist guerrillas in Malaya.

Dillon wasn't entirely ready for the reality of Saigon: the heat and noise, the blue haze hanging over the streets from the heavy traffic, the jam-packed sidewalks, the outdoor coffee shops. The city had been called the Paris of the Orient, and Dillon admired the graceful French-style architecture of many of the buildings. The streets were filled with Vietnamese on Vespas, Hondas, and Mobylette motorbikes and on bicycles, jostling for space with military vehicles—jeeps, trucks, and armored personnel carriers. Slender dark-haired women in *ao dai* garments moved gracefully along the sidewalks, as street vendors selling sugarcane, fruits, and balloons cried out their wares. There were numerous beggars, as well, some on crutches and others with missing limbs. Then, there were the pungent odors of human and animal waste, of fermented fish sauce, and of diesel and gas fumes.

At their initial meeting at the U.S. Embassy, officials had cautioned the delegation about straying too far from their hotels. The insurgents had mounted a psychological warfare campaign in Saigon, circulating leaflets that threatened "Two Americans a Day." It wasn't clear how real the threat was, they were told, but it was better to be safe than sorry.

Dillon and the other members of the mission spent the week in what seemed like endless briefings from the Country Team and military brass. He recognized that the officials were presenting the situation in the most favorable light; he discounted what they had to say by at least a factor of fifty percent. Nevertheless, Dillon was heartened by the cautious optimism of many of the Americans he interviewed. They believed that the situation in the provinces was improving. New roads. Schools. Medical clinics. Tractors. Coupled with the physical improvements would be the safety and security that the Strategic Hamlet Program could offer with its policy of relocating the rural population to defendable villages in order to isolate the Viet Cong.

"It won't be an overnight success," an earnest young Agency for International Development officer, Jack Stebbins, told Dillon. "It's going to take time. We have to be patient. You can't expect a turn-around in a few months. It's going to take years, but it can be done."

Dillon had liked Stebbins within minutes of meeting him. It was clear that he had thrown himself into the work of fashioning a new Vietnam. His enthusiasm was contagious.

There are good people, here," Stebbins said. "Many of the villagers are kind and generous. The young children are beautiful. The Vietnamese I know simply want to live their lives without fear."

"What about the security situation?" Dillon asked.

"It's dicey at the moment. But if we can push out the cadres, clear the villages of the Viet Cong, then we can institute the programs that will bind the villagers to the government. We need time. Rome wasn't built in a day."

Dillon knew that patience was in short supply in Washington. Grayson Talbott had told him on more than one occasion that the White House wanted a quick solution, an end to the insurgency and demonstrable progress in moving Diem toward a more representative government.

"We'll do our level best to give you that time," Dillon told him. "The Administration is behind you. And I think most of Congress is as well. We do need some good news to report."

"If they could see the progress we're making, they'd be sold. Give us the tools, and we'll get the job done."

* * *

Clay Blackburn, a friend of Dillon's from Charlottesville who was a Marine officer and an adviser to the South Vietnamese military, wasn't as sanguine about the situation as Jack Stebbins. Clay's father had been a Marine, and Clay had followed in his footsteps. First, the ROTC program at UVA, and then Quantico and active duty. The Embassy had been happy to contact Clay for Dillon, and they arranged over the phone to meet at the terrace of the Continental Palace Hotel.

"Sorry to hear about your father," Clay began once they were seated with cold bottles of beer in front of them. "I was in California, at Camp Pendleton, or I would have made it to the funeral."

"I appreciate that," Dillon said. "Your dad was there."

"He thought the world of your father. And he admired him, especially when you lost Wash in Korea. There are plenty of Congressmen who would have made sure their son was far from the front lines, riding a desk in the Pentagon."

"Wash was a Marine, like you," Dillon said. "There's no way he would have accepted anything other than combat leadership."

"We lost some damn fine men at Chosin. Those of us advising the South Vietnamese want to make sure there's no repeat of 1950. Of course, it's very different than what we confronted in Korea. The National Front is using Mao's tactics from the Chinese Civil War. The Viet Cong operate in small units. Hit and run. And where they have control, they work hard at building popular support, making nice with the locals."

Dillon nodded. "I've been reading about it. 'The army depends on the people just as a fish depends upon the water.' Mao's tactics. If you can get food and shelter from the locals, you don't need long supply lines."

"Exactly."

"What about the South Vietnamese troops?"

"Ninety percent of them are clueless," Clay said, shaking his head. He took a sip of his beer. "Peasants who signed for the steady paycheck. A few of the officers are top notch. Too many are corrupt or lazy or both. But there are some good soldiers, too. Unfortunately, we have a tactical mismatch. You can't fight and win a guerrilla war without confronting your enemy directly. You want to kill him and not the civilians around him. That's why relying on air power is a mistake. We need ARVN riflemen in the swamps and paddies, rooting out the Viet Cong. That ain't what's happening, but I doubt the brass is about to admit it."

Dillon nodded. "So what do we need to do in order to win? There's been a lot of talk in Washington about what worked in Malaya and the Philippines. There's a saying from Ramon Magsaysay going around, 'Win the people first, win the war second.' Isn't counterinsurgency a winning strategy?"

Clay smiled. "Well, if you could get Ho and Giap and the boys in Hanoi to agree to put their war on pause, then we could usher in the do-gooders and win the loyalty of the peasants. As it is now, the Viet Cong make the government's district chiefs and local school teachers their prime targets. So, I think we have to neutralize the guerrillas first before we can do much of anything."

"And the strategic hamlets?"

"What about them?"

"Can they make a difference? My boss is betting that they can, based on what the British accomplished in Malaya."

"It comes down to percentages. Fifty-fifty, if you ask me. Fifty percent of them will fail, fifty percent won't. It's simple mathematics. Is that enough to keep the bad guys at bay? Your guess is as good as mine."

"And the VC? How do you see them?"

"They have an advantage. They're resisting the foreign invaders. Vietnam for the Vietnamese. They've been at it for more than twenty years. The Japanese and then the French, and now us. They don't take prisoners. Come into one of your strategic hamlets and chop off the heads of the village elders, and anyone else collaborating with the government. The Reds call it Destruction of the Oppression, but it's nothing more than terror tactics. That gets everyone's attention in a hurry."

"That sort of brutality should work against them," Dillon said. "When the people see what Communism is, what it means."

"They're being told that it means a full belly of rice, and they don't have to pay taxes to a corrupt local general. And just enough terror to get the message across—don't fuck with us. It's clever, and it works. Don't get me wrong. I hate the little godless bastards. But the locals have got to stand up on their own. We can't fight this war for them."

"My boss is a lot more optimistic than you. Hilsman thinks it can be quickly turned around. A few years, at most. Based on what the Brits did in Malaya. It's not the Civil War, it's the Indian wars. Fort Apache. We become the hunters. Eradicate the VC. Pacify the countryside."

Clay raised his eyebrows. "Your boss should spend a week in the field with me, and he'd change his tune. The same goes for the chain of command and for the paper pushers at the Pentagon. I've got a decent ARVN captain to work with—at least he doesn't steal his men's pay—but the Colonel is bad. No stomach for fighting. He's more interested in his girls in Saigon and his bank account in Switzerland. But as to the larger military question, as long as we prop up the ARVN, they can hold off the Viet Cong. A stalemate. These strategic hamlets are going to take ten years. Maybe longer. Hell, we've got troops in Germany, and it's been almost twenty years since Hitler checked out."

"I don't think we have ten years."

"Maybe, maybe not. If it's not Vietnam, it will be somewhere else. The Russians and Chinese have figured out that they can tie us down in small brushfire wars. At least someone in the Pentagon is paying attention. I'm heading back to the States soon. They want me to teach a course on the winning tactics for a guerrilla war."

Clay finished his beer and motioned for the waiter. "I've got to get back," he said. "I'll walk you back to the Caravelle."

They were on the way to his hotel, when Dillon felt a sudden change in air pressure and felt himself being lifted off his feet and knocked to the pavement. A moment later, there was the sound of a massive explosion. He scrambled to his feet, slightly dazed, and found Clay by his side. Half-a-block away, down a side-street, a thick cloud of smoke obscured the view. There was debris—bricks, glass, a piece of a sign—scattered up the street.

"What the hell was that?" Dillon asked.

"A bombing," Clay said. "One of the bars that caters to Americans. The Viet Cong target them to send the message that it's dangerous to fraternize with GIs." He shook his head. "Let's get back to your hotel. There's nothing we can do, now. This area will be swarming with trigger-happy police in a few minutes."

They heard the sound of sirens in the distance. Clay peered through the smoke. "Hard to tell how bad it is." He turned back to Dillon, and took him by the arm. "Let's go."

They walked in silence. Dillon wondered how much damage the explosion had done. How many inside the bar had been killed? American soldiers? The teenage bar girls? He tried to imagine the scene: smoke, fire, bodies. He shivered, despite the warmth of the air around him.

They had reached the entrance to the Caravelle. Clay shook his hand. "What happened back there," he said. "It's the reality here. No front lines. No rules of war. It's nasty. And winning this ain't going to be easy. Take that back to Washington, will you?"

* * *

It took a week after his return from Vietnam for Dillon to fully recover from the jet lag. He hadn't slept well in the interim. He felt tired and out of sorts, depressed by his trip. It didn't stop him from going into the office and handling the paperwork that had accumulated when he was away, but he didn't feel particularly sharp.

He didn't say anything to Jill about the bombing he had witnessed. He didn't want to worry her, and he rationalized that it had been a random act. On a statistical basis, the one helicopter flight he took over the countryside had posed more danger.

He had mixed feelings about the drafts he saw of the final report of the Hilsman-Forrestal mission that would be submitted to the White House. He was struck by its contradictions: *"Our overall judgment, in sum, is that we are probably winning, but certainly more slowly than we had hoped. At the rate it is now going the war will last longer than we would like, cost more in terms of both lives and money than we anticipated ..."*

Dillon didn't agree that the U.S. was "probably winning." He couldn't square that with what he had learned. He understood the balancing act involved in crafting the report. No doubt the military advisers in Saigon were claiming success in the field. Hilsman had to avoid a fight with the Pentagon, and buy time for the Strategic Hamlet Program to show results.

Two weeks after his return, he came home early on a windy February day and found Evan Bauer and Darla Randazzo sitting in the kitchen with Jill drinking red wine. There was unfamiliar folk music playing on the phonograph. Darla had been in the same graduate program as Jill. Evan was an assistant professor of sociology. Dillon didn't care for either of them.

Jill met him at the door with a quick kiss.

"Evan and Darla dropped by," she said. "We're listening to some new music."

"So where is Sandy?" he asked, and immediately regretted asking the question.

Jill flushed in embarrassment. "She's taking a nap. Thea's in the nursery if she wakes up."

"Have some wine," Evan said. "Take the edge off."

Dillon nodded and joined them at the table. He wasn't happy to find Evan visiting—from a few things Jill had said, he suspected that Evan had been interested in her romantically before Dillon arrived on the scene. Whenever her friends visited, Dillon was wary, careful about what he said. He didn't want to be seen as an overbearing older husband, or worse, as a jealous one.

He leaned over her and touched Jill's right hand gently, a silent apology, and when he turned back he caught Evan staring at them. Dillon returned the stare, and Evan quickly looked away.

"So what's the new music?" he asked Jill.

"It's a record Evan brought. A folk singer named Bob Dylan." She paused. "I think we talked about him. About how poetic his songs are."

Dillon vaguely remembered the conversation. He had listened to one or two of Dylan's songs and hadn't been overly impressed. It was beat poetry set to acoustic guitar; Dylan had a raw, nasal voice. Dillon couldn't imagine that his popularity would last, not when he had to compete with groups like the Four Seasons and the Beach Boys.

"Jill tells us you were in Asia," Evan said. "Vietnam."

"Just back," Dillon said. He didn't like the smirk on Evan's face, as if he knew a secret that Dillon didn't.

"Where exactly is Vietnam?" Darla asked. "I know it's in Asia, but I couldn't find it on a map to save my life."

"It was part of French Indochina," Evan explained. "When the French colonialists lorded it over the people there. Exploiting them for rubber and tea. Vietnam's in the southeast, shares a border with China. We're propping up the government in the South, and the Communists run the North. Sort of like Korea."

"Why are we there?" Darla asked, turning to Dillon. "In Vietnam, I mean."

"The country was divided up after the war. Evan has it right. Like Korea. Or Germany. The Soviets and Chinese are backing Ho Chi Minh and the Communists in the North. We're helping the government in the South, and if we weren't, the Communists would take over."

"And if we'd let them hold elections, Ho would have won," Evan said. "Which means we're propping up the puppets the French left behind."

"Any election held in the North wouldn't be free and fair," Dillon said. He struggled to keep his anger in check. There was something smug in Evan's professorial manner that rubbed him the wrong way. "And if Ho had won that would have been the last election ever held in Vietnam. Once in power, he would have sent his secret police after the opposition. That's what he did in the North after the French left. You do know that a million Catholics fled to the South after the Communists took over?"

"Let's not argue," Jill said quickly. There was an awkward silence as Evan and Darla exchanged a quick glance.

"We have to be going anyway," Evan said. "A party that Mike Wiggins and some of the other Sociology grad students are throwing."

After they had left, Jill took the wine glasses to the sink and began washing them. She kept her back to Dillon.

"Is anything wrong?" he asked.

"Why do you have to argue about everything?" she asked. She turned toward him, her face set and hard. "You did a great job of chasing my friends away."

"I'm sorry," he said. "But they asked me about Vietnam. It would have been rude not to answer."

"You didn't have to lecture them," she said.

"I didn't think I was lecturing them," he said, hoping to avoid an argument.

"Please don't raise your voice. You'll wake Sandra."

"I'm sorry," he said. "I don't want to argue. Why don't I go for a walk? I'll be back in time for dinner."

She nodded silently and left the kitchen. Dillon retrieved his overcoat from the closet and headed to the street. He decided he would walk down Wisconsin Avenue. It was brisk outside, and he could see his breath. He wished he had handled the situation with Jill's friends differently. Evan had been spoiling for a fight with him, and Dillon should have steered the conversation away from Vietnam. He wouldn't make the same mistake again.

TEN

After nearly three years at Main State, Dillon had learned that to influence policy-making in a large bureaucracy you had to control the flow of paperwork. What landed on the desk of the decision makers in Foggy Bottom drove the discussion. It was through the cogent memo, the concise briefing paper, the well-argued report, that opinions were shaped and formed. More often than not, building a convincing story backed up by a blizzard of paper carried the day.

The paperwork offered the illusion of mastery. With the charts and tables and executive summaries, the answers seemed clear. Didn't the report say the number of strategic hamlets was continuing to grow? There, in black-and-white, a chart showing that ten new schools and five medical clinics had been opened in Binh Duong Province. (Or had they?) Reports of Viet Cong activity were trending down. Progress was being made. It was easy to believe. There it was, the evidence, in a neatly typed official document.

Dillon also recognized the deep and dangerous flaws in the process. From the vast flow of information coursing into Main State, from the cables, meeting summaries, intelligence estimates, mission reports, and memoranda, it was possible to pick and choose only the data that supported your argument. He saw time-and-time again that whoever was analyzing the flow tended to discount the information that undermined their preferred story. Instead, they highlighted the data that advanced their viewpoint.

Another key to influencing policy was inclusion in the inner circle, in the small group where options were discussed and debated and decisions made. Yes, the President made the final call, but the bureaucracy narrowed his choices to those options deemed possible, what the hundreds of officials in the government had committed to paper as acceptable.

He imagined that it was the same the world over—the same process, the same bland office environment with its in-boxes, chairs, desks with telephones, typewriters, and file cabinets. No different than what you would find in a large insurance agency or law firm. The tools of bureaucracy. Yet those innocent-looking pieces of paper could, in the end, condemn men to death, in the form of executive orders and directives.

Dillon tried explaining the process to Jill, but she had never worked in a large bureaucracy and didn't understand the Byzantine nature of office politics in a traditional organization like the State Department. Unless you had experienced it directly, Dillon realized, you couldn't appreciate the convoluted, complex, and opaque way decisions were often made.

* * *

A sunny March day. Dillon left the E Street complex in the late morning for a meeting with Huy Dinh Dao, a diplomat from the Vietnamese Embassy. Dao had reached out to Dillon with an invitation for lunch and had chosen the time and the place, The Colony, an expensive French restaurant on DeSales Street.

Dao proved to be a slight man, with jet black hair swept back from his intelligent-looking face. He wore a well-tailored blue suit with a handkerchief in his pocket and a dark brown silk tie. His English was quite good, with only a slight accent.

"This restaurant reminds me of Paris," Dao said. "The French have no equals when it comes to food. Or wine." He waved gracefully at the glass in front of him. "Would you like to try the Beaujolais? It is quite good."

"Thank you, but I'll pass," Dillon said.

Dillon studied the menu and settled on the Quiche Lorraine. Dao ordered for them in rapid French. After they had been served, Dao looked over at Dillon and smiled.

"Did you enjoy your visit to Saigon, Mr. Randolph?" he asked. "It is a beautiful city, is it not?"

Dillon returned his smile. If Dao hoped to impress him that he knew about his participation in the Hilsman-Forrestal mission, he would be disappointed. Dillon assumed that the South Vietnamese diplomats in the Washington Embassy had been given a list of every American who had made the trip. The lunch invitation made more sense now. No doubt Dao had been tasked with probing Dillon about any conclusions the Americans had drawn from their visit. "It was informative. We learned a great deal about the situation. Some good, and some not so good."

"I see," Dao said. "What was not so good?"

"The political atmosphere. We believe that a more accommodating policy toward the political opposition is called for, one that will encourage a more democratic environment."

Dao frowned. "We are at war, Mr. Randolph. President Diem must take that into account. A more forceful policy is necessary against those who would subvert our government. Would you have us surrender to them? Did not your President Lincoln suspend habeas corpus during your Civil War?"

"He did," Dillon conceded. "I'm impressed by your knowledge of our history, but I don't think the situation is quite the same. We held a presidential election during the Civil War, and the Democrats ran a candidate, General McClellan. It was a free and fair election."

"America as a nation was nearly one hundred years old, then. We have had our own government in the South for the briefest of times. It is more fragile. More beleaguered. Please tell me something—does Mr. Hilsman fully support our government? We have questions about his views, and those of Mr. Forrestal."

"Of course he does," Dillon said. He took a bite of his quiche. It was delicious. "You're our ally. He believes, as do many of us, that reforms are called for."

"But he presumes to tell us how to reform. How to run our government. How to govern our country."

"Don't we both want the same thing, for your government to succeed? To defeat the Viet Cong. We differ on some of the ways to do that."

"We know that you wish Ngo Dinh Nhu removed from his position in the government."

Dillon didn't respond. Dao was correct, of course, but it wasn't Dillon's place to say so. Diem's younger brother, Nhu, had a well-deserved reputation as a ruthless enforcer, eager to set loose the secret police against the regime's opponents. American officials in Saigon regarded him, and his wife, Madame Nhu, as negative influences on Diem, encouraging his authoritarian tendencies.

"Please understand. Our president will never abandon his brother. Never. There is a bond between brothers that cannot be broken. Do you have brothers, Mr. Randolph?"

"I had one," Dillon said. "An older brother. He was a Marine who died in Korea in 1950."

Dao leaned forward. "Then you should understand. The bond of brothers. Your President is no different. His brother, Robert, is the Attorney General. Is that any different than President Diem and his brother? Some criticize and call it nepotism, do they not?"

"Our Attorney General has proven his worth." Dillon had to admire Dao's ability to draw comparisons between Vietnamese and American political life. Robert Kennedy and Nhu. Lincoln's war-time measures and Diem's crackdown. He was a clever man. Dillon suspected he had benefited from a Jesuit education, with its training in argumentation and logic.

"Then we agree," Dao said. "The Ngo family is dedicated to the preservation of our country. It was not easy to establish our government. President Diem had to confront the sects, the Cao Dai, the Hoa Hao, and the brigands of the Binh Xuyen. He defeated their militias. Now, we face resistance from some of the Buddhists. Not all, you see, but the ones who crave power."

Dillon had read about the Cao Dai, a strange, eclectic religious sect that revered Lao Tse, Sun Yat-sen, and Victor Hugo as saints, and worshipped Christ and Buddha as the Supreme Being. The Hoa Hao, centered in the Mekong Delta, was a Buddhist sect that dabbled in politics. The

Binh Xuyen were nothing more than river pirates, although they had controlled portions of Saigon during the mid-1950s. All three groups had sold their political and military support to the highest bidder—and the Japanese and French, at one time or another, had paid up.

"There are many lies told about President Diem," Dao continued. "That he unfairly persecutes his opponents. That as a Catholic, he is hostile to Buddhists. Did you know that most of the members of his Cabinet are Buddhist?" Dao did not wait for Dillon to respond. "*Il faut qu'une porte soit ouverte ou fermée.* The door is either open or shut. You must choose to back us, or accept that the Communists will win."

"I don't accept your premise," Dillon said. "One man rule is not the best way forward for your country. In fact, it will stand in the way of building popular support. There must be an opposition, a loyal opposition. That's a hallmark of a healthy democracy."

"That may be true for Europe and the West. Our civilization is much older than yours, Mr. Randolph. It is based on a Confucian understanding of the world. There is an order involved. Our leaders must have a mandate from heaven, not just from the people. Many in my country believe in the stars. Astrology. Magic. They don't think the way that you do."

"And you, Mr. Dao. Do you turn to the stars?"

"I am a Catholic," he replied, his face tightening. Dillon could see that he had offended the man. "I have no use for these superstitions. But you must understand that my countrymen are different. We may need your assistance, but we would prefer a Vietnam free of all foreign influences."

"Our support is not unconditional," Dillon said. "We're convinced that only governments with popular support can withstand the Communists."

"We ask for patience." Dao lowered his voice. "We are making progress. You may hear different things from others at our Embassy. Even those with connections to our President. A word of caution—some may seek to settle old scores, not to help our country."

Dillon nodded. He knew that South Vietnam's ambassador to the United States, Tran Van Chuong, had been critical of Diem behind the scenes, as had his wife, who represented Saigon at the United Nations. What was strange about their criticism was that the Chuongs were Madame Nhu's parents. In a way it reflected the divisions, even within families, that surfaced during a civil war.

Dillon found that Dao was watching him intently across the table. "My older brother was a soldier, too," he said. "I lost him, just as you did yours."

"I'm sorry," Dillon said.

"You understand what it is to lose someone in the struggle. The cost."

The waiter arrived with the check. Dao signed the bill and smiled at Dillon. "I have an account here. The food is beyond compare. *Magnifique.*" He paused. "Should you ever have any questions about the situation in my country, I would ask that you call me. Don't hesitate. I will tell you the truth."

* * *

Dillon had lost touch with Palmer Knox for more than a month, and he was pleased when his friend called and suggested they meet at a bar in Rosslyn. When Dillon arrived, Palmer was already at a table. The jukebox was playing the Beach Boys, "Surfin' U.S.A.," and Palmer smirked. "Everybody's going surfing?" he asked. "I'm not. You couldn't get me on a surfboard for love or money. I've got lousy balance."

"Don't you like to swim?"

"I do, on a hot day," he said. "When I was a kid we used to go swimming in a place called the Quarry. We'd jump from the cliffs above into the water. Must have been a hundred feet up. Scared the crap out of me the first time I jumped. Lucky none of us drowned."

They ordered a pitcher of beer and made small talk. Ten minutes into the conversation, Palmer finished his first mug of beer and shook his head. "Do you think you can justify immoral acts for moral ends?" he asked.

"That's a pretty weighty question," Dillon said. "Not sure I know where to start."

"Why not Vietnam? You've been there. You know now how nasty it can get."

"It can."

"Can you do harsh things and remain a moral person? Things that are objectively wrong. Does it matter that your enemies are doing worse things?"

"You're a Catholic, Palmer. You know about the Just War doctrine. All the conditions to go to war. Just cause, just intentions. Then how the war is fought. Proportionality. Discrimination. There's a whole body of thinking about it. I'm sure that there's a Jesuit professor over at Georgetown who can take you through the thinking."

"I can't talk to some intellectual priest who's never heard a shot fired in anger. What's more, they wrote those rules for a traditional war. Not for what goes on in the shadows. The things we must do to keep a full-blown shooting war from happening. If I recall correctly about the Just War doctrine, one of the conditions is that there has to be a probability of success. To justify all the hard things. I struggle with that. What if I've done these things for a lost cause?"

"It's not lost yet. We're not going to win overnight. Not in Vietnam. Not anywhere else we're dealing with the Communists."

"I can tell you that in the field, it doesn't look so promising."

"It didn't look too promising for us at Valley Forge, and look what happened."

Palmer snorted in derision. "Hardly. Don't forget we're backing the Tories, not the rebels. And I don't think anyone is ever going to mistake Ngo Dinh Diem for George Washington."

"What about Cora? Have you talked about this with her?"

"Cora? How could she understand?"

"What about the men you work with?"

"Are you serious, Dillon? They'd have me seeing the headshrinker, and I'd end up at a desk reviewing expense accounts. No, I have to work this out on my own."

"Sorry I can't be of more help."

"Like I said, I need to figure this out myself. And if I can't, then I need to quit, and maybe head out to Southern California and go surfing. Like everybody, right?"

ELEVEN

Spring in Washington. It had been a hard winter, and Dillon was glad to see flowers in bloom, starting with magnolias and then, in April, the famous annual arrival of cherry blossoms—pink and white Yoshino around the Tidal Basin. In Georgetown, backyard gardens came alive with dogwood, azalea, and wisteria. May brought school tours, sightseers, and foreign tourists to the city. Along with picnickers and office workers on their lunch breaks, the out-of-towners congregated on the Mall and near Capitol Hill and the city's numerous monuments and museums.

Early in the spring, there had been rumors of changes in the leadership ranks of State. Dillon learned from Jan Nowak that Roger Hilsman would be promoted to Assistant Secretary of State for Far Eastern Affairs, replacing Averell Harriman, who would become Under Secretary of State for Political Affairs. It meant that Hilsman would shape and articulate State's policies on Vietnam and Southeast Asia, and it was no secret that the President increasingly valued his counsel.

When Dillon was offered a staff position in Far Eastern Affairs, he had to decide whether to follow Hilsman or not. He had decided that he wouldn't stay in the Bureau, for without its charismatic leader the INR would be cut off from the main action. He also didn't want to return to the German Desk. It had become a bit of a backwater with the question of Berlin having been settled for the moment by the Wall. In contrast, Hilsman had access to the President and to the corridors of power. If Dillon ever wanted to influence policy—and he wanted to—then taking up the offer made sense.

When he talked it over with Jan, his friend warned him about the risks of aligning himself so closely with Hilsman. "Roger's stepped on a lot of toes," he told him. Jan always seemed to have the inside story, the latest rumors and office gossip. He was welcome on the sixth and seventh floors of Main State and was privy to the internal thinking on personnel matters. "The Secretary isn't wild about the way Hilsman goes outside of channels and takes his case directly to the President. It's bad enough that Mac Bundy is running a Little State Department in the White House, and Hilsman and Forrestal are in the thick of decision-making about Vietnam. McNamara and the Joint Chiefs see Hilsman as an arrogant meddler who fancies himself the Lawrence of Arabia of Indochina. If you're planning on a career in State, Roger's not the best bet. Too many powerful enemies. Hilsman kicked a lot of people on the way up, and they'll be waiting for him, and his allies, on the way back down."

"I'm not worried about my career," Dillon said. "I want to help move us in the right direction. Is Roger's analysis of the situation in Vietnam correct? I think so. We can't stop the Communists through military means alone. That's short-sighted. You need land reform, education for the children, health care, all of the things that will encourage the locals to back Diem."

Jan shrugged and lit another cigarette. "I'm not sure Hilsman is going to win the argument. The changes you're talking about take time. The Joint Chiefs and McNamara and his merry band think differently. They can promise quick results. Don't underestimate the political aspects of this. Voters don't like long, drawn-out wars."

"Which is exactly what they may get with the military approach. Don't forget that Roger gets things done. He makes things happen. Action, not analysis. It may not be bullets and bombs, but it's changing policy for the better. Roger doesn't worry about who he's offending. I admire that. Otherwise, you become nothing more than a time-server. A bureaucrat."

"The government is made up of bureaucrats," Jan said, shaking his head. "State is no different. Bureaucrats are patient, and they wait for the right moment to bring down the hotshots like Roger Hilsman. And, for that matter, hotshots like you and me."

Dillon hadn't realized how much senior members of the Cabinet and State disliked Hilsman. It made sense. Hilsman had little patience for protocol and red tape.

"Remember what happened to Icarus?" Jan asked. "Fly too close to the sun, and the wax melts and your wings fall off. Roger flies high. When he falls out of favor, you may go down with him. If you stay on his staff, you're one of his hand-picked boys. No getting around that."

"Thousands of years later and we're still talking about Icarus, though, aren't we?"

"Then I take it you've made up your mind?"

"I have."

"And Jill? The baby? You're going to be working long hours. Not great for the home life."

"It will be fine," Dillon said. "Jill will understand."

* * *

Dillon learned in short order that he was wrong about how his wife would react. Jill listened to his explanation for the move, and when he had finished, didn't say anything for a long moment.

Then, she told him she didn't understand why he would follow Roger Hilsman to Far Eastern Affairs.

"You don't have to do this," she said. "You never seem to stop working. You know how demanding he is. What about your family? What about Sandy?"

"What about her? I've stayed in Washington to try to make a difference, to help shape the future. I'm doing this so Sandy grows up in a safer, better world."

"There has to be a compromise solution. A job where you can lead a normal life."

"I don't want a normal life. I don't want to sit around filing reports that no one will read."

"So your mind is made up, Dillon?

"I guess it is."

He was bothered by Jill's opposition. Following Hilsman was the smart move. What did Jill expect him to do? Resign himself to a tedious desk job? Act like a career bureaucrat? She had to know he would never accept that. He needed to be as close to the center of things as he could. That was what kept him in Washington.

"You promised we would be able to travel," she said. "Our vacation in California."

"It will only be a few months before I'm acclimated. Then we can talk about vacations."

"I don't want to talk about vacations. I want us to take one. Together. Sandy will be able to travel soon enough."

Dillon shook his head. "California would be great. Just not right now. I'm starting a new job, and I won't be able to get away. I know you're disappointed, but the time will come."

"You love to postpone things," she said. "I feel like you're postponing life, Dillon. Sandy will be this age only once. I want my mother to see her."

"Why don't you have her fly here?" Dillon asked. "We can pay for her tickets."

"That's not the same as going there."

"It will work out," he told her. "Things will settle down. I promise we'll all get to California. It's just a matter of time."

* * *

Dillon was impressed by the intelligence and knowledge of many of his new colleagues in Far Eastern Affairs. Several staffers had a deep expertise in the history, politics, and culture of the region. One of the analysts, Mary Warren, had written her master's thesis at the University of Pennsylvania on the failure of the French in dealing with the Viet Minh. She spoke fluent French and passable Vietnamese and had visited the country several times. A plain woman who wore thick glasses, Mary had an abrupt manner, but Dillon quickly realized that she was perhaps the best informed of his colleagues about Vietnamese culture and politics.

"You were on the Cook's Tour with Hilsman and Forrestal in January," she began when they first sat down to talk. "I read your report. Much more realistic than a lot of the crap that crosses my desk."

"We weren't there very long," Dillon said. "We only had time for a snapshot of the situation."

"But a snapshot in better focus. And our new leader at least knows something about Asia. Hilsman has in-theater experience, so he recognizes that Confucians aren't Presbyterians. On the other hand, I believe it was Forrestal's second trip to Vietnam. Your first?"

"My first," Dillon conceded. "I have a lot to learn. The bulk of my experience has been in Europe."

"And Australia," she said, with a slight smile. Not for the first time, Dillon wondered how far gossip about his misadventure in Canberra had spread. He could only hope that with time the rumors would fade. "They say you're a Golden Boy. Destined for bigger and better things."

"Do they?"

"I can see why. You've been in the field. Berlin Task Force. The INR with Hilsman. He must think you're good, or he wouldn't have brought you with him, and he wouldn't have asked you to focus on Vietnam. A hard charger with the right credentials."

"You're not particularly politic, are you?"

"What difference would that make? I'm a woman. I'm never going to climb the ladder in this Department, so it's not like being direct will hurt my career. I don't mind having a reputation for telling the truth. Somebody has to."

In the weeks that followed, Dillon worked long hours, trying to learn as much as he could about the ever-changing situation in Vietnam. When he was home, Jill was cool and distant. When he returned from the office after she had gone to bed, he made himself dinner and then slept in the guest bedroom.

He tried to spend more time on the weekends with Sandy. It wasn't easy—there always seemed to be another crisis, another cable that needed a response, a report that needed to be finished. The political situation in South Vietnam, already a source of significant concern to the Administration, continued to worsen. Diem and his brother Nhu apparently believed that repression was the most effective response to dissent and, despite American advice to the contrary, met political opposition with force. In May, ARVN soldiers opened fire on protesters in Hue who were demonstrating against a government ban on the flying of the Buddhist flag on Vesak, the birthday of Gautama Buddha.

"Are you sure you made the right decision?" Jan asked Dillon after a particularly stressful week. "From where I sit, I don't see how what Roger is proposing will ever work. Diem and his family seem determined to alienate half the country. I don't see them winning over the Buddhists anytime soon. Are we backing the wrong horse?"

"You're not the only one asking that question," Dillon replied. "We're all wondering if we can make any progress with the current crew."

"Then I hope someone is thinking about how to change horses," Jan said. "Or how to cut our losses. One way or the other, because we can't let the current shambles go on for much longer."

TWELVE

Dillon spent the second Tuesday of June preparing a briefing paper on Berlin's political situation in advance of President Kennedy's upcoming visit to Germany. Dillon had returned to the INR on loan for a few weeks because of his expertise in German domestic politics.

Dillon had lobbied to travel to Berlin with the President, first approaching his superiors at State and after he was turned down, he asked Grayson Talbott for help. Grayson shook his head and explained that there were no open seats on the flights to Germany.

"Sorry, but no way," he told Dillon. "Everybody and his brother wants in on this trip. It's an easy way to earn a Cold Warrior merit badge. You've already earned yours."

According to Grayson, the visit to Berlin had been designed for maximum positive publicity. President Kennedy would accompany Berlin's mayor Willy Brandt and West Germany's chancellor, Konrad Adenauer, and mount a viewing stand to gaze across the Wall at the Brandenburg Gate. Then, the President would give a televised speech to a crowd gathered in front of West Berlin's City Hall, the Rathaus Schöneberg.

"You know that I spent time at the Mission in Berlin," Dillon said. "I speak German fluently. I think I could be of help. If you put in a good word for me...."

"A good word wouldn't matter," Grayson said. "No room left in this ark. Remember, this visit is largely for show. There will be nothing of substance accomplished. It's meant to keep the Republicans from saying that the President is soft on the Reds. We're hoping for lots of photos of Jack at the Wall, staring across into East Berlin, showing strength and resolve. It will give us something to work with when the campaign rolls around."

Dillon didn't say what he wanted to: that the Berlin Wall existed to a large extent because of the President's foreign policy missteps in his first year in office—the Bay of Pigs, the disastrous summit with Khrushchev in Vienna, the indecision about what to do in Laos and Vietnam. The Soviets calculated that Kennedy would have to accept the Wall, and they had been right. Khrushchev would never have run the risk of a confrontation if Eisenhower had been in charge.

"So you think this will help Jack's reelection campaign?"

"That's how it works," Grayson said. "There's no letup. You have to keep an eye on the next election. We don't know who the Republicans are going to pick. Nixon's finished after his loss in California. Maybe Nelson Rockefeller, although his divorce makes that less likely. Maybe Goldwater, even if he's too far to the right. We need to be ready, and trust me, we will be."

Every so often, Dillon was reminded what a political animal Grayson had become. He measured every proposed course of action against whether it would help keep Jack Kennedy in the White House. Grayson was a true believer in all things Kennedy. Alex Landauer had mocked Grayson behind his back for wearing the President's favorite German 4711 cologne and imitating JFK's habit of changing his dress shirt several times during the day. "I half expect Talbott to start talking with a Boston accent," Alex said. "Or convert to Catholicism."

"You're too tough on him," Dillon said. "He admires the man. Grayson wouldn't be the only one who wants to emulate Jack. The President is putting the haberdashers out of business—he doesn't wear a hat, so half the men in America have stopped wearing hats."

Dillon was disappointed that he wouldn't make the Berlin trip, but being turned down at least meant that he wouldn't have to deal with Jill's resentment. She hated it when he traveled, and he would have faced weeks of sullen silence from her before and after. He was frustrated by her attitude. As he had reminded her more than once, he was a diplomat, albeit one assigned to Washington, and traveling overseas was part of the job. She seemed to think that Dillon could manage his schedule as he saw fit. That was absurd, of course, and Dillon made that clear whenever he could.

* * *

When Dillon returned home, after making very little progress on his Berlin report, he found Jill in front of the television set. She was watching news coverage of the confrontation in Alabama between Governor George Wallace and federal authorities over the desegregation of the University of Alabama.

He was in time to join her to watch as President Kennedy's addressed the nation about the situation in Alabama. Dillon was pleased with how directly Kennedy tackled the issues, making it clear that Wallace wouldn't be allowed to keep Negro students from attending a public university. And he then pivoted to the more profound questions about race, asking a series of rhetorical questions: *"Who among us would be content to have the color of his skin changed and stand in his place? Who among us would then be content with the counsels of patience and delay?"*

Jill had tears in her eyes when she turned to Dillon. "This is the first time I've understood why you're so enthusiastic about the President," she said. "He's showing some courage about civil rights."

"He has never lacked courage," Dillon said. "Even his enemies concede that. But Jack Kennedy knows American history. That's why he's taken civil rights slowly. It's complicated. He's a Boston Yankee, and people in the South don't particularly like being lectured to by outsiders."

"Outsiders?" She took a deep breath, her face flushed. "He's president of the country. You're from the South. Do you consider him an outsider?"

"Of course not. But it's different for Southerners. You can't rush things. You can't expect them to turn their society upside down."

"That's easy for you to say, isn't it? You're white. You heard what he asked. Would you trade places with a Negro?"

She waited for Dillon to answer her question. He hesitated, weighing his words before he responded. He had never seen Jill so agitated before.

"Uncle Leigh taught me never to answer hypothetical questions. But, no, I wouldn't change places. For the obvious reasons. I believe in civil rights. I've supported them from the start. My father did, as much as he could, when he was in Congress."

"If you were a Negro, would you accept anything less than full equality? I know I wouldn't."

"I'd want to pursue whatever course of action that would get me that full equality, if not today, then tomorrow. I wouldn't squander goodwill by pushing too hard, too soon. Honey works better than vinegar."

"That wouldn't be your attitude if you were the one facing the prejudice. You'd want justice. You wouldn't want your rights compromised."

"I think you have a choice. You can push too hard and make people dig in their heels. We saw that in Virginia. You can try to integrate the public schools overnight, but you end up with white students leaving and attending private schools. That's what happened in Charlottesville. It's better to take things step-by-step."

She shook her head. "Do you always have to win every argument? Do you always have to be right?"

"I'm sorry if it seems that way to you," he said, trying to defuse the situation. "I thought we were having a discussion. You have your opinions, and I have mine. We don't have to agree."

*　*　*

Two weeks later, Dillon intently watched the President's televised Berlin speech.

The sight of the broad plaza where the crowd had gathered brought back memories of his time in Berlin when he would visit the nearby Rathaus and meet with city officials and local politicians. He pictured the city hall, with its red-tiled roof and its bell tower, which housed a replica of the Liberty Bell in Philadelphia, a gift of the American people.

It was one of Jack Kennedy's better speeches. He struck the right note, it seemed to Dillon, not raising unrealistic expectations, but challenging the division of the city, pointedly drawing comparisons between the West and the Soviets. *"There are some who say that Communism is the wave of the future. Let them come to Berlin."* Judging from the enthusiastic applause, Berliners loved what they were hearing.

Kennedy paused for dramatic emphasis before the high point of the speech: *"All free men, wherever they may live, are citizens of Berlin, and, therefore, as a free man, I take pride in the words Ich bin ein Berliner."* The crowd waved flags and cheered with enthusiasm. It was perfect for the televised excerpts that most people would see. Grayson had to be happy.

Despite the lofty words, nothing changed on the ground in Berlin. Dillon had heard that the President had told visitors to the White House that a wall was better than a war. Harold Braun had been right about the value of the Wall—it removed the knotty question of Berlin's status from active consideration. Western politicians could proclaim their devotion to freedom, but East Berliners remained trapped, imprisoned by concrete and barbed wire.

Nonetheless, it was an impressive performance by the President. Dillon could see that he was growing into his job—he appeared more confident, more in command of the situation. After the false starts and mistakes of the first two years—the Bay of Pigs and Vienna, the Cuban Missile Crisis—it was a welcome change.

THIRTEEN

The reports from Vietnam crossing Dillon's desk turned darker that summer. The strategic hamlet and civic action programs that were a key to winning over the peasantry were faltering. Several times the Viet Cong had attacked and overwhelmed weakly garrisoned strategic hamlets. Political tensions were also rising. Instead of softening its policies toward the growing Buddhist opposition, the Diem government intensified its pressure on the dissidents. In August, after weeks of growing tension, Ngo Dinh Nhu ordered elements of the Army to raid Buddhist pagodas across the country, arresting thousands of monks and other activists. Some died at the hands of the ARVN.

Dillon was staggered by the sheer arrogance and stupidity of the crackdown. Did Diem and Nhu not understand that whatever momentary advantage they gained over their domestic adversaries came at the cost of alienating American officials in Saigon and Washington? Did they not care about the damage to the regime's already battered public image? Or did they not worry about the consequences, confident that the Americans had no choice but to back them?

The raids on the pagodas came on August 21st, the day before Henry Cabot Lodge, the new American ambassador, arrived in Saigon to take up his duties. Mary Warren shook her head when they discussed the latest developments over a cup of coffee in the cafeteria. "I think Diem wanted to show Lodge that he calls the shots," she said. "That's a grave mistake on his part. Lodge is just as much a mandarin as the Ngo brothers, and he's used to getting his way. There's that old saying in Boston: 'The Lodges talk only to the Cabots, and the Cabots only to God.' He won't take kindly to the raids."

"Lodge's reputation is that he suffers no fools," Dillon said.

"My bet is that he'll make a very forceful case that Diem has to allow the democratic process to work. No more attacks on the Buddhists. No more arrests of the opposition. Diem has to rein in his brother, and that awful woman, Madame Nhu, the Dragon Lady."

"Will Diem listen to him?"

She shrugged. "Who knows? Lodge speaks fluent French. Maybe he and Diem will get along. Miracles do happen. But Lodge won't be very patient. Every time Nhu orders some repressive measure against the opposition, the regime loses credibility. Ho Chi Minh and Giap have an advantage—they're not held to Western standards. There's no opposition left in the North to persecute. They're all dead or in prison camps."

Dillon thought about calling Huy Dinh Dao at the Vietnamese Embassy but decided against it. What could Dillon say that would make any difference? Dao could pass along a message of disapproval, but it didn't seem anyone in Saigon would care to listen.

"There's only so far you can push," Mary said. "Diem is never going to hold Vermont town hall meetings. It's a Confucian culture. They're accustomed to hierarchy. To expect them to embrace Western-style democracy is absurd."

The following day it was front-page news that Tran Van Chuong, South Vietnam's Ambassador to the U.S., had resigned his post in protest over the campaign against the Buddhists, as had his wife, Nam Tran Van Chuong, the country's observer at the United Nations. Chuong's successor was the chargé d'affaires, who would serve until Saigon could appoint a new ambassador.

"They say that Chuong's replacement is loyal to Diem," Mary said. "Like your buddy, Huy Dinh Dao. Chuong may be Madame Nhu's father, but he has broken with her and the government. He and his wife are Buddhists and sympathize with the demonstrators. They're also schemers. They've been all over Washington running down Diem, saying he's the wrong man for the job. They have their reasons for hating him. They had some prime rice land taken from them during the initial land reform, right after Diem took power in the mid-fifties."

"What happens next?"

"You mean, will we intervene?" She shook her head. "I don't know."

Dillon frowned. "Roger is pushing the President to act. To back away from Diem and to throw our support behind a leader who can unite the country and will end the persecution of the Buddhists. Paul Katzenberg of the Vietnam Task Force has been arguing that if Diem stays in power the U.S. will be out of Vietnam in six months. He suggested that leaving wouldn't be such a bad outcome. Rusk shut that line of thinking down. We're staying, we won't pull out until the war is won. But Rusk wouldn't come out and endorse a coup."

"There are some nasty rumors floating about Ngo Dinh Nhu," Mary said. "That he's using heroin and opium. That he's cracking up under the stress. That he hates Americans. He's upset that our soldiers don't come with passports. Then, there are stories that he's been talking to the North about neutrality."

"What do you believe is the truth?"

"Half of the rumors are probably true," she said. "I just don't know which half."

* * *

Dillon took Jill and the baby to Far Ridge for a long weekend. She had seemed happier, focused on Sandy, who had begun to crawl and babble. Sandy had settled into a routine, sleeping through the night, and starting to eat baby food. On a sunny Saturday afternoon, they drove to Charlottesville and walked through the University's Grounds, with Sandy in a carriage. They stopped for ice cream at the end of their impromptu tour. Jill gave Sandy a taste of her chocolate ice cream, and she broke into a delighted smile.

Dillon returned to the office on Tuesday, relaxed and in a great mood. He had been at his desk only for a half hour when Mary pulled him aside.

"A wild weekend," she said. "Some strange things are going on. Hilsman, Forrestal, and Harriman cooked up a cable to be sent to Ambassador Lodge. They got the President to agree to it and George Ball to send it.

A change in policy. Cable 243. Lodge was told that he has the authority to talk to the generals about a change in government. That we aren't wedded to the Ngo brothers. The generals will interpret it as a withdrawal of our support for Diem."

"And the President approved this?"

"He did. For all intents and purposes, they're telling Lodge that we're okay with a coup. Diem won't leave voluntarily, or quietly. Not with his brother and Madame Nhu at his elbow. The military will have to depose him, and to do that the generals need to line up enough support to neutralize the troops loyal to Diem."

"What about McNamara? Taylor? McCone? Did they endorse the change in policy?"

"There was a high-level meeting yesterday. They were furious. They apparently weren't consulted about the cable. I wouldn't be completely surprised if the policy is reversed."

"It sounds a bit slap-dash. The Secretary of Defense and the Chairman of the Joint Chiefs of Staff aren't involved in a decision of this magnitude? A cable sent over the weekend? That won't sit well."

"It's not what they teach in civics class. By the way, there's word from France that De Gaulle will soon propose a peace conference in Paris, bringing the leaders of the North and South together. The idea is to negotiate reunification and a government of national unity. Vietnam would become neutral, like Cambodia and Laos."

Dillon shook his head. "That would be tantamount to surrender."

"A slow-motion surrender," she said. "The French are quite good at surrendering. They've had lots of practice."

* * *

While Dillon and his colleagues concentrated on an insurgency halfway across the world, there were signs of discord closer to home. On the last Wednesday in August, some 250,000 civil rights demonstrators, mostly African-American, descended on the capital city. The March on Washington for Jobs and Freedom, organized by Dr. Martin Luther King, represented the culmination of more than two years of increasing activism for equality for black Americans.

Dillon was occupied by meetings all day at Main State, and he caught only a few minutes of the massive demonstration on the small office television. He missed Dr. King's speech, which one of the secretaries told him was quite inspiring.

When he reached home, well after seven o'clock, he found Jill in the kitchen finishing a glass of red wine. Her face was flushed with excitement. She explained that she had gone to the Mall and listened to several of the speakers.

"I went with Darla," she said. "It was an amazing scene. A huge crowd, as far as the eye could see. There was something grand about the whole thing. Uplifting. For all those people to come to Washington and ask for justice. I just hope that the men in power were listening. It's long past time to right the wrongs we've done to the Negroes."

He nodded, not trusting himself to say anything. He was disappointed that she had attended the March without letting him know in advance. There had been some speculation in the newspapers that the rally on the Mall could turn violent if black nationalist groups confronted the police. Did she even think about the potential risk? She was a mother, now, no longer a carefree graduate student like Darla. He was annoyed with her.

He had mixed feelings about her spending time with Darla. Jill had complained about feeling isolated, being trapped at home with Sandy, and not having many friends in Washington. Dillon had encouraged her to go out, and Jill had turned to Darla for companionship. But whenever Jill socialized with her friend, in the following days she would be short-tempered, impatient with Thea, and critical of Dillon. Did Jill envy Darla's freedom to go where she wanted when she wanted, her lack of responsibility? Dillon worried that it was so.

"Is the President going to do something about civil rights?" Jill asked. "Take some real action?"

"You know he can't just snap his fingers and fix it," he said, his irritation growing. "Jack Kennedy supports civil rights, but he's not a king. He can't command people to do things. He needs support in Congress, and he has to be careful not to lose the South. It's going to take some time."

"Don't the Negroes in the South deserve the same rights and benefits as we do? Why should they wait any longer?"

"Of course I believe in civil rights. I wish it were that simple." He struggled to keep the annoyance out of his voice, but he wasn't sure that he had succeeded.

"How can doing the morally right thing be complicated?"

Sometimes he wondered if she chose to quarrel with him over the question of civil rights because it put him on the defensive. He was at a disadvantage, a Southerner burdened by his ancestors' complicity in the horrors of slavery. There was tension in every marriage, he knew, and it surfaced in different ways.

"It should be simple," he said. "But we live in a fallen world, or so I'm told. So we'll have to hope that the Kennedy brothers can work some magic in Congress on civil rights, and not lose the House, Senate, and Presidency in the process."

FOURTEEN

A week later, Roger Hilsman called Dillon into his office for a brief conversation. Hilsman suggested that it was time for another on-ground assessment of the Strategic Hamlet Program, and he thought Dillon should make a trip to Saigon to meet face-to-face with the American officials responsible for its progress.

"Secretary McNamara and General Taylor will be on a fact-finding mission that will overlap with the time of your visit," Hilsman said. "Mike Forrestal had been designated the chief of staff for the mission by the President, and he has agreed to include you in the larger meetings of the delegation whenever he can. You'll attend in a quasi-official capacity."

Dillon remained silent. He wasn't sure what Hilsman wanted him to do. What did he mean by "quasi-official capacity"?

"I'd like you to be the proverbial fly on the wall," Hilsman continued. "Keep your eyes and ears open. See what you can find out from the junior members of the mission. When you get back, I'll expect a summary report with your impressions. No holds barred. Along with what you learn about the strategic hamlet business, of course."

"That could put me in an awkward position." Dillon hoped that he was making it clear that he wasn't comfortable with the idea.

Hilsman grinned. "You're a diplomat. I'm told you have a reputation for tact. I'm confident that you can deal with any issues that may arise. It's important that you be there. I believe that the President wants to encourage McNamara and Taylor to apply more pressure to Diem so that we can advance our goals in the countryside. I'd like you there as an observer. An interested observer."

"I'll do what I can."

"I have no doubt of that," Hilsman said, flashing another grin.

Mary Warren laughed out loud when Dillon told her about the genesis of his trip. "So Hilsman wants you to spy for him," she said. "It's amazing how much political infighting there is at the moment. It seems like half of Washington is headed to Saigon. One mission after another. General Krulak and Joe Mendenhall of State are just back. They were also sent to assess the situation. Both old Vietnam hands, by the way. Once they were there, they heard different things. It got fairly contentious when they returned to Washington. They reported their findings to the National Security Council, with President Kennedy there to hear what they had to say."

"How did that go?"

"Krulak, the tough Marine, told them that the people loved Diem, that we were winning the war, and that Nhu wasn't the bad guy everyone made him out to be." Mary raised her eyebrows. "Imagine that. Mendenhall then reported that the regime was about to collapse, the war effort was flagging, and that Nhu should be removed."

"How did the President react?"

"He looked at them and asked: 'Were you two gentlemen in the same country?'"

* * *

When Dillon told Jill about his trip to Vietnam, she didn't say anything at first, but she quickly made her displeasure known. "You know that you'll miss Sandy's birthday," she said. "I had hoped that you'd be here for that. I wanted to have a little party."

"I'm sorry," he said. "Why don't we postpone the party until I come back? Sandy's not going to know any better."

She made a face. "I want it to be on her birthday. I've already invited a few people. We'll have to go ahead without you."

"Sorry about the timing. I wasn't given a choice."

"It's always like that, isn't it? When Roger Hilsman says 'jump' you ask 'how high?' I'm no longer surprised by it."

Dillon shrugged. He wasn't going to argue with her. As it was, he expected a sullen silence from Jill in the days leading up to his trip.

He tried to sleep as much as he could on the long flights to California, Hawaii, and then across the Pacific to Southeast Asia. On the morning of his arrival in Saigon, Dillon ran into Alex Landauer in the lobby of the Caravelle Hotel. Alex smiled when he saw him.

"Small world, it seems," he said. "What brings Dillon Randolph to Saigon?"

"I'm checking in on the Strategic Hamlet Program. A progress report. And you?"

"I'm here to provide staff support for Secretary McNamara. His mission with General Taylor." Alex had adapted well to Washington. He had become one of McNamara's Whiz Kids, known for his ability to analyze data and quickly produce a crisp summary detailing the implications of a proposed policy.

"As it happens, I may be sitting in on some of the meetings. At Mike Forrestal's invitation."

Alex smiled again. "Maybe we can compare notes."

In the days that followed, Dillon managed to get himself invited to most of the briefings by the Country Team and MACV, the U.S. Military Assistance Command, Vietnam. He kept to the back of the room, maintaining a low profile. From what the diplomats and officers shared with the delegation, it seemed that rapid progress was being made in the struggle with the Viet Cong, at least from a statistical perspective. Dillon was skeptical—he didn't put much faith in the numbers provided by the South Vietnamese military, particularly the volume of reported VC defections and casualties. In the few interviews he conducted about the strategic hamlets, he learned that the program was in trouble, plagued by incompetence, underfunding, and resistance from villagers who didn't want to leave their ancestral homes. That came as no surprise.

At dinner, Dillon learned from Alex that earlier in the day General Taylor had gone off to play tennis with General Duong Van Minh, with McNamara as spectator and scorekeeper. Whatever they discussed about the current political situation wasn't shared with anyone else on the mission.

"Judging from the glum looks of General Taylor and the Secretary when they came back to the delegation, I'd guess Big Minh played it coy about his intentions," Alex said. "He's smart. He knows better than to show his cards now."

There were two interesting developments near the close of the mission. From Rome, Madame Nhu—who had been sent on a trip to Europe by her husband as a way of lowering her profile—called the American troops in her country "little soldiers of fortune." Ambassador Lodge responded angrily to her comment, saying Madame Nhu should be thanking the soldiers, not insulting them.

Then, there was a moment of clarity about the military situation. When the delegation reached Can Tho, the large American base in the Mekong Delta, one courageous major spoke up about his frustrations with the progress of the war. He questioned the commitment of the South Vietnamese Army and suggested that the fight against the Viet Cong was faltering. Taylor and McNamara listened but didn't say much. Dillon imagined that the major had just effectively killed his chances for promotions.

Dillon and Alex had a final dinner together where Alex discounted much of what they had heard in Can Tho.

"There's progress when the South Vietnamese military listens to our advisers," he said. "The numbers show that. They have to abandon the tactics of the French—hunkering down in forts and letting the insurgents control the countryside. You can't expect to win if you're starting your morning with coffee and croissants."

"Aren't the problems a bit deeper than that?" Dillon asked. "From what I can gather, Diem has lost much of whatever support he had in the countryside."

"The villagers respect strength. We need to pressure Diem to get more aggressive. Take the fight to the enemy. Read your Caesar. *Gallic Wars*. Think of the barbarian tribes. Caesar gave them a choice—accept Roman rule or be annihilated. We have to convince the Viet Cong that if they continue to fight, they'll face a similar end."

Dillon shook his head. "I don't think that's going to work," he said. "Do you think that bombing villages and killing peasants will be a winning strategy?"

"There's only one way that we lose, Dillon. If we back away. General LeMay is right—we can bomb them back into the Stone Age, if need be. We don't need measures that drastic. As long as we have air superiority, we can keep the government in Saigon in power. That will buy time to consolidate the gains. Prove to the peasants in the bush that they can be protected. And at some point, Ho and Giap will cry uncle."

* * *

Once back in Washington, Dillon read the McNamara-Taylor mission report in an afternoon. As he skimmed the document, he grew increasingly disturbed. It claimed that the "military campaign has made great progress," while at the same time admitting that the Diem regime had become increasingly unpopular, a fact seized upon by the Viet Cong in their propaganda. There was nothing in the report that reflected what the delegation had heard at Can Tho.

The report's overly optimistic view of the military situation was coupled with a reluctance to confront the question of Diem directly. It suggested that the U.S. pressure Diem by suspending the financial assistance given directly to him. If he refused to deploy his elite Special Forces unit outside of Saigon, the recommendation was to cut off the $200,000 in monthly cash he used to supplement their pay and ensure their loyalty.

Dillon typed out a short, candid memo to Hilsman. He recounted what he had learned about the failures of the Strategic Hamlet Program, and what he saw as overconfidence on the part of MACV. Near the end of his memo, he noted the rumors that Diem and Nhu were negotiating with the North.

After sending the memo, he phoned Grayson Talbott, and they met for coffee. Grayson shook his head after Dillon shared his impressions of the mission.

"For once I'd like someone to return from Vietnam with some half-decent news," he said.

"What are you hearing?" Dillon asked. "What is the President thinking?"

"Our policy remains unchanged until after the election. The President will campaign on whatever progress we've made, but he'll resist any calls to double down on our involvement. The Republicans can talk big, but voters don't want American boys dying in Asia. Hell, Douglas MacArthur told the President that we should never fight a land war there."

"I hope that you're right," Dillon said.

Grayson grinned. "Not to worry. Jack is as smart as they say. He's not going to blunder into an unwinnable war. Remember, Jack and Bobby visited Saigon back in the early fifties, when the French made that mistake. Not a second time. Wait and see. He knows what he's doing."

FIFTEEN

Washington, D.C.
November 2, 1963

On Saturday morning, as he drank his second cup of coffee and finished his scrambled eggs and toast, Dillon listened intently to a radio update on the coup d'état in South Vietnam. The end of the Diem regime had come suddenly on All Saints' Day, the first day of November, after months of rumors. The rebel generals made their move with surprising efficiency, ringing the Presidential Palace with troops and tanks, and seizing the radio station. Despite some resistance by the soldiers defending the Palace, it soon became clear that the Ngo brothers had lost the backing of the military.

When he reached the office that morning, Dillon got a blow-by-blow account of the events of the day from Mary Warren, who had been on the phone with her friends in the Department and the Pentagon. When Diem called Henry Cabot Lodge during the early stages of the coup, the Ambassador had offered the Vietnamese leader safe passage out of the country on an American plane. Diem had countered that offer with a request for military assistance, but Lodge had told him that it was 4:30 in the morning in Washington, and no decisions could be made. Diem must have realized at that point that he and his brother had been abandoned, that the U.S. had decided to back the rebels.

Diem and Nhu escaped from the Palace through a secret tunnel, and found sanctuary in a church, St. Francis Xavier, in Cholon, the Chinese district of Saigon. From there, Diem negotiated with the generals and offered to surrender in exchange for safe passage out of the country. The end came swiftly for the Ngo brothers. After being taken into custody, they were executed.

"The killings appear to have been a mistake," Mary told Dillon. "The officer, Captain Nhung, sent to escort the Diem brothers to meet with the rebels hated Nhu. They put the brothers in an armored personnel carrier, with their hands tied. Nhung got into an argument with Nhu, and things escalated. Nhung stabbed Nhu to death and then shot Diem. The generals didn't want that. They knew it wouldn't look good."

"That's an understatement," Dillon said.

"They've planned this coup for some time," she said. "After the cable in August, Lodge started talking with the generals. He let Tan Van Don, the former army chief of staff, know a few months ago that we wanted a change. That was the clear signal the generals were waiting for."

"What about the Special Forces?" Dillon asked. "I thought Diem could count on their loyalty. That's how he beat back that coup attempt three years ago, isn't it?"

"Do Mau, the director of military security, convinced Diem to move the Special Forces out of Saigon to block a rumored assault by the Viet Cong. It was a pretext, of course. Do Mau had gone over to the rebels."

"It sounds like something out of the Borgias. A hall of mirrors. Betrayals. Plots within plots."

Mary laughed. "Is it any different than the jockeying that goes on in this town? Rusk versus Bobby. Bobby versus LBJ. McNamara versus half of the Joint Chiefs. We have enough internal intrigue to delight the Borgias. Except we don't shoot the losers. I'll admit that this coup was a bit macabre. The coup on All Saints' Day. Today, All Souls' Day, is the Day of the Dead."

"Are you a Catholic, Mary?"

"Nope. My Puritan ancestors would roll over in their graves at the thought. Although if I was ever tempted to become religious, I might convert to Catholicism. Have to admire the Jesuits. They've got their mumbo jumbo down pat. They've had several hundred years to come up with an answer for nearly everything."

* * *

At dinner Sunday night, Dillon faced questions about the coup in South Vietnam from Jill. He was surprised—she rarely asked him about his work, and he knew that other than occasionally watching the nightly news, she had little interest in the ins and outs of international politics.

"Did you know it was going to happen?" she asked. "The coup."

"Of course not. Why would you think that?"

"Aren't you and your boss advising the President about Vietnam? I would think that you would know what was going on. You went to Saigon just a month or so ago. I just wondered if you knew in advance about the coup."

"Absolutely not."

"Did they have to kill Diem and his brother?"

"The generals play for keeps. They worried that Diem might engineer a counter-coup."

"The whole thing is ghastly."

"Diem and his brother were corrupt. They weren't doing what needed to be done. That was no secret. Things should improve now. If we're going to keep the country out of the hands of the Communists, the common people have to begin to support the government in Saigon."

"I wish you didn't have anything to do with it," she said. "It's ugly."

Dillon nodded. "I agree that it can be ugly. But with any luck, things are going to get better. By this time next year, if things stabilize there, I'll be working elsewhere in State."

"That can't happen soon enough."

* * *

That next Thursday on poker night, differences within the Group over the wisdom of the coup in Saigon quickly surfaced. Jan Nowak defended Diem's removal, and Alex Landauer questioned its wisdom. State versus Defense. Dillon and Grayson Talbott listened to the two men make their points. (Palmer Knox was once again absent; he had told Dillon that he would be overseas for several weeks.)

Alex shook his head. "Diem was the best show in town. Removing him was a mistake. We've abandoned the one leader that the locals respect."

"The local Buddhists would disagree with you," Jan said. "They didn't particularly care to have their pagodas and temples burned down. We've had to work hard at the United Nations to head off a vote condemning the Diem government for its persecution of the Buddhists."

"The U.N. shouldn't be the arbiter of our foreign policy," Alex replied. "Half of the countries in the General Assembly brutally repress their own people. Why would we ever allow the U.N. to stand in judgment of what we do, or what our allies do? And I hardly think that summary executions of Diem and his brother strengthened our reputation for morality."

"There's some thought that it was a rogue captain who killed them," Grayson said.

"I don't buy that," Alex said. "Even in exile, the brothers could stir up trouble. The generals ordered their execution."

"By most accounts, the people of Saigon are happy about the change," Jan said. "I'm sure the political prisoners that Nhu's secret police tortured are resting easier. And the students and the Buddhists. There should be an opening now to establish a healthy political system."

"Well, it's our mess, now," Alex replied. "Stamped with 'Made in the U.S.A.'"

"I don't think so," Grayson said. "The President insisted that we stay clear of the coup. It had to be a Vietnamese action, not an American one."

"You can believe that if you like," Alex said. "No one else does. Do you think Big Minh and the other generals would have acted without encouragement from Lodge? And who gave Lodge the green light? The generals would never have moved ahead if they hadn't been told that the dollars would keep flowing. They wouldn't lift a finger against Diem and Nhu without approval from Washington."

"What about the demonstrations in the streets of Saigon?" Jan asked. "Seems the people are thrilled. Handing flowers to the soldiers. A tyrant deposed."

"A tyrant?" Alex smirked. "Hardly."

"What do you think, Dillon?" Alex turned to him.

Dillon hesitated before answering. He didn't want to be drawn into the debate. "I understand why the coup happened. To stop the Viet Cong, there has to be a government that the people will support. The Strategic Hamlet Program, economic development, a military willing to fight—they require a clean government, not a bunch of corrupt autocrats."

"I see nothing wrong with installing a puppet government," Alex said. "But our puppets need to be competent, or we'll never be able to cut their strings and see them stand on their own. Like Pinocchio. I just question whether this new group is competent."

"The Military Revolutionary Council has made the vice president, Tho, the head of the provisional government," Jan said. "The real power will be with Big Minh and the junta. Twelve generals."

Alex made a face. "That will never work. In Asia, you need a strong man at the top. A committee can't run the country. It sounds like Minh will have to negotiate with the other generals if he wants to make changes."

"Ambassador Lodge believes that we're going to get movement on the reforms that Nhu blocked," Jan replied. "The generals will make nice with the Buddhists. No more monks setting themselves on fire."

"That may be so," Alex said. "But I've heard some calling it the Asian Bay of Pigs. The Joint Chiefs, Max Taylor, McCone at the CIA, the Vice President, and the President's brother all think the coup was a bad idea. One of the few times Bobby Kennedy and Johnson have agreed on anything. So maybe we shouldn't count this as a victory quite yet."

"Our people in Saigon think differently," Jan said. "I've seen the dispatch from the Ambassador. He argues that the South Vietnamese military performed well in the coup, showed some discipline, so there's no reason that they can't meet the challenge of the Viet Cong equally well."

"Ambassador Lodge should remember that Notre Dame wins when they play college teams," Alex said. "Not the same if they have to play the Green Bay Packers."

* * *

The following Monday, Huy Dinh Dao called and left a message inviting Dillon to lunch. Dillon pulled Mary Warren aside and asked her whether she thought he should go.

She shook her head. "It will be awkward at best. Dao is a Diem loyalist. His family has supported Diem since '54. They're Catholic and Westernized, perhaps even more than the Ngos. Dao was educated in France, and I believe he spent a year or two in the U.S. in graduate school."

"Do you think I should accept?"

She sighed. "Why not? You'll get a read on what the Diem loyalists are saying and thinking. Their attitude toward us, and toward the junta."

This time Dillon met Dao at a different French restaurant, Bonat's, on Vermont Avenue, a popular lunch spot that was known, jokingly, as the poor man's Colony.

Dillon could not see Dao's eyes behind his tinted glasses. The diplomat fiddled with his silverware and quickly dispensed with casual conversation.

"It is a dark time, Mr. Randolph. A time of betrayal. Your government has made a grave mistake. One of our poets, Nguyen Dinh Chieu, wrote that he would rather face eternal darkness than see the face of traitors. Like Homer, Chieu was blind. By betraying President Diem, these generals betrayed their country. And you Americans engineered this, did you not?"

"There were no Americans involved in the coup," Dillon said. "It was a Vietnamese matter. Your generals made the change, not us."

Dao shook his head vigorously. "They would have never acted without approval from your Ambassador."

Dillon saw no point in denying the obvious. "It's common knowledge that President Diem was resisting reform."

"Ah, yes, reform. The magical word for Americans. How many times have you been to my country, Mr. Randolph?"

"Twice."

"I see. Your postings were in Australia and Germany before your current job?"

"You've done your research."

"I ask questions. It is important to know these things. You are a cultured man. We respect and admire men of integrity. Men of letters. You wield influence."

"I'm flattered that you believe I'm that influential. I work with others in the State Department who know more about your country and its culture. I don't pretend to be an expert on Vietnam, and I certainly don't set policy."

"But you believe in the magic of reform. After two visits to my country. Why should we reform? So that our adversaries can use our weakness to achieve their aims? Do you think reforms will convince the Cao Dai or the bonzes who have always hated us to support the government? If that is the case, you are sadly mistaken, Mr. Randolph."

"We are of different opinions, then."

"Spoken like a diplomat. I will not speak like one and mince my words.

Americans are ignorant. A willful ignorance, as you've made no attempt to understand us. President Diem and his brother were *si*, scholars. The Ngo family is known for its learning. These puffed-up generals are *binh*, lowly soldiers. They will never be respected. But you believe you can impose your will through these soldiers. You are wrong. You cannot. And there will be a steep price to be paid."

Dillon shrugged. "The die is cast. For better or worse, we will work with the new government. We have to."

"You know that General Mai Huu Xuan has been made the director general of the police? It is common knowledge that he gave the orders for the assassinations. I do not see clean hands. I see bloody hands. And like Pontius Pilate, there is no washing them clean."

"There could have been a different outcome. Many in Washington hoped that President Diem would ask his brother and his wife to step aside, for the good of the country."

"I told you before that he would never do that, betray his brother, dishonor his family."

"I'm sorry that it has come to this," Dillon said.

Dao took off his glasses so that Dillon could see his eyes. He leaned forward. "Someday, you may be called upon to make decisions about my country. Your family is powerful. Your father was in Congress for many years. I can only hope that you learn more about us. Study our history and our culture. In the meantime, we will work with you, even if what you have done is wrong. Saving my country from its enemies must come first."

* * *

Two weeks after the coup, Dillon met Palmer at Martin's Tavern in Georgetown, at his friend's request. Palmer said he needed to talk through something that was bothering him. When Dillon arrived, he found Palmer sitting in the back of the restaurant, away from the bar, with a half-filled mug of beer in front of him. He waved Dillon over to join him.

After the waiter had brought him a whiskey sour, Dillon waited for Palmer to explain why he wanted to talk. His friend seemed restless, shifting in his seat, looking around the restaurant, avoiding eye contact.

"We've thrown our lot in with some pretty hard characters," Palmer began. "They say Big Minh's bodyguard, Captain Nguyen Van Nhung, killed the Ngo brothers. You wouldn't want to meet him in a dark alley. He puts a notch on his pistol handle for every man he kills."

"No one here wanted Diem or his brother killed," Dillon said. "The idea was for them to go into exile."

"When you start the avalanche, people get buried. That's how it works. Washington made a mistake in getting rid of Diem. Sure, he was a son of a bitch, but he was our son of a bitch. The Vietnamese are Confucian. They respect the strong man, even if he is corrupt."

Dillon nodded. He wasn't going to argue with Palmer, even though he believed that he was wrong.

"Cora has left me," Palmer said, abruptly. "I came home, and she had cleared out. You'd never know that she was ever there. Took all her things."

"I'm sorry to hear that."

"I'm not," Palmer said. "We fought all the time. She hated living here. She's gone to San Francisco to live with her sister. At least that's what her note said."

"Jill isn't wild about Washington, either," Dillon said.

"We've been at odds for a while. Cora hates what I do, or what she thinks I do. She wants me to quit. Move to California. Start over." He paused to drink from his mug. "I'm thinking about getting out. I don't sleep well. Don't have much of an appetite. Sometimes I don't feel like a human, I feel more like a robot. Push my button, and I follow orders. Is that any way to live?"

"Can you take some time off?" Dillon asked. "A vacation?"

"They want me back in Vietnam," Palmer said. "I've told them I'm not wild about the idea. It's ugly work. Really ugly. They're telling me I'm the only man for the job. They've offered more money."

"What are you going to do?"

"I don't know. I'll probably go. Ours not to reason why, ours but to do and die. Isn't that what they say?"

"No, that's Alfred Lord Tennyson. A lousy poem and lousy advice."

"I'll drink to that," Palmer said. "To lousy poems and lousy advice."

SIXTEEN

Friday, the twenty-second of November, the week before Thanksgiving. A mild day for so late in the fall, with slightly overcast skies and temperatures nearing sixty degrees. Dillon had taken the day off from work to join Palmer Knox for trap shooting at a gun range in Virginia, a thirty-minute drive from the city. Palmer had invited him a few weeks before, and Dillon had finally arranged his schedule to allow for the outing.

Dillon hoped that they could talk over lunch before they started at the range, but Palmer was in no mood for conversation. They ate a quick meal of ham and cheese sandwiches and bottled Coca Colas, sitting at a battered outdoor table. Palmer answered Dillon's questions about his current status with grunts or brief answers, and so Dillon gave up after a while. He wasn't going to force the issue.

Palmer came alive once they were on the range, knocking down the clay targets with ease. He was a great shot, and while Dillon knew he couldn't match Palmer's accuracy, he nonetheless enjoyed losing himself in the routine of loading the shotgun, bringing it to his shoulder, following the flight of the target with the barrel slightly ahead, and squeezing the trigger. He got used to the feel of the gun recoiling into his shoulder. When the buckshot hit the clay targets, he couldn't help but grin.

They had been shooting for an hour, when the owner of the range, a man named Hendricks, suddenly appeared. He called out to Sammy, the young man who had been pulling the trap handle for them, and asked him to stop.

"You gentlemen might want to come inside," Hendricks said, gesturing toward the shack that was his office. "There's news on the radio. Terrible news. It's about the President."

Dillon glanced at this watch—it was five minutes before two o'clock. When they entered the shop, Hendricks motioned toward a transistor radio sitting near the counter. An announcer was talking about President Kennedy and Dallas. The reports were sketchy, but it was clear there had been a shooting. The President had been riding in an open car in a motorcade when he was struck by rifle fire. They listened in stunned silence. Some thirty minutes later, the announcer read a bulletin from the Associated Press—despite the efforts of the surgical team, the President had died at Parkland Memorial Hospital.

Dillon and Palmer looked at each other, dismayed. Hendricks made a sound of disgust. "Bastards," he said.

Palmer kept shaking his head. "How could they let this happen?" he asked. "Where the hell was the Secret Service?"

"Mark my words," Hendricks said. "It had to be planned. They found someone damn good with a rifle to be able to hit the President in a moving car. It just doesn't happen by chance. Maybe the Russians?"

"You never know, but I doubt it," Palmer said. "They wouldn't risk a war, which is what they'd get if they were behind this and we found out. We won't know until they catch someone. The assassin. Or assassins."

"Do you think there was more than one gunman?" Dillon asked.

Palmer shrugged. "If it was a planned hit, then they would want multiple shooters, to make sure the job got done."

They left the building and walked to the gravel lot where they had parked their cars. "I've got to get to Langley," Palmer said. "It'll be a fire drill there. I'll call you if I learn anything."

"Likewise. What do you think? Who could be behind this?"

Palmer shook his head, ruefully. "Hard to say. If you play with fire, you can get burned."

Dillon turned on him, angry. "What the hell does that mean?"

Palmer stepped back, his hands up, palms facing Dillon. "Forget it," he said. "I just meant that every President has his enemies. The right wing in the South hates him because of civil rights. I read that in the paper that some protester in Dallas hit Adlai Stevenson on the head last month with a placard. A woman, mind you. There were flyers circulating in Dallas accusing Kennedy of being a traitor. And if it's not the Birchers, it could be the Mob. They've hated Bobby ever since the Hoffa hearings. Who knows?"

"But this isn't some banana republic," Dillon said. "Our presidents don't get shot down in the street."

Palmer didn't respond. He waved as Dillon pulled out of the parking lot to head back to Washington.

On the drive, Dillon listened to the news on the car radio. There was little in the way of further detail. The more he listened, the angrier he became. How could it have happened? How could the President of the United States be murdered in broad daylight? Where was the Secret Service? He pulled over to the side of the road when the arrest of a suspect was announced, a man who had shot a Dallas police officer.

When he arrived at the office, one of the secretaries was weeping at her desk, her head bowed. There was an eerie silence in the halls. When people spoke, it was in hushed tones. Dillon sat at his desk, listening to the radio. After an hour or so, he decided there wasn't anything he could do, so he left the office.

He found Jill at home, cradling Sandy in her arms, tears streaming down her cheeks as she watched the network news from Dallas on their television set.

"How could this have happened?" she asked. "It's impossible."

"I don't know," he said. "I can't explain it. It's beyond belief."

"His children," she said. She pulled Sandy closer to her. "Caroline and John John. They're so young. It must be such a nightmare for Jackie."

"It's a nightmare for all of us, for the country."

"What will happen now?"

"The Vice President takes over," he said. "That's what happens. The King is dead. Long live the King."

* * *

Nothing Dillon learned over the next few days made any sense out of the catastrophe in Dallas. How could one man, an inconsequential loner by the name of Lee Harvey Oswald, have killed the leader of the greatest power on earth? There had to be larger forces at work. Oswald had lived in Russia—was there a Soviet connection to the killing? Dillon quickly rejected the idea—the Kremlin had to know that such a provocation would mean war. If it wasn't the Russians, then who? Oswald had been part of a group in New Orleans called Fair Play for Cuba, demonstrating against U.S. policy. Could the assassination be linked to anger over Kennedy's anti-Castro policies?

Then, he began to wonder whether organized crime was involved after Jack Ruby, a Mafia-connected nightclub owner, shot and killed Oswald on live television in the basement of the Dallas Police Headquarters. A move to silence Oswald? Incompetence on the part of the police? Eliminating the chief suspect in the case meant that investigators would have fewer leads to follow.

In Washington, thousands of mourners filed past Jack Kennedy's bier in the Capitol Rotunda. The state funeral was held the next day. School was canceled. Businesses closed. People gathered around television sets to watch. Jill persuaded Dillon to stay home with her and not join the throngs in Washington's streets.

They watched together in their living room. Dillon was struck by the symbolic weight of the ceremonies. The caisson drawn by six gray horses carrying the coffin. The tear-streaked faces of the crowds, men and women bewildered and dismayed. Then the funeral and its aftermath. The muffled drums and bagpipes. The raw grief of the onlookers. The riderless black horse, the empty boots reversed in the stirrups. The veiled widow. The daughter and son dressed in blue. The little boy saluting his father's coffin. They buried Kennedy at Arlington National Cemetery, his grave marked by an eternal flame.

Dillon continued to struggle with the meaning of what had happened. He understood the skepticism of his friends and colleagues that it could have been a lone assassin. Surely Oswald must have had help, must have been part of some larger conspiracy. How could one troubled man, a nonentity who had failed at every job he ever held, plan and execute an assassination of the most powerful figure in the world? It made little sense.

* * *

In the days that followed, the nation continued to mourn. In Washington, the permanent government slowly returned to its routine. The tried-and-true offered some measure of comfort and security. Civil servants didn't have to worry about getting elected. Their job was to keep the machinery of the state running.

The political appointees worked very hard to show the world that while one American leader might have fallen, it hadn't paralyzed the government. The new President was describing himself as a trustee. Not surprisingly, then, Lyndon Johnson quickly announced that the U.S. would continue to support the South Vietnamese government. Dillon and his colleagues could only hope that there would be a strategic review at some point in the near future. Johnson also established a commission, headed by Supreme Court Chief Justice Earl Warren, to investigate the assassination.

There was a stark contrast between Johnson, a gangly man with a prominent nose and large ears, and his appealing and handsome predecessor. Dillon was not surprised by the thinly disguised disdain that many of the Kennedy team had for LBJ. They had gone from grace to gracelessness, from wit to crude barnyard humor, or so it seemed.

Jill had been shaken by Dallas, and to Dillon's dismay, her response to the tragedy widened to include aspects of their life in Washington.

"This place generates darkness," she said. "The Republicans didn't have anything to say that was positive about Jack Kennedy when he was alive. And the Democrats aren't much better. The people running things, all they care about is power. They call it government service, but all they're doing is serving themselves. Getting ahead by controlling the lives of others."

"That's a bit simplistic."

"I guess I'm simple, then," she said. "But I know what I feel. This isn't a healthy place."

"It's a dark time," Dillon said. "I won't deny that. But things will get better. We'll get back to normal."

"That's just it," she said. "I hate what you call normal. The last few weeks have helped me see that. It's made me confront my feelings."

"We can talk about what I can do to make things better at home after things settle down."

"When things settle down?" She looked away.

Jill wasn't alone in her disillusionment. Nearly everyone Dillon encountered seemed depressed and anxious. It was important, he told himself, that it did not turn to despair. The initiatives of the Kennedy Administration had brought hope to Americans and people around the world. The Nuclear Test Ban Treaty. The Peace Corps. Progress on civil rights. The space program. The sense that America could accomplish great things. But the man behind that progress was gone. His loss was being felt far and wide.

When Dillon called Leigh in Charlottesville, he found his uncle in a reflective mood.

"I've been thinking about it," Leigh said. "Like everyone else, I guess. In some ways, I'm not surprised. Jack Kennedy stirred things up. All that charisma. The sex appeal. It attracts more than admirers, you know. The demented, the jealous, the little men. Like this Oswald. If you kill the King, you're in the limelight. You're on the stage, front and center."

"Was it a lone gunman?" Dillon asked. "A nut? There's something about the randomness of it—if it was random—that's very disturbing."

"History says otherwise. Don't forget a crazy five-foot-tall Italian bricklayer shot at FDR in Miami, tried to murder him. And there was an assassination attempt on Truman. Out of the blue, Puerto Rican nationalists attacked Blair House, where Truman was staying while they renovated the White House. I think it was in 1950?"

"It would make more sense if Oswald had a cause, like the Puerto Ricans. Or John Wilkes Booth."

"But Oswald didn't," Leigh said. "He was at the bottom of the heap. A loser. This was his way to stand out. After practicing law all these years, I know his type. They turn up in court all the time, charged with stupid crimes. It's almost as if they want to be caught so the world will finally pay attention to them."

"What about Johnson?" Dillon asked. "Can he handle the job?"

"I know him only by reputation," Leigh said. "A wheeler-dealer. Self-made. A bit crude, and a bit of a bully. He has to be on the defensive—Jack was murdered in Texas, Johnson's home state. I expect that he'll be a caretaker for now. Most likely he'll run for the job next fall, and he'll have an excellent chance of winning. The Republicans don't have a candidate, not with Nixon out of politics after losing in California."

Dillon didn't share his uncle's optimism. Johnson seemed a throwback to the southern Senators of the 1940s, poorly equipped to lead a nation that had grown accustomed to the style and grace of the Kennedys. It wasn't fair to judge him against his charismatic predecessor, Dillon knew, but the inevitable comparisons wouldn't be flattering.

In one sense, it would never be the same again. Jack Kennedy was one of a kind, vigorous and virile, so unlike the bland, tired, and overly cautious political leaders of the near past. Nothing like him before or, Dillon imagined, after. Yet, there was so much of Jack's ambitious program left to complete. Kennedy had attracted some of the brightest minds to Washington, and it didn't seem right to Dillon that this vision of a renewed America should come to a grinding halt. He felt a sense of duty, an obligation, to continue on when the challenges remained. He didn't see how he could walk away now and live with himself. So he would stay and serve, and trust that what they had begun with such high hopes, they could find a way to finish.

PART TWO

SEVENTEEN

Washington, D.C.
December 31, 1963

Dillon had always hated the forced gaiety of New Year's Eve. The frantic revelry at the party thrown by Eliot and Gloria Garrison that he and Jill attended in Georgetown, just blocks from their house, seemed particularly strained and false. The jokes were too loud, the drinking too hard, the conversations too animated. Was it an attempt to dispel the gloom caused by the tragedy of Jack Kennedy's death in November? It certainly seemed that way. At the same time, Dillon sensed a barely submerged anger at the senselessness of what had happened in Dallas. It made him think of the refrain in Dylan Thomas' most famous poem: *Rage, rage against the dying of the light.*

He had arrived at the party in a foul mood after quarreling with Jill earlier in the day. Dillon didn't particularly want to attend the gathering, but with all of the tension at the State Department over potential changes in policy by the new Administration, he felt that he needed to make an appearance. Jill had balked at the idea, and they had argued. Dillon pointed out that she had skipped the Christmas celebration for the staff of Far Eastern Affairs.

"I don't want to get a reputation as being standoffish," he told her. "If you don't come with me, I'll be the only man at the Garrisons without his wife. That will look very strange."

"I'll go if you insist," she said. "I certainly wouldn't want to hurt your precious reputation."

He ignored her sarcasm. "It will be a night off for you."

"I don't like being away from Sandy. She doesn't understand why I have to leave her."

"She'll be fine," Dillon said. "Thea loves the baby. And Sandy will be sound asleep by eight."

"She's very young, Dillon."

He frowned. "She's almost sixteen months old. Other wives with even younger children manage to socialize. I don't see why you can't. It's only for a few hours. We don't want her to become clingy."

"All right," she said, her mouth pursed. "If you insist, I'll go."

"Thank you," he said. He was angry, but he knew better than to prolong the argument. He was frustrated by her moodiness. He knew it wasn't easy to deal with a small child, but Thea was there to help Jill around the house and care for the baby whenever she needed a break.

She took her time dressing for the party, choosing a light blue-colored evening gown that accentuated her slim figure. When Dillon complimented her on how she looked, she made a face. He felt a sudden surge of resentment. Jill had been a reluctant partner in bed since Sandy's birth. When they did make love, she wasn't very responsive. It made him feel that he was imposing on her, and he hated that feeling.

The Garrison party was a disaster, from start to finish. Jill quickly drank two martinis, and when Dillon tried to slow her down, she ignored him and drank another. Within minutes, she was slurring her words, and she wobbled across the room in her high heels and plopped down in a chair in the corner. He was embarrassed and surprised by her behavior. He had never seen Jill so drunk before.

She sat in the chair, martini glass in hand, and continued to drink. Dillon circulated around the party, keeping an eye on her. He saw Gloria trying to talk with her, but it was clear that Jill wasn't responding. After another thirty minutes, Dillon decided that he had had enough. He checked his watch—it was 11:15.

He made his excuses to Gloria and Eliot, and then shepherded Jill out of the party, propping her up as they slowly made their way back to their house. Once inside, she staggered into the bathroom, and he could hear the sounds of her vomiting. When he went to check on her, he found her on her knees, leaning over the toilet. She waved him away. "Leave me alone."

He went into the living room and turned on the television to the celebration in Times Square. Guy Lombardo was leading his band from the ballroom of the Waldorf-Astoria Hotel in New York City. As the ball dropped at midnight, the band began playing "Auld Lang Syne." Dillon heard fireworks crackling in the distance, the sounds of Washington celebrating.

He went into the bedroom and found Jill lying on the bed on her stomach. Her dress was on the floor. She had stripped down to her bra and panties. When he put his hand on her arm, Dillon felt her stiffen and then pull away. "I've been sick," she said. "Don't touch me. The idea is disgusting."

"I wasn't looking to seduce you," he said.

"Good. I have no interest in that. None whatsoever. Why would I?"

"You've had too much to drink."

"Have I? What do you expect? You forced me to go out. I didn't want to go to that damn party. Do you blame me? Drinking is the only way I could stand it, listening to all of your smug friends who aren't really your friends."

"I'm sorry it's such a burden for you," he said. "But do I ask that much of you?"

"I guess you don't," she said. "But I don't ask much of you, either, and I don't get much in return."

"That's absurd. You don't want for anything."

"So you say. I don't want to talk about this anymore. You wouldn't understand."

"Is there someone else? Are you seeing someone?" He studied her face, watching her reaction. He wondered if he would be able to detect it if she were deceiving him.

"Why do men always think there's another man when a woman is unhappy. Can't we have feelings that don't involve a man? I won't let myself be defined by you. I have my own life."

"Did I say otherwise?" he asked, puzzled. "Now, I truly don't understand."

"You wouldn't."

He decided to leave the bedroom before he could say something that he might regret. He would sleep on the couch in the living room. It certainly wouldn't be the first time—he was used to returning late enough from the office that he would spend the rest of the night there, not wanting to disturb Jill's sleep.

* * *

In the morning, a pale and drained Jill was apologetic. She slept late, and when she arrived in the kitchen, Dillon silently handed her a cup of hot coffee. She took a small sip.

"I had too much to drink last night," she said. "I'm sorry. I apologize for embarrassing you in public."

"I don't care about that," he said. "And it's not as if you made that much of a scene. There were lots of drunken people there. What's important to me is how you feel about us."

She sighed softly. "I know that I'm lucky to have you, Dillon. I'm trying my best to be a good mother and a good wife. It's just that at times I feel overwhelmed and trapped."

"Do I make you feel that way?"

"Not directly, no. It's the situation. Being a mother. Stuck in the house. Sometimes I feel the days are slipping by and I'll never get them back."

"You're raising a small child. As she grows older, it will become easier."

"Are you happy, Dillon?" she asked. "With your job? With me? With your life?"

"Of course I am," he said. "The job takes a lot out of me. You know that. But it will get better, I promise. I'll spend more time with you and Sandy. We can go to California on vacation in the spring."

"I'd like that."

That night when Dillon came to bed, Jill was awake, waiting for him. When he slipped under the covers, he found that she was naked. She kissed him gently on the lips, pulling him toward her, and they made love silently.

"I want you to be happy," he said later, as they lay in the bed, shoulders touching.

She turned away from him. "I hope you're right. That it gets better. I do hope."

* * *

Lyndon Baines Johnson didn't wait long to put his stamp on the government. In his State of the Union address, just eight days into the New Year, Johnson declared an "unconditional war on poverty" and proposed wide-ranging social programs as a solution. At the same time, he retained the key members of Kennedy's Cabinet. Dillon saw it as smart politics on Johnson's part: he could reassure the country that he wasn't abandoning the New Frontier policies of his predecessor while staking out his own ground with his War on Poverty. It also removed any principled reason for Bobby Kennedy to challenge him for the nomination. While some of Jack Kennedy's inner circle, like Theodore Sorenson, his chief speechwriter, and his close adviser Arthur Schlesinger, decided to leave the government after the transition, most, including Rusk, McNamara, and CIA director John McCone, elected to stay.

Johnson's focus on domestic issues heartened Dillon and his colleagues in Far Eastern Affairs. They figured that the new President would be less likely to seek a costly military solution in Vietnam, and that would strengthen the hand of Roger Hilsman and the other moderates in the ongoing debate over strategy with the hawks in the Pentagon. While

Johnson hadn't been a force on foreign policy matters during the Kennedy years, he had opposed the Diem coup.

There were some troubling developments. Paul Katzenberg was removed as chair of the Department's Vietnam Task Force. Bill Bundy, who was considered a hawk, replaced him, and the rumor was that Katzenberg had been deemed too pessimistic about the prospects for success in the war. Dillon remembered that six months earlier Katzenberg had argued for an honorable withdrawal from Vietnam, an approach rejected outright by Rusk, General Taylor, and the then-Ambassador to South Vietnam, Frederick Nolting.

* * *

Jill reacted poorly when Dillon told her near the end of the month that he once again needed to make a return trip to Saigon to assess the status of the Strategic Hamlet Program.

"I don't like it," she said. "You'll be gone two weeks, and then you'll be tired for another week or so when you get back. It's losing you for a month. Can't someone else go? Why does it always have to be you?"

"It's a crucial part of my job. I'm supposed to monitor the hamlet program. We need to know what's going on, and it's my responsibility to stay on top of things."

"Evan says that what you do is immoral. That you and the men around you are propping up a puppet government."

"I wasn't aware that Evan was such an expert on Southeast Asia." Dillon fought to keep his temper. He wasn't happy that Evan was in contact with Jill. He had been pleased when Jill's connection with Darla had seemed to fade.

"He called me on the phone last week. He invited me to a study group on Vietnam. Evan has been involved in organizing several demonstrations."

"That's his right," Dillon said. "I think the demonstrators are misguided. Misinformed. Did you agree to go to the study group?"

"No, I didn't. Then Evan and Darla asked me to go a demo next week. They are very sure that we shouldn't be in Vietnam."

"Do you agree with them?"

"Some of what they say makes sense. Some of it doesn't."

"If you ever want to talk about it, I'm here."

"Not now. Maybe later."

"I'd rather that you didn't go to the demonstration," he said. "For obvious reasons."

"I have the right to my own views."

"There's no question of that. But you are my wife, and what you do reflects on me."

"Darla said you would try to stop me from going."

"But I'm not stopping you. Go if you feel you must. It's your choice."

She sighed. "I already decided that I wouldn't go. I told Darla that yesterday. I also told her that it was my decision, not yours. And it is."

Dillon nodded. He didn't want to quarrel with her. Since their blowup on New Year's Eve, things had been better. Jill had been less moody, but there were still times when she was quite difficult. He was relieved that he had been able to avoid another argument. He didn't need tension at home when he was experiencing more than enough of it at the office.

EIGHTEEN

Saigon, Vietnam
February 1964

Dillon landed at Tan Son Nhut airport just after the close of the Tet holiday. It had been less than five months since his last visit, but it seemed like a lifetime. Much had happened. The coup in South Vietnam and the fall of the House of Ngo. Jack Kennedy's assassination. A nation stunned and disheartened. The change in administrations.

Before he left Washington, Mary Warren had reminded him that the Vietnamese believed that 1964—the Year of the Dragon—would be a very difficult and dangerous time. Astrologers maintained that every sixty years war and natural disasters would visit Indochina. In 1904, there had been a cyclone and widespread famine, so there was the expectation of a troubled year ahead.

Dillon arrived in Saigon better prepared for the heat—he had packed tropical weight clothing and dark sunglasses. He was also prepared for bleak and inconclusive interviews in the field.

A week earlier, General Nguyen Khanh had pushed Big Minh and the junta generals aside and assumed control of the South Vietnamese government. Some of the newspaper stories speculated that Khanh had acted because he hadn't been given the position and power he had expected after Diem's overthrow. Other accounts suggested that he was the choice of Ambassador Lodge and the American Embassy staff to lead South Vietnam.

By all accounts, Khanh was more tractable, more willing to follow Ambassador Lodge's lead. He had agreed to cede operational control in the countryside to American officers down to the company level.

The junta generals had resisted that concession, and it was said that General Harkins, the top U.S. military commander, had concluded that the junta was rudderless and ineffective after the debacle at Thanh Phu in mid-January. South Vietnamese troops had been defeated in fierce fighting, with some 600 killed or wounded and numerous helicopters downed. There were persistent rumors that some of the junta's leaders, particularly those educated in France, were open to Charles de Gaulle's calls for a unified, independent, and neutral Vietnam.

At least this time, Dillon thought, the losing side of the internal power struggle didn't face summary execution. That had to be considered progress. Big Minh was allowed to stay on as head of state, a figurehead, free to play as much tennis as he liked.

As he interviewed American officials in Saigon, Dillon learned that since the coup in November, some fifty strategic hamlets had been abandoned. Many of the peasants had returned to their home villages. The junta had purged the officer corps of Diem loyalists, dismantled Nhu's secret police, and curbed or eliminated the grassroots organizations, like the National Revolutionary Movement, established by the Ngo brothers.

Luke Bridgewater, an Agency for International Development officer in Ben Tre province, southwest of Saigon, told Dillon that he was disturbed by what he saw as a lack of commitment by the government and provincial officials, to say nothing of the peasants, in the Strategic Hamlet Program. Bridgewater wasn't anywhere near as upbeat as Jack Stebbins had been on Dillon's earlier tour.

"The local people aren't willing to stick their neck out," he said. "They know that the Viet Cong will execute anyone seen as supporting the government. They don't believe that we can protect them. And the program isn't being properly supported. The provincial officials divert funds meant for the hamlets into their own pockets."

"That's a grim picture."

"I'm not going to lie to you, Mr. Randolph. There's too much of that going on already. How can we fix things if we avoid a full accounting of what is going on?"

"Do you still believe it's a sound concept? The hamlets?"

Bridgewater nodded. "With the proper backing, I think it'd be a winner."

Bridgewater's qualified optimism wasn't shared by all. Another American official told Dillon that he feared much of the past data about the strategic hamlets had been fabricated. For example, it turned out that the number of secure hamlets in Long An province was not the 200 reported in the fall, but only ten. Dillon wondered, not for the first time, about the accuracy of the statistics collected and sent to Washington. How could they assess progress, or adjust policy, if they couldn't rely on the numbers?

* * *

Dillon was pleased to discover that Clay Blackburn was in Vietnam, on a month-long assignment to assess the readiness of several ARVN units. They met at the Caravelle's rooftop bar late in the afternoon.

"I'm not surprised that Big Minh only lasted three months," Clay said. "He was a lousy leader. Lazy. Ineffective. They say he'd rather play Mahjong or hit the tennis courts at Cercle Sportif than run the country. The betting is that Khanh holds on longer. But who knows? What goes on with these people is a complete mystery."

Dillon told him what he had learned about the flagging Strategic Hamlet Program. "It seems like we've lost considerable ground."

"In some ways, we have. But many of those hamlets were poorly sited. General Harkins doesn't like the fixed, isolated posts, where resupply had to be by convoy or helicopter. Lots of them are in the Mekong Delta. Diem resisted him on that question, and the junta generals weren't wild about it either. Harkins would rather withdraw from the outposts, concentrate forces, and hit the Viet Cong hard wherever they surface."

Dillon heard his name being called. He looked up to find Palmer Knox approaching their table. Palmer wore a white shirt and dark green pants.

"Small world," Palmer said. "Imagine bumping into you here."

Dillon introduced Clay and invited Palmer to join him, but his friend shook his head.

"No can do. I'm late for a meeting. Then it's off to the boonies." He slapped Dillon on the back. "I'll see you back in civilization."

As Clay watched Palmer leave the bar, a strange, puzzled look crossed his face. "Where do you know him from?" he asked Dillon.

"From Washington. We've been friends for a while. We play poker with a group of guys."

"What do you know about him?"

"He's former military. Works for the CIA now."

"Knox has a formidable reputation," Clay said. "One of the Agency's cowboys. They send him out to fix problems. He's very good, from all accounts, but he plays rough. He works with the Provincial Reconnaissance Units. They make up their own rules. One of their favorite tricks is decapitating any VC they catch. They've been told to cool it, because headhunting wouldn't sit too well with the American voting public. It's a struggle to get my ARVN officers to respect the Geneva Convention when it comes to prisoners and civilians. No torture. No out-of-hand killings. I don't always succeed, but I try. On my dark days, I wonder if your friend Knox and the others may be right, that to win a war like this means getting our hands dirty."

"Do you believe that?"

"The VC target the local district chiefs and their families. Teachers. Aid workers. They stage public executions. Beheadings. Grisly stuff. We know in the territory they control, they create their own political structure, with cadres and leaders. Some of my buddies think we should target their top echelon, hunt them down and execute them. Put the fear of the Lord in them."

"That would be a mistake," Dillon said quickly. "If we do that, we're no better than them."

"Don't worry," Clay said. "I haven't crossed the line. Don't plan to. Still, I feel sometimes like we're fighting with one hand tied behind our back." He paused. "Please don't repeat anything I've said to your friend. It's all rumors. It's impossible to say what's fact and what's fiction when you're talking about what goes on in the field."

The waiter brought them another round of drinks. As he was serving them, a middle-aged man and a younger dark-haired woman approached their table.

"Journalists," Clay said. "Remember to watch what you say."

Clay invited the pair to join them for a drink. Al Orenstein of the Associated Press peered at them through a pair of thick, black-rimmed glasses, blinking rapidly. The woman, Isabelle Lavalle, was a photographer for Agence France-Presse. She had striking Eurasian looks, with delicate features and dark brown hair. She wore a Nikon camera on a strap around her neck.

"Dillon's from Washington, but he's okay," Clay told them. "State Department. We're friends from way back. From my hometown. Charlottesville, Virginia."

"Randolph," Orenstein said. "Any relation to Congressman Randolph? His district covered that part of Virginia."

"My father," Dillon said.

"So what do you do for the State Department?"

"He works with Roger Hilsman," Clay said. "A hot shot. A guy with answers." He grinned at Dillon and raised his glass to him in a mock toast.

"Hardly," Dillon said. "Just part of his staff."

"What brings you to Saigon?" Isabelle asked. She spoke English with a slight French accent.

"I'm here on a fact-finding trip. Checking in on the Strategic Hamlet Program."

"And what have you discovered?"

"Still gathering facts," Dillon said. "And what brings you here, Miss Lavalle?"

"Please, call me Isabelle. I'm here to take photos. As you can imagine, Vietnam is of great interest to AFP, considering our history in the country."

"The French just want to gloat," Orenstein said. "They told us it would be a mistake to get involved here. We didn't listen." He glanced over at Dillon, who remained silent.

Isabelle shrugged. "I'm not political. I take photographs."

"Well, we're here," Clay said. "I say we make the best of it. No one said it would be easy, but I see some progress."

"Not enough," Orenstein said.

Clay turned to Isabelle. "Haven't seen you around much. Where have you been?"

"I've been in Paris," she said. "I'm back here for the last time, I think."

"And why is that?" Dillon asked.

"I've had enough of it," she said. "Hungary. Algeria. Suez. The Congo. It's become too much. I'm ready to make images of beautiful things."

"Can't argue with that," Clay said.

"Perhaps I can take your photograph," she said to Dillon and Clay. "Two friends from Virginia, far from home."

"Sure," Clay said. He moved his chair, and he put his arm around Dillon's shoulder. "Two Cavaliers."

Isabelle focused her camera and clicked the shutter twice. "I'll send you a print, Major," she said.

Orenstein finished his drink and stood up. "I'd love to stay, but I've got to get over to the Rex," he said. "Don't want to miss the military command's daily news conference." He looked around. "I like the rooftop bar here more than the one at the Rex. A better crowd. Less brass." He glanced over at Clay. "No offense."

"None taken," Clay said. "I probably have less use for headquarters types than you do. I agree with General Patton—no good decision was ever made in a swivel chair."

They watched as Orenstein left the bar. Isabelle Lavalle waited until he was out of earshot before she spoke.

"I've heard that the convoy to that ARVN post near Dong Xoai is overdue," she said to Clay. "They say you're going out to look for it."

"You have good sources," he said. "First thing in the morning."

"I'd like to tag along," she said.

Clay glanced over at Dillon. "I was going to invite Dillon to join me. To see what we're facing."

Dillon nodded. He was curious about the state of affairs in the countryside. "I'd like that."

Clay looked at them both. "In the morning, then. I'll pick you up in front of the hotel at six o'clock sharp."

* * *

They left Saigon at first light. Clay pulled up in a green sedan at the curb of the Caravelle, where Dillon and Isabelle were waiting. He drove at a fast clip until they reached the outskirts of the city. There, they found the relief column.

At the front, and back, of the column were M113 troop carriers with .50 caliber machine guns. In between were two trucks with Vietnamese Marines, and a jeep with a mounted machine gun. Clay placed the sedan near the back of the line of vehicles.

"Believe it or not, this may not be enough firepower," Clay said. "The bad guys like to rig explosives along the roadside and then attack once the column has stopped." He grinned and pointed skyward at two Huey helicopters flying above. "Insurance," he said. "Sometimes the VC ambush a first convoy as bait, and then wait and hit the rescue column hard. The choppers can hit them hard with their rockets and machine-gun fire if we run into another ambush."

"Is that likely?" Dillon asked. "A second ambush?"

"In this war anything's likely. They don't play by our rules, not the ones they taught us at Quantico. Take ambushes. They don't pick the logical spots. You'd think they'd hide in the trees just around the bend, but instead they're waiting for you crouched in drainage ditches on the other side of the road where there's little cover and where you don't expect them. They seem to have an uncanny sense of when we'll drop our guard."

"They sound a bit like Quantrill's Raiders."

Clay nodded. "They're damn good at bushwhacking." He paused. "Didn't Jesse James ride with Quantrill?"

"He did."

"Well, he and Captain Quantrill met the same fate. Hunted down and killed. That's what you have to do with guerrillas. Flush them out. Keep them on the run. Kill the leaders."

They had been on the road for an hour when the column came to an abrupt stop. Above them, the helicopters swooped by and banked and turned. An overturned jeep blocked the road ahead where two abandoned cargo trucks sat side-by-side. Dillon could see bodies dressed in green uniforms lining the side of the road.

Clay cursed and brought the sedan to a stop. He got out of the vehicle and Dillon and Isabelle followed him. Clay unholstered his sidearm. He walked over to the South Vietnamese officer who had emerged from the other jeep. The officer wore aviator sunglasses and was dressed in freshly-pressed fatigues and spit-polished black boots. The two had a brief, but intense, conversation.

Further up the road, they encountered a cloying, putrid odor. Isabelle covered her mouth and nose with a handkerchief. Dillon fought back the urge to retch. Dead ARVN soldiers lay by the roadside. They had been stripped of anything of value. The drivers of two of the trucks were slumped over the steering wheels of their vehicles. Dillon looked away from the bodies, focusing on the rice paddies that stretched out on the other side of the macadam. Above, the helicopters flew in a lazy circle.

Clay wore a look of intense disgust. The convoy had been heavily armed, with armored cars—Ferrets with .37-millimeter cannons—and heavy machine guns mounted on the cab of the four two-and-half ton trucks. The commander had been riding in a jeep right behind the first armored car, and his body remained in the vehicle—he had been decapitated.

"You behead a Vietnamese and their spirit wanders forever," Clay said. "It's a move designed to terrorize the locals. Not that our little allies don't return the favor when they get a chance. Tit for tat. It's the law of the jungle."

He warned Dillon and Isabelle not to leave the road, explaining that the Viet Cong often placed sharpened bamboo foot traps where they thought soldiers might try to escape an ambush.

Isabelle began taking photographs. She kept to the road and worked her way closer to the burned-out vehicles. Dillon noticed that she didn't point her camera at the headless body of the column's commander. He couldn't imagine any magazine in the world that would publish a photograph that grisly.

Clay picked up a few brass shell casings. He said something to the Vietnamese officer and then turned to them. Isabelle had stopped taking photographs.

"The VC had good intelligence," he said. "This was a well-planned, well-executed ambush. Professional. They knew when the convoy was coming, how well-guarded it was going to be, and what it was carrying."

One of the Vietnamese Marines was talking on a walkie-talkie. The helicopters wheeled in the air and made a sharp turn toward the tree line. Two missiles sped toward the ground beyond Dillon's line of sight and exploded with a flash of light. Smoke rose into the air.

"There's a so-called strategic hamlet on the other side of those trees," Clay said. "The pilots spotted some men in black pajamas, and they took some fire."

He walked over and talked with the South Vietnamese officer, who kept shaking his head. When Clay returned, he motioned to Dillon and Isabelle toward the sedan.

"We're turning around," he said. "Back to Saigon. There's nothing we can accomplish here."

* * *

They drove back to Saigon through an afternoon rainstorm. Clay made no attempt at conversation, and Dillon and Isabelle remained silent, occupied in their own thoughts.

Hours later, Dillon and Clay sat in the rooftop terrace bar of the Caravelle, taking in the sweeping view of the city and the Saigon River. Dillon found it strange to be in such a comfortable setting, drinking bourbon, when only hours before they had witnessed the aftermath of a massacre.

"I know what you're thinking," Clay said. He motioned toward the well-dressed people at the tables around them. "How can this exist? How can they be so oblivious? How can we? While out there you can encounter such violence? Such terrible cruelty?"

"It crossed my mind."

"It's the contradiction inherent in war. We think of ourselves as civilized, and yet we slaughter each other like animals. I've come to believe it's just two sides of the same coin. Human nature. 'Red in tooth and claw.' Hobbes had that right."

"The fighting seems right out of the Indian wars," Dillon said. "Instead of scalping, beheadings."

"It will harden you fast," Clay said. "The Communists understand how to use terror. They're convinced that they can do no wrong in the pursuit of their objective. History is inevitably on their side. There's no such thing as good or evil, not as we understand it. They can justify exploding a bomb in a crowded theater or butchering the pregnant wife of a government official as part of the dialectical imperative, as part of the path to the Marxist paradise. Is it worth trying to stop them here? To make the sacrifices necessary? I think so. There are innocent, decent people who will suffer if the Viet Cong win."

"But do the locals have the will to fight?"

"Maybe not enough of them." Clay shook his head and drained his glass. "If you'll excuse me," he said. "I'd love to stay, but I have a prior engagement. She doesn't like being kept waiting."

"Call me when you get back to the States."

"You bet," Clay said.

After his friend had left, Dillon sat alone for a moment, glancing at his watch. It was nearing six o'clock and darkness had begun to descend over the city. Just as he was about to get up, Isabelle Lavalle slipped into the empty seat next to him, a drink in hand. She had changed into a light blue ao dai and silk trousers.

"It was an ugly scene today," she said. "The ambush. It is always that way with civil wars. Brother against brother. Cain and Abel. I've seen it before, sad to say."

"I haven't."

"I remember the first time I saw an atrocity like this. In Algeria. The editors could not use my photographs, they were so gruesome." She stopped talking for a moment and took a sip from her glass. "I was anxious today," she said. "When Major Blackburn told us not to step off the road. I remembered that was how Bob Capa was killed years ago when we French were fighting the Viet Minh. Perhaps the best photographer of our time, and it didn't matter when he stepped on a land mine. So random. After all the wars he had covered, to die in such a stupid way."

She stopped abruptly, and they sat in silence for a while. Then she stirred. "President de Gaulle has called for Vietnam to become neutral," she said. "One country, neither capitalist or Communist. It would at least cut the knot for you."

"Does De Gaulle propose this for the good of Vietnam, or because he wishes to see us humiliated?"

"A mixture of both, I suppose," she said. "But it would be foolish to dismiss the idea out of hand. It preserves American face. You could leave with a clear conscience."

"And Uncle Ho will be sitting in the Independence Palace within six months."

"I know that your intentions are good, and I have no illusions about what will happen if the Communists win. There's a reason that a million Northerners came south after the Viet Minh won at Dien Bien Phu." She paused and studied Dillon. "You've backed the wrong people, the Vietnamese who have been to the West. They know how to speak to you, but not to the people. You have made many other mistakes. You've armed the NLF with your own weapons—captured, stolen, bought on the black market."

"We've made mistakes," Dillon conceded. "But, like you said, our intentions are good. I'd hope that the people here can see that."

"What do they see? They see that your Negro and white soldiers don't socialize with each other. The French were not prejudiced like that. And they see that you will sleep with their women, and then abandon them. And what do they make of the barges on the river with generators so that you Americans can have air conditioners and refrigerators in their villas? You have created a vast black market. Your cigarettes, beer, whiskey, and your dollars. It has corrupted your countrymen as much as the Vietnamese. Everyone pilfers from the hundreds of tons of supplies that arrive on those ships in the Saigon River. It's amazing how much is diverted from your PXs. Just go to Cholon, and you can find anything American that you might want."

The sky to the west was suddenly illuminated by phosphorus flares, and then there was the rumbling sound of explosions and flashes of light. The sound continued for several minutes.

"A light show," she said, looking at the sky. "*Son et lumière*. Beautiful in its way. Except that bombs are dropping and people dying. Innocent people along with the insurgents."

"It's a war."

She sighed. "With whatever influence you have, Mr. Randolph, I hope you warn against escalation when you return to Washington. I covered the war in Algeria. We sent hundreds of thousands of troops there, the cream of France's military, and we failed to defeat the insurgents. The population of Algeria is ten millions, much smaller than that of Vietnam. I do not think that even with thousands of brave men like your friend, Major Blackburn, that you can win under these conditions."

"I agree with you on that."

She put her glass down on the table. "This was my mother's country. My father was a diplomat. When my mother died, he brought me back with him to France." She shook her head. "My Vietnamese is rusty. The moment I speak, the people know I'm an outsider. There's nothing here for me. Today convinced me that I should not stay. I've decided to fly back to Paris tomorrow. I had planned to leave before the end of the month, but I've moved up my departure. I'm done with taking photos of death."

"What will you take photos of? Those beautiful images you talked about?"

"A mix. Simple people on the street. Perhaps I'll go backstage at the Opera and photograph the singers in their dressing rooms, when they're not performing under the lights. Or lovers along the Seine. Perhaps people in the cafes. An older woman walking her dog. There are a million subjects that don't involve pain and death. Images of beauty and light. I can find them there, but not here."

NINETEEN

Washington, D.C.
February 1964

It was chilly and wet in Washington. Dillon returned in a bad mood, which didn't get any better in the days that followed as he battled jet lag and a lingering cold. Jill was distant and aloof; clearly resentful over his extended absence.

He spent two days drafting his report to Roger Hilsman. He tried not to be overly influenced by the ghastliness of what he had seen on the road to Dong Xoai. He stuck to the facts. The statistics on the Strategic Hamlet Program spoke for themselves. Even if they were accurate (which Dillon doubted), they showed a stark, downward trend. It was clear that the program was failing, and that the Vietnamese government officials involved had given up on the idea, and were only making a show of complying with American wishes.

Dillon was careful in the way he couched his conclusions. He recognized that he had been in-country for the briefest of times, and he made sure to quote those AID officials, like Luke Bridgewater, who had spent years in Vietnam. He was frustrated by the gap between the concept of establishing strategic hamlets, which he considered to be sound, and the reality of its faltering execution. His report wouldn't come as any surprise to Hilsman and the upper echelons at State. The National Liberation Front publicly claimed control over two-thirds of South Vietnam, and more than half of the country's population. Even if the insurgents were exaggerating their success in the countryside for propaganda purposes, it was clear that they had gained considerable ground since Diem's ouster.

Dillon found a tense office atmosphere upon his return. There were rumors that Hilsman had fallen out of favor, that he might be fired.

"It'll be any day now," Mary Warren told him. "Roger has alienated the powers-that-be. McNamara and the Joint Chiefs hate him for challenging the Pentagon's estimates. He has ruffled Rusk's feathers in the past by going around him to lobby for his programs with President Kennedy. And he's blamed for cheerleading for the coup against Diem and the black eye it has meant for the U.S. He might survive all of that if Johnson liked him, but he doesn't."

"Did Johnson have much contact with him? I didn't think the Vice President was part of Jack's inner circle."

"When Johnson was brought into the high-level discussions, he and Hilsman were never on the same page. LBJ likes to play the tough guy. Support the Joint Chiefs. He didn't like the Diem coup, and he's part of the group that blames Hilsman and Forrestal. And Harriman, but the Old Crocodile is nigh untouchable."

Hilsman's departure from the government came in short order. On a gray February Monday, it was announced that an interdepartmental committee had been formed to "coordinate policies in Vietnam." The committee would be chaired by William Sullivan, a State Department official with some experience in Southeast Asia. The move sent a clear message that Hilsman was being sidelined.

Two days later, Dillon was not surprised by the front-page headline in the *New York Times* that Hilsman had resigned from his State Department position. He was quoted as saying that he wanted to return to academic life. It was telling that the announcement emanated from the White House and not Main State—the new President wanted to make it clear that he was cleaning house. The story noted that Hilsman had been offered the ambassadorship to the Philippines, and had refused the appointment. Hilsman claimed he had no policy quarrels with the current Administration, but that wasn't true, of course. The *Times* added that "informed sources" said Hilsman had resigned under pressure because Administration officials were critical of his performance as a policy coordinator.

Mary Warren argued that Hilsman's mistake was to continue to argue for a strategy of counterinsurgency, even when it was becoming clear that

Johnson, backed by the military, didn't have the patience for winning hearts and minds. Taking the fight to the North was being promoted as the key to victory, and that meant a war conducted from the air.

"Give him credit," Dillon said. "Roger stood up for what he believes."

"At least he'll end up in an Ivy League political science department," she said. "Back in the day, it would be straight to the chopping block. Thomas More. 'I die the king's faithful servant, but God's first.' I would imagine that tenure is a distinctly better fate."

Hilsman's replacement was William Bundy, the older brother of McGeorge Bundy, the National Security Advisor to the President. Educated at Groton and Yale and Harvard Law School, Bundy had served in the Army Signal Corps in the Second World War, and then in the fledgling Central Intelligence Agency. He had been deputy to Paul Nitze, the assistant secretary for International Security Affairs at the Defense Department. When Nitze became the Secretary of the Navy, Bundy had joined his staff. He was married to Dean Acheson's daughter, Mary. It was hard to conjure up a better-connected appointee, one already trusted in the White House.

"Looks like they've replaced one spook with spectacles with another," Mary said. "Is there some sort of machine that cranks these guys out? Hilsman in the OSS. Bill Bundy in CIA."

"It's called the Establishment," Dillon told her.

He remembered what Grayson Talbott had said, that when Hilsman fell out of favor, those around him would as well. Would Dillon be regarded as a Hilsman loyalist? He had joined the State Department well before Hilsman's arrival, so it was possible he wouldn't be seen as beyond reclamation. Not that it mattered that much to him any longer.

"Are you going to leave us?" Mary asked. "No one would blame you. I certainly wouldn't."

"I'm not sure what I want to do," he replied. "I'm willing to stay on in Far Eastern Affairs for a short while, during the transition to Bundy, but I eventually want out."

"Back to European Affairs?"

"I'm thinking of asking for a leave of absence. I need to think some things through. Roger isn't the only one attracted to the academic life."

"Lucky you," she said. "I'm here for the duration. At least, I'll have a front-row seat for what comes next. I don't think it will be pretty."

* * *

Two weeks after Bill Bundy's arrival at Far Eastern Affairs, he summoned Dillon to his office. Bundy was a tall, handsome man with dark-rimmed glasses and a surface charm.

"I read your last report on the strategic hamlets," he began. "You didn't pull any punches."

Dillon nodded. "I just reported on what I found in the field."

"You did, indeed. I appreciate the candor. Quite rare in Washington. It made me realize that we need a comprehensive look at the program—a full and detailed report. The highs and the lows. What we can learn from its failures. Here, and in Vietnam. Lord knows there's enough data collected to let you draw some conclusions."

"To what end?"

"To educate. To inform. My predecessor believed strongly that this was the route to defeating the Communists. He was wrong. I think that's clear, now. But why? Why did it work in Malaya and the Philippines and not in Vietnam? Was it Diem and his brother? Something different about the peasants there? Our tactics?"

"When do you want this report?"

"I want it to be comprehensive. Interview the key people. Read all the reports. Draw on your colleagues when necessary. I imagine this will take you several months, perhaps even six months. It's worth taking the time. You can make a significant contribution. Remember Santayana. 'Those who cannot remember the past are condemned to repeat it.' We need to learn from our mistakes."

"And I'm free to draw my own conclusions?"

"An honest appraisal. That's what I'm looking for."

"Under those conditions, I'm more than willing," Dillon said. "Give me a week to clear my desk, and then I'll start in on it."

"Excellent," Bundy said. "I look forward to reading it. It will be quite helpful as we set policy in the future. You can make a significant contribution, and it will be appreciated."

Later, when he described the conversation to Mary, she smiled and looked up from her pile of paperwork. She sighed.

"Smart man," she said. "He picked the one project that would keep you here. He doesn't want to fire you, and he doesn't want you resigning. You're well regarded in the Department. It's better this way."

"Better for whom?"

"Better for all concerned." She peered at him over her reading glasses. "What are you going to do?"

"I'm going to write the damn report, and I'm going to set the record straight. We should have stayed the course with the strategic hamlets. It was the flawed execution that torpedoed the program. I'll give it to them unvarnished. Then I'm going to take a leave of absence and figure out what's next."

TWENTY

Washington, D.C.
April 1964

There were storm clouds overhead, and a very light rain had begun to fall when Dillon left Main State on his way to a late lunch with Huy Dinh Dao. By the time the cab deposited him in front of Bonat's, rain was cascading down. He had neglected to bring his umbrella, and in his dash to the restaurant's door, he had been caught in the downpour. The maître d' brought him a few napkins to dry off his hair and shoulders, and then escorted him to a corner table where Dao awaited.

When Dao had invited him to lunch, Dillon had debated whether to accept. He didn't want a repeat of their lunch after the coup, when he had been put on the defensive. He figured that enough time had elapsed since Diem's ouster that Dao would be less confrontational, and Dillon might learn something useful about the situation in Saigon.

Dao wore a white linen suit and a pair of horn-rimmed glasses. There were dark circles under his eyes. He had nearly finished a glass of white wine.

"I'm flattered that you were willing to join me," he said after Dillon had taken a seat. "After our last conversation, and after what has transpired, I thought you might decline my invitation. I would not have blamed you."

"I'm here," Dillon said.

Dao nodded. "Thank you for coming." He took a final sip from his wine glass and beckoned to the waiter to refill it. "You worked for Mr. Hilsman, did you not? Was it not his office that campaigned against

President Diem? That encouraged the generals? Mr. Hilsman and Mr. Forrestal and Mr. Harriman. I know that Mr. Harriman always detested President Diem."

"The coup originated in Saigon, not Washington," Dillon said. He wasn't going to say anything that might suggest that he agreed with Dao, that any American officials had been involved in planning or encouraging Diem's removal. If Dao wanted to argue, he would be disappointed, because Dillon was prepared to cut the lunch short.

"Is that so?" Dao asked, with a trace of a smile.

Dillon didn't respond. The waiter arrived, and they ordered from the menu and sat in an uncomfortable silence until he returned with their lunch. Dillon had chosen the Nicoise salad, and Dao selected the sole.

"And now Mr. Hilsman is gone," Dao said. "To Columbia University, to teach."

"Roger always said he was on temporary leave from the academic life."

"You have stayed on after a change in command, just as I have." Dao took a bite of his sole, and then put his fork down. He drank more wine. "You Americans are no longer innocents abroad, as Mr. Twain called you. You have become the new imperial power. But there is something amiss, and we both know it. President Diem's death marks the beginning of dark days for my country."

"I understand that you are disappointed by what has happened. Perhaps even discouraged. But there's a deeper commitment on our part in many ways, now. There is no reason to give up."

"I have no intention of giving up," Dao said. "*Jamais*. That doesn't mean that I will close my eyes to the danger. I'm told there was a war game held in Washington recently. I believe it was called SIGMA I-64, and the players took sides in our conflict. Bundy. Wheeler. McCone. LeMay. A red team and a blue team. To see what escalation of the war might accomplish. Would it lead to victory?" Dao fiddled with the silverware, straightening it on the table. "Do you know the outcome, Mr. Randolph? I'm sure that you do. This exercise concluded that bombing the North would not end the war, that the Viet Cong would fight on, and that Hanoi would send arms and men to help them."

"What you're describing, the results of a war game scenario, would be classified information," Dillon said. "You know that I can't discuss it."

In fact, Dillon had heard about the SIGMA simulation. After it concluded, Robert McNamara had rejected the negative results, deeming them too subjective. McNamara preferred the statistical model developed by one of his favorites, Alain Enthoven of the Office of Systems Analysis, that showed that the North Vietnamese, and the Viet Cong, would be defeated by American firepower, on the ground and from the air.

"You cannot comment," Dao said. "Fair enough. It must concern you as it does me. I fear for the future of my country. The view of the struggle is quite different from your Pentagon, where all is reduced to rows of numbers in a ledger. Guerrillas killed. Weapons seized. Villages pacified. You wage your war with accountants. In the field, it is quite different. I know what my family tells me, and it is not promising."

"Do you know the film *Rashomon*?" Dillon asked. "It tells the story of a crime from multiple viewpoints, none with the same interpretation. That's how I view information about the war. There are many different truths."

"Or is it the same story, with different actors this time? General Maxwell Taylor has been given authority both military and civil to conduct the war. Did you know that the French did the same in 1954, appointing General Ely to a similar post? It did not work."

Dao stood up suddenly, swaying slightly. He had hardly touched his food, and it was clear that he had drunk too much on a relatively empty stomach.

"Did you know my daughter is attending college here?" he asked. He didn't wait for Dillon's response. "Linh is at Wellesley College in Massachusetts. A very good student. She has made all of us proud." Dao retrieved a snapshot from his jacket pocket and showed it to Dillon. His daughter was pretty, with long black hair and the delicate features of many Vietnamese women.

"Congratulations," Dillon said. "You have reason to be proud."

"Linh hopes to become a diplomat some day," Dao said. "Perhaps as an ambassador representing a free and independent Vietnam. You can see why I believe so strongly in our cause, in resisting the Communists. For now, she will stay here, in the United States. After the coup, my status remains uncertain. I will not risk bringing her back to Saigon. Even if I am duty-bound to return myself."

Standing by the table, he motioned to the waiter for the check. He bowed to Dillon and wobbled his way to the front door of the restaurant.

* * *

At home, it had been a difficult winter and early spring with Sandy. She seemed perpetually sick, either with a cold and cough, or an upset stomach. She was a frail child, but very pretty, with Jill's blonde hair and long arms and legs. She clung to her mother or Thea, and didn't take to strangers. At times, she wouldn't stop crying unless Jill held her.

Jill's mood increasingly depended on how Sandy was feeling. When her daughter was sick, she was short-tempered and quarrelsome, and Dillon felt like he couldn't do right in her eyes. He recognized his marriage was in trouble, but he didn't know what to do to repair it. All that he and Jill had in common now was their daughter. Jill had little interest in his world. Jill had stopped complaining about his long hours at the office. On the few occasions when they went out to dinner, Dillon found it hard to keep the conversation flowing.

They rarely slept together. She maintained a deliberate distance from him both emotionally and physically. It frustrated Dillon, and he knew it made him more likely to argue over trivial matters.

Jill blamed the weather in Washington in large part for Sandy's sickliness, and it seemed to Dillon that she was blaming him for where they lived.

"Children are never sick like this in California," she said. "It's the cold and wet, and then the temperature goes up suddenly and it's terribly humid. I can see why Sandy doesn't respond well to it."

"Does Dr. Matthews think it's our weather causing Sandy's problems?" Dillon asked.

"I don't need a doctor to tell me that my daughter is suffering from the climate." She glared at Dillon. "She needs to be in the sunshine. It's overcast here for months at a time."

"That's an exaggeration."

"Don't you want to see Sandy get better? Aren't you as frustrated as I am with her health?"

"Of course I want her better. Didn't Dr. Matthews say it was something that she would grow out of? Her immune system will get stronger as she gets older."

"You always have an answer, don't you? I'm her mother. I think I know what's best for my child."

"She's my child, too," he said, softly.

"I wish you would act more like it, then."

Dillon shook his head. "That's not fair, Jill. I'm disappointed that you would say that."

"And I'm disappointed that you don't listen."

* * *

The last weekend of the month found Dillon in Charlottesville for the baptism of Charlie and Molly Woods' baby girl Caroline. Dillon had agreed to be Caroline's godfather. He couldn't persuade Jill to join him, and, in the end, Dillon drove out to Far Ridge by himself on Saturday night.

Charlie and his family had begun attending Christ Church, no doubt influenced by Leigh. It made sense to Dillon—Charlie was in line for a partnership at McFarlin & Randolph, and the Episcopal church carried much greater social cachet than First Presbyterian did. Charlie and

Molly had other good reasons for their move—there were lots of children in the Christ Church Sunday school.

On Sunday morning, Charlie and Molly greeted him warmly at the church, and he quickly explained that Jill had stayed in Washington to look after Sandy. They didn't seem surprised. Molly had never warmed up to Jill. She was an outsider, not from Charlottesville, not part of the circle of young married couples there.

The baptism went smoothly. Dillon and Molly's sister, the godparents, gathered around the baptismal font with Charlie, Molly, their five-year-old son, Hillyer, and the baby for the brief ceremony. Caroline dozed through the ritual, stirring only when the minister took her in his arms. After the conclusion of the service, they gathered in the undercroft for refreshments. Dillon twice caught a glimpse of a pretty woman with reddish-brown hair in bangs, a thick fringe cut that framed her brown eyes, staring at him; he was flattered by her apparent interest. He was surprised when she came up to him and introduced herself.

"Naomi Friedman," she said. "And no, I'm not part of the congregation. Or parish. Or whatever you call it. Far from it. I'm here because I'm one of Molly's friends. The truth is that my father would shudder at the thought of his Jewish daughter spending any time in a church."

"Don't worry. No one will try and convert you. No speaking in tongues. No snake-handling. The Episcopal Church is said to be the ruling class at prayer."

"So you admit that you're part of the ruling class," she said, grinning, and bobbing her head.

"I believe that I was quoting others."

She kept her eyes fixed on his. "Did you know that Molly says that you're the one that got away?"

Dillon shook his head. "Molly and I never dated. So I'm flattered in one sense, but..."

"I think she means that a local girl, a girl from Charlottesville, should have caught you."

"I'm married, now. I'm sure Molly told you that. My bachelor days were many moons ago."

"Many moons ago you had quite the reputation," she says. "Quite the ladies' man."

Dillon laughed. "All hearsay."

"Are you staying for the weekend?"

"An early dinner with Charlie and his family. Tomorrow, I'll head back to Washington in the morning. We still have a house here."

"You mean *you* still have a house. A mansion, Molly says. Far Ridge Farm." She smiled. "After you finish dinner at Charlie's, why don't you drop by my place? The night will still be young. We could continue this conversation over a glass of wine. You're a poet. Maybe we can listen to my new Dylan Thomas recording. A discovery the other day in a discount bin at the record store."

"Dylan Thomas, not Bob Dylan?"

"The one and only."

"So you met Molly college?"

"I did. And now I'm a graduate student. I've spent the spring struggling with writing my thesis. It's about how tight-knit communities operate." She smiled. "I'm a sociologist."

"A social one, it seems."

Naomi laughed. She rummaged through her pocketbook and found a ballpoint pen and a slip of paper and wrote down her address. She let her fingers linger on his when she handed the paper to him.

He thought about her during the dinner with Charlie and Molly. He tried to make small talk, but he knew he must have appeared distracted. Dillon made his farewells and got into his car. He considered Naomi's invitation and what it might promise. He was intrigued by her, but the smart thing would be to drive straight home and avoid temptation. He looked at the address on the piece of paper she had given him. He would pass by it on his way to Far Ridge. Why not stop by?

When he rang the doorbell to her apartment, Naomi opened the door with a smile. She had changed into a peasant blouse and blue jeans. She took him by the hand and drew him into the apartment. There was a framed poster from the movie *Giant* on the wall, with James Dean, Elizabeth Taylor, and Rock Hudson looking properly dramatic. The door to her bedroom was open, and there was a light on by the nightstand.

"I was hoping you would come by," she said. "I'm quite curious about Dillon Randolph. To hear Molly tell it, you're quite something. A diplomat. A poet."

"Among other things."

"What other things?"

"As I told you at the church, I'm married."

"Of course you are. Very respectable. But here you are at my front door. Alone. Is that something a respectable married man does?"

Dillon didn't respond. She moved next to him, their bodies almost touching. She tilted her head so she could look into his eyes. "Maybe you're not interested in being respectable," she said. "At least for tonight. We're alone, here. We can do whatever we like, and no one's the wiser. As far as I'm concerned, that's what matters. I think maybe you feel the same way."

"You don't waste any time," he said, his voice suddenly husky with desire.

"I don't."

"This can't go anywhere," he said. "After tonight."

"I'm on the pill. A modern girl. So don't worry. There won't be any surprises. You're married. That's your problem, not mine. Just don't keep reminding me about it. It's not the sexiest thing, you know."

"Are you an expert on the question? About the sexiest things?"

"Try me," she said, and reached over to his belt and unbuckled it. "Now, this is sexy. What we'll do in my bed is sexy."

It didn't take long for them to end up between the sheets in her narrow bed. Naomi was an aggressive lover, telling Dillon what she wanted him to do, and how. Of all the women he had slept with, she was the most uninhibited.

Later, as they lay on the bed together, she whispered softly in his ear, "That was so nice."

Dillon found himself smiling—Naomi was a free spirit, with no care for convention. He knew that he had been drawn to her for that very reason, the contrast with Jill's reserve. Naomi was dark and full-figured, and she clearly enjoyed sex, in a way Jill never had.

"I'm glad I finally got to meet you," she said. "I was really curious. I'm glad I scratched that itch."

"So am I."

Naomi sighed. "I'm leaving for California next week. Back to Berkeley to finish my master's. So I guess this will be one of those one-time things."

"I don't do this sort of thing," he said. "Not since I've been married. This is the first time."

"I should be flattered, then," she said. "You broke the rules for me."

"I did. I can't say that I regret it. You've made me feel alive again."

Dillon had kept secrets before, and he could keep this one. While he didn't regret sleeping with Naomi, he knew that it carried with it a measure of risk. He had crossed a line. If he wanted to keep his marriage intact, there could be no revelations, no confessions, although a part of him wondered whether Jill would actually care.

TWENTY-ONE

During a long weekend at Far Ridge in mid-July, Leigh had announced that the Democratic National Convention, to be held in Atlantic City in August, would be the last that he would attend as a delegate. He invited Dillon to join him.

"It should be fascinating," Leigh said. "Almost as interesting as '48. We'll learn where Johnson wants to take the country, and how he's going to handle the Kennedys and their supporters."

Dillon had attended the 1948 Democratic Convention in Philadelphia, along with his father and uncle. There had been plenty of drama: after Harry Truman had been nominated as the party's presidential candidate, Senator Strom Thurmond of South Carolina led members of the Mississippi and Alabama delegations in a walkout to protest Truman's support of civil rights. Dillon had been proud of John Custis and Leigh for voting for Truman, and for rejecting the idea that all Southerners reflexively opposed integration.

"I'd like to come," Dillon told Leigh. "Although, it's probably going to be more of a coronation than a convention. We know who the presidential nominee is. When Johnson announced he wouldn't consider any Cabinet members for vice president, he ruled out Bobby as his Number Two."

They were sitting on the porch; Dillon with ice tea in hand and Leigh with a bourbon and water in his. Jill and Sandy had stayed in Washington. It was becoming harder and harder to convince his wife to make the drive out to Charlottesville, a clear reflection of the frayed state of their marriage. Leigh must have wondered about Dillon's situation at home, but he hadn't said anything.

"You never know with a convention," Leigh said. "There's the platform on civil rights and Vietnam. And it's not like the country is in a good place. Johnson needs to address that."

For Dillon and his colleagues at State, it had been a summer marked by a mounting uneasiness about the war in Vietnam. Just weeks earlier, the Defense Department had admitted that American casualties were now hovering around 1,400, with almost 400 dead. That troubling admission was followed quickly by the announcement of the dispatch of another 5,000 military advisers.

Dillon wondered why the Democrats in Congress hadn't questioned the drift toward escalation. The President didn't have to worry about criticism from the Republicans. Dillon had watched on television the Republican National Convention in San Francisco, where their right-wing faction nominated Senator Barry Goldwater. The delegates in the Cow Palace booed Nelson Rockefeller, the moderate governor of New York, and Goldwater gave a harsh and bellicose acceptance speech where he defended extremism in the "defense of liberty." If anything, Goldwater was advocating a wider war in Vietnam.

"I worry that the military will persuade Johnson to ramp up the bombing of the North," Dillon said. "They're like a child with a hammer—everything needs pounding."

Leigh frowned. "I'm not as worried. At least, not yet. Johnson has promised he's not going to send American boys to fight and die in the place of the Vietnamese. There's no stomach for another Korea. Johnson knows that. Your father told me that in 1954 Eisenhower had refused to send troops or planes to help the French at Dien Bien Phu. All of his advisers said it was the thing to do. Nixon was gung ho for it. But Ike told them that Vietnam would be a morass, and he wouldn't do it. No land war in Asia. Johnson has to know that history, and he's as shrewd an operator as they come."

"We'll see," Dillon said. "I hope you're right. But I think he's surrounded by hawks, and they're influencing him."

"Well, he has a choice between guns and butter. I would bet that he's going to pick butter."

* * *

Dillon and Leigh had arrived in Atlantic City in the late afternoon, along with most of the Virginia delegation, the day before the opening of the Democratic National Convention. After a nondescript buffet dinner at their hotel, Dillon and Leigh watched the surf from a porch on the boardwalk and talked. The sky matched the dark blue of the ocean. A few people were lying on the beach, and some were swimming, but the day-trippers who flocked to the resort on the weekends were absent.

The situation in Vietnam had worsened. Earlier in the month, there had been the Gulf of Tonkin incident, where three North Vietnamese gunboats had attacked the destroyers *USS Maddox* and *USS Turner Joy* and were driven off by jets from the carrier *USS Ticonderoga*. One gunboat had been sunk. President Johnson didn't waste any time in going to Congress and asking for broad war powers. With the presidential election only months away, the Gulf of Tonkin Resolution sailed through.

The political games in Saigon continued. General Khanh, a swaggering figure with his aviator glasses and red beret, had declared a state of emergency and proposed a new constitution giving him more power. He had to back down after objections from his fellow generals. Khanh didn't seem capable of governing the country. In comparison, Ngo Dinh Diem's government had been a model of stability.

It wasn't only Vietnam. There had been signs that summer of fractures in the Great Society. When a New York City police officer shot and killed a fifteen-year-old black student, there had been unrest in Harlem, six days of what the newspapers called "race riots." It appeared that America's inner cities, its ghettos, were simmering with rage over the justice delayed and denied that Martin Luther King, Jr. had talked about during the March on Washington.

"Give Johnson some credit," Leigh said. "He's doing more for the poor and the Negroes than any president since Roosevelt. Johnson grew up dirt poor. He knows what it's like to not have two nickels to rub together. Not like Jack Kennedy."

Dillon was surprised. "I didn't know that you had warmed up to Johnson."

"He's a mean bastard, but he gets things done. Laws passed. He wants to finish what FDR started with the New Deal. And it needs to be a Southerner pushing to fix the race problem. He's got the best chance of convincing the good old boys that things have to change."

* * *

On the last night of the convention, Dillon and Leigh sat side-by-side in the seats reserved for the Virginia delegation, waiting for Bobby Kennedy to introduce a short documentary about his brother, the late President. There wasn't an empty seat in Convention Hall, a cavernous facility best known for hosting the Miss America Pageant and now showing its age. There were three large photos of Franklin Roosevelt, Jack Kennedy, and Harry Truman posted above the stage with a banner below them proclaiming "LET US CONTINUE..." and two huge photos of Lyndon Johnson flanking the podium.

The convention had run smoothly for the most part. The delegates had confirmed the presidential and vice presidential nominations—for Johnson and Senator Hubert Humphrey of Minnesota. Dillon found the only drama in the proceedings to be quite familiar, as the party struggled with the difficult issue of civil rights. The all-white Mississippi delegation had been elected in primaries that excluded African-Americans. A compromise, seating two members of the integrated Mississippi Freedom Democratic Party, had angered both sides of the dispute. Many members of the Mississippi and Alabama delegations refused to support the party ticket and left the convention.

"Good riddance," Dillon had remarked to Leigh. "You'd think that they would have learned something from '48. The party is better off without them."

"I agree in principle," Leigh said. "In practice, it's going to hurt us in the Deep South, but they'll come around. Sooner or later."

Dillon glanced around the convention floor—it was standing room only everywhere he looked. Replacement delegates had filled the seats left vacant by the Mississippi and Alabama walk-outs.

The delegates began cheering and whistling for Bobby Kennedy the moment he appeared on the stage, waving placards and hats and pennants. Everyone around them rose to their feet. Kennedy stood at the elevated rostrum with a half-smile, nodding his head slightly, trying several times to begin his speech (never getting past the words "Mr. Chairman") as the standing ovation continued. Just when it seemed that it would end, another wave of applause would sweep through the hall.

Dillon checked his wristwatch—the sustained applause had lasted a good twenty minutes or more. After the crowd quieted down, Kennedy began his remarks, talking about his brother Jack's legacy, and how his goal was to leave the world a better place for the young people of the U.S. and of the world. He said that when he thought of his brother, he was reminded of what Shakespeare said in *Romeo and Juliet*: "*When he shall die, take him and cut him out into little stars, and he shall make the face of heaven so fine that all the world will be in love with night and pay no worship to the garish sun.*"

Dillon felt tears forming. Kennedy's speech brought back so many memories. Bobby finished gracefully, closing with Robert Frost's words, "*the woods are lovely, dark and deep, but I have promises to keep, and miles to go before I sleep, and miles to go before I sleep,*" and then telling the delegates that Mrs. Kennedy had wanted the film they were about to see dedicated to them, and all who had helped elect Jack Kennedy president.

The lights went down and the documentary, "A Thousand Days," began, projected onto a massive screen at the back of the stage. Dillon found it hard to watch, the images of the Kennedy years flickering in front of them—the confident young man in the Oval Office, the sound of his voice and its nasal Boston twang, the soaring rhetoric of his speeches, the dark and somber scenes of his funeral. The film concluded with a montage of footage of Jack and his family, Jackie and the children, in the White House and in Hyannisport with Richard Burton singing "Camelot," a song from the Broadway musical that had been one of the President's favorites.

When the film ended, there was a brief moment of silence and then thunderous applause. Dillon had never seen so many men and women cry in public, tears streaming down their cheeks. He realized that he had joined them, eyes brimming over with his own tears. Dillon hadn't expected to be so moved.

"If they had played that film at the start of the convention, we would have nominated Bobby for president," Leigh said. "And Teddy for vice president."

"Johnson's smart," Dillon said. "He made sure that Bobby didn't appear until after the delegates had voted on the nominations. He wasn't taking any chances with the Kennedy charisma."

"LBJ can't be happy about it. Bobby's speech and that film are all anyone is going to be talking about tomorrow."

As Dillon and Leigh left the convention hall to return to their hotel, they ran into Grayson Talbott, who was attending the convention as a member of the New York delegation. Dillon introduced him to Leigh. Grayson wore a seersucker suit with his PT-109 pin on the label. His hair was wet from perspiration.

"I was bawling like a baby during the film," he said. "God, it brought back the memories. Bittersweet."

"It makes you realize how much we've lost," Dillon said.

"We wanted Bobby as vice president, damn it," Grayson said. "It's frustrating as hell that Johnson has been so petty. He took Humphrey as a bone to throw to the liberals because he wouldn't risk being upstaged by Bobby. Pure ego."

"Bobby's time will come," Leigh said. "He'll still be a young man when Johnson's done. He should start by winning that Senate seat in New York."

"He will," Grayson said. "We're all behind him. No question that he can beat Keating."

"First things first, then," Leigh said.

"As it so happens, I'm off to New York tonight," Grayson said. "I wanted to see Bobby give his speech. I've volunteered for his campaign. I'm done with Washington. Once we've got Bobby elected to the Senate, I'll be back to pitching ad campaigns over three-martini lunches."

"If you wanted to stay in D.C., I'm sure there were other places in the Administration where you could land," Dillon said.

Grayson nodded. "I thought about that, about perhaps moving over to Justice. I'm not a lawyer, but there was a slot in their press office. But I'd rather work on Bobby's campaign. We're going to move heaven and earth to put him in the Senate. It's what helped position Jack for the presidency, and with any luck, it'll do the same for him."

TWENTY-TWO

When he returned home from Atlantic City, Dillon found an unwelcome domestic surprise awaiting him. While he was away, Jill had visited a nearby beauty salon and had her hair cropped short, almost as short as the pixie cut of the actress Jean Seberg in *Saint Joan*. She knew how much Dillon liked her long hair, and he couldn't mistake the message she was sending, the assertion of her independence and her discontent with their marriage.

When Jill greeted him at their front door, she wore a black turtleneck and black pants. Dillon didn't say anything about her altered looks. If she had wanted to provoke a reaction, he hoped to disappoint her.

"We need to talk," she told him.

"I'm all ears," he said.

"I did a lot of thinking when you were away with Leigh. I want to take Sandy with me to California. I want to live there for a time."

"Is this about our not going there on vacation?"

"No, it's deeper than that. I need a change."

"Are you saying you want to leave me?"

"No, that's not it. I want to make changes in my life. How I dress. My hair. How do you like my new haircut?"

"It's lovely," Dillon said.

"You're lying. You hate it."

"What if I did? You've already cut it off."

"The shorter hair makes me feel lighter. It's part of becoming a happier person. I need some time, and some room to do that. By myself. I miss art. I want to try my hand at painting. Feel the sun on my back. Right now, I don't want to live here with you."

"You've made that clear in a number of ways."

"It always comes back to sex with you, doesn't it?"

"I would have left long ago if that was the case," he said.

"Aren't you tired of fighting? I know that I am." She shook her head. "Let me go to California. It'll give us both some time to think. I have friends there. My mother is there."

"Are you sure about this?"

"I feel like I'm drowning here. I've come to hate this place and what it's doing to you and to me."

"I would like you to stay." Even as he said it, Dillon wasn't sure he meant it. Perhaps Jill was right, and time away would help.

"I can't do that. It wouldn't be right for Sandy or for me. Please listen to me, Dillon."

"When did you decide to do this? Is this your idea? Or your mother's?"

"This is my decision. Completely. My mother thinks I'm making a huge mistake. She says I'm jeopardizing my security, and Sandy's. She always worries about money, as if it's all that matters. I won't be like her. I can't go on living like this and I won't."

"You don't have to worry about that, about money. You'll always have what you and Sandy need."

"I know that. You've always been very generous." She hesitated. "We rushed into marriage. Part of me knew it was too fast. I wasn't as certain as you were, but I got swept along. We should have waited. Now, I don't want to make any decisions until I've had a chance to think things through. I don't want to have any regrets over whatever I decide to do."

He nodded. Dillon knew that if he forced her to stay—and he wasn't even sure that he could—it would effectively end their marriage. He was tired of returning home to a resentful wife, of the strained silences and tense quarrels. Perhaps time apart would help. It wasn't that he wouldn't miss her or Sandy, but he believed not fighting her move to California represented their best chance at salvaging the relationship.

* * *

They had missed two poker nights in a row, and then three, and it became apparent that the spirit behind the Group of Five was waning. Grayson spent most of his time in New York working on Robert Kennedy's Senate campaign and rarely could attend. Palmer Knox was a consistent no-show. It was Alex Landauer who first suggested that they meet for one last time before they disbanded the Group of Five.

On a Thursday night with all members present, Alex handed each of them a plaque, entitled "The Group of Five 1961-1964." Underneath the title, each of their names had been embossed on five blue poker chips.

"I wish we had stuck with the New Frontiersmen as a name," Grayson said, examining his plaque. "That's what we were. That's the only reason I would have left a great job in the greatest city in the world to come here. We had a purpose. 'Don't ever let it be forgot, that once there was a spot, for one brief shining moment that was Camelot.' That's how I'm going to remember it."

Dillon didn't share Grayson's overly romantic view of the Kennedy years, but he did remember the heady early days of the Administration, the excitement, the sense of being part of history. It was hard to accept that it had all ended so abruptly.

"Well, nothing lasts forever," Jan said.

"I think it hurts more because of the unfulfilled promises," Dillon said. "What could have been."

"And still can be," Alex said. "We can still make progress, even without the Kennedys."

Grayson snorted and was about to say something in response when Jan interjected. "I'm going to miss taking your money," he told them. "My Chicago buddies are much harder to bluff than you Washington types."

"Hell, I'm a country boy," Palmer said. "I don't remember losing too often to you, Nowak."

"You've been here long enough to have been corrupted by the District of Columbia. That makes you a Washington type in my book."

"Never," Palmer replied. "Not in a million years."

Later, Dillon and Palmer walked back to Dillon's place in Georgetown. They talked on the way, and Palmer confided that he was ready to leave the Agency.

"I'm quitting," he said. "Getting out while the going's good. I need to. I'm at a point where I can't do what they want me to do. I've been out on the edge for too long. I'm not proud of what I've done. To what end? It's hard to come back to the States after time in Vietnam, and you see the people walking around safe and sound in their nice clothes and driving shiny, nice cars. They have no clue. You wonder if you're living in the same world."

Dillon remained silent. He had no advice to give.

"I haven't been sleeping very well," Palmer said. "Too many damn nightmares. And I'm drinking too much. I figure I'll head out to San Francisco. Look up Cora. See if she'll give me a second chance."

"I wish you luck with that."

"Thanks. I know you've got your own situation with Jill to deal with. I hope that works out for the best."

"It's really up to her, now. She has to figure out what she wants, and if I'm part of it."

* * *

With Jill and Sandy in California, Dillon threw himself into work. He made significant progress on his strategic hamlets report, spending long hours in the office, and writing large sections of it on the weekend at Far Ridge. He worked in what he still considered his father's den, setting up his typewriter on the wide mahogany desk, and keeping his research papers in a large cardboard box on the floor for easy reference.

He met Charlie Woods one Sunday afternoon, and they played a quick set of tennis. When they were done, relaxing over a beer, Charlie asked about Jill and Sandy.

"What's going on?"

"Jill's living in California for now. I guess you could call it a trial separation."

Charlie shook his head. "Hate to ask this, Dillon, but did she catch you stepping out on her?"

"No, it wasn't that. The irony is that I'm not sure whether she'd care if she did catch me."

"You don't mean that."

"I'm afraid I do. She's never been jealous. She's not a passionate woman—at least when it comes to me."

"Every marriage goes through its rough patches, Dillon. Hell, it hasn't always been smooth with Molly. She wasn't overjoyed when she found out she was pregnant with Caroline. She already had her hands full with Hillyer." He paused. "Molly says you've been in touch with Naomi."

"That's one way of putting it."

Charlie gave Dillon a long look of appraisal. "Naomi has one saving grace. She's not a kiss-and-tell girl. No broadcasting her latest triumph. Or triumphs. Only her closest friends know anything."

"Discretion is an under-appreciated virtue," Dillon said with a slight smile.

"I'll bet," Charlie said. "Of course, people gossip. Word gets around. A word to the wise." He frowned. "Have to admit that I don't quite get the friendship between Molly and Naomi. They're so different. Night and day. I'm glad Naomi has gone to California. I think she's been a bad influence on Molly. Naomi has a way of making her feel that she's wasting her life as a mother, caring for the kids at home."

"I've gotten some of that with Jill. Having Sandy meant leaving her master's program. She hated it when I traveled. We've had other disagreements, too. Some of it has been political."

"Political? Seriously?"

"She thinks I'm too timid on civil rights. And we disagree over Vietnam. I think that she's been influenced by some of her friends on that."

Charlie nodded. "It's a tough call. Vietnam. You don't have to be Bob Taft to question whether we should be the world's policeman. I'm not sure I've ever believed the falling dominoes argument. If the Reds win in Vietnam, will we really be fighting the Commies in Honolulu a year later?"

"But you agree we have to make a stand somewhere. Draw a line and defend it."

"Draw the line where it matters. Where it is worth it. Where the locals are willing to fight for themselves." Charlie looked over at Dillon. "Have you thought about coming back home? To friends and family."

"Did Leigh suggest you work on me?"

"He wouldn't need to encourage me. Why wouldn't I want my best friend back where he belongs? And whether you're ready to admit it or not, this is your true home, Dillon."

TWENTY-THREE

Washington, D.C.
October 1964

An overcast Friday night. Earlier, the skies had threatened rain, and there had been the sound of distant thunder, but it had remained a gray, cool day. Dillon had walked home from Main State and was finishing his supper—a Swanson TV dinner—and catching up on two days of the *New York Times* when he heard the doorbell ring.

When he opened the front door, he found Naomi Friedman perched on the top step. She was dressed casually, in jeans and a black blouse. She had changed her hairstyle, dropping the bangs, combing her hair back, and she wore tortoise-shell glasses. It made her look older, more serious, but Dillon found her no less appealing.

"I heard you were by yourself," she said. "I thought I'd drop by and say hello."

"Molly told you that I was alone?"

"Of course. Good old Molly. My spy on all things Dillon Randolph. May I come in?"

"Of course," he said, and opened the door wide, ushering her into the foyer. Dillon caught the scent of lemon and sandalwood as she brushed by him. She carried a small light brown suitcase.

"I was on the way to a hotel," she explained.

"How long are you in Washington?"

"The weekend. Two nights."

"I have a guest bedroom," he said. "You can stay here if you like. Save on the hotel bill."

"That's some offer," Naomi said, smiling. "Guess that I'll take you up on it." She moved closer to Dillon. "Molly says you could use a little cheering up, and I think I might be able to do just that."

She hugged him tight to her, and then she raised her face to him, eyes closed, to be kissed. Dillon kissed her hard on the lips, aroused.

"You're glad to see me," she said. "Where's this guest bedroom?"

"Upstairs," he managed. "I can show you."

"I'll bet you can," she said. "I'd like that."

Once upstairs, in the guest room, she looked around at the flowered wallpaper and mahogany furniture. "Nice," she said. She took his hand and led him to the bed, and she kissed him on the lips. She pushed her body onto his, and moved her hand down to his belt buckle. He kissed her. "I can tell that you've missed me," she said. "You must have been lonely. Let's see what we can do about that."

They quickly undressed each other, pausing momentarily to kiss. Dillon pulled the covers away and guided her onto her back. Naomi gasped in pleasure as he pushed into her. They made love urgently and until, arching her back and clinging to Dillon, she cried out twice. Moments later, Dillon climaxed. He rolled over onto his back and lay still for a moment.

"You're so right. I missed you." He touched her thigh. "I missed this."

Naomi retrieved her jeans and sat on the edge of the bed. She rummaged through the pockets and found a rolled joint. She lit it up and took a long drag, offering it to Dillon who shook his head.

"I'm not sure who enjoyed that more," he said.

"Didn't you have a classical education? Remember that Tiresias, the blind prophet who lived as a man and a woman, told Zeus and Hera that women enjoyed sex more. When your lover knows what he's doing, there's nothing better."

"Do I know what I'm doing?"

"Don't be cocky," she said. "On second thought, I like that idea." She looked over at him and took another puff from the reefer. "We're good in bed, aren't we? You know I decided that I was going to have you the first time I saw you at Caroline Woods' baptism. Just like that."

"Just like that."

"Don't worry. It's not a trap, Dillon. I find you attractive enough, but I don't want anything lasting. It's better that way. No complications. I don't need a husband, and I'm not ready for kids."

"You don't worry that you're missing something?"

She laughed. "Half of my married friends are miserable. Maybe someday I'll want children, but that can wait. I'm not ready to give up my independence."

"You're not the only woman who feels that way. It's one of the issues in my marriage. Independence."

"And sex. That's the other issue, if I had to guess. She's frigid, or close to it. You don't have to say anything. It wouldn't be gentlemanly."

Dillon remained silent. He wasn't about to discuss Jill or his marital problems with her.

"Don't blame her," Naomi said. "I'm sure that your wife was taught from an early age that she needed to keep her knees together. That sex was dirty. Sexual repression courtesy of our plastic, bourgeois upbringing. In this uptight country, no one is in touch with their bodies, let alone their emotions. And as women, we're taught to block our sexual urges, you know. I'd bet that your wife has that in spades. Smiling while inside she's furious. Agreeing when she didn't want to. That will drive you crazy."

"You don't know her," he said. "And I don't particularly want to talk about my marriage."

"Sure," she said. "All I'll say is that you should make the changes that you need to make. Get in a better place. That's all. I saw a psychotherapist for a while. I finally figured out that there wasn't anything wrong with me. I wasn't going to let other people decide how I would live my life. I want to experience things to the fullest, and I have. You know, we're not here on earth for that long. If I see something I want, I don't hesitate. If I want to sleep with a man, then I do. It's my choice."

"You're more impulsive than me. Not that there haven't been times when I acted impulsively. Always there was a woman involved. But in the other aspects of my life, I've been rational, or at least I thought I was being rational."

"So you think too much, and I think too little?" Naomi smiled. "Are you living the life you want? Or the life your father wanted for you? I see the man that you could be. He isn't a government bureaucrat. You should get back to writing poems."

"I have one thing left to do here," he said. "A report on our failures in Vietnam. Then, I'm going to take a leave of absence."

"And do what?"

"Figure out whether I should stay in Washington, or go, and start over."

* * *

In his dream, they are dancing the foxtrot in a smoky nightclub in Berlin.

He holds Christa close, her arms around his neck. It's a slow number—Frank Sinatra singing "Night and Day"—and they sway, bodies touching.

She whispers something in his ear, but it's too loud in the club, and he can't hear what she is saying, but he knows it's important. He asks her to repeat herself, but she can't hear him, either.

Then the music stops abruptly, and Christa steps away from him, turning her back to him.

The door to the club opens, and suddenly there is a cold breeze sweeping through the room. A woman enters and stands in the doorway. He can't make out her face, and then she moves into the light, and he realizes that it's Jill, her eyes locked on him. Her face, a silent mask of anger and resentment.

He is confused. What is she doing there? How did Jill get to Berlin? It didn't make any sense. Where is Sandy?

He looks around for Christa, but she has disappeared.

"It was always her," Jill says, contempt in her voice. "It's your fault. You should have never married me."

He tries to speak, but he can't get the words out.

She begins to cry. The tears roll down her cheeks, but she doesn't try to brush them away.

"No," he says. "That's not so."

"Is that so? Then why do you dream about her? And not me?"

"But I do dream about you."

"You think you're so clever, but you're not fooling me."

"I'm not trying to fool anyone."

Then the dance floor is suddenly empty. Dillon is left alone, and he knows he has failed—he has lost them both. He feels a wave of sadness.

* * *

Dillon woke first, confused. It took a few moments before he realized that he was in the guest bedroom of his Georgetown house, with a naked Naomi Friedman sprawled out next to him in bed. The dream had been so real and yet so strange that he was left at a loss. What did it mean? It had been quite some time since Christa had appeared in one of his dreams.

Next to him, Naomi stirred. She rolled over and smiled at him.

"Did I tire you out?" she asked. "Or is there some fight left in the old man?"

"Old man? You're going to pay for that. In the nicest of ways."

They took their time, making love again slowly. He waited until she had cried out in pleasure before he finished. They lay on the bed, side-by-side, her leg over his.

"You were talking a lot in your sleep last night," she said.

"Sorry. A dream."

"Who's Christa?"

"Did I say her name? She's someone from the past. From years ago. When I dream these days, people from my past seem to surface. She's one of them."

"I won't take offense that you weren't calling out my name."

"You shouldn't. It wasn't the happiest of dreams. It didn't end well."

"You don't have much luck with women, do you?"

"I've been lucky with you. And you're very lucky this morning—I'm going to cook breakfast for you."

He put on his bathrobe and went downstairs to the kitchen, where he cooked a meal of cheese and tomato omelets, home-fried potatoes, and dark toast while Naomi watched.

"That smells great," she said.

He served them both, pouring two small glasses of orange juice, and watched her eat with relish. He hid a smile—Naomi was a woman of very strong appetites.

"I'm glad you stopped by," he told her.

"The truth is that I didn't have a hotel reservation," she said. "I figured it wouldn't be a problem."

"You figured right."

"What are you doing this weekend?" she asked. "Anything planned?"

"Tennis this afternoon at the club. Then I'm heading to the office for a few hours to work on that overdue report I told you about."

"That sounds boring. I'm meeting a girlfriend for dinner tonight. And my uncle and his family want to take me to brunch tomorrow. The rest of the weekend I'm free." She smiled. "I don't want to tire you out for your tennis, but I wouldn't mind spending the rest of the morning in bed with you."

"A considerate host is supposed to look after his guest's needs," he said. "And I certainly want to be considerate."

TWENTY-FOUR

After Dillon sent his final report on the Strategic Hamlet Program to Bill Bundy, he made an appointment to meet with him on the last Friday of October. Dillon was proud of the report and primed to answer any questions Bundy might have. He had made what he considered a compelling and convincing argument that the idea of pacification in South Vietnam remained a sound one, based on several examples of successful strategic hamlets becoming safe havens. The program could have worked to neutralize the National Liberation Front in places like the Mekong Delta and the provinces near Saigon if it had been properly executed. Dillon quoted Mao about the people being the sea that the revolutionary swam in, and how any strategy that failed to take this central fact into account—and drained the sea—would fail.

In his conclusions, Dillon argued that governments without broad popular support couldn't win a guerrilla war. He pointed to the successes of the British in Malaya and the U.S. in the Philippines as examples of how a coherent policy could produce the desired results. He directly chronicled the mistakes that the Diem government and its successors had made in managing the program, and he was equally blunt in his assessment of American blunders.

When he arrived at two o'clock that afternoon, the appointed time for the meeting, Bundy's secretary greeted him politely. Dillon could see over her shoulder that Bundy wasn't at his desk.

"I'm sorry, but Mr. Bundy was called away to a meeting at the White House," she said. "He'll get back to you to reschedule a sit-down when he's had a chance to review your report."

Dillon nodded and returned to his office, a copy of the report in his hand, certain that Bundy had deliberately missed their scheduled meeting.

The concept of strategic hamlets had been discredited; the policy was now considered an embarrassment. No doubt Dillon's report would gather dust on a shelf somewhere. He understood the nature of the game—ambitious men were always quick to put distance between themselves and any hint of failure. It didn't matter, he told himself. He had done what Bundy had asked, and the report was the best work he had produced while at Main State.

He was ready to take some time for himself, to think things through. He wasn't prepared to abandon his career at State, but he wanted to consider all his options.

He sent a brief note to Bundy explaining that he would be approaching the Undersecretary to seek a brief unpaid leave of absence. Dillon didn't expect a reply and didn't get one.

He had to wait a week for the meeting with the Undersecretary, who didn't seem surprised at Dillon's request. As Hilsman's fair-haired boy, Dillon had fallen out of favor—for those with an eye on the future, he had become radioactive.

"How long do you anticipate the leave will last?" the Undersecretary asked. He had a reputation for courtesy and caution. His wavy gray hair, aquiline nose, and square chin gave him a distinguished, patrician look. He had been Dean Rusk's colleague and friend in the mid-1950s, and those in the bureaucratic know claimed that even if Rusk were to leave State, he would keep his job.

"I've asked for a month," Dillon said. "There are some family issues I need to attend to."

"I understand," he replied, and Dillon was sure that rumors about the tattered state of his marriage must have reached the sixth floor, if not the seventh. "We've all faced these sort of things. Unavoidable. Part of life. Best that you get that cleared up."

"Thank you, sir," Dillon said.

"I remember your father. A good man. A shame that we lost him. Always a friend of the Department. Not every Congressman felt that way. We make an easy target at appropriations time. Cookie pushers in striped pants."

Dillon nodded. The Undersecretary didn't need much encouragement to ramble on with his musings.

"The country needs us," he said. "I've always thought that if we were fully utilized, there would be a lot fewer wars. Jaw, jaw, as Churchill used to say, is better than war, war." He paused. "Presidents come and go. I recognize the assassination has been jarring for many of our younger men. I would hope that it not dissuade anyone from soldiering on in the Department."

"It was a terrible day," Dillon said. "But my request for a leave is related to personal matters."

The Undersecretary looked down at the pile of paper neatly arranged on his desk and sighed. "It keeps piling up," he said. "I'm like Sisyphus except that instead of rolling the stone up the hill, I'm confronted by an endless stream of paper. Bumf, I believe our British friends call it." He didn't make eye contact, and Dillon realized that the interview was over.

* * *

He drove to Far Ridge on Election Day in time to vote at his regular polling place in Charlottesville. Dillon wasn't worried about the outcome of the presidential race. The polls suggested that Lyndon Johnson and the Democrats would win a substantial victory. Dillon couldn't imagine Barry Goldwater, a man who joked about lobbing a nuclear weapon into the men's room of the Kremlin, as Commander-in-Chief. He had heard the joke that Goldwater's slogan, "In your heart, you know he's right," should have been, "In your guts, you know he's nuts." After the election, he hoped Johnson, now bolstered by winning the Presidency in his own right, could lower the temperature with the Russians and rethink the strategy for Vietnam.

The first week of his leave wasn't what he had expected. While he felt a sense of relief, Dillon could no longer plunge into work as a way of avoiding the questions about his life he didn't want to address. The more he thought about the events of the past several months, about the ruin of his personal life, the more depressed he became. He had been sad before—who hadn't?—but this dispiritedness seemed different, more profound in its weight.

After two weeks of feeling detached from everything around him, as if he was watching people and things around him from a distance, he finally decided to see the doctor. His physician, Dr. Tilton, listened intently as Dillon described his symptoms. He checked Dillon's vital signs and scribbled a few notes on his chart.

"You say you've been under stress of late?" he asked.

"My wife and I have separated. There's that. I've been working too much. I just took a leave of absence to think things through."

"I see. You have been under some pressure, then."

"I have, on several fronts. What do you think?"

"It's quite natural for slight depression to set in, considering what's been going in your life. It's situational in nature. I've seen other cases like this. More among my female patients. The sensitive ones." He realized what he had said, and quickly apologized.

"I take no offense," Dillon told him. "I have my creative side, after all. Poets should be slightly sensitive."

"Give it some time," Tilton said. "Time is a great healer. Why don't you come back and see me after the New Year if your mood hasn't improved? But if you take it easy, perhaps a vacation someplace warm, I think you'll find you're feeling better."

"A vacation."

"It will help in reducing the stress level. Fresh air and sunshine, preferably by the ocean. It can do wonders."

* * *

Dillon arrived in Key West on a Friday. He had rented a car and drove south from the Miami airport along U.S. 1, marveling at the shifting turquoise and green colors of the Atlantic on one side and the Gulf of Mexico on the other. He stopped in Marathon for a lunch of fried fish and beer.

He had never been to the Keys before, although he had been curious about the islands after reading Wallace Stevens poem "The Idea of Order at Key West" in college. Key West was known as a writer's town, attracting the likes of Ernest Hemingway, Robert Frost, Tennessee Williams, and Elizabeth Bishop. Dillon hoped that while he was taking it easy, he might be inspired to begin writing again.

His travel agent in Charlottesville had made reservations for him at the Highsmith Inn, a small resort that included a restaurant and several cottages. When he arrived, a lovely dark-haired woman in her early thirties greeted him at the front entrance of the restaurant. She introduced herself as Maria Collins and motioned for him to follow her into a small office. It was decorated with watercolors of beaches and palm trees. On the wall over a small desk, there was a framed, faded eight-by-ten photograph of three men in combat fatigues, arms draped over shoulders, in what looked like the tropics.

She saw that Dillon was looking at the photo. "My husband and my father, and one of their friends," she said. "Okinawa. Almost twenty years ago. We used to hang it out by the bar. Dennis, my husband, made me bring it in here."

"Why is that? It's a great photograph."

"He got tired of answering questions about it. Dennis doesn't like talking about the war. Any war, for that matter."

"I see."

"We don't stand on formalities much around here," she explained. "Let us know if there's anything we can do. We're happy to make recommendations for restaurants, although we think our food is quite good."

"Are you a local?" he asked, intrigued by her.

"My mother was. I was born in California at Twenty-Nine Palms when my father was in the Marine Corps, but I spent a lot of my childhood here. So I guess I'm sort of a Conch. A half-Conch, maybe. And where are you from, Mr. Randolph?"

"Virginia," he said. "Although I live in Washington, now."

"I see," she said, her smile fading. "Do you work for the government?"

"I do. The State Department. But the idea behind this vacation is to put that out of mind."

"Then you've come to the right place," she said. She retrieved a set of keys from the desk and handed them to you.

"Cottage Six," she said. "My son will take you there."

A freckled-faced boy with dirty blonde hair guided Dillon to his cottage. It faced upon the street but was screened by banana trees, Travelers Palms, and tropical foliage. As they neared the porch of the house, a wild rooster strutted past them, ignoring them.

Dillon unpacked and took a quick shower. He didn't like the image staring back at him from the bathroom mirror, the dark circles under his eyes and his pale skin.

For the first several days, he kept to himself. He spent much of the day at the beach, reading poetry, and watching the ships passing by in the Atlantic. His face took on some color. Dillon loved the late afternoon sun, the way it bathed the streets and houses of the town in soft light.

He found the raucous nightlife on Duval Street to be what you would expect from a town with a large military contingent. He didn't care for the drunken scene and retreated to his cottage to read more poetry. He didn't feel the urge to write anything, but that didn't surprise him. He wasn't in the mood.

He decided he would spend a day on the water. Maria Collins recommended a fishing guide, Captain Frank, and made a reservation for Dillon over the phone for the next day. "He's a bit pricey," she said, "but he's the best. My father swears by him, and he's been fishing since the early fifties." She nodded at the wall of photos near the bar. "Went out fly fishing with Ted Williams once or twice."

Dillon met the guide at the docks by Garrison Bight. Captain Frank turned out to be a heavy-set, deeply tanned man with gray hair spilling out from under the sides and back of his bill cap. Dillon was surprised that he appeared to be in his fifties or early sixties. He had expected a younger man.

"Francis Curzon," he said, shaking Dillon's hand. "Most people call me Frank."

"You come highly recommended by Maria Collins," Dillon said.

"They're good people, the Highsmiths," he said. "Maria's a wonderful gal."

"I thought her name was Collins."

"It is," Curzon said. "She married a newspaper guy from New York. Denny Collins. He's a travel writer, now, when's he's working. Her father, Jim Highsmith, knew Collins in the Pacific, and that was the connection. Jim was a Marine major. Retired here after the war and has run the Inn and restaurant for almost fifteen years. Denny and Maria started helping out a few years ago, then moved down from New York."

Curzon showed Dillon on a marine chart where they would be fishing—pointing to the shallow waters around Snipe Key on the Gulf of Mexico side of Key West. He rummaged in a bag and retrieved another long-billed cap and handed it to Dillon. "You better wear this," he said. "Or you'll come back looking like a lobster."

Dillon looked up at a clear blue sky as Curzon drove his flats boat toward the spot on the chart. He enjoyed the heat of the unrelenting midday sun on his back and shoulders. They were alone, with no sign of other boats or people in their line of sight. Curzon let the boat drift over the flats, where the water stood only two or three feet deep. He handed Dillon a rod, and they began fishing, casting plugs toward the shoreline.

Dillon asked Curzon how long he had been a fishing guide.

"Ten years," he said. "Late to the game. I grew up in New Mexico. Then came East for college and medical school. Until ten years ago, I was a headshrinker in Boston. A Jungian. In a different life, you could say. Then I retired here and decided to do something completely different. When I was a kid, my father used to take me trout fishing on the Red and

Hondo rivers. Taught me a lot. Surprising how much of that transferred to fishing in the Keys."

"On the level?" Dillon asked. "You were a therapist?"

"I was." Curzon grinned. "I guess I don't look the part now. I can pass for a local with the tourists. The Conchs know better."

"Do you miss it? Your practice, I mean."

"Some days. Fishing can be therapeutic, you know. Spending a day on the water puts everything in perspective. For me, and for my customers. Makes you appreciate how good we have it."

"It's beautiful out here," Dillon said.

"What do you do, Mr. Randolph?" He motioned to the shoreline. "Back there? In what they call civilization."

"I work in the government. State Department."

"And do you enjoy the work?"

"I did. Not so much these days."

"What has changed?"

"The war. I'm on the staff of Far Eastern Affairs, and we've all been focused on Vietnam. Relentlessly. I haven't been able to shake the feeling that I'm complicit in a huge mistake, one that is costing a great deal in human terms." Dillon surprised himself by how much he was confiding in Curzon. He found him easy to talk to, a man he instinctively felt he could trust.

Curzon grunted but didn't say anything.

"What do you think?" Dillon asked. "About the war."

"All I know is what I read in the newspapers," he said. "It seems like a blind alley. Halfway around the world."

"There's nothing clear-cut about it," Dillon said. "It seems that no matter what policy you try, it doesn't produce the needed results. I've been working on this for years, and I feel like any progress we've made slips away before you know it. Like building sand castles at the tide line. It hasn't helped my marriage. I've been quite down of late. My doctor suggested that I take a vacation. That's why I'm here."

"By yourself."

"By myself. I wanted to be alone so I could think. I guess the Black Dog has paid me a visit. I think that's what Churchill called it. A bit depressed. The idea was to put some distance between me and my troubles."

"And is it helping?"

"It is. So is having this conversation."

"Perhaps it was meant to do just that. You know what Jung taught about coincidence? *Synchronizität*. So our meeting may be a connection with more meaning than a few hours of fishing."

"That's a bit mystical."

"Yes, I suppose it is. There's a story about that. Jung had a young patient, a fiercely rational woman, who was resisting moving forward in her therapy. At one session, she told Jung about a dream she had of receiving a costly piece of jewelry, a golden scarab. As she was talking, there was a tapping on the window. When Jung opened the window, he found a large flying insect there, a scarabaeid beetle, colored gold-green. He handed it to his patient saying, 'Here is your scarab.' It was enough to get her to stop resisting, and he was able to treat her successfully."

"I've been dreaming more," Dillon said. "Vivid dreams. Some about my unresolved issues, and some about the war."

"You've been to Vietnam?"

"Briefly. A few times. Visits long enough to give me nightmares. It's a very strange place. I don't think we have a clue about the way the Vietnamese think. And then there's the legacy of colonialism. You can blame the French for mucking things up royally."

"We seem to be guilty of that as well."

"Of mucking things up? No question about that. The question is whether we can turn things around." Dillon took his cap off and ran his fingers through his hair. "My uncle worries that we may do as much damage at home as we're doing there."

"Do you think you will stay the course?" Curzon asked. "With your job?"

"I don't know. That's why I came down here. To try to figure things out. Any advice?"

"Keep asking yourself questions. That's all. You'll arrive where you need to if you do that. You might consider talking with a therapist. I can give you the name of someone I know in Washington. I believe he's still practicing. He had a pretty substantial clientele from the government, as I recall. But it's up to you. In the end, it's always up to you."

"I get that," Dillon said. "I don't expect someone else to solve my problems."

"I'm glad to hear that," he said. "Contrary to popular belief, psychiatrists don't have the answers. You must find them yourself. I'm still grappling with a golden scarab or two of my own. I expect that I will until I shuffle off this mortal coil."

Curzon looked directly at Dillon. "It will work out," he said. "In the end, you'll find yourself where you need to be."

He opened a tackle box and rummaging through it, considering a few lures before settling on a shiny spoon.

"We're here to fish," he said. "Let's fish. They say there's nothing better, except maybe an ice-cold beer and the love of a good woman."

TWENTY-FIVE

On the flight from Miami to Washington, Dillon sat in the window seat and drank three bourbons on ice, watching the coastal landscape passing thousands of feet below. His vacation had relaxed him. He no longer felt exhausted and depressed, but he had little enthusiasm for plunging back into the bureaucratic fray. He had decided to stay in his job in the State Department for at least another six months. If things didn't improve, he would leave. In the meantime, he would explore the possibility of teaching a poetry seminar in the English Department of Georgetown or American University.

He learned on his second day back in the office that he wasn't the only one who had struggled over whether to stay or go. Jan Nowak had resigned from the State Department and would return to Chicago to finish his doctorate.

"I wasn't sure until last week," he told Dillon. "It's partially the change in administrations, but it's more than that. I miss the University. I stopped working on my dissertation to come to Washington, and I don't want to postpone finishing it any longer."

"Sorry to hear that. I'm going to miss you. Always liked having an ally in the building."

"I'll miss you, as well. Did you make any decisions about your future while you were on leave?"

"For now, I'll stay. The future? I'm working on it. Nothing concrete yet."

"I don't have a good feeling about what's ahead," Jan said. "I think that the Joint Chiefs and McNamara are going to convince Johnson that we need to send combat troops to Vietnam. Lots of them. Rusk won't stand up to the hawks. Jack Kennedy would never have agreed to American troops unless it was as a last resort."

"I like to think that Jack would have resisted the military. But he was a political animal. Wouldn't he have worried that the Republicans would say that he lost Vietnam? Like they claimed that Truman lost China?"

Jan shook his head. "Maybe not. There's a report circulating from Sherman Kent of the CIA. They're calling it the 'Death of the Domino Theory Memo.' Kent has been arguing that losing Vietnam to the Communists wouldn't trigger the fall of Thailand or Burma or Indonesia. No dominoes. You may hear the Domino Theory from the politicians, but no one in the Administration will make that argument anymore. It's more about how we have to live up to our commitment to the South Vietnamese. How our credibility is at stake." He looked over at Dillon with a half-smile. "I don't have to worry about that anymore. Not professionally, at least. You don't have to either if you don't want to. Remember that."

* * *

Dillon found the holiday season difficult. Jill had discouraged him from flying to California, and so he spent the last two weeks of December at Far Ridge. His phone calls with her were brief and unsatisfactory. She was evasive about nearly everything of importance—about how she felt about him, about when he could visit, about what the future held for them. When Dillon pressed her, she went silent. So they stayed on safe topics: on Jill's progress in her painting classes; on how she was dealing with Sandy's teething pains; on Dillon's plans to replace Far Ridge's ancient furnace and to repaint the bedrooms.

He didn't know where he stood with her. Jill would quickly cut him off if he tried to talk about their relationship, explaining that she wasn't ready for that discussion. He didn't think she wanted a permanent break, but he couldn't tell. He thought about asking her to come back to Washington, but decided against it—he didn't want to force her to make any choices, not yet. At some point, however, they would have to close the distance between them, geographically and emotionally, if the marriage was going to survive.

* * *

Dillon spent the first few months of the New Year writing summary reports documenting the growing instability in Vietnam. He would send them to Bill Bundy. Were they circulated on the sixth and seventh floors? Did Bundy or any of the senior leaders of the Department read them? Dillon had no idea.

"You're in limbo," Mary Warren told him. "You do hold some value for Bundy and the seventh floor. If the wind starts blowing the other way, and Johnson cools on the idea that we can bomb our way to victory, you're one of their experts on counterinsurgency. Maybe they'll take a second look at the strategic hamlets idea."

"Or maybe they won't," Dillon said.

The situation in Saigon would have been laughable if the stakes weren't so high. In February, another coup forced General Khanh from power. It had been only a year since Khanh had seized control of the government from the junta. It was clear that Ambassador Taylor and the Embassy had backed the ouster of the ineffectual Khanh, who was made an ambassador-at-large and exiled from Vietnam.

"That Khanh didn't face a firing squad counts as progress," Mary said. "It's the second coup without a bloody transfer of power. Maybe the generals should take turns. Three months each as the supreme leader."

"What I don't understand is how they can play musical chairs when they're in the middle of a shooting war."

"They play their games because they know we're going to back the winner, no matter what. We prop up the regime, at the same time robbing them of any true independence. We advise the Vietnamese, which is a euphemism for our brass making the major decisions. When they execute poorly, we step in with more advisers. At some point, we'll grow even more impatient and start to do the fighting ourselves."

In the field, an emboldened Viet Cong had become more aggressive. During McGeorge Bundy's first visit ever to Saigon in early February, the insurgents raided Pleiku airbase, catching the troops there by surprise. Employing a captured American mortar, they shelled the base. Eight Americans were killed, and more than 120 were wounded. Some twenty-four aircraft were damaged or destroyed.

Mary shook her head after reading the cables on Pleiku. "They flew Bundy to the base, and it really shook him, seeing the bodies and the damage. Enough so that he pushed for a reprisal raid. Bombing the North. Operation Flaming Dart. I don't know who dreams up these names. It means an escalation of the war, to be sure."

"Any reaction from Hanoi?" Dillon asked

"They've denounced the bombing. Called us imperialist warmongers."

"Maybe it will work. Bring enough pressure on the North, and they'll conclude that it's time to back off."

"You don't believe that," she said. "And neither do I. We both know this is just the beginning, and it's a mistake."

Mary was proved right. Operation Flaming Dart was followed, in March, by Rolling Thunder, which sent Air Force and Navy jets over North Vietnam to bomb a broader range of targets. That month, two battalions of U.S. Marines were ordered to Da Nang airbase, the first American ground combat troops in Vietnam.

* * *

The newspapers that spring were filled with small stories that, taken together, suggested that a significant escalation of the war had begun. The bombing of the North continued. South Korea sent troops to support the Saigon government. In early May, the Pentagon sent soldiers from the 173rd Airborne Brigade to provide security for the Bien Hoa airbase and the port of Vung Tau. President Johnson halted the bombing for five days in May to signal to Hanoi that the U.S. was willing to talk about a negotiated peace. That initiative failed, and the air strikes resumed.

On a weekend at Far Ridge, Dillon discovered that the worsening picture hadn't gone unnoticed outside of Washington. Charlie Woods asked him whether the Administration had a strategy for winning in Vietnam.

"People are uneasy," Charlie said. "There's a joke going around—they told me that if I voted for Goldwater that in a year we'd have thousands of men fighting in Vietnam, and by God, they were right."

"I think sending ground troops is a mistake," Dillon said. "It's going to be hard to keep our troops on a leash, keep them out of combat. The bombing is another mistake. Johnson has listened to McNamara and Westmoreland. Don't forget there's always someone talking about Neville Chamberlain and Munich."

"Hell, it's completely different," Charlie said. "That was Europe. This is Asia. A million miles away. A war between Orientals. I'm as patriotic as the next guy. I get that we have to stand up to the Russians, but we can't be the world's policeman." He shook his head. "No one wants another Korea. Did you see they had 30,000 people show up in Berkeley for that teach-in against the war? That's a lot of people."

"The idea is to keep the Viet Cong at bay. Make them pay a terrible price. Force the North Vietnamese to the bargaining table."

"Seems like they're willing to pay that price," Charlie said. "If it means more of our boys getting shot up and killed, I'm not sure we are."

TWENTY-SIX

Dillon sat down at his typewriter and began composing his resignation letter from the State Department on a balmy Sunday evening in late May. There was no point in remaining in the government. He no longer believed in the current Vietnam policy, and in what he was doing. It was time to go. He had stayed longer than he should have; he had stubbornly hoped that things might change. They hadn't.

He tore up two drafts of the letter. In his first try, he wrote about his opposition to pursuing a military solution in Vietnam, and how that made it impossible for him to stay at State. When Dillon read the letter out loud, it sounded like sour grapes over losing a bureaucratic struggle over the direction of policy.

In a second draft, he raised a series of specific questions about the direction of the war and the morality of escalation. Did the bombing campaign of the North meet the test of proportionality? Was it being employed only as a last resort? What was the probability of success? He believed that the Administration's current approach failed those classic tests of a Just War.

He sat for fifteen minutes considering the second letter. It was pointless, he realized, unless he was going to go public with his concerns, and send the letter to the *Washington Post* and *New York Times*. He couldn't stomach that idea. Going public would be grandstanding of the worst sort. He would have a brief moment of celebrity. The antiwar activists would lionize him, invite him to speak at their teach-ins and protests. But to what end? It wouldn't matter.

Calling the war immoral, it seemed to Dillon, was too simplistic, too reductive. The initial motives for intervening hadn't been immoral. Ho Chi Minh and his cadres weren't angels: they had demonstrated that once they had wrested control in the North and established a Stalinist regime. Persecution of political opponents. An active secret police. Indoctrination in the schools. Encouraging neighbor to inform on neighbor. Repression of the Catholic Church and its priests. If they won, the Communists would quickly establish a similar police state in the South.

If the reasons for American intervention were sound, then the morality of the war relied on the prospects for success. If the Strategic Hamlet Program had worked, if the Saigon government had been reformed, if the counterinsurgency plans had worked, then would there be any moral questions? It was the failure of those efforts, and the doubling down on tactics like the bombing, that made it ethically troubling.

The last letter he wrote, and the one he decided to send, was only a few sentences long. It stated simply that he was resigning, effective immediately, and that he would always cherish his time in the Department and the opportunity it had offered him to serve his country.

On Monday, he placed his letter in the interoffice mail, cleared out his desk, packing everything in a cardboard box, and found his way out of the building. Dillon put the box in his car and walked over to the park near Main State where he and Feliks Hawes had sat and talked. He found the same park bench, and stayed there for half-an-hour, enjoying the shade under the trees. He had few regrets about leaving. After more than a decade at State, it was time to go, to start over.

* * *

That night he called Jill in California to tell her that he was finished at State. She listened in silence as he explained about his resignation. When he had finished, she asked only one question.

"Are you coming here? To California?"

"Do you want me to?"

She didn't respond for a long moment. "I think it would be better if you didn't," she said. "I don't think I'm ready for that. I promise that I will tell you when I am."

"I'm willing to try again," he said. "Whenever you are. Just say the word."

"When I feel that's it's right for me, for us, I will. Just not yet."

"I miss you. I miss Sandy. I'd like to visit so we can talk things out, face-to-face."

"Let me think about it, Dillon. I'd like to see you, but I want to get straightened out myself. I'm starting therapy. To work on *my* issues. Then, when I'm feeling better about myself, perhaps we can start on us."

* * *

Later that week, on Thursday, Palmer Knox called and asked to meet. Dillon told him that he had quit his job at State, and they could get together any time during the day.

"I'm completely out," Dillon told him. "I've become a gentleman of leisure."

"That makes two of us."

Palmer picked an Irish bar on Newspaper Row, and Dillon found him waiting in one of the booths. Dillon hadn't seen Palmer in months and was shocked by the changes in his appearance. His hair fell almost to his shoulders, and he wore a torn BDO jacket over a faded plaid shirt. He didn't look at all like the clean-cut version of Palmer Knox of the past; Dillon would have walked past him on the street without recognizing him.

"Hey, man," Palmer said. "Long time, no see."

"Where have you been?" Dillon asked. "You haven't been around."

Palmer grunted and took a swallow of his beer. "I went out to San Francisco. I thought I could patch things up with Cora. It didn't work. It was a goddamn total disaster. We tried. Hell, I even dropped acid. She said I'd see things differently. I tripped on the colors and the images, but it didn't change things for us. We kept fighting. I had to hear a hundred times about how she hated waiting around for me to get back from whatever Godforsaken hellhole they had sent me to. The fact that I had quit the Agency didn't seem to register with her."

"I'm sorry to hear that."

"Her sister Arlene is a witch. She's never liked me, and the two of them ganged up on me, complaining that all I ever did was sit around and drink." He grinned. "Some truth to that. I figure I'm owed some R&R. Maybe a decade's worth. I'm not easy to live with, and I get that. But it's not like Cora is any better."

"Where does it stand between you and Cora?"

"It's over. Done. One day I came back to the apartment, and Cora tells me that we're finished. Just like that. She wants a divorce. She wants nothing to do with me. I pack a bag, and I split. I gave her what she wanted, getting out of the Agency, and then she dumps me. Ironic, isn't it?"

Palmer didn't make eye contact. His hands were trembling, and he kept moving his legs restlessly.

"Is everything all right?" Dillon asked. "You seem jumpy."

"I haven't been sleeping well. A nightmare or two. It's been hard to concentrate."

"What's going on?"

"I think they've started watching me," he said. "And no, I'm not paranoid."

"They? Who is watching you?"

"If I had to guess, my ex-boss has sicced the FBI on me. They're being obvious about it. Stationing a car across from my apartment. Asking my neighbors questions."

"Why would they do that?"

"They're sending a message. How I need to keep my mouth shut. I sent a letter to some of the higher-ups in the Agency when I was in California. How I realized that much of what we have been doing was not only illegal but immoral. I told them like it is. Didn't pull any punches. I imagine that they took it as a threat of some sort. They hate it when you put that sort of thing in writing."

"Was that wise?"

"When have you known me to be particularly wise, Dillon? 'Where angels fear to tread.' That's my motto. I told the truth. They don't want to hear it because they're all hypocrites. They're happy to make use of you when there's dirty work to be done. But there's a catch. They don't want to have any of it on their conscience. Never a direct order from the top. Like I said, nothing in writing. So they can go home at night to their pretty wives and cute children and sleep soundly. Out of sight, out of mind."

"That's harsh."

"You should know, Dillon. They're your people. Your friends. For Christ's sake, your father was in Congress. You were in the State Department. You never got your hands dirty. It's been different for me. I've done some hard things. Crossed the line. Blood on my hands. You haven't had to worry about your soul."

"Your soul?" Dillon was surprised. He had never thought of Palmer as being either religious or particularly sensitive.

"You can't do certain things, and see certain things, and not begin to question your own humanity. You can be cynical and tough, but it wears away at you. Day after day. You remember faces. Their eyes. It isn't easy to square what you've done with who you thought that you were."

"You did what you were asked to do."

"I did. I followed orders. But that wasn't much of a defense at Nuremberg, was it? I could have said no to the worst of it. And I didn't." He paused. "I have a favor to ask."

"A favor?" Dillon wondered if Palmer needed money. He hadn't said anything about being employed. It certainly didn't look like he was working.

"What with the situation with Cora, I figure I need a change in my will. I can't have her as my executor. I thought about it, and you fit the bill."

"A bit morbid, wouldn't you say? At your age."

"Realistic, not morbid. If I'm going to have a will, I should have someone I trust to close out all the loose ends. In the event that I buy the farm."

"Loose ends?"

"I've left instructions about that. The lawyer who drew up the new will is a bit of an ass. Ignore him."

"I haven't said yes."

"But you will," Palmer said. "Never let it be said that Dillon Randolph didn't do his duty."

Dillon nodded. "All right. I'll do it. Anything else? Do you need money? A loan? To tide you over?"

"I wouldn't turn one down. How about five hundred? I'm good for it. I've got a line on a job back in Indiana."

Dillon retrieved his checkbook from his inner jacket pocket, and wrote out a check and handed it to Palmer. He folded it and put it in his wallet. "Is there anything else I can do?" Dillon asked.

"Do you ever wonder about karma?"

Dillon shook his head. "I don't know what you're driving at."

"What goes around, comes around. Take the assassination of the President. Did you ever wonder about the truth of that? What actually happened? And why?"

"Another gunman on the grassy knoll? A conspiracy to kill Jack? All of that? I read the Warren Commission report. It's hard to accept, but I do think that Oswald acted alone. I think he was a pathetic loser, hoping to become famous."

Palmer shook his head. "Maybe he was. Maybe he wasn't. I don't think that Dallas happened completely by accident. Maybe because I know too much. I put that in the letter I sent to Langley. That was probably a big mistake. But at least I gave the bastards something to think about."

TWENTY-SEVEN

Dillon remained in Washington for several weeks after his official departure from the State Department. He took long walks, played tennis three times a week, went sailing on the Potomac, and caught up on his reading. Dillon had known men who left the government and quickly regretted it—they missed being in the know, no longer privy to the secrets of state, no longer walking the corridors of power. That wasn't the case for Dillon. He felt a sense of relief, of a burden lifted.

He thought that freed from writing memos and reports and white papers, he might begin writing verse again. He was wrong. When he sat down and confronted a blank piece of paper, the words didn't come or, worse, when they did, they rang false. He wasn't completely surprised. He wanted to write about his experiences and the changes he had seen—in his personal and professional life—but he wasn't ready. Not yet. So he busied himself on other things. He had always wanted to read Dante in the original, and he found an elderly Italian man to tutor him in the language.

None of his former colleagues stayed in touch, with the exception of Mary Warren. He had expected that. He was an outsider, now. He was pleased when Mary called with an invitation to join her at a televised debate on Vietnam being held at Georgetown University. McGeorge Bundy, the President's National Security Advisor, would debate critics of the Administration's policy, including Hans Morgenthau of the University of Chicago, a legendary figure in the field of international politics, known for his realist outlook. Mary had a friend in the Georgetown administration who reserved two seats in the second row for her.

Dillon met Mary outside Healey Hall, and they walked over to the debate site together. Several large trucks with the CBS logo on their sides were parked outside. One of the network's most experienced correspondents, Eric Severeid, would moderate the debate.

Once the debate was underway, Dillon was disappointed by its awkward, disjointed format. There were other panelists besides Bundy and Morgenthau, and that meant answers from the participants had to be kept brief. Bundy was a skilled debater, and he argued quite persuasively that the U.S. had to honor its commitment to the South Vietnamese. His glasses flashing in the harsh television lights, he exuded confidence as he cited facts and figures to support his position. Dillon wondered whether Bundy was coming across to the television audience as arrogant. Or in command? Morgenthau wasn't as smooth in his presentation, and yet Dillon found himself agreeing with many of the points he was making. The war was not going well. The South Vietnamese government didn't have the support of the people. The conflict was as much about nationalism as it was about which political system the Vietnamese would choose.

When the debate ended, Dillon and Mary waited as the room cleared out. Mary sighed. "Bundy won the debate on style points," she said. "That doesn't mean he was right on substance. Pointing out that Morgenthau was initially wrong about the prospects for success with the Marshall Plan doesn't mean that he's wrong about Vietnam."

She shook her head. "We're too close to it. We know too much. The people at home are going to believe Bundy's numbers, even if they're suspect and don't paint an accurate picture."

Only a few audience members remained in the room. As they were leaving, Dillon was surprised to find Evan Bauer standing at the main door, glaring at him. Bauer moved slightly to block his way, keeping his eyes on Dillon.

"Here to cheer on Bundy as he defends the indefensible?" he asked.

"No," Dillon said. "I came to hear what both sides had to say."

"Is that so? Having second thoughts about supporting an immoral war? Pretty late in the day for that."

"I'm no longer in the government. I'm here as a private citizen." Dillon moved to step around Evan, sure that he could see that Dillon had no interest in continuing the conversation. Mary stood next to them. Evan continued to block the door.

"So you've left the government. Big deal. Do you think that absolves you of the guilt? You've been part of the war machine. Anyone who supports Johnson and his policies is complicit in the atrocities. That means you. Can you deny that you had a hand in it, in keeping the war going? It could end tomorrow if we'd get out."

Dillon shook his head. "It could end tomorrow if the Viet Cong put down their arms and agreed to enter the political process. They don't want a negotiated peace, nor does Hanoi. That's become clear. Their goal is to 'liberate' the South."

"And why not? They deserve a country free of foreign invaders and their puppets."

"I don't see it that way," Dillon said. "We agree to disagree, then."

Evan wasn't done. "I hear that Jill has dumped you. She's gone to California."

"I don't see how that's any of your business." Dillon could feel his face flushing with anger. He clenched his fists. He didn't want a scene with Evan, but he wasn't going to put up with much more.

"I always thought she was too good for you. I told her that. I guess she finally wised up."

Before Dillon could respond, Mary turned to face Evan. She said something to him, and he shook his head, not comprehending what she had said. "I asked you why you are acting like such a bastard," she said. "In Vietnamese. Which you can't speak or understand. But you've read a few newspaper articles, and that makes you're an expert on Vietnam? In my book, that makes you a fraud. You're wrong about the nature of the regime in the North. You're wrong about our motives. And you're dead wrong to make public comments about another man's marriage."

She turned to Dillon, pushing by Evan. "Let's go," she said. "I could use some fresh air."

* * *

Later in the month, Huy Dinh Dao called Dillon at home. He had heard about Dillon's resignation from the State Department and asked if Dillon would meet him for drinks at the Hay-Adams. Dillon agreed, curious about what Dao might have to say.

"I'll be leaving Washington," Dao announced once they had cocktails in hand. "I'm returning to Saigon. Whether there is a place for me in the Foreign Ministry is an open question. It does not matter. I've been away for too long."

Dillon raised his glass in a toast. "To returning home."

After a sip of his drink, Dao fixed his gaze on Dillon. "I have many questions," he said. "About what you and Mr. Hilsman counseled before you left the government. You are free to talk about it now, are you not?"

"It's not a mystery. You know what we advocated. The Strategic Hamlet Program. Proving to the people in the countryside that the government is on their side. A free press. Free elections."

"And the coup? Did you not advocate for it?"

Dillon remained silent.

"Do you have any regrets?" Dao asked. "Any second thoughts?"

"I think you know the answer to that."

"You can never win with the generals in power. They fought for the French as sergeants. The people know that. They do not respect them. If they did, the young men would fight, the countryside would not help the Viet Cong. And we are left to wonder whether we're simply pawns in a struggle between China and the United States. A continuation of Korea. The Chinese supply Hanoi with guns and bombs and you supply Saigon with the same. It is we Vietnamese who die. A proxy war, they call it."

"And Americans," Dillon said. "Our young men are fighting and dying there."

"Yes, you have made that mistake. More will die. Your generals believe that they have a simple solution. More bombs. More troops. Can I tell you that the French generals thought the same?"

"You wouldn't have us leave, would you?"

"*Comme on fait son lit, on se couche.* You have made this bed, now you must lie in it." He motioned to the waiter for another drink. "Since we last met, I've learned more about your brother," he said. "Captain Washington Randolph. A war hero. A great loss for you and your family."

"He was my best friend," Dillon said.

"I have an older brother, too," Dao said. "Thanh is lost to me, although he still lives. A soldier, as well. He joined the struggle against the French when he was a student in Paris. We disagreed about the proper course for our country. I supported President Diem. He supported Nguyen Ai Quoc—the man now known as Ho Chi Minh. After the partition, he stayed in the North, and I moved to Saigon."

"Your family is Catholic. Yet your brother supports the Communists?"

"Sadly, he does. My brother's wife died in childbirth. He lost his faith and became convinced there was no God, that there is nothing more than the material. It is easy to see how he was attracted to Marxism. The discipline. The explanation for the ills of society. The promise of heaven on earth. Now, he is a general in their Army." He looked directly at Dillon. "I fear for my country should my brother and his comrades win. They will do what they did in the North. They do not care how much more suffering that will cause. They will bring their secret police and their concentration camps. There will be harsh measures against merchants, teachers, journalists, believers. If we lose this war, I don't expect any mercy from Thanh. He would do whatever the Party asked him to."

Dao shook his head. "I pray that does not happen." He gave Dillon a half-smile. "I have a favor to ask of you. When I return to Saigon, my daughter, Linh, will remain here at school. Will you intervene on her behalf, for her to stay in America, should it become necessary?"

"Should it become necessary, I'll do what I can."

"Thank you," Dao said. "I'm in your debt."

"Not yet," Dillon said. "And for all of our sakes, I hope it never comes to that."

TWENTY-EIGHT

Thousand Oaks, California
July 1965

It was clear to Dillon within minutes of arriving at Jill's place that his daughter didn't recognize him. Sandy clung to Jill's leg and hid her face in her mother's skirt. It took several minutes of coaxing before she would look at him. Jill didn't seem concerned that Sandy no longer knew her father. That bothered Dillon greatly, and he told her so.

"What do you expect?" Jill asked. "It's been more than nine months since she last saw you. She's little. They don't remember all that well at this age."

"I am her father."

"Who hasn't been around for quite some time."

"Not by my choice."

"My therapist says I shouldn't let other people make me feel guilty about my choices in life. That includes you, Dillon."

Dillon had flown to Los Angeles and rented a car for the drive to Thousand Oaks, where Jill was living with Sandy in a small one-bedroom cottage near her mother's apartment. Jill had agreed to the visit, but she hadn't expressed any enthusiasm about Dillon coming to see them.

"I'm not trying to make you feel guilty," he said. "I just wish she knew who I was."

"She'll warm up to you," Jill said. "Give her a little time."

Dillon smiled at Sandy and was rewarded with a shy smile in response. "I'm afraid we only have a little time for that."

Jill frowned. "I agreed to a short visit. Let's not fight. We can get caught up, and you can play with Sandra. That's why you're here, isn't it?"

Dillon nodded. He didn't want to quarrel with Jill. She had only reluctantly agreed to his visit, and she had made it very clear that he should rent a hotel room during his time with them. He figured he would take it slowly in trying to rebuild his relationship with Jill.

She and Sandy made a lovely picture. Jill had grown her hair back, and she was tanned and fit. Sandy had grown much taller, and she was walking and saying a few words. It hurt Dillon to see the changes in his daughter, but he was careful not to say anything to Jill. He was resolved to make his abbreviated visit a success. He wouldn't confront Jill, or question her, about the way she continued to keep him at a distance.

* * *

Dillon left Thousand Oaks after five days without knowing when he would get to see Jill and Sandy again—Jill had been noncommittal—but he felt he made some progress. He had invited her to come to Far Ridge in the fall, and she said that she would consider the idea. Dillon hadn't expected her to agree immediately, but at least she hadn't rejected his offer out of hand.

Dillon's flight back to Washington was uneventful. He had collected his luggage and was walking past a newsstand in National Airport when he spotted a large photograph of Evan and Darla on the front page of the *Washington Post*. They had led a "teach-in" on the Vietnam War at a local college. He stopped and purchased the paper.

As he read the article, Dillon was troubled by the harshness of the quotes attributed to Evan. He had told the crowd that Lyndon Johnson was responsible for a murderous policy of indiscriminate bombing and violence. "We must stop the war machine dead in its tracks by any means necessary." Dillon studied the photograph above the article. Evan's hair was much longer, and he was raising a clenched fist. Darla stood next to him, gazing at him intently. It seemed as if Evan was enjoying his moment in the limelight.

The story mentioned that the teach-in had become an increasingly popular way of protesting the war. The Students for a Democratic Society had staged a well-publicized one at the University of Michigan in March, and within weeks, teach-ins had been held on college campuses across the country.

Dillon doubted that the teach-ins would make any difference to the men advising the President. They certainly wouldn't alter policy based on what a few left-wing professors and their students thought. They would only pay attention when the war, and the way they were waging it, became unpopular with middle-class voters. Dillon didn't see that happening—not yet, not until many more young Americans had died.

* * *

On Saturday, Dillon rose before dawn and drove to Far Ridge. He made the trip in just over two hours. Leigh wasn't around, but Lucy welcomed him with a bright smile. Dillon relaxed on the back deck, drinking coffee, and reading the newspapers. Lucy appeared with a basket of freshly baked muffins.

"It's nice to have you back home, Mr. Dillon," she said. "I know that Mr. Leigh is very glad when you visit."

"No place like home."

"Miz Jill and the baby," she said. "Will they be coming here? We miss them."

"They're still in California. I just visited them, and they're doing well."

"There's lots of room here. Plenty of room for babies."

"I hope for that, too, Lucy. Perhaps someday. Things are a bit difficult at the moment. You understand."

She nodded, but he could tell that she was puzzled. She had to be thinking that something had gone terribly wrong for Jill and Sandy to live so far from Dillon.

He finished his coffee and decided to go through the recently-delivered mail that Lucy had collected in a wicker basket and left in the den. There was a lone postcard mixed in with the magazines and bills. The photo on the front of the card was of Sather Gate, the main entrance to Cal-Berkeley. On the reverse side there was a message: *Dillon, If you make it to San Francisco, come look me up. We can read some poetry together. Naomi.* He had to smile at the directness of her invitation. She was a woman who knew what she wanted.

Dillon drove into Charlottesville after lunch. He had arranged to meet Clay Blackburn, who was back on leave, in front of Cabell Hall. The late afternoon sun bathed the Lawn in a golden light. The University was not yet in session, so only a few students were crossing its Grounds, enjoying the day. Dillon and Clay sat on a wooden park bench. Dillon felt the sun warming his back, and he was tempted for a moment by the thought of taking a nap.

"It's so damn beautiful here," Clay said. "You don't know how many times I've pictured this place during the hard times in-country." He waved toward a young couple walking near them, hand-in-hand. "Look at them. So innocent. They can enjoy the day without worries."

"You're home, Clay. It's as it should be."

"As it should be. Picnics and baseball games. Peace and quiet." Clay paused. "We've been told that we need to fight thousands of miles from here in the jungle to preserve this. I don't know whether that's true, Dillon. Is it? I can see intervening in Latin America. The Monroe Doctrine and all that. That's our backyard, so send in the Marines. And after Hitler, keeping the Reds out of Europe makes sense. But Vietnam is a long damn way out there. Too far."

"You're having doubts?"

"Who wouldn't? Let me tell you a story. There was an intense firefight near Da Nang. Our guys killed more than fifty Viet Cong. When they checked the bodies, they found a young Vietnamese boy, maybe thirteen years old, who had a sketch of their positions in his pocket. He was the same kid selling cold drinks to the Marines the day before. That's what we're up against. At the same time, we're fighting on behalf of the corrupt and incompetent in Saigon."

Dillon nodded. He had followed, with dismay, the accounts of the political infighting in the capital. How could there be any progress in the fight against the Viet Cong and their North Vietnamese backers if the leaders of South Vietnam were consumed by internal bickering? "It's the last thing in the world that we need," he said. "But I'm out of it now. I try not to think too much about it."

"So what are you doing with yourself?"

"I'm going to try my hand at teaching. A seminar on poetry next year at Georgetown. See if I like it."

"I'm happy for you," Clay said. "Not happy that you're out of the government. You understood what we're up against. You've been there, seen it with your own eyes. The irony is that on one level, it's getting better in the field. The air support is impressive, and we're decimating the Viet Cong whenever they stand and fight. But killing more guys in black pajamas isn't going to work, not over the long haul. You get that. I can only hope there are other Dillon Randolphs still in Washington."

* * *

The next morning, Dillon joined Leigh for the eleven o'clock morning service at Christ Church. Leigh rarely missed a Sunday service, and he had become one of the church's lay-readers.

Dillon daydreamed through much of the service, standing, sitting, and kneeling, switching between the Book of Common Prayer and the Hymnal. He listened to a forgettable sermon and took communion next to Leigh. After the service, he joined Leigh for the coffee hour as his uncle chatted with his friends.

On the drive back to Far Ridge, Leigh thanked Dillon for attending the service with him. "It was great to have you there," he said. "I look forward to Sunday. Perhaps when you reach my age, you'll understand.

It's very comforting. We become part of the Communion of Saints with the wine and wafer. When I'm gone, that will continue. The Lord's Supper stretches back in time, centuries, and if we don't blow the world up, it'll survive into the future with those who take my place."

"I envy you that certainty," Dillon said.

"Certainty?" Leigh laughed. "I wouldn't call it that. I would call it hope. Hope and a prayer. I do pray. I heard once that you don't change God when you pray, you change yourself. I've changed because of it. I've become more patient, more loving, less inclined to despair."

"Despair?" Dillon asked, shocked. He couldn't imagine Leigh despairing about anything. He seemed so calm, so wise.

"I am human, Dillon," he said, clearly amused by Dillon's response. "I'm flawed. A sinner. We all are."

"You don't need to remind me of that. My visit to the West Coast was proof positive. I'm no model husband and father. I had hoped Jill would be more receptive to living together again, but she isn't ready."

Leigh nodded. "It's always been a mystery to me about what keeps couples together and what pulls them apart. I've seen marriages that seemed perfect on the outside fail, and I've seen marriages last where the husband and wife fight like cats and dogs."

"We've had our differences," Dillon said. "I'm more than half to blame. Not spending the time at home I should have. And I've my weaknesses, as you know."

"Naomi Friedman being one?"

Dillon tried not to look surprised. He wasn't about to lie to Leigh. "Did Charlie say something to you?"

"No, Charlie didn't say anything. I have two eyes. I saw the way the two of you were looking at each other at the baptism of Caroline Woods. And opposites do attract. Mind you, it's a risk you take. Did Jill find out?"

Dillon shook his head. "She doesn't know. I doubt that she would be surprised. There hasn't been much passion in the marriage for quite some time. Her preference, not mine."

"So you strayed." It was Leigh's turn to shake his head. "Secrets in a marriage can be corrosive. I've handled enough divorces to know that."

"I didn't go looking for trouble," Dillon said. "It found me. Or, I should say, Naomi found me. It wasn't anything serious, and it's over. It won't stand in the way of fixing my marriage. I'm certainly going to try."

"You're going to try?"

Dillon nodded. "It may be too late, but there's Sandy. She deserves to have a father who's present. If the teaching goes well next year, it's something I can do anywhere. Even in California."

* * *

A week later, back in Georgetown, Dillon was strolling up Wisconsin Avenue when he heard someone calling his name. He turned around to see that it was Alex Landauer, dressed in a conservative gray suit and wearing dark sunglasses.

"I heard that you had left town," Landauer said.

"I've been splitting time between here and Charlottesville, but I'm sticking around for a while. Taking it easy. You're the only member of the Group still in government. Last of the New Frontiersmen."

"These aren't easy times," Alex said. "We're all feeling the strain. The war. The protests. At least things are looking up on the ground. We're able to bring the war to the enemy."

"Is that so? From what I read in the *Post* and the *Times*, it doesn't look so good."

Landauer shook his head. "Don't believe the newspapers. What do they know? General Westmoreland has assured us that we're on track to eliminate the Viet Cong. We've been pounding the Ho Chi Minh trail and their infrastructure in the North. Interdicting their supplies. The body counts are way up in the Delta and Central Highlands. I just don't think they can continue to take such punishment. At some point, Uncle Ho will say 'uncle.' When he does, we should be able to negotiate something along the lines of Korea."

"What if you're wrong?" Dillon asked. "What if Ho is willing to sacrifice ten Vietnamese for every American? Or a hundred Vietnamese? Where does that leave us? You must know how unpopular this war is becoming. Do you think we'll accept an endless war?"

Alex raised his eyebrows. "We?"

"Americans. I'm an American."

"Are you going to take the Hilsman line on this? Claim that Kennedy would never have approved American combat troops? Piss all over us because President Johnson didn't choose his, and your, pet counterinsurgency strategy? It's easy to be a dove when you don't have the responsibility. It turns my stomach to see all the Harvard and Yale liberals who started the war and don't have the stomach now to finish it."

"Weren't you teaching at Harvard before you came to Washington?"

"I've never been one of *them*. I don't shy away from the consequences of what I recommend. I'm not a bug-out type." Alex took off his sunglasses and looked at Dillon. "Have you seen your buddy Palmer Knox?"

"It's been a few months."

"He's off the rails. He confronted me in a restaurant a few weeks ago. His hair to his shoulders. Needing a bath. He spouted the antiwar clap-trap. Claimed we were losing our souls by staying in Vietnam."

"He feels strongly about it."

"Good for him. He should be careful what he says, though. He swore an oath, and he shouldn't be airing dirty laundry. If you see him, tell him that. You can also tell him that I called a guy I know in Langley and filled him in on some of the crazy things Palmer is saying. So they know."

"Is that a threat, Alex?"

"Not a threat. A fact."

"If I see Palmer I'll tell him this—that you bad mouthed him and that

I told you that you were full of shit. Palmer Knox has done more for this country than you ever will in a lifetime of pushing paper and acting tough."

"Screw you, too," Landauer said. He put his sunglasses back on, turned on his heel and walked away, moving briskly up the street without a backward glance.

PART THREE

TWENTY-NINE

Washington, D.C.
October 1966

Dillon took the call just before midnight. A detective, Jack Trevino, from the Metropolitan Police Department came on the line, explaining that there had been an accident involving Palmer Knox and that Dillon's name and phone number had been on a folded piece of paper found in his trouser pocket. Detective Trevino asked if Dillon would be willing to come to the site of the accident.

"How serious an accident?" Dillon asked. "Is Palmer okay?"

"We can discuss that once you're here."

Dillon didn't ask any more questions. He figured that Trevino's reluctance to say anything more was because he had very bad news to relate: Palmer was dead, or perhaps severely injured. Dillon found a cab on the street, and twenty minutes later, when he arrived at the address Trevino had given him, he spotted several police cars and an ambulance parked by the curb.

"Mr. Randolph?" A stocky man in a light gray suit approached him. He had dark circles under his eyes. "I'm Jack Trevino."

Dillon nodded. "I got here as quickly as I could. What's happened?"

"I'm sorry. It appears that Mr. Knox fell or jumped off the roof." Trevino looked up at the top of the nearest building. "From that height, four stories up, it was fatal. We've put him in the ambulance."

Dillon shook his head. "I don't know what to say. What was he doing up on the roof?"

"We don't know. Again, I'm sorry to say that it appears that he planned it."

"Suicide?"

"It looks that way."

"You don't think he could have slipped and fallen by accident?" Dillon asked. "That it was an accident?"

Trevino frowned. "He left some of his clothing on the roof. His jacket. And there was an envelope addressed to you in his pocket." The detective reached into his jacket pocket and produced a letter, which he handed to Dillon.

Dillon found his hands were trembling as he opened the envelope. Inside, there was a folded note and a business card for a lawyer, Samuel X. Scully, Esquire, with an address on H Street. Dillon read the note: *Dillon, The weight is too much. Set it right. Palmer.* He gave the piece of paper to Trevino, who read it and nodded.

"This is a terrible thing," Dillon said. "To take this step. He must have been in a dark place."

"Did he use drugs? We've seen a lot of that of late."

"Not that I know of. More likely he was drinking."

"Well, the coroner will check for drugs and alcohol."

Dillon knew that Palmer had been struggling. He had not heard from him in months, but Dillon had never imagined that his friend was troubled enough that he would take his own life. Then again, what did anyone know about the inner life of another person? Wasn't it always a mystery?

"When did you last talk to him?" Trevino asked.

"It's been a while. Perhaps two months."

"How did he seem? Did he sound depressed?"

"He wasn't happy with things, but he wasn't despondent. He had been through a lot. He spent time in Vietnam, and that was bothering him. But I'm having a hard time with the idea of him committing suicide. It doesn't seem like him. He wasn't the type to give up."

"Does he have any family? Wife? Children?"

"An ex-wife. That's it. His parents are gone."

"That's a relief in one sense. If there's no family that needs the insurance, that's better. The insurance companies won't pay when it's a suicide." Trevino hesitated. "I wonder if you would be willing to identify him. Just to be sure. He's in the ambulance."

Dillon nodded his assent. Trevino led him around to the back of the ambulance. A young man opened the door, and Dillon could see a body inside covered by a blanket. Trevino gently pulled the top of the blanket back to reveal Palmer's face, pale and composed in death. One side of his face was severely bruised and scraped, and his hair was matted with blood. Dillon motioned for the attendant to cover him up again. He turned to the detective. "It's him," he said.

"Thank you," Trevino said. "I appreciate it." He patted Dillon's arm. "We can give you a ride home." He handed a business card to Dillon. "I know this must have been a shock. Call me if you need anything."

"He made me the executor of his will, not too long ago," Dillon said. "I should have realized what that might mean. The message he was sending. I could have encouraged him to get some help."

"I've been at this for a while," Trevino said. "It never gets any easier. I've learned some things along the way. When they want to go, they go. No hesitation. So don't beat yourself up. There's nothing you could have done."

* * *

Samuel X. Scully, Esquire had a one-room, second-floor office on H Street near Chinatown. It was simply furnished with a battered oak desk, a file cabinet, and two wooden chairs neatly arranged before the desk. Scully gestured with his hand toward the empty chairs, not bothering to rise from behind his desk when Dillon arrived.

"Sit down." Scully had white hair, a bulbous nose topped with plastic reading glasses, and an officious manner. He looked down at a file, and then back up at Dillon.

"You're his executor," he said. "How well did you know Mr. Knox?"

"We were friends."

"Just out of curiosity, how long did you know him?"

"We met about six years ago, here in Washington. We would socialize as couples, Palmer and his wife Cora, before their divorce."

Scully nodded. "He talked about his ex-wife. Some regrets about that, I think." He picked up a stack of papers. "Since you're his executor, I'm going to turn over copies of the will to you. From what I can tell, Mr. Knox didn't have what you'd call significant assets. No real estate. One bank account with a few hundred dollars. There's a sealed letter with further instructions for you. I haven't read it."

Dillon shifted in his seat. "What about a service? A funeral?"

"Nothing in the will. If there's going to be a memorial of some sort, I imagine organizing that would fall to you since there's no immediate family."

"Cora is living somewhere in California."

Scully nodded. "Mr. Knox made me aware of that when we drew up the will. He was clear that while their divorce was relatively amicable, she was out of his life. He did leave her a gift, but it had conditions."

"Conditions?" Dillon was surprised. It didn't seem like something Palmer would do, out of character.

"The gift is conditioned on her providing you with some documents that are in a safe deposit box at a bank in San Francisco. It's a joint account, so she has access. Her gift and the documents are in the box."

"What sort of documents?"

Scully shrugged. "I don't know. He didn't say, and I didn't ask."

"It seems somewhat convoluted. Why didn't Palmer keep these documents here, in Washington?"

"Who knows? I've handled probate matters for years, Mr. Randolph, and I've seen much stranger things. I have no idea why he would arrange it this way. I believe the safe deposit box dates from a year or so ago when he was living in San Francisco."

Dillon shook his head. What was Palmer thinking? It didn't make any sense.

"Here are his personal effects," Scully said. He produced a large manila envelope. "From the police. A wallet. A wristwatch. Mr. Knox was living at the YMCA. There was nothing in the room, other than a shirt and trousers."

Dillon accepted the envelope from Scully.

"This should be relatively easy to wrap up," Scully said. "The estate is quite small. There's the matter with his ex-wife, there's my fee, and the disposition of, ah, his ashes. He wanted to be cremated and asked that you spread the ashes over the Potomac. That's in the will. That should be it. As probate matters go, nothing messy or complicated. When it's been an ending as bleak as this one, that's a blessing."

THIRTY

They held the memorial service for Palmer Knox at the Georgetown Presbyterian Church on a chilly November Saturday. Dillon had made the arrangements. While Palmer had been a nominal Catholic, Dillon knew that the Church refused funerals and burials for those who had committed suicide. He asked around and found a minister willing to hold a memorial service, the Rev. Russell Stroup, who had served as a chaplain in the Pacific during the Second World War and was also a Virginia native.

Stroup had listened in silence as Dillon explained the tragic end of Palmer's life, and what Dillon believed had brought his friend to such a state of despair. The minister didn't hesitate before responding. "I learned during the war that there are wounds to the mind and soul that linger," he said. "Some never heal. I'd be honored to conduct a service for your friend here, in this church."

When the memorial service began, at eleven o'clock, Dillon looked around the chapel. He counted ten mourners in attendance. Grayson Talbott had flown down from New York, and Jan Nowak had made the trek from Chicago. Alex Landauer didn't show up, but that was no surprise. Palmer and Alex had never warmed up to each other.

Dillon didn't expect a crowd. Palmer had few friends in Washington, and after he left the Agency, he had alienated many of those he did have with his erratic behavior. Dillon didn't know a great deal about his background; Palmer was an only child, and his parents had died years ago. Dillon had contacted Palmer's uncle on his mother's side, but he was in poor health and couldn't make the trip from Des Moines to Washington. In his will, Palmer had stipulated that if there was a service of any sort, he didn't want Cora to attend.

Dillon had placed a paid death notice in the *Washington Post* which included the details about the service. He glanced toward the back of the church and noticed two middle-aged men in dark suits in one of the pews. They had an Ivy League air about them, and Dillon assumed that they were from the Agency. Friends of Palmer? Colleagues? Had they been sent to monitor who attended?

The service was brief. Rev. Stroup gave a eulogy that focused on sacrifice and faith and was short on details. It wasn't much of a farewell for his friend, Dillon thought, but it was better than letting his passing go unmarked. After the service's end, when Dillon turned around, he noticed the men in the dark suits had already left the chapel.

Grayson and Jan joined Dillon in his car for the five-minute ride to the Tombs, a bar and restaurant near the University that was a popular nightspot for Georgetown students. Dillon ordered a round of drinks.

"To Palmer, may he rest in peace." Dillon raised his glass, and his friends followed suit. The whiskey burned his throat.

"I hope that I get a better turn-out at my funeral than Palmer's," Grayson said. "More than a bit depressing, to be honest."

"Palmer didn't come from a large family," Dillon explained. "And he wasn't the most social creature. He didn't make friends easily."

"What about Cora?"

"Palmer didn't want her there. Those were the specific instructions he left. As his executor, I felt I had to honor his request, even if I think it's a lousy decision. Cora deserved to at least decide for herself if she wanted to come back East for the service."

"Where is she?" Jan asked.

"San Francisco." Dillon paused. "Palmer said I should contact her only after the funeral."

"The spooks sitting in the back didn't stick around very long," Grayson said.

"Palmer wore out his welcome across the river," Dillon said. "He burned some bridges."

"Any idea why he did it?" Jan asked. "Why he would take his own life?"

"He'd been disturbed, depressed, for some time. He wasn't doing too well the last time I saw him."

"We all get down. But to take your own life." Jan shook his head. "He must have been pretty far gone."

"He was sick. That's the only explanation."

"I know for a fact that he was very troubled at the end," Grayson said. "I was here in D.C. for a meeting about a month ago. I'm having lunch with a client, a decent-size account, at the Old Ebbitt Grill, and Palmer walks in out of the blue and sees me and marches over to the table. He starts jabbering about how we had to get out of Vietnam. How it was a trap. That we were doing terrible things. How he had experienced the heart of darkness. How we were destroying America's soul. Crazy stuff. The client isn't happy with the interruption, to say the least. I manage to pull Palmer aside and calm him down and walk him to the door. Then I patched things up with the client."

"He saw too much," Dillon said. "Did too much. His last time in Vietnam was hard. Very hard."

"Is there any hope of us disengaging?" Jan asked. "When will the situation be stable enough for us to leave? I think Senator Aiken's right. Let's just declare victory and get out."

"That isn't going to happen," Grayson said. "Not with this president."

"I'm afraid you're right," Dillon said. "Johnson's too stubborn."

"I'm glad I came for the service," Jan said. "Palmer was a good man. And Dillon, you've gone the extra mile for him. Remind me to make you the executor of my will."

"Once is enough," Dillon said. "I have a few items I need to clear up. A trip to the West Coast. While Palmer didn't want Cora at his funeral, he did want me to give her a message of sorts. In person. If I had known what being an executor involved, I would have told Palmer 'no' when he asked."

"No, you wouldn't have," Jan said. "You would have agreed. Palmer knew that, and that's why he picked you."

"There's one other thing," Dillon said. "Palmer asked that his ashes be scattered over the Potomac. It's a bit ghoulish, but I brought them along in the car, and if you're willing and able, you can help me."

"Jesus," Grayson said. "That's some kicker."

"What the hell," Jan said. "I'll do it."

Grayson nodded. "Count me in."

Dillon settled their bill, and they left the restaurant. He retrieved the urn with Palmer's ashes from the car. They walked down Prospect Street and turned on 34th Street. Halfway across the Key Memorial Bridge, with the Potomac flowing swiftly below them, Dillon reached into his jacket pocket for a slip of paper.

"I thought we'd send Palmer off with some Yeats. *'Think where man's glory most begins and ends/And say my glory was I had such friends.'* So here we are, his friends."

He carefully took the top off the urn and shook some of the ashes out of it, letting them drift out into the wind. Then, Grayson and Jan did the same. When they had finished, Dillon turned the urn upside down, making sure the container had been emptied.

"Thank you, gentlemen," he said. "We kept the faith. If Palmer's watching from above, I'm sure that he's smiling."

THIRTY-ONE

The day after Palmer's memorial service, Dillon sat down and wrote a letter to Cora Knox breaking the news about Palmer and asking her to call him. He mailed it to the San Francisco address of her sister Arlene. When he hadn't received a response by the end of the first week of December, he called directory assistance in San Francisco and was surprised when the operator insisted that there was no listing for Arlene White.

He wondered whether Arlene had moved, or the letter had somehow gotten lost in the mail. He couldn't imagine that Cora wouldn't respond. He reluctantly decided that he would have to fly to California and try to find her.

Dillon held the final meeting of his poetry seminar on the Wednesday before Christmas. He had enjoyed the experience of delving into some of his favorite poems with his students, and the good-natured give-and-take of the discussions that followed. Dillon particularly liked the class session when they reviewed poems written by the students. The word-of-mouth about the seminar must have been positive because the department chair had asked Dillon if he would like to teach it again in the next fall semester. Dillon agreed to return without hesitation.

During the holidays at Far Ridge, he and Leigh had a long conversation about his future, personal and professional. Dillon still held out hope for a reconciliation with Jill. He didn't want to concede that their marriage had failed without making another attempt at a reconciliation. "Either way, I need to see her face-to-face," he told Leigh. "If it's over, I want to hear it directly from her."

He explained to Jill over the phone that he would be visiting the West Coast to wrap up Palmer Knox's will, and asked if he could stop by. She agreed and gave him her new address—she had moved to Santa Monica from Thousand Oaks—and asked that he call the day before he planned to come. When Dillon asked about Sandy, Jill told him that she was doing fine. The call ended quickly.

* * *

Dillon arrived in San Francisco late in the day, bleary-eyed and fatigued from the long flight from Washington. He took a cab from the airport to the Fairmont Hotel and checked in. He ordered a hamburger, french fries, and a beer from room service, and after his dinner, fell asleep in front of the television set.

In the morning, he showered and shaved and set out to find the apartment of Cora's sister. Arlene lived in the Haight-Ashbury neighborhood, which had become a mecca for runaway teenagers, hippies, street musicians, and college dropouts drawn to its freewheeling, "anything goes" atmosphere. Dillon found Haight Street crowded with long-haired young men and women wearing jeans and beads and the tie-dyed clothing of the moment. The scent of marijuana lingered in the air. Dillon passed one dazed boy sitting on the sidewalk staring vacantly into space, his eyes blank. A block away, he saw a group of three young black men with Afro hairstyles striding through the crowd. Hare Krishna in orange robes chanted near where a black-jacketed musician with curly hair strummed a guitar and sang a Dylan song off-key. A girl in overalls danced awkwardly, out of sync with the music, moving to a rhythm that only she heard.

The address he had for Arlene brought him to a storefront head shop, with pipes and bongs and rolling papers in the front window display. He heard sitar music coming from inside the shop, and he smelled incense. There was a second floor above the shop, and he figured that was where Arlene lived. He opened a side door and noticed that a mailbox labeled "A. White." He climbed the stairs to a second-floor landing. At the first of two doors, he knocked and got no response. An older version of Cora opened the second door.

"Arlene?"

"Who's asking?" she asked.

"Dillon Randolph. A friend of your sister Cora. From Washington. Is she here by any chance?"

"Here?" She shook her head. Dillon wondered whether she would invite him inside, or whether they would continue to hold their conversation in the hallway.

"Did she get my letters?"

Arlene shrugged. "I toss her mail in a cardboard box. She'll read it when she gets back."

"I need to find her," he said. "I've some bad news. About Palmer."

"Palmer Knox is the bad news," she said.

"He's dead."

"Palmer is dead?" She whistled softly. "For real?"

She stepped aside and motioned for Dillon to come into her apartment. He looked around—the place was a mess, with clothing strewn over the floor and the sink filled with dishes. A glass bong sat on a small table next to a narrow couch.

"Palmer passed away in October," he explained. "I'm looking for Cora to wrap up some unfinished business. I'm Palmer's executor."

"I'm not surprised," she said flatly. "Considering what Palmer did for a living. Cowboys and Indians."

"So Cora doesn't know? She hasn't heard?" It was always possible that one of Cora's Washington friends had seen the death notice for Palmer in the newspaper and telephoned her, although Dillon doubted it.

"She left to go north in October, so I wouldn't know. North of the city."

"Is she there now? Can I call her?"

"Does Cora get anything out of this? Did he leave her anything?" She paused. "You know that he was an inconsiderate asshole, right? Never treated her right. Cora should have ditched him long ago."

Dillon wanted to tell her to go to hell, but he stopped himself. He needed her help. "I'd like to talk to Cora, if I could."

"You and me both. She left with her new guy, Greenie. They were excited about moving to a place called the Haven, near Santa Rosa. Greenie had met some guru who he kept talking about. Name of Carvey. You'd think he walked on water. The guru, not Greenie."

"How can I get in touch with Cora?"

"The Haven isn't the kind of place that has a telephone," she said. "I can draw you a map, and I guess you could go up there and see Cora." She shrugged. "My sister has terrible luck with men. Greenie's a loser if I ever saw one. Not that Palmer Knox was any prize."

* * *

Naomi Friedman's apartment was only blocks from the Berkeley campus, in Elmwood, a neighborhood filled with student housing. As he walked up College Avenue, Dillon felt overdressed in his blue blazer and gray trousers. He had telephoned Naomi from the Fairmont, explained that he was on the West Coast for business, and wondered if he could stop by.

"I want to take you up on your offer of a poetry reading," he said. "The two of us."

She laughed. "I like that idea," she said. "Come on over and see me."

As he neared her address, Dillon heard his name being called. He looked up and saw Naomi waving to him from the third-floor balcony of her apartment building.

"I'm up here," she said. "I left the door unlocked."

Her cramped apartment was filled with cheap furniture and piles of books. Naomi had decorated her walls with movie posters. James Dean and Julie Harris in *East of Eden*. Jean-Paul Belmondo and Jean Seberg in *Breathless*. Dillon noticed her bed, situated in the corner, was unmade.

She motioned for him to sit in one of her two wooden chairs by the kitchen table.

"Coffee?" she asked, and Dillon nodded.

She busied herself pouring them cups of coffee, and invited Dillon to sit on her battered couch. They sat facing each other, cups in hand.

"Welcome to Berkeley," she said. "How are you, Dillon?"

"Things are a bit up in the air. I've left the government. Made a clean break. Spent the fall teaching a poetry seminar at Georgetown. I enjoyed it immensely. On the other hand, my personal life's a bit of a mess. Jill and Sandy have been living in Santa Monica."

"So is it over between you and Jill?"

"I don't know. I haven't seen her in months. It's not looking good."

"Are you visiting her while you're in California?"

"I am." He paused. "I don't think it's going to be a happy visit."

"Poor Dillon," she said with a slight smile.

"What about you?" he asked. "How are you doing?"

"Me? I'm just another struggling graduate student. I like Berkeley. I feel free here. You can be whoever you want to be. No one cares about whether you come from a 'good family' or went to a 'good school' or any of that crap."

"Are you seeing anyone?"

"I'm not looking for anything permanent," Naomi said. "I don't need a steady boyfriend. That would get in the way of my research and my studies. I'm making progress on my thesis. It's narrower in scope, now. Child-rearing in tight-knit communities." She looked at him. "I don't think you came all the way to Berkeley to talk about my research. Did you?"

Dillon didn't say anything but smiled at her. She stood up, slowly stretched her arms over her head, and yawned.

"So let's go to bed," she said. "You're an itch I do like scratching."

They took their time. She kissed him on the lips, and he pulled her closer and unbuttoned her shirt. He slipped his hand inside her shirt, and caressed her left breast and then her right, feeling her nipples harden. She moaned softly, and took his hand in hers and moved it to the buttons on her jeans. He didn't need any more encouragement.

Later, they lay in her bed, the sheets rumpled around them. Naomi propped herself up on one elbow. Dillon leaned into her and kissed the nape of the neck. "The naked female, the human form divine."

"Is that from one of your poems?" she asked.

"William Blake. I've had my students read *Songs of Innocence and Experience*."

"First time I've had a man quote poetry to me in bed. Before or after." She put her hand on his forearm. "Been writing any poems yourself?" Dillon didn't answer her. "I thought so. Still blocked?"

"I have to be patient. For now, teaching is enough. If I can reach my students, help them see the world anew in poetry, then I'll have accomplished something. Maybe not by some standards, but by my own."

"That's good," she said. "Speaking of new worlds, I'll be spending the summer in Israel, of all places. A professor at Tel Aviv University has invited me to work on a research project. Interviewing women in kibbutzim about raising children in a communal setting. I've never been, and it's the trip every good Jewish girl is supposed to make. Except that's not me, the good girl part. I'm curious about the place. I don't remember much of *Exodus*, except that Paul Newman had the most amazing blue eyes."

"You're full of surprises," Dillon said. "Israel is a long way from here. Not just the geography. It's a bit tense. Nasser has been threatening to close the straits of Tiran, blocking Israeli ships from the Red Sea. Let's hope he backs down."

"I wouldn't know about that, Mr. State Department," Naomi said. "I guess I'll get up to speed on the politics once I'm over there." She smiled at him and stroked his chest. "Enough politics. What do you think we try again? If you're willing, that is?"

"I'm willing," he said. "Willing and able."

THIRTY-TWO

As Dillon left San Francisco in a rented Chevrolet Impala, the morning skies opened up—first an intermittent drizzle, then a hard, driving rain. When he crossed the Golden Gate Bridge, the rain and fog obscured any views of San Francisco Bay. He drove cautiously with the windshield wipers at their maximum speed and kept his eyes fixed on the road ahead. On the radio, the forecaster claimed the rain would stop by noon. Dillon hoped so. He had no desire to spend the day driving in a downpour.

He followed Route 101 through Marin County and San Rafael. The weather had begun to clear up by the time he reached Petaluma with the sun peeking out from behind fluffy white clouds. From Santa Rosa, he drove west on Route 12 and stopped at a gas station outside Sebastopol. He asked the attendant, a burly man with a wrinkled face and a crew cut who looked to be in his late forties, how far he was from Freestone and the Bohemian Highway.

"Not much up there," the man answered. He glanced over at Dillon, clearly curious.

"I'm headed to a place called the Haven. Heard of it?"

The man grimaced. "I've heard of the Haven," he said. "Hippies. Dropouts and losers. They say it's a farm, but if they're growing anything, it ain't legal crops. They're high all the time, is what I hear. That's where you're going?"

Dillon didn't see any point in denying it. "I'm visiting a friend there."

The attendant shrugged. "A friend? No disrespect, but you don't look the type to have any friends there."

"Takes all types, I guess," Dillon said, annoyed. He didn't see how it was any of the man's business and was about to say more when the attendant shook his head.

"I wish they'd all go back to the city," he said. "We don't need their fuckin' kind here. They're what's wrong with the country. Deadbeat hippies on welfare."

Dillon didn't respond. He wasn't about to get into an argument with the man. He paid him in cash and got back into the car. He studied the rough sketch Arlene had drawn and compared it to the AAA map they had given him at Hertz. Her drawing showed a side road on the right of the Bohemian Highway, marked by a sign for the Haven. Dillon hoped she had it right.

He was two miles up the highway before he realized that he must have passed the turnoff, the dirt road leading to the Haven. He hadn't seen any sign by the side of the highway. He pulled over and looked at the crude map again, cursing, hoping that Arlene hadn't been high when she drew it and that it was accurate.

Dillon turned the car around and drove in the opposite direction. He kept an eye on the odometer. He spotted what looked like a break in the trees ahead to his left, and then saw the gravel path leading off the highway. Dillon slowed down and crossed the highway and turned onto the path, which led to a dirt road. A wooden sign laid on the ground with "The Haven" painted on it in crude lettering. There were holes in the sign as if someone had shot it with a small-caliber rifle.

The road ahead was rough, with potholes and ruts, and Dillon was glad that he was driving a rental car. After four or five minutes on the dirt road, he reached a clearing with several buildings. There was a school bus, one wheel propped on cinderblocks, sitting in a corner. Someone had painted it in garish, psychedelic colors. The buildings all needed repainting. There was what appeared to be a farmhouse to the north of the clearing. It had a sagging wrap-around porch, with a pile of lumber, two-by-four studs and plywood sheets, haphazardly stacked up by its side. One section of the porch had been repaired, but it looked like someone had abandoned the project just after it started.

From inside the ramshackle farmhouse came the sound of rock

music—the Byrds, "Mr. Tambourine Man," the twelve-string guitar riffs and vocal harmonies carrying out into the yard.

Dillon parked the car and got out. He noticed a rail-thin young woman with curly brown hair and hoop earrings sitting cross-legged on the farmhouse porch. She wore a tie-dyed shirt and a long skirt. She ignored him until he was ten feet from the house.

When Dillon said hello to her, she turned her head slightly and squinted at him.

"Hey, man, what's up?" she asked. When he moved closer, he found that she reeked of patchouli oil and marijuana and sweat. Dillon guessed that it had been some time since she had last bathed.

"I'm looking for Cora Knox," he told her.

"Cora?"

"Cora Knox. I know she's here."

"Carvey's in town, and he don't like it when strangers come around when he's not here. Not at all. What's your name?"

"Cora," he called out to the house, ignoring the woman's question, hoping that Cora might be inside. "Cora, it's Dillon Randolph."

"Carvey is going to be pissed," the young woman said. "This ain't cool."

The screen door to the house opened suddenly, and a woman appeared. It was Cora, except a Cora altered from the one Dillon had known in Washington. Her braided hair fell to her shoulders, and she was wearing a floral blouse, a leather fringed vest, and blue jeans.

"Dillon, what the hell are you doing here?" She threw her arms around him and kissed him on the cheek.

"Hi, Cora," he said. "Your sister told me you were here. How are you?"

"I'm groovy. What's going on?"

"I'm afraid I have bad news."

She frowned. "Bad news. Is this about Palmer?"

"It is." He took a long breath and slowly exhaled. "I'm sorry. Palmer died at the end of October. I've tried contacting you, sent a few letters, but got no response. I came out to San Francisco to find you."

She gasped and slowly lowered herself to the porch steps. "Did he get killed playing soldier?" she asked. Her eyes filled with tears. "Did he go back to them? Did the bastards send him to Vietnam again?"

"He died in Washington." Dillon told her the truth, that Palmer had ended his own life. She shook her head.

"That can't be so," she said. "Palmer wouldn't do that."

"I'm sorry," Dillon said. "He left a note. He was in a bad way. None of us realized how far his mental health had deteriorated. He must have been desperate at the end."

"Did he shoot himself?" She glared at Dillon. "Did he shoot himself?"

"Nothing like that."

"What then?"

"Does it make a difference?"

"It does."

"He jumped off the roof of a four-story building. He was killed instantly on impact. They called me from the scene, and I went over to identify him."

"I see," she said. She wiped tears from her cheeks. "You came all this way to tell me this?"

"Palmer left instructions with his will. He asked me to take care of something. He said he had mailed you a key to a safety deposit box at a bank in San Francisco. Wells Fargo. There's a binder inside with documents that he wanted me to have. And there's a gift for you. I think it may be some money."

"A gift?" She looked puzzled. "Money? I doubt that. Palmer never had any. At the end, we didn't part on the best of terms. I made a clean break. Didn't even keep his photo."

"Did you get any mail from him? Possibly in the last few months?"

She shook her head quickly. "I've been here since October."

"Arlene said she has a box of mail for you. If Palmer mailed you a key, it's probably in the letter he sent. Can you come back to the city with me? Open the safety deposit box?"

"I'd like to go with you," she said. "But I don't know..."

"What's the problem?" Dillon asked. Cora looked away, avoiding his gaze.

"Carvey doesn't like us leaving the Haven," she said. "I can ask, but he'll be pissed off. He says he doesn't want us corrupted by the system." She sniffed. "He and Poncho go into town when we need supplies. That's where they are now, I think. They should be back any minute now."

Dillon studied her, wondering why she seemed so anxious. He didn't like what he had heard—it sounded like she had somehow come under this man Carvey's control.

"I can't do this without you," he said. "I think you should come with me. Stay in San Francisco with your sister. You shouldn't be in a place where you have to ask anyone permission to leave."

"Carvey can get very angry. One of the girls, Rainbow, tried to leave, and Poncho got rough with her. She stayed until Carvey kicked her out. That's the story I heard."

"Who is this Poncho?"

"He's Carvey's right-hand man, his bodyguard. They say he's done some prison time. He's tough—that's for sure."

"Why is he called Poncho?"

"It's his nickname. The first time he came here, he was wearing a poncho." She paused. "I think a better name would be Bullet. His head is shaped like a bullet."

"It's up to you," Dillon said. "I can't make you go, but as a friend I think you should. I'll handle Carvey and Poncho. They can't stop you from leaving if that's what you want."

She hesitated for a long moment and then gave him a faint smile. "Dillon Randolph to the rescue, is it? Okay, I'll go back to San Francisco with you. I'll get my stuff. Maybe we can get out of here before Carvey comes back. That would be best."

THIRTY-THREE

Dillon waited impatiently for Cora by the farmhouse porch while she collected her clothing and belongings. When she emerged from the house, carrying a worn green duffel bag, she flashed a smile at him. "Let's go," she said.

As they walked over to Dillon's rental car, they heard the sound of a poorly-tuned engine in the distance, and a minute or so later, a battered Chevrolet truck rolled into the clearing and came to a stop. Cora looked over at Dillon and grimaced.

"Carvey and Poncho are back," she said. She took a deep breath. "We need to stay calm."

"I'm calm," Dillon told her. "Don't worry. We're leaving."

The arrival of the truck drew several people out of the farmhouse. The young woman from the porch appeared, along with two companions, a busty blonde in denim overalls and a skinny teenage boy with a bad complexion. They waited on the porch.

The driver of the pick-up truck had a stocky build and a shaved head—Dillon figured that he was Poncho. From the passenger side, a shorter, long-haired man got out of the truck. Carvey was handsome in a dark Irish way, with deep-set blue eyes and black hair that fell to his shoulders. Dillon was surprised at how short Carvey was—he guessed that the Haven's leader was no more than five feet six inches tall. Poncho, on the other hand, was almost Dillon's height, although he had a more muscular build.

Cora was right—Bullet would have been a better nickname for Poncho, with his odd-shaped bald head, sharp beak of a nose, and jutting chin.

Poncho wore a tie-dyed shirt, jeans, and a pair of stained cowboy boots. Dillon didn't like the look of him, and he was sure the feeling was mutual.

Carvey strode toward them, with Poncho trailing behind him. He had a smile on his face.

"What's happening, man?" he said, looking directly at Cora.

"Dillon's a friend of mine," Cora said. "From back East."

Carvey glanced over at Dillon. "We don't get many visitors. So what brings you to the Haven?" The smile had vanished.

"A personal matter involving Cora," Dillon said. "We're going to drive down to San Francisco and take care of it."

"Is that so, Cora?" Carvey asked, turning to Cora.

She moved closer to Dillon and nodded silently. Dillon could sense her fear, and when he looked at Carvey's stern face and his hooded eyes, he understood why that might be so. Something was intimidating about the man, despite his small size.

"Cat got your tongue, Cora?" Poncho asked.

"No," she said. "I need to go to San Francisco."

"You *need* to go?" Carvey asked. "Why is that? Whose idea is this little trip? His or yours?"

"How is that any of your concern?" Dillon asked.

Carvey pursed his lips. It was clear that he had been sizing up Dillon, trying to decide how to handle him, a stranger, an interloper. "Cora is one of us. We took her in and cared for her. We look out for each other in this community. It's based on love, man. That's how we live in the Haven. So I feel like we have a say in what goes down. A big say. Do you dig?"

"I don't. I think Cora should decide whether she stays or goes. She's agreed to come with me to San Francisco. I don't see how that it's any of your business."

Dillon looked around the clearing and back at the farmhouse—where three silent figures on the porch watched them—and Carvey must have interpreted the look on his face as one of disdain.

"You don't like it here, do you?" he asked.

"Not particularly. Not that it matters."

"We hate what you stand for, man," Carvey said. "You know that, don't you? We don't want to live like you. I'd tear down your sick society in a heartbeat if I could. All of it. The rat race. A bunch of rats fighting over who's buying the bigger house. It's sick, man. We want nothing to do with it. We want to live freely. Cora was desperately unhappy when she came here, man. Can you dig that?"

"I'm not here to debate with you. I don't care, one way or the other, what you think. Cora has agreed to help me out."

"This is a fuckin' bad trip," Poncho said.

Carvey shrugged and walked away from them and stood by Dillon's car, looking it over. Poncho followed him.

Carvey turned back and glared at Cora. "If you're leaving with him, don't ever come back," he said. "We don't want you here."

"Then I guess I'm gone for good," she said.

"Cora owes us," Carvey said to Dillon. He folded his arms across his chest. "She's been here for months. She's been eating our food and smoking our weed. I figure $500 would be about right. Cash."

"That's a joke," Cora said. "I've paid my own way. Just in the time I've spent cooking your meals."

"I'm not talking to you," Carvey said.

"Cora says she doesn't owe you any money," Dillon said. "I take her at her word."

"You're on my property," Carvey said. Poncho moved a step closer, his fists clenched.

"We're going to leave," Dillon said. "If you try to stop us, it becomes a police matter."

"A police matter," Poncho said mockingly in a high-pitched voice. "I'm so scared."

"We don't need the pigs to settle anything." Carvey looked over at Poncho. "We take care of our own business."

Poncho advanced on Dillon. "Last chance, pretty boy. Pay us what she owes, or I'm going to fuck you up."

Dillon was shaking his head when Poncho shoved him with both hands, staggering him backward.

"I don't want any trouble," Dillon said.

"Then pay."

"Come on, Cora," Dillon said. She picked up the duffel bag.

"She ain't going fuckin' anywhere," Poncho said.

Dillon looked over at Carvey, who shook his head. "You heard the man."

Then Poncho moved quickly, swinging at Dillon and punching him in the side of his face before Dillon could get his guard up. Dillon was stunned for a moment, and Poncho rushed at him, looking to tackle him. Scrambling backward, Dillon moved to the side and threw an uppercut into Poncho's gut, slowing him down. Poncho grabbed his stomach, enraged. He rushed at Dillon and tackled him. They fell to the ground and rolled around until Poncho used his bulk to straddle Dillon, pinning him to the ground. He hit Dillon once in the mouth with a stinging blow, and Dillon struggled to wrest free. Then he heard a sudden thud and Poncho slumped over, falling on top of him.

Dillon pushed Poncho's body away and to the side and sat up, trying to catch his breath. Cora stood nearby, a two-by-four board from the woodpile in her hand. Dillon realized that she must have smashed Poncho in the head with the wood, knocking him out. Dillon scrambled to his feet and dusted off his clothing. He felt the left side of his face. It hurt, but there was no blood.

Carvey hadn't budged from his spot near the car. When Dillon advanced on him, Carvey stepped aside.

"You have anything you want to say?" Dillon asked. He could feel a throbbing sensation in his face where Poncho had hit him. He was angry, ready to fight.

Carvey didn't respond, his eyes burning with hatred.

"If there's anyone else who wants out, they can get a ride to town or the city with me," Dillon called out to the people on the porch. They looked at him blankly and didn't move. Poncho was still out cold.

"Time to go," Dillon said to Cora.

Once they had reached the highway, Dillon pulled over for a moment so he could face her. "Thanks," he said. "I appreciated the help back there. With the two-by-four."

"He had it coming," she said. "He hit you with a sucker punch at the start. I thought I'd just even things up. Good thing there were some spare boards nearby."

"A very good thing."

On the drive to San Francisco, Cora wanted to talk. She explained how she had ended up at the Haven.

"It sounded groovy when Greenie described it," she said. "Leaving the city and all the noise and crime and hassles. Getting some fresh air. Being with people who dig the things I did. A little grass, maybe a chance to trip. And sex, don't forget that, without any of the guilt or judgment."

"What happened to Greenie?"

"He and Poncho didn't get along, so he split. Greenie, that is."

"I understand why he wouldn't want to stay around with Poncho in the picture. But you stayed?"

"It was okay for a while. Taking acid was wild. It blew my mind. Made me see things I hadn't ever imagined. Colors. Lights. You feel at one with the Universe when you're tripping. I know that's trite, but that's how I felt."

"But it wasn't paradise?"

"It wasn't. When I wasn't high, I began to see that Carvey, our wonderful and generous leader, was more interested in banging underage runaways than building a community. He had Poncho as his enforcer to make sure everyone did what Carvey said. The women ended up doing all the work, all the cooking and whatever cleanup we did."

"Is the Haven his property, like he said?"

"I don't think Carvey holds the title to the land, but he acts like it. He convinced one of his rich friends from Santa Rosa to buy the farm. An older guy with family money from a manufacturing business. They make the rubber bulbs that go into toilet bowl tanks."

"Seriously?"

"Carvey calls him the Toilet King behind his back. Anyway, Carvey made sure this guy had a supply of weed and invited him to party with us at the Haven."

"And money? What did Carvey do for money?"

"He had us sell weed in town. Some odd jobs. Shoplifting. Sometimes Carvey made the girls go work as chambermaids at a local motel. They gave him their pay. One for all, and all for one. Except, it's all for Carvey." She glanced over at Dillon. "I'd never go back. I can get stoned just as easily in the city, and I'm tired of cooking and doing the dishes for a bunch of lazy men."

"Are you worried he might come after you?"

She shook her head. "He's the cock of the walk at the Haven. King of the roost. He knows that once he leaves the Haven, he loses all of that power. He's not going to chase after me. There are plenty of sixteen-year-old runaways to take my place."

They had reached the turnoff for Route 12. Dillon asked if Cora wanted to stop for dinner along the way or wait until they reached San Francisco. She shook her head.

"I don't want to stop," she said. "I want to put as much distance between the Haven and me as I can."

THIRTY-FOUR

By the time they reached San Francisco, night had fallen. Dillon drove directly to Nob Hill and the Fairmont. He pulled over in front of the hotel and turned to Cora.

"I thought we'd visit Wells Fargo in the morning," he said. "The branch office is downtown, just a few blocks away. I can drop you off at your sister's, or I'd be happy to get you a room here at the hotel."

"You don't need to pay for another room," she said. "Not in an expensive place like this. We can double up in yours."

"Another room is no problem," he said.

"But one room, one bed, would be a lot cozier."

Dillon frowned. He didn't need any more complications in his life. He wasn't going to spend the night in a hotel room with the widow of one of his closest friends. He wasn't sure why she was signaling her availability. Some kind of delayed revenge on Palmer? He didn't know what her motives were, but he could easily see how messy it could become. She was an attractive woman in her own right, and Dillon knew his own weaknesses.

"I don't think that would be a particularly good idea," he said.

"I'm going to smoke a little weed," she said. "Then you could make love to me. I'm sure you've thought about it. Wondered what I'd be like in bed."

"Cora, let's not complicate things."

"Complicate things?" she asked. "Just the opposite. It's simple. You need to loosen up. Smoke some weed with me, and then go to bed. Simple."

"No thanks," he said. "It's not simple."

"Suit yourself. I always thought you were too uptight for your own good."

"Sure," he said. "I'm uptight. But I've learned the hard way to steer clear of trouble."

"How is getting laid trouble?"

"And what would Palmer think about it?"

"He's not around to care, is he?"

Dillon shook his head. "That's not the way I see it. I've done some things in my past that I regret. Sleeping with you would become one of them. I don't need to add any more."

"Fine. It's no big deal. You're not interested. That's cool." She ran her hands through her hair. "Get me a room, next to yours. All you have to do is knock on the door if you change your mind."

In the morning, after a light breakfast of coffee and pastries, they took a cab to Haight-Ashbury and Arlene's place so that Cora could retrieve her mail. When she returned to the waiting taxi, Cora held up a bank deposit box key with a smile. At the Wells Fargo branch, a young woman joined Cora to unlock Palmer's safe deposit box. They waited until she had left the small side room before Cora opened the metal box.

Sitting on the top was a black plastic binder with an envelope clipped to it, addressed to Dillon. Cora handed the binder to Dillon. Then, she showed him a small Tiffany jewelry box. "This is for me, I guess," she said. When she opened it, she smiled. "This must be the gift. These are gold earrings that I had always wanted. Palmer was a romantic bastard. Sentimental."

There were two fat manila envelopes at the bottom of the box with Cora's name on them. She opened the first one slowly and gasped. She held the top open so Dillon could see that it was crammed with cash.

"That's a surprise," Dillon said. "He had less than a hundred dollars in his bank account in Washington. I guess he wanted you to have a tax-free gift."

She looked up. "These are fifty-dollar bills. Between the two envelopes, it must be twenty-thousand dollars." She shook her head. "I assumed Palmer was broke. When I divorced him, I told him I didn't want any of his money. Not that I thought he had any."

Dillon nodded. He opened the envelope Palmer had left for him, and read the note inside: *Dillon, I'm counting on you to stop the bastards. Palmer.* Dillon quickly looked through the binder. The first document, entitled "A Confession by Palmer Knox," was a typewritten manuscript with hand-written corrections in the margins. At the back of the binder were several pages of memos with classified designations stamped at the top of each page. They appeared to be copies of the original documents.

"Did Palmer ever show you this binder?" he asked Cora. "Did he let you read it?"

"Nope. First time I've ever seen it. I remember when he dragged me to the bank to sign the paperwork for the safety deposit box. Wouldn't tell me what was going on. I remember I was pissed off at having to come over here. A waste of my time. I'd forgotten about the box until you reminded me."

"You're positive he never showed this to you?"

"I'm positive. What's it about? What's the big mystery?"

"It's better if you don't know. It looks like it involves what Palmer was doing for the Agency. It has nothing to do with you. You can honestly say that you've never seen it."

"Why would it matter whether I'd seen it or not?"

"It appears that Palmer took some classified materials when he left Langley."

"So what? I don't get it, Dillon. He's dead and gone."

"He thought I could make use of what he left behind to force them to make some changes in policy. I don't know that he was thinking straight at the end."

"You can't be serious. Palmer laid this on you? Some friend."

"He did what he thought was right. It's a bit muddled. I'm not sure what he thought he could accomplish with this." Dillon motioned to the binder. "He went around the bend a bit."

Cora made a wry face. "Palmer was more than a bit around the bend. He was nuts. Convinced there was a conspiracy to get him. Convinced that the phones were tapped, that spooks had been sent to watch him. I couldn't deal with it. That and the drinking. He finally quits the Agency, but he's so messed up that he can't think straight." Tears welled up in her eyes. "I tried. I did. He was impossible."

"I know you tried."

"What are you going to do about it?"

"I don't know."

"Well, that's Palmer Knox for you. Even when he's dead as a doornail, he's finding ways to screw up your life. It's infuriating." She paused. "You know that you don't have to do a damn thing he's asked. You don't owe him anything."

"I'm his executor."

"And if he left instructions for you to jump off a cliff, would you?" She sighed. "He picked you because he knew you would feel honor-bound to follow through. He always said you were the one friend he could trust to do the right thing, whatever the consequences.

"We'll see," Dillon said. "And you?"

"For now, I'm going to leave most of this cash in the deposit box," she said and grinned. "It'll be my private piggy bank. I'll take enough to rent my own apartment. Then I'll try to figure out what I should do next with my life."

* * *

After he returned to his room in the Fairmont, Dillon read through Palmer's binder. It was divided roughly into two parts. The first was Palmer's meandering account of his career in the CIA. Then there were twelve pages of memoranda labeled either SECRET or TOP SECRET that Palmer had apparently taken from Langley.

In his "confession," Palmer listed several CIA operations he considered immoral and illegal. He wrote about ZR/RIFLE, an "executive action project" tasked with the assassination of foreign political leaders. Palmer claimed OPERATION MONGOOSE, aimed at overthrowing Fidel Castro, had been orchestrated by Robert Kennedy. It was hard for Dillon to tell whether Palmer's claims were exaggerated. Some of what he reported was clearly conjecture, based on rumor. But there was enough detail about his involvement in targeted killings in Vietnam to ring true.

The classified documents were a different matter. They were written in a dry bureaucratic tone, filled with bland phrases about "moving into the next phase" and "deploying operational assets." In some cases, they referred to other reports and memos, and it was hard to place them in context. Nonetheless, Dillon could see that portions of them validated Palmer's account.

He got up from the hotel desk, closed the binder and walked over to the window and gazed out at the city. He thought about Palmer and what it must have been like for him during the early Kennedy years. In one sense, Dillon wasn't surprised by what Palmer related in his confession. There had been signs, hints, that he was involved in some nasty business. There had been the time in Saigon where Clay had told Dillon about the ARVN reconnaissance teams created to hunt down and execute Viet Cong sympathizers. Palmer had been part of that program. Dillon had enough experience with the shadowy world of the intelligence agencies to know that they operated with a grim pragmatism. They wouldn't have hesitated if the hunting down and killing of Viet Cong officials had been deemed necessary.

If what Palmer related was true—and Dillon had no reason to believe otherwise—these clandestine programs had been well outside the bounds of the law, domestic and international. The contradiction between Jack Kennedy's soaring, idealistic rhetoric and the cold-blooded reality of assassination plots and targeted killing couldn't have been more stark. Palmer's involvement must have cost him greatly in psychic terms. He had come to believe that what he was doing was immoral, wrong. He wanted it stopped.

Dillon thought about destroying the documents in the binder. It would be a simple solution. An easy out. No one would ever know. And who could blame him? Palmer's request was unreasonable. What did he expect Dillon to do? When it came to matters of national security—and that was how these CIA programs would be categorized—there would be very few, if any, who would lend support. Where would Dillon find allies in the government? Then, there was the problem of Palmer's credibility. The Agency would brand him a renegade, a rogue officer who had lost his way, distraught, unhinged. There was enough truth to it, Dillon had to concede, to give a reasonable person pause. Only a deeply disturbed man jumped off the roof of a four-story building.

He decided to keep the binder, at least for now. Before he did anything, he needed to think it through, consider the complications. Dillon wanted to honor Palmer's request, within reason. He wasn't sure what that meant, not yet.

THIRTY-FIVE

Jill had rented a place at the edge of Santa Monica, close to the border with Brentwood. Her neighborhood was an advertisement for sun-drenched Southern California prosperity. Palm trees lined quiet streets. There were lovely flowers in front yard garden beds and shiny new cars in the driveways. Dillon imagined the hidden backyards most likely featured barbecue pits and in-ground swimming pools. New money. A neighborhood filled with stockbrokers, real estate agents, small business owners, and their families.

The gritty Haight-Ashbury street scene seemed far away. Ozzie and Harriet would be quite at home living next door to Jill, Dillon thought, but he wondered if the placid exteriors of the suburban bungalows and houses hid the same generational and cultural tensions being experienced by much of the rest of the country.

When he parked his rental Ford Falcon in front of the address Jill had given him, he noticed that the mailbox had FAIRCHILD, her maiden name, painted on its side. Jill appeared at the front door and stepped forward and gave him a slight wave. When he reached the door, Jill made no move to hug him.

"Hey there," she said. "How did your trip work out?"

"I accomplished what I needed to accomplish."

"I'm very sorry about Palmer. I know you were close. A very sad thing."

"He had dropped out of sight near the end. I wish he had asked for help."

"Palmer was different from the rest of your Washington friends," she said. "He wasn't a schemer. Wasn't trying to climb the ladder."

She invited him to come into the house. The living room was tastefully decorated with modern art and teak and glass furniture. A soft light cascaded through large picture windows.

"Can I get you a cup of coffee?" she asked.

"I'm fine."

"You look tired, Dillon."

He nodded. "It's been a long trip." He studied her for a moment. "What have you been up to?"

"There's Sandy," she said. "A few jobs, here and there."

"You're working?"

"You'll laugh. I've helped decorate the houses of a few friends. They paid me for my time, so I guess I'm an interior decorator."

"I'm not laughing. You've always had good taste." He looked around the room and nodded. "I can see how you would be quite good."

"It's not bringing in a lot of money," she said. "Not yet. But I'm being considered for a very large engagement. One of the movie producers. He has a new place in the hills. Very modern. A sweeping view from the living room. I think I could do something with it."

"I hope you get the job." Dillon hesitated. "Sandy. Is she around? I'd like to see her, if I could."

"She'll be taking her afternoon nap in about fifteen minutes. You can see her now, but she may be cranky."

Dillon was surprised by how much Sandy had grown. She gave him a shy smile, but ran to her mother and hugged her leg when Dillon reached out to her. He was hurt. Was Jill turning her against him, or was it the natural caution small children develop around strangers? And he was a stranger.

"Give your father a hug," Jill said to Sandy. "He has come a long way to see you."

Sandy walked over to him and gave him a soft hug. He kissed her on the top of her head.

"Time for her nap," Jill said. "We can talk in a few minutes."

Dillon waited in the living room, leafing through a coffee table book filled with photographs of lavishly decorated coastal homes. After ten minutes Jill returned and took a seat across from him.

"She's going through a phase," Jill said. "She fights taking a nap, but she needs to."

"Perhaps I could come back tomorrow. In the morning, before my flight."

"I don't think that would be a good idea."

He didn't know what to say in response. "She's my daughter. I'd like to see her."

"Now, you would. Before, in Washington, you never made the time. Do you think it's healthy for you to show up here now and then and confuse her? You won't be here long enough to make a difference. Children need consistency in their lives. People who are there for them every day. What am I supposed to tell her? Your job is so important that you can only get away once a year?"

"That's not fair," he said.

"Fair or not, it's how I see things."

"So where do we go from here?" he asked.

"I've learned a lot about myself in therapy, and how I need to assert myself. I know now that I married you in large part because I craved security. I lost my father when I was a little girl. We only scraped by. When you came along, I remember thinking that I'd never have to worry about money again. Not that I was ready to marry. I was ignorant about the world. And I was perfect for you—the innocent virgin who could play the part of the fashionable wife of a rising young government official. A wife who smiled and kept her mouth shut as her husband climbed the ladder."

"That's quite harsh."

"I have to be harsh. I'm tired of being nice. I'm tired of not saying what I think. I can't do that any longer. I won't stay silent."

"I knew you were unhappy, but was it all bad? We had some good times."

"There were good times," she said, softening. "Back then, I blamed myself for the problems in our marriage. If only I could be a better wife, I'd be happy. We'd be happy. I know that's wrong, now."

"It takes two to make a marriage work. I didn't hold up my end."

"I've decided to file for divorce," she said in a flat voice. She crossed her arms. "That will let us both live our lives the way we want."

"And Sandy?"

"Visitation rights. But with you living on the East Coast that might be difficult."

"It seems you've made up your mind. Are you sure this is what you want?"

"We haven't lived together for quite some time. My lawyer tells me that will hold up as abandonment. I assume that you'll not contest it."

Dillon remained silent, thinking. He couldn't claim to be surprised. Their marriage had been over for some time—Jill was only ending the fiction that they were husband and wife. He had been willing to give it a try, because of Sandy, but it was clear that Jill was not. He couldn't blame her.

"I don't think it would be hard to prove that you're an adulterer," she said. "I don't think you want your girlfriends deposed. Airing dirty laundry in court wouldn't do for Charlottesville's favorite son."

"I've nothing to apologize for," he said. "You made it clear that you didn't want me in your bed. Did you expect me to remain celibate?"

"My lawyer is going to start on the paperwork," she said.

"Is there someone else?" Dillon asked. "A boyfriend? Someone you plan to marry?"

She shook her head. "I'm not going to rush and make another mistake.

I'll take my time. I would never bring anyone in Sandy's life who isn't going to stay. She deserves that." She paused. "And you? Do you have someone waiting in the wings?"

Dillon looked over at her, wondering whether she was mocking him, testing him.

"Absolutely not. My life is enough of a mess without having to complicate it further. I won't fight you over this." He paused. "I that we can't turn the clock back and start over."

"It doesn't work that way. What's done is done. We'll both be happier. Sandy will be fine. It's not as if you've been there for her. It's time for us to move on. You can start over, and I can start over. It's best for all concerned."

He didn't want to fight. He wondered if she had half hoped that he would. Jill seemed to be spoiling for a battle. Or did some part of her want him to resist a divorce, to demonstrate that he cared, to suggest that she and Sandy were worth fighting for? It didn't matter. He had come to California knowing that the chances of salvaging the marriage were slim. So be it.

"If this is what you want," he said. "I won't stand in your way."

* * *

They made strained small talk until Sandy woke up from her nap. Dillon played with her for an hour or so, reading a picture book to her, and listening to her explain how things stood with her small collection of dolls. Jill left them alone, and he could hear her talking quietly to someone on the phone. Her mother? A friend? Her life in California was a mystery, and it would remain that for him.

He turned down her half-hearted invitation to dinner, kissed Sandy goodbye, and drove away as the sun was beginning to set. He found his way west to Santa Monica Boulevard and then to Ocean Avenue, and parked the car. He figured he might as well see the Pacific before he flew back East.

There were only a few stragglers on the beach. The air smelled of the sea. In the distance, he could see the Santa Monica Pier and the Looff Hippodrome, an ornate building that enclosed a carousel. The ocean stretched in front of him, whitecaps stirred by a light breeze, clouds visible to the west. Dillon took off his socks and shoes and rolled up his trouser legs and let the cold ocean water sweep over his bare feet.

He stepped back and watched as the surf rolled in, the waves hissing and rapidly advancing up the beach until they died at his feet. He ran his hands through his hair, thinking. At least there was no ambiguity, no confusion, about his relationship with Jill. The marriage was over, and it was likely that he would see his daughter only when he could make a trip to the West Coast. Jill was right—it was time for both of them to start over. Dillon knew that he should have accepted that reality earlier. He had been too stubborn, hoping against hope to repair the marriage. Now he could leave that behind. Dillon felt a sense of relief, a burden lifted.

THIRTY-SIX

Dillon went directly to Far Ridge after his return from the West Coast. It had snowed the night before, and a white frosting covered the evergreens in the nearby foothills. He stepped into a brisk wind as he made his way from his car to the front door of the house—the chill stood in stark contrast to the warm weather he had left behind in California.

In the den, he made space for Palmer's binder on the bookshelf next to his father's law volumes. He knew it would sit there, undisturbed, until he figured out what to do. His initial instinct had been to ask for Leigh's advice on the matter, but he decided against involving him. Not yet, at least. He wanted to hear from the remaining members of the Group first. They knew Washington, and they would understand the risks, and consequences, of whatever action he decided to take.

Leigh was curious about his trip, and Dillon shared the bad news about his marriage at their first meal together.

"It didn't go well with Jill," he explained. "She's going to file for divorce. I don't plan to contest it. What's the point? I'll have visitation rights for Sandy, but Jill made it clear that she's not coming back East. She'll be staying in California."

"I'm sorry to hear that," Leigh said.

"It makes me feel like a failure. Hell, I have failed."

"You can't take all of the blame. You tried to meet her more than halfway. It's a cliché, but it takes two to tango. You can't fix a marriage by yourself. I know that better than most."

"There's blame on both sides, but I'm responsible for it getting to this point. I neglected her and Sandy for work when we were in Washington. There's no sugarcoating that."

"So you learn from your mistakes, Dillon. You're still young." Leigh sighed. "How did the rest of the trip go?"

"A mixed bag. I resolved most of Palmer's unfinished business. I'm still struggling with how it ended for him."

"It's this damn war," Leigh said. "I always thought Korea was a bad mistake, and not just because of your brother. This war is worse. From what I can tell, the Vietnamese generals who are supposedly running the country are feathering their own nests. Bank accounts in Switzerland. Jewelry for the wives and mistresses. We're backing the wrong horse. And worse, it's stirring up things here."

"Do you think people are paying more attention to the war?" Dillon asked.

"They are," Leigh said. "Not just the students and the liberals. It's clear that Johnson has decided on escalation. The bombing of Haiphong and Hanoi. Drafting hundreds of thousands of young men. LBJ, the peace candidate. I was dead wrong about him, Dillon. He's plunging us deeper into the quicksand, and I don't think he knows how to get us out."

* * *

Days later, Dillon joined Clay Blackburn, who was back from Vietnam on leave, for a drink at the Tune Inn on Capitol Hill. The bar was dimly lit and smelled of beer and cigarette smoke. Some of the owner's hunting trophies hung on the walls.

Clay had noticeably aged since Dillon had last seen him. There was gray in his crew cut and more lines in his face.

"I'm staying with my little sister, Grace, at her place in Silver Spring," he told Dillon. "She's not so little anymore, I guess. A nurse at Walter Reed."

"I don't think I've ever met her."

"You have. You just don't remember her. She was the tow-headed girl with my parents at our graduation."

"I don't remember much of that day," Dillon said. "I think I may have had a drink or two. A long time ago. It seems like a million years."

Clay nodded. "We were young and innocent, then, weren't we? Thought God was in his heaven, and all was right in the world. But life teaches you otherwise." He looked over at Dillon. "How's the family?"

"Jill's in California with my daughter. We're separated. And I expect divorce papers in the mail any day now."

"Sorry to hear that," Clay said. "It seems to be catching. Half the guys I know seem to be in the middle of getting divorced. Or on the way there. You can blame the war, but it's more than that. I'm single, so I don't have those worries."

"It's been tough," Dillon said. "I want to do what's best for Sandy."

"All you can do is try. If Jill stays in California after the divorce, she won't be making it easy for you."

Dillon nodded, eager to change the subject. "So what's it like on the ground these days? Are we winning?"

"How do you define winning? We can win on the battlefield. At the company level and above they can't deal with our superiority in the air, or our firepower. There's no shortage of ammunition. Whenever we get the chance, we decimate them. But can we win the war? That's another question."

"What do you think?"

"I ain't paid to think. Just to fight."

"Come on, Clay."

"Can we bring the troops home—that's the important question, isn't it? How long do we have to prop up the South Vietnamese government? Decades? Will people back home accept that more and more of their sons would be coming home in body bags? It's not like Korea, it's not a peninsula where we can shut off any movement from north to south as we have with the 38th parallel there. Charlie has the Ho Chi Minh trail. He can sidestep us and infiltrate from Laos and Cambodia. It makes me wonder what they're thinking in Washington. No matter what we do, we're screwed. And that's really, really bad for the South Vietnamese."

"General Westmoreland has been telling the newspapers that we're making steady progress."

"Westmoreland has it wrong. We should use the Combined Action Program that's been taught to Marine officers for years, the approach we took in Haiti and Nicaragua back in the '20s and '30s. You focus on the coastal areas, make 'em safe. You cut off the supplies coming from the North. And you only engage the enemy when you have the terrain and the numbers in your favor. Westy doesn't care about safe areas or cutting off the supplies. He wants big battles with the North Vietnamese. Meantime, we're losing the countryside. Why would they trust Saigon? You've seen the photos of Ky, right? The sunglasses and the slick-backed hair and the scarf. He's like the Red Baron in the Peanuts comic strip."

Dillon laughed. "That's some picture. Ky as the Red Baron."

"I envy you," Clay said. "You're doing something constructive. Teaching. Writing. I can't say that about myself. I'm good at what I do, don't get me wrong. But I've been soldiering for too long. I've been thinking about what I may do after I retire from the Corps, when I come back to Virginia. I've kept my dad's cabin outside Bridgewater. I don't know if I'd get tired of fishing."

"And hunting?"

"No, I'm done with hunting." Clay looked over at one of the mounted deer heads on the paneled wall. "I've heard enough gunfire to last a lifetime."

"Do you remember when we met Palmer Knox at the Caravelle?" Dillon asked. "You told me about the rumors. His work with the Provincial Reconnaissance Units."

"I remember that."

"Palmer died here in Washington. Took his own life."

"Sorry to hear that."

"How much do you know about what he was doing there?"

"No more than what I told you before. I've tried to stay as far away from that whole operation as possible. I'm a Marine officer. I stick to the rules of engagement. The straight and narrow."

"I made a quiet call to a friend at State," Dillon said. "The CIA continues to run the program. If anything, they've expanded it."

Clay nodded. "That's what I've heard in the field."

"What if I told you that they were using assassination as a tool in other places? Not just in Vietnam?"

"I wouldn't be surprised. The CIA boys seem to make their own rules. In my book, that's wrong. That's why there's a Uniform Code of Military Justice and the Geneva Convention. That's why we prosecuted the Nazis and the Japanese for war crimes. What I worry about in Vietnam most is contagion, that my Marines will be tempted to copy their tactics. Fighting fire with fire." He looked directly at Dillon. "I take it you know more than you're saying."

Dillon nodded silently.

"Can you prove any of it?" Clay asked, lowering his voice.

"Some of it. Sort of. Palmer left me some documents."

"Are you going to do anything?"

"I feel that I have to take some action. Alert somebody. I owe that to Palmer. But I'm not going to do a damn thing until I can figure out the best way to do it. The right person to approach, at the right time."

Clay nodded. "Pick your spot carefully. The farther up in the chain of command you go, the less they want to hear bad news. And you'll be bearing some really bad news."

"I've got a few friends left here in the city," Dillon said. "I'm going to turn to them. See what they think. Get the lay of the land first. I don't need more trouble than I can handle."

PART FOUR

THIRTY-SEVEN

It took three weeks before the remaining members of the Group could meet at Dillon's Georgetown place for a Friday night dinner. He had explained to his friends that he had a serious matter to discuss that involved Palmer, and he needed their advice and counsel. He was careful not to say more on the phone. Grayson offered to fly down from New York. Dillon wasn't sure that Jan would be able to make it, but at the last moment, he announced that he would come from Chicago and join them. To Dillon's surprise, Alex agreed to join him, apparently willing to overlook the nastiness of their last encounter.

They caught up at dinner. Grayson had plunged back into the New York advertising world. Jan was near to finishing his doctorate and considering a return to the East Coast. Alex had remained at the Defense Department, where he had the ear of the senior leaders. Dillon filled them in on his experience teaching his poetry seminar at Georgetown.

He waited until after dinner, when they settled down in the living room with drinks, to get to the heart of the matter concerning Palmer. "I asked you here tonight for your help," Dillon began. "Palmer left behind what he called a confession. About some of the things he did when he was at the Agency. It makes for some difficult reading. Plots to assassinate Fidel Castro. Targeted killings in Vietnam. All well outside the bounds of the Geneva Convention. He wanted me to do something, to find people in the government who could stop the wrongdoing."

"Are you sure you can rely on his account?" Alex asked. "How much is real and how much is imagined?"

"If even half of it is true, it's bad," Dillon said.

"He was obsessed with the war," Grayson said. "I told you about him interrupting my business lunch and ranting about the immorality of Vietnam. He was unhinged."

"His conscience was bothering him," Dillon replied. "He believed what he had done in Vietnam was both immoral and illegal."

"Assuming it's true, it sounds to me like par for the course in a guerrilla war," Alex said. He was smoking a cigar, and he let out a little puff. "It's common knowledge that the Viet Cong cadres were beheading village officials and butchering school teachers. Turnabout seems fair play."

"And Cuba?" Dillon asked. "Trying to assassinate Castro and the other Cuban leaders? It's hard to believe, but Palmer claims the CIA worked with the Mafia on some of the plots."

"Do you have any proof of this?" It was Grayson, a frown on his face. "That's an extraordinary claim to make."

"Palmer left some documentation. Fragmentary. A few CIA reports. There were several operations aimed at Castro." Dillon hesitated. "He claims Bobby Kennedy led one of them."

"I don't believe it," Grayson said. "Palmer was a very troubled man. I can't believe that Jack or Bobby ever would have agreed to assassination plots. Look at how Jack reacted to Diem's killing. He was aghast. Jack was a Catholic, first and foremost. And I can't see Bobby getting mixed up in something so sordid."

"I can," Alex said with a slight smile. "Bobby has a well-deserved reputation for ruthlessness."

"What is it that you want to do, Dillon?" Jan asked.

"I want to honor Palmer's wishes. There has to be someone in the White House, or at State, who will listen, who will see that these sorts of operations need to stop."

Jan frowned. "I still have a few connections. I can make some discreet inquiries. But I don't think you're going to find anyone willing to take this on."

"What about finding someone on the Hill?" Dillon asked.

"Only if you want this on the front page of the *Post*," Jan said.

"I don't."

"You have other worries," Alex said. "You're no longer part of the government, now, Dillon. That puts you in a very awkward position. You're not cleared to possess classified documents. You're breaking the law by keeping them, and not immediately turning them over to the FBI."

"Where are they?" Grayson asked. "The documents?"

"In a safe place," Dillon replied. "It's better if you don't know where." He had removed Palmer's confession and the other documents from the binder and transferred them to his leather satchel bag that he took with him to class. At night, he left the bag by his nightstand. He wanted to keep the documents close at hand.

"Let's assume for a moment that the Cuban operations are dormant," Jan said. "There's no pressing need to deal with them. What's going on in Vietnam is a different matter. You'd need the White House to rein in any counterinsurgency programs being run by the Agency."

"If these programs are successful, I doubt there'd be any support to shut them down," Alex said. He looked over at Grayson. "They were approved by Saint Jack when he was president."

"Saint Jack?" Grayson stood up, his face flushed with sudden anger. "Who the hell are you to talk that way? You bastard."

Alex didn't appear ruffled. "I'm a bastard? It's true that I'm not a pretty boy, with the J. Press shirts and regimental ties. That was the problem with the White House under Saint Jack. Too many pretty boys."

"I ought to punch you in the nose," Grayson said. "Your big ugly nose." Jan moved quickly to get between the two.

"My big nose?" Alex asked, his face reddening. "I always thought you were an anti-Semite. Hiding behind your country club manners. Now, you're out in the open with it."

"This has nothing to do with you being Jewish. It has to do with you being a sarcastic bastard."

"That's enough," Dillon said. "I didn't ask you here to quarrel. I asked you for your help."

"Burn the damn papers," Grayson said. "We all know Palmer wasn't thinking clearly at the end."

"He's right," Alex said. "Grayson's only out to protect the reputation of the Kennedys, but there are sound reasons to destroy them. You're not going to find anyone receptive in the Administration. Going public with this sort of information would be a nightmare, and you could face federal charges. And to what end?"

"To set things right," Dillon replied. "To keep faith with Palmer."

"You feel you owe something to Palmer." Alex waved his cigar in the air. "Okay. If you want us to tell you that you're not bound by whatever requests he made, I'm happy to absolve you. He had no right to dump this on you. He should never have left you with this mess."

"I agree," Jan said.

"So what are you going to do?" Grayson asked Dillon.

"I don't know," Dillon admitted. "I'm not going to rush into anything. I want to think it through. Obviously, this has to be kept confidential."

"I hope that you've ruled out going to the *Times* or the *Post* with this," Grayson asked.

"Only as a last resort," Dillon said. "If I decide to go through official channels and I'm stonewalled, then I would consider it. But I haven't decided on any course of action yet."

"At the very least you should check with a lawyer," Jan said. "Someone you can trust. I'd be guided by what they have to say about the personal risks. For what it's worth, I think they're considerable."

* * *

On Wednesday, Leigh called Dillon to tell him that there had been a break-in at Far Ridge on Monday or Tuesday. It hadn't been discovered until that morning, when the cleaning ladies, Myrtle and Rose, had arrived to find the kitchen door ajar.

"I think you should come back to see this," Leigh said. "It's very strange. They smashed a window to open the kitchen door. Other than that, you wouldn't have known they were there, except for the mess they made in the den. They went through the bookcases and the desk in a hurry. They left papers strewn about everywhere."

"What did the police say?"

"They were puzzled. Not a typical break-in. It doesn't look like they took anything of value. I don't think the burglars even went upstairs."

Dillon immediately thought of Palmer's papers, safe in his satchel bag. If he had left them at Far Ridge in the binder on the shelf in the den, they would have been discovered and taken. He was sure that the intruders had to be connected to the Agency. Operating domestically would be a violation of federal law, but Dillon didn't believe that would stop the CIA. Not if Langley had any idea of what Palmer had left behind.

"Did the Jacksons see anything?" They were the closest neighbors to Far Ridge, two miles down the road, an elderly couple.

"No. They told the police that they heard nothing, saw nothing. You know I rarely come by when you're not home. The house is only open when you come down. So if someone has been casing out Far Ridge, they'd know it was empty much of the time."

"I'll drive out this afternoon," Dillon said. "Let's meet at Far Ridge."

"What were they after?" Leigh asked. "They must have been looking for something in the library. You know, don't you?"

"I think that I do," Dillon admitted. "Best not to talk about it on the phone. I'll fill you in when I see you."

"Good," Leigh said. "In the meantime, I'll get the window fixed. I'll let you deal with the mess in the den."

THIRTY-EIGHT

The sunlight pouring through the French doors illuminated the living room well enough that Leigh didn't need to turn on any lamps to read the documents Dillon had given him. It was the most comfortable spot in Far Ridge for reading, with wingback chairs that could be positioned by the windows or, in the winter, by the fireplace.

Leigh took his time, a pair of reading glasses propped up on this noise. He paused once or twice to take a sip of his coffee. When he had finished, he handed the stack of papers to Dillon.

"It makes for an ugly story," he said. "If it's true. Assassinations. Torture. The government of the United States of America consorting with mobsters. It boggles the mind. Again, assuming that it's true. Hardly the recommended way to run foreign policy."

"You question his story's authenticity? Why would Palmer fabricate any of it?"

"Who knows? He left the Agency under a cloud, didn't he? The classic disgruntled employee, ready to settle grudges in any way he can. He had a motive."

Dillon shook his head. "I knew Palmer fairly well. Revenge wasn't his motivation. He knew what he was doing was immoral and illegal, and he just wanted it stopped."

"Who knows what he wanted? Your friend jumped off the roof of a four-story building. What did he leave you with? A jumbled account by a disturbed man, one troubled enough to take his own life. He tells some tall tales but offers little proof. A few classified internal CIA documents. They appear to back up portions of his story. But there's a problem—Palmer, the star witness, is gone. He can't be questioned or cross-examined. You have very little here without him. It's thin, Dillon."

"It may be thin, but I'm convinced that it's real, and it's disturbing as hell. I'm the executor of his will. I feel that I have a moral duty to do something. I can't ignore his last wishes."

"Sure, you can. You need to listen to me, Dillon. I see little legal risk with Palmer's document, his confession. You have the only copy. It's clearly yours. You can destroy it, hide it, do whatever you like with it. The problem is with the CIA materials." Leigh shook his head. "Who knows that you have them?"

"Besides us? Cora, Alex Landauer, Grayson Talbott, and Jan Nowak. And I mentioned to Clay Blackburn that Palmer had left behind some documents."

Leigh shook his head. "That's not good. Too many people know. Have any of them seen the documents?"

"No. I gave them a general description. The documents have never left my possession."

Leigh considered his answer for a moment. "Are they originals? The classified papers?"

It was Dillon's turn to shake his head. "They're carbon copies."

"So you don't know for certain that they're authentic, do you?" Leigh raised his hand to keep Dillon from answering. "You can't be sure. They were marked classified, but only the CIA would be able to confirm their authenticity. If you destroyed them now, you could honestly say that you were never in possession of any actual classified government documents. Any knowledge about the legitimacy of these copies came from Palmer Knox. When you mentioned them to your friends, you were relying on Palmer's characterization."

"More than a bit lawyerly, Uncle Leigh."

"It's how a good attorney keeps his client out of trouble and out of jail."

"And what's my reason for destroying the documents? If I'm questioned?"

"Upon reflection, you realized how delusional your friend, Palmer Knox, had become. You thought it best to destroy the papers to protect his reputation. So his friends and family wouldn't know how far gone he was at the end."

"Flimsy."

"I disagree. It would be a natural thing to do. People would understand it. You acted to protect the good reputation of your friend. And if the documents are gone, you're in the clear. How could the government prove you had classified documents in your possession? There's no evidence whatsoever. All they have is hearsay from your friends."

"There has to be someone in the government I can go to with this. Someone who can intervene. If I don't pursue this, I've betrayed Palmer's trust."

Leigh frowned. "You're too damn romantic for your own good. Is it worth ruining your life? Do you want to go to prison? Over this?" He gestured toward the documents on the table in front of them. "And do you want to be part of blackening the memory of Jack Kennedy? God forbid anything about this gets out."

"Don't worry. I've ruled out going to the newspapers. Either I pass this on to someone in the government, or I stay silent."

"It appears that someone in the government already knows what you have," Leigh said. "The break-in here. It's clearly connected. You've attracted the attention of people willing to step well over the line."

"Most likely the break-in was orchestrated by someone in the CIA. They must have been told that I had Palmer's confession."

"So someone you told, told them." Leigh grimaced. "And betrayed you. Do you have any ideas who it was?"

"I do." Dillon remembered that Alex Landauer had alerted the Agency about Palmer's behavior. It seemed logical that Alex would have been the one to have tipped them off. "There's nothing I can do about that, except to know that I can't trust him again."

* * *

Dillon took Palmer's documents from his satchel bag and hid them in one of the kitchen cabinets, underneath a stack of plates that hadn't been used in years. He figured they would be as safe there as anyplace else in Far Ridge.

In the early afternoon, Dillon fielded a call about Palmer Knox not from one of his former colleagues at the CIA but—to his surprise—from an FBI agent in the Richmond office named Darlington. He asked if Dillon would be available for a brief interview.

"What's this about?" Dillon asked.

"We're following up on aspects of Mr. Knox's departure from the government. We understand that you were close friends."

"We were friends."

"This won't take more than thirty minutes. We'd appreciate your cooperation."

Dillon agreed to meet Darlington at Leigh's law office in Charlottesville. He wanted to keep the agent at a remove from Far Ridge. When he explained the situation to Leigh, his uncle gave him a thin smile.

"For the purposes of this interview, I'm now your attorney," Leigh said. "I'm going to sit in. You need to keep your answers as brief as possible. The more you say, the more likely it is that you'll inadvertently reveal something that you shouldn't. You have to fight your natural tendency to explain things."

"Isn't that going to make me look like Jimmy Hoffa? Like I have something to hide?"

"I'm not suggesting that you take the Fifth Amendment." Leigh grinned. "At least, not yet. Nonetheless, you must be very careful. It's a felony to make a materially false statement in the course of an FBI investigation. You can imagine how wide a net they can cast with that. They don't have to prove you did anything illegal, just that you lied to them."

Fifteen minutes before the appointed time for Dillon's interview, two men wearing dark suits and white shirts arrived at McFarlin & Randolph's front door. Leigh's secretary ushered them into Leigh's private office.

The older agent introduced himself as Harvey Darlington. His sidekick, Francis O'Brien, produced a notepad and pen.

"I've asked my uncle to sit in," Dillon said. "For this conversation, he'll act as my counsel."

"Do you feel that you need a lawyer to talk to us?" Darlington asked.

"These are troubled times," Leigh said quickly. "It was my idea. I'm a bit protective of my nephew, and as an old country lawyer, I wanted to make sure all goes well."

"I see," Darlington said. He turned to Dillon. "We have a few questions for you, Mr. Randolph. As I told you over the phone, they concern Palmer Knox. You were close friends?"

"At times we were close. Not so much near the end of his life."

"Did Knox ever discuss his work with you?"

"His work? Let's not fence. Sure, I knew that Palmer worked for the Central Intelligence Agency, but he never talked about what he did there. I never asked. No specifics. The same with my job at State."

"Did you think that he was disaffected?" O'Brien looked up from the notepad after he asked his first question. "Disgruntled? Angry?"

"He committed suicide," Dillon said. "I think it's safe to say that he wasn't a happy man. He was struggling with personal demons."

"Personal demons?" O'Brien raised his eyebrows.

"Palmer drank too much. He had seen things in Vietnam and elsewhere that he wanted to forget. He had regrets about his life. He never got too specific, like I said, and I never pressed him about it."

"Was he seeing anyone about it?" Darlington asked. "A psychiatrist? Did he mention a therapist in Washington?"

"Never to me. Was he?"

Darlington ignored his question. "Did he ever say anything that could be considered disloyal to the country? Did he have strong feelings against the war? Did he talk about it?"

"I don't think disagreeing with our current policy in Vietnam is disloyal," Dillon replied. "There are a fair number of Congressmen and Senators who oppose what we're doing there. Palmer had questions about the wisdom of our policies. So do I. But he was a patriot. He put himself in harm's way for his country, which is more than I can say for lots of the hawks in Washington."

"Did he ever leave documents with you?" It was O'Brien. "For safekeeping?"

Leigh coughed. "One moment," he said. "I know that my nephew wants to help you with your inquiries. But I'm his attorney, and I think that it's best to set some boundaries. Dillon was the executor of Mr. Knox's estate. He dealt with all the paperwork involved in that role. If you're asking about written records, I think a court order of some sort would be in order."

"A court order?" O'Brien made a face. "That's a bit much, isn't it? I asked if he had any documents and you immediately jump to that. Does your nephew have anything to hide?"

Leigh shook his head. "It's been my experience that you never go wrong observing the letter of the law."

"You didn't answer the question, Mr. Randolph," Darlington said to Dillon.

"Yes, I was the executor of Palmer's estate. So I've had to handle a fair amount of paperwork."

"What sort of paperwork might that be?" Darlington's tone was hostile.

"Do you read your Bible, Mr. Darlington?" Leigh asked. "The prophet Isaiah suggested that we reason together. My nephew has done nothing wrong. You may have been misled about his relationship with Mr. Knox. As to documents, I think it's reasonable for him to ask for more specifics.

An executor deals with many documents. Are there specific documents in question?"

"Classified documents." Darlington glared at them both.

"My nephew will make an inventory of Mr. Knox's papers in his possession and ascertain if there are any classified documents. We will inform you, immediately, if he finds anything. In any event, you can expect a letter from my office detailing the results of his search."

"It seems like you're about to make a serious mistake," O'Brien said to Dillon. "Impeding a federal investigation."

Dillon shook his head. "You heard what my uncle had to say. That sounds like cooperation to me."

"This won't end today," O'Brien said. "You haven't been very forthcoming. What is it you have to hide?"

"Nothing." Dillon shook his head. "Like my uncle said, I'm cooperating."

The two agents rose to their feet. "We'll see ourselves out," Darlington said. Leigh didn't say anything for a few moments, waiting until the men were safely out of earshot.

"What do you think?" Dillon asked.

Leigh shook his head. "I don't know what to say. It's clear that someone has told them that Palmer Knox left you classified documents." He polished his glasses, quiet for a long moment, lost in thought. "We can assume the break-in at Far Ridge was someone looking for the documents. And now the FBI comes calling. Disturbing. As long as you have them, you're at legal risk. In theory, you could be prosecuted for violating the Espionage Act."

"Seriously? The Espionage Act? Doesn't that date back to Woodrow Wilson?"

"It does. 1917. Your friend Palmer Knox violated it. Your situation is somewhat different. You were out of the government when, if, you received the documents. You haven't made them public." He paused. "On the other hand, you haven't returned them to the government. They could also prosecute you under federal law for the theft or misuse of government 'things of value.' In your defense, I would point to all the government officials who retired and brought classified documents home to help them write their memoirs."

"What are the odds they come after me legally?"

"I'd be surprised," Leigh said. "They'll want to keep things very quiet. They'll hope that you've gotten the message from today's interview. They'll wait and see if you contact anyone in the government. Or worse, from their perspective, the press. You could give the documents back to the government. Not to the FBI or the Justice Department, but to someone in Congress. Maybe a Senator. Let him make the call."

"What would you do?" Dillon asked.

"I'd burn every single blessed piece of paper Palmer left you."

"You would?"

"It's best for you, and it's best for the country. We're divided enough. I can't see what good would come from it. Whatever happened is best kept secret."

"But exposing what they're doing in Vietnam, and what they tried to do in Cuba, would put Johnson and whoever is the next President on notice that they couldn't use assassination as a tool."

"I don't have your experience in Washington, but even I think that's pretty damn naive. What's more likely is that they would do everything they can to discredit Palmer. And you. I worry about what will happen to you, Dillon, if you pursue this. They can make your life quite difficult."

* * *

Two days later an agitated Grayson Talbott reached Dillon on the phone. Grayson got straight to the point.

"What the hell is going on?" he asked. "I had some visitors from the FBI's New York field office. They had lots of questions about you and

Palmer and what the two of you talked about on poker nights. Were you antiwar? What did you say about LBJ? Did Palmer talk about his problems at work? That sort of thing."

"They've been to see me, as well," Dillon said. "Leigh sat in on the interview. I think Palmer's former employers are concerned about what he may have left behind. The agents who talked to me were most interested in whether I had classified documents in my possession."

"Same here. I told them that I hadn't seen anything labeled classified since I left the White House. They asked directly whether I had any knowledge of CIA documents that you might have."

"What did you say?" Dillon asked.

"That you had mentioned something about Palmer leaving you some personal papers. That was it."

"Someone must have called the FBI and alerted them. I don't think Jan would. That leaves Alex. It's easy for me to think the worse of him, and I hope I'm wrong. I can't believe that he would sic the FBI on you. On us."

"Has Alex called you? About the FBI talking to him."

"No."

"Well, that's a tell, isn't it?" Grayson paused. "You would think that they would have gone to see him. If Alex hasn't called you to warn you, there's a reason for his silence. Not a good one."

"That's a logical conclusion."

"Dillon, I wish you'd do what your friends are telling you to do. Get rid of Palmer's papers."

"I've given it some thought," Dillon said. "Believe me, I'm considering it. But I'm stubborn. I don't like being bullied. It gets my back up. But don't worry—I'll figure something out."

* * *

While Dillon resisted the idea of destroying Palmer's documents, he recognized that he was in an awkward position. He had to respond to Darlington in the near future. He didn't want to risk approaching anyone in the government, not with an FBI field investigation underway. He decided on a middle way, one that would relieve the pressure from the FBI but would preserve his options. At some point in the future, he vowed that he would do what Palmer had asked—when the time was right.

He recovered the documents from their hiding place in the kitchen and put them in a file folder. Then, he wrapped the folder in wax paper and placed it in a metal canister. Dillon took the canister and a shovel and walked several hundred feet from the back of the house and climbed the hillside. Near a large pine tree, he dug a deep hole. Dillon carefully lowered the canister into the ground and covered it with dirt. He spread pine needles over the spot. He marked the tree, carving a cross into its trunk with his jackknife.

When he returned to the house, he telephoned Leigh at his office. "I've taken care of my problem," he told him. "So you can rest easy."

"I see."

"As my lawyer, you can write Darlington and tell him that I'm not in possession of any classified documents. There's nothing further to discuss. Nothing to produce. They can search Far Ridge from top to bottom if they like, but they're not going to find anything."

"I'm pleased that this is the way you're handling it."

"Did I have much of a choice? Please send the letter. I'm not going to tilt at windmills, Leigh. Not now."

THIRTY-NINE

Dillon spent the rest of the summer at Far Ridge, and he didn't return to Washington until September when it was again time to teach his poetry seminar at Georgetown. Leigh had dispatched a brief letter to Agent Darlington stating that Dillon had reviewed all of Palmer Knox's documents in his possession and had found nothing classified. There was no response from Darlington.

The Washington newspapers were filled with news about Vietnam. In early September, the leaders of the military junta, General Thieu and General Ky, won the presidency and vice presidency respectively in national elections. The two men, who hated each other, had been pressured by U.S. officials to run on a combined ticket. Those same officials hailed their victory as proof that the country was moving toward democratic norms. The second-place finisher, a lawyer named Dzu, won some 17 percent of the vote on a platform of negotiating with the Viet Cong. After the election, Dzu had been arrested on charges of illicit currency transactions, including setting up a bank account in San Francisco. He had been sentenced to nine months in jail. That most ARVN generals had accounts in Paris and Zurich somehow didn't warrant prosecution.

In the field, a bloody battle in the Que Son Valley between North Vietnamese troops, the Viet Cong, and U.S. Marines cost the lives of more than 100 Americans. As Mary Warren remarked in a brief phone call with Dillon, the American bombing of the North had provoked Hanoi to send troops south, escalating the conflict.

"There are rumors that McNamara is having second thoughts," Mary said. "He's resisting Westmoreland's demand for more troops and an invasion of the North."

"What is Westmoreland thinking? An invasion could provoke the Chinese to intervene. We don't want another Korea."

"When you don't know where you're going, any road will take you there."

In his first week back in Washington, Dillon made separate calls to Grayson and Jan to tell them that he had decided not to take any action with Palmer's documents. He recounted his FBI interview and explained that his uncle had convinced him that he would risk prosecution if he disclosed what Palmer had left him.

"I'm glad to hear that," Grayson said. "It's not worth the risk."

"I don't know," Dillon said. "I don't exactly feel like a 'Profile in Courage.' I'm not honoring Palmer's wishes."

"You're doing the right thing."

"The expedient thing."

"Sometimes they're one and the same," Grayson said. "This is one of those times."

For his part, Jan had listened quietly when Dillon explained his thinking. He hesitated before responding.

"I think you're making the smart choice," he told Dillon. "It's not your responsibility. You're no longer in the government. You're not in the chain of command."

"Is there anyone in that chain who will act?"

"I did ask around like I said I would. To see if there might be anyone at the White House or State who might be an ally. No luck. Johnson's people are one hundred percent behind the war effort, or at least that's their public position. Whatever the CIA is doing in Vietnam is seen as moving us closer to victory."

"And the Cuban operations?"

"Ancient history," he said. "Who wants to dig up old bones?"

Dillon didn't bother to call Alex Landauer. Dillon was convinced that he had been the one to contact the FBI. Alex had admitted alerting the CIA to Palmer's erratic behavior in the past, after all. Dillon didn't want him to have the satisfaction of knowing that his betrayal had worked—that Dillon had backed down when confronted by government agents. Perhaps it had been the prudent thing to do, the smart thing, but it didn't sit well with him.

* * *

The phone was ringing in the late afternoon when Dillon returned to his house after his third seminar session. It was Naomi Friedman, back in Washington from her time in Israel. They made small talk, and Dillon invited her over to his place, wondering if they would end up in bed—it seemed that was where they inevitably found themselves.

When Naomi arrived, she gave him a quick kiss on the cheek but didn't hug him. She had lost weight, and her skin was a golden brown.

"My life has changed," she began. "All for the better. I'm only in the States for a few weeks, and then it's back to Israel. I can't stay too long with you today, but I didn't want to miss a chance to say hello to you. And, I guess, goodbye."

"Back to Israel?"

She smiled broadly and shook her head. "I agree it's a bit surprising. I didn't expect to become a Zionist. If anything, I thought I'd hate living there. But it was so different. When I walked through the Old City in Jerusalem, I immediately felt at home. We had been kept from our holiest places for too long. Of course, living through the war changed me. We all knew that it was life-or-death."

Dillon nodded. Israel had emerged victorious from the Six-Day War in June. The Israel Defense Forces had occupied Jerusalem, and for the first time since 1948, Jews could openly worship at the Western Wall in the Old City.

"And the people of Israel," Naomi said. "They're so brave. So aware of the moment."

"Your friends in Berkeley would probably argue that they're fully aware of the moment."

"It's so different. California isn't reality, Dillon. Israel is. There's no 'keeping up with the Joneses,' no mindless consumption. Everyone knows they're building a country. That isn't to say that Israelis have traded one kind of conformity for another. It's still two Jews with three opinions. Arguing. Kvetching. But when it matters, there's no confusion about who our enemy is."

"*Our* enemy?"

"I'm a Jew, Dillon. I always knew that before—you can never completely forget that, even in America—but it became so very clear living in Israel that I'm Jewish to my core. It makes me who I am."

"You can be Jewish in California or Virginia," Dillon said. "There's no contradiction."

"It's different. I feel more Jewish in Tel Aviv and Jerusalem than I do in San Francisco. And Israel is the only place in the world where we can defend ourselves, and not have to rely on others. Who else will protect us? Not the United Nations. Not the United States. We have to stand on our own two feet."

"It's a bit complicated, Naomi. I think the world learned from what happened with the Nazis. There's good will toward Israel. On the other hand, the Arabs have their own claim to the land that was Palestine."

She made a face. "Have you looked at a map? There's plenty of land in Jordan. Lebanon. Even Syria. The Arabs who left in '48 could settle there. They've kept them in camps as a tactic. You must see that. I know the State Department is chock full of Arab lovers and anti-Semites, but I hope they haven't overly influenced you."

"I like to think that I make up my own mind," Dillon said. "There are two sides to the question, as you know. I'm sympathetic to Israel, like most Americans. You know my father always voted for assistance for Israel when he was in Congress."

"Sorry," she said. "I'm very emotional about this."

"I'll confess that I'm amazed at the changes in you."

"Good changes. The war was scary." She took a deep breath. "What was amazing was how connected we were then. All the petty stuff disappeared. People shared. They would give you the shirt off their back. That's partially why I'm going back. I have a purpose, there. And I've met someone. Avi wants to marry me, and he wants children."

"I'm glad you've found someone," Dillon said. "Congratulations."

"I would have thought it was a crazy idea six months ago. Now, I'm not so sure." She looked directly at him. "You're different, too," she said. "Not quite as sure of yourself. I like it."

"Life has a way of doing that," he said. "It beats you up. Takes the edges off."

She kissed him on the cheek. "We had some good times together. I won't forget them."

"Nor will I. And I wish you the best, Naomi. If there's ever anything I can do, do let me know."

After she had left, he poured himself a beer and sat in the living room and thought about Naomi and the twists and turns in her life. He wondered how it would work out for her in Israel. She might think she could shed her American identity and assume a Zionist one, but would it be that easy? Would her new-found fervor fade over time? How would she handle marriage and children in her new homeland?

Part of him envied her. Naomi believed in something, and she had dared to act on it. She didn't hold back or seek the easy route. He admired her passion. Dillon didn't have that in his life, that purpose, not since he had left the government. He wondered whether that would change. He hoped that it would.

FORTY

Washington, D.C.
Fall 1967

A crisp autumn day in Georgetown, and the shade trees on the side streets—red oaks, maples, willow oaks, and dogwood—had turned brilliant shades of yellow, orange, and scarlet. Dillon took a deep breath; the fall had always been his favorite time of the year in Washington.

He was feeling more relaxed about the situation with Palmer's documents. Leigh hadn't been contacted by the FBI or the Justice Department since the summer. "I think you may be in the clear," he told Dillon. "If they were going to pursue this, they would have come back quickly with a court order looking for the documents. You need to lay low. Stay off their radar."

"I doubt I'm going to attract much attention teaching poetry to Georgetown students," Dillon replied. "That hardly can be classified as subversive, even by J. Edgar and his G-men."

"At least you've kept your sense of humor about it," Leigh said. "Let them forget about you. That's the best for all concerned."

Dillon's second foray into teaching had gone well. He was more comfortable in working with the students in his seminar. He kept the focus on interpreting classic poems, although he did spend one week on poems by Lawrence Ferlinghetti, Allen Ginsburg, LeRoi Jones, and Anne Sexton (who had just won the Pulitzer Prize). On the few occasions when they discussed politics, it was clear that his students were becoming increasingly concerned about the war. A few of them were open about their opposition to American involvement. The draft had become a looming issue. There had been protests at many colleges, although not

299

at Georgetown. Resistance to the war effort was spreading. A group of young men had gathered on the Boston Common to burn their draft cards.

It was not surprising that opponents of the war decided to demonstrate in the nation's capital. They announced plans for a protest march on October 21st. One of the protest leaders, Jerry Rubin, claimed that he and the poet Allen Ginsberg would attempt to "levitate" the Pentagon as part of the protest. It seemed the demonstration was meant to be political theater, the absurd mixed with the serious.

On a Monday morning, posters appeared on stop signs and walls in Georgetown promoting the upcoming march on Washington. Several signs advertised a fundraiser sponsored by the "Artists of Conscience" at the Ambassador Theater to benefit the march organizers (the National Mobilization to End the War in Vietnam, or the Mobe). It would feature appearances by Robert Lowell, the renowned New England poet, and other literary types. Dillon had the evening free, a Thursday, and decided to attend.

He took a cab to the Ambassador Theater, which had been rented for the antiwar literary gathering. It had seen better days. Now a psychedelic dance hall and nightspot, with a head shop on the premises, the owners had hoped to mimic New York's Electric Circus. Groups like The Doors and The Jimi Hendrix Experience had appeared there.

The pungent smell of marijuana and unwashed bodies greeted Dillon after he had paid for his $5 ticket and entered the auditorium. The theater's orchestra seats had been removed to create an open space for dancing. Young people sat on the floor, leaving a makeshift aisle. A rock group had just finished playing and were leaving the stage when he arrived. He checked his watch—the event was running late. Dillon found an open spot against the side wall where he could see the stage. He estimated that there were more than 500 people in the audience.

The meeting began when a middle-aged man introduced the author Paul Goodman to polite applause. Goodman's book, *Growing Up Absurd*, had challenged the suburban status quo of the 1950s. Dillon had tried reading it, but abandoned the book after a few chapters, annoyed by Goodman's strident certainty. Goodman began by reading a poem proclaiming his contempt for "the misrulers of my country."

Then, the novelist Norman Mailer stumbled out onto the stage, a mug in hand. He had decided to play the role of court jester. Mailer, who was wearing a three-piece pinstripe suit, appeared much heavier in person than he did in his book jacket photographs. He addressed the audience without using the microphone, giving a rambling, expletive-filled talk filled with equally sharp attacks on the war in Vietnam and the Washington press corps. Mailer took over as master-of-ceremonies and introduced Dwight Macdonald, the radical social critic and author, who proceeded to read Rupert Kipling's poem, "The White Man's Burden."

Finally, it was Robert Lowell's turn. In the spring, Lowell had refused an invitation to a White House garden party because of his opposition to the war. Dillon was looking forward to hearing Lowell read his poetry aloud. A tall, gangly man with a large head and glasses, Lowell started with his poem "Waking Early Sunday Morning," his voice dropping to a whisper at times. A few people in the crowd called out for him to speak up, and Lowell responded archly that he would bellow, but that it wouldn't do any good. Dillon was surprised at how detached, how diffident, he seemed. When Lowell finished, the audience gave him a standing ovation.

Dillon left after the reading, happy to escape the crowded theater and its musty smells. He had been disappointed at how poorly organized the evening had been. Mailer had played the buffoon, Lowell had seemed disengaged, and the young people sitting on the stone floor seemed more interested in smoking pot and hooting and hollering than in protesting against the war. Dillon wondered if the march would be as disorganized as the Ambassador Theater event. A chaotic demonstration wouldn't impress those in the government deciding current policy.

* * *

On Saturday, Dillon rose late and ate a breakfast of scrambled eggs, Canadian bacon, and buttered toast, washing it down with two cups of coffee. Then, he made his way through crowded streets to the National Mall. It was a sunny day with few clouds. There were helmeted police all around, watching and waiting, and the nearby side streets had been closed off. At the Mall, Dillon was surprised at the size of the crowd that had gathered for the march. As far as the eye could see, demonstrators filled both sides of the reflecting pool. They carried signs that read GET THE HELL OUT OF VIETNAM and BRING OUR GIs HOME NOW! and END THE DRAFT. Dillon spotted banners and placards announcing the presence of organized political groups: SANE, the American Friends Service Committee, CORE, the Southern Christian Leadership Conference and the Students for a Democratic Society. A few demonstrators carried the blue-and-gold flag of the National Liberation Front. He remembered that Evan Bauer had joined the SDS, even though he had to be one of its older members. It wasn't all young people and students. Dillon spotted some well-dressed men, in suits and ties, and middle-aged women in "sensible" clothing.

A platform had been erected in front of the Lincoln Memorial, facing the reflecting pool, in the same location where Martin Luther King had given his "I Have a Dream" speech in 1963. Dillon found a spot where he could hear and see the speakers. They uniformly attacked the war and either advocated a negotiated peace or an immediate American withdrawal. David Dellinger, a radical and pacifist, called for a teach-in for the troops guarding the Pentagon. The crowd stirred, and people began shouting their support for a confrontation across the river.

Dillon heard the sound of a trumpet in the distance, and many in the crowd began to move in the direction of the Potomac. He was curious about what was going to happen at the Pentagon and maneuvered his way to the head of the column, which was led by veterans of the Abraham Lincoln Brigade who had fought against Franco in the Spanish Civil War. A large group of protesters followed them to the Arlington Memorial Bridge, where they crossed the Potomac, and headed to the Pentagon. It was the Old Left and the New Left uniting in opposition to the war.

A helicopter flew overhead. Dillon noticed several photojournalists were taking photos of the demonstrators. He wondered if some of the men with cameras were undercover government agents. It wouldn't help to have the FBI spot him in a photograph in the midst of an antiwar protest. He decided that the odds were incredibly long against that happening, and he continued to follow the crowd. Dillon looked back to a sea of people and placards headed toward the Pentagon.

The crowd surged into the north parking lot near the Pentagon. A ring of soldiers and federal marshals in dark suits and white helmets protected the entrances to the massive building. Dillon watched as some of the demonstrators pulled down the temporary security fences erected around the Pentagon. They approached the soldiers and called out to them to cross the lines and join them. There were no defections. A pretty girl in a peasant blouse stuck flowers in the muzzles of the rifles held by some of the soldiers.

Dillon stepped back to let a few long-haired young men pass, and was surprised to find himself suddenly face-to-face with Evan Bauer. They looked at each other for a long moment. Evan wore a green military field jacket with a button that read "Victory to the National Liberation Front."

"Well, look who's here," he said, sizing up Dillon. "You haven't joined us, have you?"

Dillon didn't know what to say. It was a stroke of bad luck to have encountered Evan. He hadn't forgotten his open hostility at the Bundy-Morgenthau debate. What were the odds that Dillon would run into him in the vast crowd?

"I wanted to see what it was all about," Dillon said. "What the speakers had to say."

"That's bullshit. We don't need spectators. Either you're with us against this fuckin' war, or you're not."

Dillon remained silent. He was sympathetic to some of the demands of the demonstrators—he thought the Administration needed to acknowledge that the current strategy of bullets and bombs was failing miserably, but he couldn't see how immediate withdrawal, or even accepting a neutralist government in Saigon, was anything but a fig leaf for abandoning the South Vietnamese to an ugly fate.

"I don't think it's that simple."

"But it is," Evan said. "Not that what you think matters. You're not in the government, so you can't do a damn thing. But we're going to stop Leviathan. We're going to bring the war home and force Johnson to withdraw the troops."

"And what about the people of South Vietnam?"

"What about them? Except for the corrupt elite, the people support the NLF. They support the revolution."

Dillon shrugged. "Millions of them don't. I think it may be a bit more complicated than you think."

Evan shook his head. "No, it's not. We must stop the fuckin' war machine. Let the Vietnamese make their own choices. Not ones dictated by fat cat capitalists, by imperialists, and their stooges in Washington."

"We have an election next fall," Dillon said. "That will be the test, won't it? From what I see of the polls in the newspapers, half of the country thinks Vietnam is a mistake. If they turn out, you'll get peace candidates elected to Congress."

Even as he made the argument, Dillon knew that Evan would reject it.

"We can't wait for that. We aren't going to rely on fake peace candidates. Do you believe that fuckin' crap? Johnson ran as a fuckin' peace candidate last time and then escalated the fighting. They all lie. This immoral war needs to end now, long before next fall. We're going to use whatever means necessary to accomplish that."

Evan turned and began to move toward the Pentagon, looming ahead of them. "Leave now," he said. "We don't need anyone spying on us. You've been warned. I won't be responsible for what happens if you stay."

* * *

Stories about the march dominated the Sunday newspapers. There had been some violence at the Pentagon. The police had clubbed and arrested some of the demonstrators, with several hundred hauled off to jail. While much of the coverage was hostile, Dillon believed that the size of the march, estimated at 100,000 people, sent a message that the opposition to Johnson's policies was growing. The increased bombing and the troop build-up in Vietnam had caught the attention of more than just the radicals.

Dillon got up early and attended services at St. John's. After church, he was walking down M Street when he spotted Alex Landauer coming out of the front of the City Tavern Club. Dillon considered crossing the street to avoid him, but decided against it. Dillon wondered if Alex was a member of the club, an exclusive private organization, or had been there as someone's guest.

They greeted each other warily. Alex wore dark sunglasses, and Dillon couldn't see his eyes. He asked Alex if he had seen the march.

"I wasn't at the Pentagon," he said, shaking his head. "I missed the barbarians at the gates. I watched some of it on television. A joke. They're lucky that the police and paratroopers were as gentle as they were."

"Gentle? They're saying several demonstrators ended up in the hospital."

"That's what happens when you deliberately break the law, provoke the cops. Everyone has coddled these students. Parents, teachers. Now they're discovering that they're not so special."

"We're losing, what, two hundred men a week in Vietnam? I can see why they would be concerned."

"It's a war," Alex said. "Men die. What did you expect?"

Dillon felt himself flushing with anger. He decided to speak his mind on a different matter. "After that dinner at my place, the last time I saw you, someone broke into Far Ridge looking for Palmer's documents. Then, the FBI came by and questioned me."

Alex didn't respond.

"Did you tell them about what Palmer had left me?" Dillon asked. "You and Jan and Grayson are the only ones that knew about it."

"Do you think I informed on you?" Alex shook his head, disgusted. "I'd never do that. You can't blame me for your troubles. I told you that you should have destroyed whatever Palmer gave you. Who knows how the FBI found out. What about Cora? Maybe she told them."

"Cora?" Dillon stared at him. It was his turn to be disgusted. "That's absurd."

"If the FBI questioned her, who knows what she might say. You said that she was mixed up with hippies in California. Druggies. She'd have every reason to cooperate and get the Feds off her back. So she tells them about Palmer's Washington buddy and how he left San Francisco with some mysterious documents. And this buddy has a White Knight complex. They could have put two and two together."

"And why would they bother to talk to her in the first place?"

"Maybe they're thorough."

"I don't buy that for a moment."

"Then maybe it was a consequence of Palmer shooting his mouth off. He was nuts at the end, you know. We all heard the stories. He probably went around button-holing anyone he could find. Telling them crazy stories about assassination plots and covert operations."

"Crazy stories?"

"Unsubstantiated stories." Alex adjusted his sunglasses and then took them off. "Palmer made enough noise that I wouldn't be surprised if the Agency asked the FBI to look into whatever mischief he was up to."

"After Palmer died? Why would they care, then? No, I think someone tipped them off about what he left me."

"And you think it's me who called them?" Alex shrugged. "Believe what you want. I didn't. But I'd say you deserve to be called on your bullshit. You've always wanted to play by your own set of rules. You and Palmer. Not the ones the rest of us have to follow. If you've got yourself in a jam because of Palmer Knox, don't expect any sympathy from me. As far as I'm concerned, you're responsible for whatever happens. It's your jam."

Dillon shook his head. "Thanks for nothing."

"I'm glad you left the government," Alex responded. "You never had the stomach for what we needed to do. You're like Bobby Kennedy and Javits and the others who keep calling for a bombing halt. As if we haven't tried that. And all Kennedy and the others do is embolden Ho and Giap. We have to stay the course. If anything, we need to bomb them more. Destroy their will to fight."

"If this continues, you'll lose the country," Dillon said. "Can't you see that?"

Alex put his sunglasses back on and turned to leave. "So it's Dillon the dove. Can't say I'm surprised. You've always been a bit soft. But you're wrong on this. Trust me. Wait and see."

FORTY-ONE

Charlottesville
Winter 1968

Back at Far Ridge, Dillon began the New Year with a new project—translating poetry from the German, Latin, and Italian. His inspiration was Robert Lowell's *Imitations*, with its eclectic collection of translated verse. He began with poems by Heine and Rilke. He decided he would turn to the Roman poets next, and he purchased Loeb Classical Library volumes of Catullus, Propertius, and Ovid. Dillon decided to wait before trying his hand at Italian poetry—he needed to brush up on his facility with the language first.

He continued to struggle with his own poetry. He had written a love sonnet or two, but they lacked genuine emotion, and he hated their artificiality. At least the translation project offered him an outlet for his creative energy while he waited for the return of what he thought of as his fickle muse.

He enjoyed the challenge of trying to capture the spirit and imagery of a poem in a language not his own, of refashioning it into English line by line. Above his desk, he posted a note card on the wall with a quote from Robert Frost: "Poetry is what is lost in translation." Dillon spent the late afternoons and early evenings in his office, a mug of coffee on the desk, piles of poetry books, foreign language dictionaries, and reference works surrounding him. There were days when he ignored the newspapers and nightly televised news, instead losing himself in solving the latest creative puzzle. He welcomed the intellectual challenge and the feeling of escape it gave him.

On the next to last day of January, Dillon was crafting an English version of Catullus 51, one of the series of poems addressed to Lesbia, when the phone rang. It was Leigh.

"You might want to turn on the television," Leigh said. "There's big trouble in Vietnam."

"What sort of trouble? Another coup?"

"No, much worse. From what they're saying, the Viet Cong and North Vietnamese have launched all-out attacks throughout the country. Coordinated. They've hit Saigon and Hue."

"Saigon? That's an unpleasant surprise."

"It's all a surprise. It appears to be a major offensive."

When Dillon turned on the television, he found that Leigh was correct and there was heavy fighting raging across Vietnam. In the days that followed, Dillon followed the desperate battle: scenes of soldiers and Marines pinned down under heavy fire; the breaching of the U.S. Embassy grounds in Saigon; the reality that neither American or ARVN military intelligence had anticipated the sudden attacks. For Dillon, it was a validation of his worst fears.

In the middle of February, he called Mary Warren for her insights on what the newspapers had begun calling the Tet Offensive.

"It's been a shock," Mary told him. "Westmoreland and the Joint Chiefs kept telling the world that the end of the war was near. This attack has put the lie to that. It was quite grim at first, but the latest reports have been more encouraging. The North Vietnamese counted on a popular uprising, but that hasn't happened. Won't happen. Some of the ARVN units have stood up fairly well. I hear that the Pentagon is confident we'll retake whatever ground we've lost, but the damage has been done to their credibility. And Johnson's. A battlefield victory, but a political defeat."

"At best, our generals have been deluded about progress. At worst, they've been lying to Congress and to all of us."

"I vote for worst," she said. "They haven't wanted to admit that we've been caught in a vicious spiral. When we expand the bombing and increase troop levels, Hanoi sends more men down the Ho Chi Minh trail. Neither side gains an advantage. A classic stalemate."

"How is morale in the office?"

"Lousy. It's hard to put a good face on what's happening." She paused. "I'm leaving Main State, Dillon. I'll be in Saigon next month, working for AID on rural development. I speak the language, and I can't sit back at a distance any longer. I want to contribute however I can in a more direct way."

"Good luck," Dillon said.

"Thanks," she said. "Good luck seems in short supply these days. I'll take however much of it I can get."

* * *

In late March, Dillon met Charlie Woods for a round of golf at the Farmington Country Club. Charlie had recently been made a member at Farmington and wanted to show Dillon how much his golf game had improved.

After their eighteen holes, they relaxed in the Clubhouse with a lunch of roast beef sandwiches, potato chips, and sweet tea. Their talk turned to politics, and Charlie mentioned how he and many of his friends had been deeply troubled by the Tet Offensive.

"How the hell did that happen?" he asked Dillon. "How could we have been caught by surprise?"

"We haven't been getting the straight story from the generals."

"The photo of the execution of that Viet Cong prisoner on the street in Saigon turned my stomach," Charlie said. "It was grisly. I made sure my kids didn't see the newspaper that day."

Dillon nodded. The executioner had been South Vietnam's chief of National Police, Nguyen Ngoc Loan, and he had shot the handcuffed prisoner in the head with his sidearm. An Associated Press photographer, Eddie Adams, had captured the grisly scene and the photograph had been widely reprinted.

"It brings the nasty reality of war home," Dillon said. "How savage it can be. If Loan were an American, he'd be prosecuted for a war crime. You can't shoot prisoners."

"You know what I hear from some of my friends and clients? They don't like this war. They want it to be over. They don't want their sons drafted. They think it's a fight for the South Vietnamese, not for us."

"What about you?" Dillon asked.

Charlie shrugged. "I think we're doing the right thing. More or less. You know Southerners aren't afraid of a fight. We want to fight to win, or get out." He took a sip of his ice tea. "What about Bobby Kennedy? Can he win the nomination?"

That Charlie could even ask the question suggested to Dillon how quickly the national political landscape had changed. Johnson had only eked out a win in the Democratic New Hampshire presidential primary, edging out Senator Eugene McCarthy of Minnesota, an antiwar candidate. Kennedy entered the presidential race in mid-March, a move that had angered many of McCarthy's young supporters.

"I think Kennedy is sincere about wanting to end the war," Dillon said. "He doesn't think McCarthy can beat LBJ, or for that matter, Nixon. I think Bobby has guts, running for the Presidency after what happened to Jack."

"All of the Kennedys have that in spades," Charlie said. "Guts, that is. I wonder if that will be enough."

* * *

It proved to be a very strange spring, one filled with contradictions and surprises. As Dillon immersed himself in translating centuries-old love poetry, there was a dizzying train of events in the political world. At the end of March, Lyndon Johnson halted some of the bombing of North Vietnam and called for peace talks with Hanoi. In the same nationally-televised speech, Johnson shocked the Washington establishment by announcing that he wouldn't run for reelection. The vice president, Hubert Humphrey, entered the race weeks later. In early April, Martin Luther King, Jr. was assassinated in Memphis by a white man. In the days that followed, American cities burned: Chicago, New York, Baltimore, Cincinnati, Kansas City, Detroit. In Washington, there were four days of rioting, looting, and violence. Dillon called his next-door Georgetown neighbors and learned that the skies over the District of Columbia had filled with smoke, and in the streets the police and National Guard were battling the rioters.

There was one moment of light. In Indianapolis, on the night of King's murder, Bobby Kennedy had addressed a grieving crowd, eulogizing Dr. King and calling for an end to violence and social injustice. He talked about the pain of dealing with the death of his own brother, quoting a passage from Aeschylus by heart: *"In our sleep, pain which cannot forget falls drop by drop upon the heart until, in our own despair, against our will, comes wisdom through the awful grace of God."* Kennedy had closed his improvised speech with a call for love and wisdom, and compassion, and to "to tame the savageness of man and make gentle the life of this world." And Indianapolis didn't burn.

* * *

Dillon spent more time in Georgetown as the weather improved. He took his books and dictionaries with him and kept working on his translations. Thinking ahead, he hired a graduate student to tutor him in Italian. At some point, Dillon hoped to translate portions of Dante's *Divine Comedy*.

Grayson Talbott was traveling with Senator Kennedy's campaign. He sent postcards to Dillon from the campaign trail, from Kansas, Nebraska, Wisconsin, South Dakota, Oregon, and California. Kennedy had proven to be an unconventional candidate. It seemed that the Senator from New York had been transformed into a crusader for the poor and downtrodden. A man who had been called the Irish Roy Cohn by his liberal detractors, the hard-edged political operative known for his ruthlessness, had become a hero to the young and many of the intellectuals (who had previously despised him as complicit in Joe McCarthy's Red Scare). Bobby challenged the war, challenged America's indifference to poverty, quoting Bob Dylan and Marshall McLuhan while appealing to the better instincts of his countrymen. Dillon wondered whether it had been the impact of Jack's death that had changed him. Whatever his reasons, Bobby Kennedy had become a symbol of a new inspirational politics, one that appealed across class and racial lines.

Then, abruptly, on the night of the California Democratic presidential primary, the unthinkable happened—another Kennedy assassinated, cut down in his prime. Dillon couldn't understand how after Dallas a man with a gun could get so close to the candidate. The assassin, a Jordanian-American named Sirhan Sirhan, had targeted Kennedy over his support of Israel. Dillon had assumed that any threat to Bobby would have come from the Kennedy haters on the right, or perhaps from organized crime because of his prosecution of Jimmy Hoffa and the Teamsters. It didn't make sense that he would be killed over the jumbled politics of the Middle East.

There was renewed talk of conspiracies. Was there a link to his brother's death in Dallas? Or to Dr. King's murder? The two men who had most directly challenged the status quo in American society had met the same fate within months. Coincidence? It was hard to believe that an angry loner had again changed the country's destiny. Dillon didn't believe in a grand conspiracy, but he did think that the politics of the day had become dark and toxic, an encouragement to extremism.

Once again, the country mourned the loss of a dashing young leader. Dillon watched the televised coverage of the New Yorkers, rich and poor, who filed past Senator Kennedy's casket in St. Patrick's Cathedral. A haggard Grayson Talbott showed up on Dillon's doorstep a few days later. He had been on the train from New York that brought Robert Kennedy's body to Washington for the funeral, and Dillon invited him to stay with him in Georgetown for as long as he wanted.

"I haven't been able to sleep since he was murdered," Grayson confessed. "I was at the Ambassador Hotel, on the other side of the ballroom. We heard people screaming and yelling. I've never experienced anything like it. The shock and disbelief. Again? A second fucking time?"

Tears began rolling down Grayson's cheeks. He brushed them aside. "The train ride was amazing. People lined the tracks all the way to Washington, holding American flags and signs. People from all walks of life. They knew Bobby was there for them. The last few weeks of the campaign in Oregon and California were amazing. Never seen anything like it. We'd arrange for the Senator to visit places like Watts, to meet with Cesar Chavez and the farmworkers. Bobby would ride in convertibles so the people could see him. Shirtsleeves and a tie. They would crowd next to the vehicle, and reach out. They wanted to touch him. To see the looks on their faces, Dillon. They had hope. They had a champion. For the first time since FDR, they had someone who cared deeply about the poor. *Some men see things as they are, and ask why. I dream of things that never were, and ask why not.*' God, what a tragedy to lose him this way." He paused and mopped his face with his handkerchief. "I'm going on and on, aren't I?"

"You have a lot to get off your chest."

"I do. It's not only the country who has lost him. His family. Ethel and his children. And Jackie and hers." He stared off into the distance. "Bobby would have led us to a better place."

"What about Senator McCarthy? Will he inherit Bobby's supporters?"

"It was never about just ending the war. It was changing the country. McCarthy doesn't feel that in his bones. He's an intellectual. He'd rather write a poem than help the poor." He glanced over at Dillon. "No offense meant."

"None taken."

"Once in a generation, Dillon. Bobby was the leader who comes along once in a generation. Even more so than Jack, he could have accomplished marvelous things."

"I understand there's a move by some of the Kennedy delegates to support Senator McGovern. To try to keep Humphrey from getting the nomination."

Grayson shook his head. "That's not going to work. It's over. And I'm done with politics. I'm going back to New York, and I'm going to try to live a normal life. I won't pretend that I'm not bitter, because I am. I'm bitter as hell. But there's no changing the bad things that happened, and I'm just going to have to live with it. Like it or not. We all are."

FORTY-TWO

They arrived at Corolla, a small town located on the Outer Banks of North Carolina, in the last week of August. Leigh had convinced Dillon to join him for a brief vacation by the ocean.

"I want to sit on a porch, feel the breeze, and watch the surf," Leigh said. "I haven't been to the Outer Banks in twenty years. It'd do us both some good to get away."

"That's the week of the Convention."

"They have television sets in North Carolina. Besides, I think it will be pretty cut-and-dried. Humphrey has the nomination locked up, from what I can gather. It should be relatively smooth sailing."

"Maybe," Dillon said. "The wild card is the protesters."

There was the potential for trouble at the Democratic National Convention. While the beginning of peace talks with the North Vietnamese in Paris had given opponents of the war some hope, the more radical elements of the protest movement weren't satisfied. They had announced that they were coming to Chicago to disrupt the proceedings. Students for a Democratic Society. The Mobe. The Black Panthers and the Young Lords. The Yippies, who promised a "Celebration of Life," complete with pranks and theatrics. Chicago Mayor Richard Daley and the local authorities decided to ring the International Amphitheater, the site of the convention, with a chain-link fence and barbed wire—hardly a promising symbolic touch, as Leigh noted—and brought in private security guards to supplement the Chicago police and the National Guard.

Dillon and Leigh drove to North Carolina on Sunday and settled into their seaside cottage. The first days of their vacation were idyllic. Dillon played two sets of tennis with a local pro on Monday, and Leigh stationed himself in a rocking chair on the front porch and read the Sunday *New York Times* and watched the ocean. That night, they grilled steaks and fresh corn for dinner. Dillon went swimming in the Atlantic the next morning, bracing for the initial shock of the cold, and then enjoying his time in the water.

On Wednesday, they left the television tuned into the Democratic Convention in Chicago. Dillon had to adjust the antenna to better pick up the signal from a nearby CBS affiliate. They watched as the delegates voted to give Vice President Humphrey the presidential nomination and rejected Senator McCarthy's antiwar platform, instead endorsing the Administration's Vietnam policies. Outside of the convention hall, trouble was brewing. A group of demonstrators who had been denied a permit sought to march from Grant Park to the convention hall. The Chicago police confronted them on Michigan Avenue in front of the Hilton Hotel. The showdown quickly deteriorated into violence, as the helmeted police clubbed the mostly young protesters to the ground. Huge clouds of tear gas covered the streets. Many of the protesters began chanting: "The whole world is watching."

Leigh shook his head. "This is a disaster. A televised disaster."

"The police are out of control," Dillon said. "What is Mayor Daley thinking?"

"He thinks that it's his city, and he'll be damned if he lets college kids and hippies show him up. Daley thinks in terms of power. He has it, and he's going to use. You can see why. The demonstrators are nihilists. The lot of them. Spoiled children who don't know how good they've got it, and are trying to burn down the house around them out of spite because they didn't get what they wanted."

"I understand why they're protesting," Dillon said. "The students want the war to end. They're angry about that. Can you blame them? They're tired of the lies and the killing."

"Will this accomplish anything?" Leigh asked, gesturing toward the scenes of violence and protest flickering across the television screen. The cameras caught a glimpse of a long-haired young man, blood dripping down his face, being dragged to a waiting police van. "Rioting.

Smashing windows. Throwing rocks. Fighting with the police. It plays into the hands of Nixon and his demagoguery about law and order. Do you think the average American watching this at home sees this as anything but anarchy?"

"I see the Chicago police running amok."

"More than half the country will say the hippie troublemakers had it coming. When it comes time to vote, they'll remember the chaos. The cops look like their friends and neighbors. Not the protesters."

Leigh switched off the television set. He found glasses and ice and poured two bourbons, handing one to Dillon.

"I can't watch this any longer," he said. "It's going to put that bastard Nixon in the White House."

"Humphrey has a chance," Dillon said. "He has to put some distance between himself and Johnson's policies."

Leigh frowned. "He won't. To do that, he'd have to admit the war is a mistake and Big Lyndon has been dead wrong."

"We're off course," Dillon said. "That's clear."

"Humphrey has other problems. Like it or not, people are going to blame him for what's going on in the country. The attack on tradition and on values. Small-town lawyers see it all, you know. The family troubles. Adultery. Divorce. Children arguing with their parents, dropping out of school, using drugs. It's gotten worse. It's not pretty." He looked at Dillon. "We all have our disappointments. Personal ones. I hoped that you would follow in your father's footsteps. You would have been a sight better than that nonentity we've sent to Washington."

Dillon shook his head, surprised. "That was supposed to be Wash. You full well know that. Not me. I never wanted that."

"It hasn't worked out the way it was supposed to," Leigh said. "Not with the country. Not with you. Or your marriage. I'm sorry about that. I had hoped that you'd be raising a family at Far Ridge by now." Tears came to his eyes. "I wish I knew how it went off course. All of it. It's a damn mystery to me. A mystery."

* * *

After Leigh had gone to bed, Dillon left the cottage and went for a walk along the shore. Moonlight illuminated the beach and the surface of the Atlantic Ocean, stretching beyond as far as the eye could see. The surf rolled in and out, and he breathed in the smell of the ocean. He was unsettled from the images of the violence at the convention, and from his conversation with Leigh.

It stung to know that he had disappointed his uncle. It wasn't fair. Dillon had honored the family tradition of service—his years at State had to count for something. He made no apologies for not entering elective politics; he wasn't suited for it. He was happiest teaching and writing, and he wouldn't sacrifice that to pursue a job he didn't want.

There wasn't anything he could do about his personal life, and the failure of his marriage, his distance—geographical and emotional—from his daughter. He felt a sense of defeat when he thought about it. Did his uncle's past, his own divorce, play some part in the keenness of his disappointment with Dillon? There was nothing Dillon could do now to change any of it. He had to accept the situation and live with it and his regrets. Who didn't have regrets? Who hadn't made mistakes?

He looked up at the stars, wondering about the pain and tragedy of the past months, the assassinations, the racial tension, the alienated young people, the division in American society. He had to agree with Leigh, there was a darkness, a despair, an anger in the country, as if someone had opened a modern Pandora's Box and evil spirits had flown out. They seemed to have spread around the world, for the discontent and the violence hadn't been confined only to America.

Dillon stood for a moment at the water's edge. On the horizon, he could see the lights of a distant cargo ship blinking. The surf kept rolling onto the beach, hissing as it retreated, returning with another surge moments later. He thought about the next day, and whether it would be awkward between them. Perhaps he could rent a boat and a guide and convince Leigh to go fishing. He remembered how Captain Curzon, his fishing guide in the Keys, believed that getting out on the water simplified everything, put things in proper perspective. It was worth a try.

FORTY-THREE

New York City
Fall 1968

When Jill had called on short notice and asked Dillon to meet in midtown Manhattan, he had hesitated before agreeing. A trip north would be inconvenient—he would have to drive from Charlottesville and fly from National Airport to LaGuardia. He would have preferred that she come to Georgetown—he knew that her returning to Far Ridge was out of the question—but he suspected that she would want to avoid Washington with all of the memories a visit there would trigger.

During the past year, she hadn't encouraged contact from Dillon beyond occasional phone calls to Sandy. He tried to stay in touch as best he could, but the distance made that difficult. He sent his daughter birthday and Christmas gifts and wrote her brief letters every couple of months. In return, he would get thank you notes in Sandy's childish scrawl. It was far from what he wanted.

Jill didn't bring Sandy on her trip to the East Coast, and she was evasive when Dillon asked why. He agreed to meet her on a Tuesday afternoon at the Carlyle Hotel, where she was staying with her boyfriend, Austen Sanderson, a divorce lawyer in the Los Angeles firm that had represented Jill. At least he hadn't been directly involved in their case, or so Jill claimed.

Dillon waited for her in the hotel's Art Deco bar. Its walls featured murals of Central Park, painted by Ludwig Bemelmans, the creator of the classic Madeline children's books. After Jill arrived, slender and lovely in a light blue dress, they ordered drinks; a glass of white wine for Jill and a whiskey sour for Dillon. After the waiter had left, they sat in uncomfortable silence for a long moment.

"How are you, Jill?" Dillon asked.

"I'm fine," she said.

"And Sandy, how is she?"

"She is doing well."

"I'm disappointed that you didn't bring her. I'd like to come out to California and see her."

Jill didn't say anything. She took a sip of her drink. "I saw your buddy Alex Landauer on television the other day. He's back at Harvard, talking about how immoral Vietnam is, how he could no longer stay in the government. A matter of conscience. He sounded very high-minded."

"High-minded? Alex is an opportunist. His change of heart is because he's worried about his academic career. Supporting the war would make him radioactive on any campus in the country."

"So you don't think it's sincere?"

"Anything is possible, but mark me down as a skeptic. Alex was one of the original hawks."

Alex's hypocrisy didn't surprise Dillon. Ambition had been his guiding light. Alex was clever enough to turn the fact that he had been one of the architects and cheerleaders of the policies he was now denouncing into a story of redemption. He had seen the error of his ways. He had seen the light.

"And you, Dillon? What responsibility do you have?"

"Some. I don't deny that. But I never supported escalating the war. That wasn't Hilsman's approach, or mine. You know that. We thought the way to win was to build popular support for the Saigon government. When Johnson took over, we lost the argument and the Pentagon won. They sold LBJ on the idea that with enough troops and bombs they could get the war over fast so that he could get back to building his Great Society."

She sighed. "Men and their politics."

"I ran into your friend Evan Bauer last year at the March on the

Pentagon. He's as radical as they come. He claims he's ready to do whatever it takes to end the war."

She wrinkled her nose. "Evan was always trying to get me into bed. Trying to get me alone. He thought he was irresistible with all his talk of Sartre and Michel Foucault and how we needed a revolution. I told him that it was never going to happen. Us, in bed, that is. I finally let Darla know what he was up to behind her back. I didn't see much of him after that, and I can't say it was a loss."

"So why am I here?" Dillon asked. "You told me over the phone that it involved Sandy. An important matter."

"I thought I should tell you face-to-face. Austen has asked me to marry him, and I've said yes. Because of Sandy, I thought it might be awkward for you."

"No reason for it to be."

"We would expect the child support and other financial arrangements to continue. No interruption."

"I'm good for my commitments," Dillon said, flushing with anger. "Haven't I supported you and Sandy financially without complaint since you walked out on me? Have you ever wanted for money? Did you think the divorce settlement was unfair? Not a word of complaint from you at the time."

She wouldn't meet his gaze. "It's not about the past, Dillon. Circumstances have changed. Austen has more experience in these matters. He says people can be unpredictable. There can be friction when there's a remarriage. A new husband."

"Sandy will always be taken care of," Dillon said. He rose to his feet. "If that's all, I'll be on my way. I didn't need to come all the way to New York to be insulted."

"I'm sorry," she said. "I didn't mean to insult you. Please stay a little longer. I don't want you to go away mad."

Dillon opened his wallet and placed a twenty dollar bill on the table. "For the drinks," he said. "In his own way, Leigh tried to warn me about this. He pegged your mother as mercenary to the core. I told him that you were different. It looks like I was wrong."

"You've never known what it's like to be poor," Jill said. "To not have nice clothes and have the other girls mock you. To eat macaroni and cheese because it's cheap and fills you up. To move from one sad and shabby rental to the next. You have no idea what that's like. Do you think it was easy for me to leave you?"

"Have you ever wanted for anything from the day I married you?"

"No," she conceded. "Not for anything material."

"I have a question. Has your boyfriend been married before?"

Jill blushed. "What does that have to do with anything?"

"You didn't answer my question."

"His divorce came through last year. They didn't get along. She was very difficult. There were no children, so it didn't get messy."

"Good luck, then," Dillon said. "It sounds like you're well matched."

"I'm sorry, Dillon, that it's come to this. I truly am."

"No more than I."

* * *

Dillon took a cab downtown to the Minetta Tavern on Macdougal Street, where he was to meet Grayson Talbott for an early dinner. He found Grayson at a corner table in the back, a martini on the table in front of him. Dillon glanced over at the faded fresco of scenes of historic Greenwich Village that decorated the walls—it seemed he was destined to spend the day in rooms with murals. Grayson motioned for Dillon to take the seat opposite him.

"I thought about inviting you to dinner at the White Horse Tavern," Grayson said. "But it's not a great place for poets named Dillon. It's where Dylan Thomas drank himself to death. Eighteen shots and a quick trip to St. Vincent's Hospital."

"That's a cheery welcome," Dillon said.

Grayson signaled the waiter, and Dillon ordered a whiskey sour. He might as well stick with the same drink. Grayson nodded when the waiter asked if he wanted a refill.

"It's been a cheery day," Dillon said. "I just spent some time with Jill at the Carlyle. She's getting remarried. To a divorce lawyer. A recently-divorced divorce lawyer who wanted Jill to make sure I wasn't going to renege on the child support."

"Did you meet him?"

"No, and I didn't particularly want to. If he sticks around, I guess that eventually I will."

The waiter returned with their drinks, and they ordered dinner. Grayson wanted to hear the latest Washington gossip and made a wry face when Dillon admitted he spent very little time in the city.

"They say Nixon is leaning toward William Rogers for State," Grayson said. "It's hard to believe that son of a bitch is going to be president, let alone that he's picking a Cabinet. Rogers is a lawyer, not a diplomat, so I guess it means Nixon will run his own foreign policy show."

"You're still politically active?" Dillon asked.

"Not at all," Grayson said. "I'm done. I can't take any more pain and disappointment. I'm tending my personal garden, just like you. After what happened to Jack, and then Bobby, I don't have the heart for politics. And I've concluded that the damn country didn't deserve them. The country deserves Nixon."

"The country would have been immeasurably better off with Humphrey, flawed as he is."

"Would it?" Grayson took a sip of his martini. "Maybe Nixon can extricate us from Vietnam. Declare victory and finally get us out."

"His secret plan?" Dillon snorted in derision. "I doubt that."

"Well, we'll see soon enough."

The waiter returned with their steaks and side orders. After he had left, Grayson picked up the conversation.

"Do you miss State at all?" he asked.

"I don't. I paid a price for my stay there. It cost me my marriage, among other things."

"I'm sorry to hear that. My time in the White House, working for Jack, was golden for me. That and Bobby's last campaign. I felt like we were moving the country in the right direction. If only Bobby had lived."

"And you? How is Marion?"

"It's over between us," he said. He avoided looking at Dillon directly. "She kept the apartment on the East Side, and I moved down here, to the Village."

"I'm sorry to hear that."

Grayson cleared his throat. "I'm not, Dillon. Marion is a fine woman, and it's not her fault that the marriage broke down. It wasn't her. It was that I wasn't being true to myself. I know that sounds like a cliché." He looked down for a moment, embarrassed. Then he took a gulp of his martini. "In my case, it's the truth. It's taken most of my life to admit this to myself, but I'm attracted to the male of the species. I haven't wanted to acknowledge that, but I had a health scare recently, and I realized that I didn't want to keep on living a lie."

Dillon remained silent. He had no inkling of the turmoil in Grayson's inner life. There wasn't anything overtly effeminate about his friend. Grayson had always been impeccably dressed, but Dillon had chalked that up to his advertising agency background. There had been no other signs, at least none that Dillon could think of.

"And yes, I've been through therapy," Grayson said. "It's not my relationship with my mother or my father. I've fought this since I was ten years old. I knew I was different. There were a few, ah, episodes when I was in my late teens. I compensated by throwing myself into my work. I was a monk when I was in Washington, and then I met Marion. I told myself that maybe she could cure me. Of course, that was absurd. I tried. I did try. The funny thing is that when I finally told her, she wasn't surprised. She said she had always suspected, always wondered."

He stopped and looked at Dillon. "You haven't said anything."

"I'm your friend," Dillon said. "That will never change. Remember, I had a posting in Berlin. They're a lot more open there about such things. They're right. To each his own. It's not my business what you do in bed."

Grayson sighed, clearly relieved. "Thanks. I've only told a few people. Most have been supportive, although I guess you never know what people really think." He paused. "Do you remember that fight I had with Alex Landauer last year at your place? When he made the nasty comment about the pretty boys in the White House. I don't know whether he had figured it out about me, but it terrified me that he could expose me. Even now it bothers me."

"Alex was just trying to be a tough guy," Dillon said. "Overcompensating for his Harvard connections. Anyone associated with Kennedy or the Ivy League was considered soft by LBJ. They say he used to mock McGeorge Bundy for playing tennis on the Vineyard. Called it a sissy sport."

Grayson nodded. "Well, I see that Alex is crusading now against the war. He's on television and in the papers talking about how sorry he is that he was part of a mistaken approach. If I didn't know better, I'd think he had a change of heart."

"What about your work?" Dillon asked. "I assume that you're very careful about what's known about your personal life."

"I am. I'm very discreet. You know how office gossip spreads. If it got to some of our clients, it could be a problem. I'd hate to lose an account because some vice president thinks I'm a pervert who likes young boys."

"I don't see how they would know. You don't come across like you're different. Like that."

"But I am different. You mean I don't lisp or wave my hands around. You'd be surprised how many macho types are secretly homosexuals, Dillon. You'd never guess when you met them."

"And Marion? How is she doing?"

"She's moved on. A new, younger boyfriend." He smiled broadly for the first time. "I guess that's the something we have in common, now. A younger boyfriend." He took a sip of his whiskey. "When I was working at the White House, Jack gave an inscribed plaque to Dave Powers that read: 'There are three things which are real: God, human folly and laughter. The first two are beyond our comprehension, so we must do what we can with the third.' I've come to see that was great advice. So I'm trying to laugh as much as I can, for as long as I can."

As they were leaving the restaurant, Grayson placed his hand on Dillon's coat sleeve. "One other thing," he said. "It's a day for telling secrets. You should know that I was the one who called the FBI about Palmer and the documents. Not Alex. I wanted them to scare you off because I didn't want Bobby damaged."

"That was a shitty thing to do, Grayson."

"I'd do worse to protect Bobby. Now, it doesn't matter. He's gone."

"You know what? Someday it's going to come out. All of it."

"I hope not. Jack and Bobby aren't here to defend themselves. Who knows what happened? Who knows who gave the orders? And if there were excesses, there was nothing venal about it. Their motives were pure—they did whatever they did in the national interest." He paused, his handsome face drawn, and his eyes glistening. "I know you must feel that I betrayed you, Dillon. I didn't. I saved you from doing something that you would have regretted. Something that would have caused terrible damage."

"It's going to come out," Dillon said. "Too many lies have been told by too many people. Not just then, but now. No one in Washington has been telling the truth about the war. There's going to be a reckoning, and it won't be pretty."

* * *

When Dillon returned to Charlottesville, he found a basket of mail waiting for him at Far Ridge. Buried among the magazines and bills, he discovered a postcard with a photo of the Western Wall in Jerusalem. When Dillon turned it over, he saw there was a brief message written on the back. *Dillon, We have a son, Jacob Solomon, born in the Promised Land, November 12, 1968. Come to Jerusalem and meet him! Yours, Naomi.*

He was composing a letter to Naomi when the doorbell rang. It was his friend, Charlie Woods, with a somber look on his face.

"I'm afraid I've got terrible news," Charlie said. "It's Clay Blackburn. He was killed in Vietnam two days ago. They contacted his mother, and I just heard about it. Word is that she's pretty torn up about it."

Dillon felt a wave of sadness. He knew Clay was at risk when he was in the field, but somehow his friend had always managed to duck the proverbial bullet—until now. "Any details on what happened?"

"Killed in action during a search-and-destroy operation. He was with Task Force Yankee in the An Hoa area. An ambush."

Dillon shook his head. "Clay was a fatalist, Charlie. He told me once that he didn't worry about dying, that if it was his time there was nothing he could do about it. I'm going to miss him. He was a good man. A good Marine."

Charlie grimaced. "Much too good a man to waste in that Godforsaken place. It's not worth another American life. Not a single one."

"This year can't end soon enough for me," Dillon said. "It's been a bad one. And now the news about Clay. They say when it rains, it pours. It's been a hell of a storm."

PART FIVE

FORTY-FOUR

Charlottesville
Winter 1975

In late January, Leigh's health began to noticeably fail. He came down with a nasty cold, and when it persisted, he had to be hospitalized for pneumonia. After a course of antibiotics, he recovered well enough to return to Far Ridge, where he spent another two weeks in bed. Dillon arranged for a nurse to stay at the house so Leigh could get around-the-clock attention. His uncle protested that it was a waste of money, but it was clear that Leigh was still too weak to see after himself.

Dillon spent as much time with him as he could spare. Leigh had better days where he had the energy to come downstairs for breakfast. On the third Tuesday in February, Dillon found him at the breakfast table, a copy of the newspaper next to his plate of scrambled eggs. He peered at Dillon over his reading glasses. "You might want to read this," he said, handing him the front section of the *Washington Post*. Leigh pointed to the lead story, which was about the formation of a special Senate committee chaired by Idaho's Frank Church to investigate past abuses by America's intelligence agencies.

Congress was responding to a *New York Times* story by Seymour Hersh, claiming that the government had been illegally spying on thousands of Americans. Hersh was the investigative reporter who had exposed the horror of My Lai, where American troops had massacred hundreds of Vietnamese villagers. Dillon had been sickened by the details of the atrocity exposed at the trial of the officer in command, Lt. William Calley. He had been deeply troubled by those who tried to defend the killings as part of fighting a dirty war. My Lai didn't occur in a vacuum. In a conflict where body counts and kill ratios were used to measure progress, and where brutality was met with more brutality, it wasn't surprising that some descended into barbarism. That Calley only served three years of his life term under house arrest and that more officers in the chain of command didn't face punishment struck Dillon as a clear perversion of justice.

"They're looking at the entire alphabet—CIA, the FBI, the NSA, and the IRS," Leigh said. "Senator Church is a tough cookie. A maverick. There's no telling how far he's willing to go." He sighed. "Things were just starting to settle down. Jerry Ford in the White House. Students getting back to studying."

Leigh had the mood right—campuses around the country had settled down. Despite his opposition to the war, Leigh had mixed feelings about the protests against Vietnam that had come to the University, and Charlottesville, in May 1970. A crowd of several thousand students had gathered at the Rotunda to hear William Kunstler, the radical lawyer, and Jerry Rubin, the Yippie activist, speak. Leigh saw the pair as political opportunists using the protest movement to attack the values and traditions he held dear. In fact, Virginia was never in danger of becoming Columbia or Berkeley. Students briefly occupied Maury Hall, the Navy ROTC building, but there had been no sustained campus-wide unrest.

"It is quieter now," Dillon said.

"We've got nearly all the boys back home. Too late, but we're out of that sinkhole."

Leigh had taken some comfort in the belated withdrawal of American combat troops from Vietnam after the Paris Peace Accords. He had always disliked Richard Nixon, and he blamed him for prolonging the war and for ordering the "incursion" into Cambodia. "Incursion?" Leigh had asked incredulously at the time. "What poppycock. It's a full-scale invasion." He was pleased when Nixon resigned in disgrace, even though he thought that the proposed articles of impeachment in Congress overstated the extent of his wrongdoing.

"The Church Committee hearings could be a positive thing," Dillon said. "Perhaps the start of an overdue reckoning. Shining the spotlight on the dark corners. I'm all for that. I'd like to help that process."

Leigh frowned. "What are you thinking, Dillon?"

"I'm thinking that this might be the time to turn over what Palmer left me to this committee."

Leigh gave him a hard stare. "How can that be? You told me that you destroyed the documents. I remember the conversation distinctly. I wrote a letter to the FBI stating that you didn't have them."

"I told you that I didn't have Palmer's confession and classified documents in my possession at Far Ridge. I didn't. I buried them in a metal canister on the hillside, about a quarter of a mile from here."

"So you deceived me."

"You heard what you wanted to hear. I never said I destroyed them. I could never do that because I hoped that this day might come."

"I'm disappointed in you, Dillon. Why would you ever want to get involved in this mess? Are you looking to salve your conscience? What Palmer asked you to do wasn't reasonable. You owe him nothing. If you go ahead with this, have you thought about the damage airing our dirty laundry can cause?"

"*Our* laundry?"

"You know what I mean. I don't deny that some of our leaders made mistakes in judgment, but they thought they were advancing the national interest. Sometimes they overstepped, but men do hard things during times of war. They bend the rules. Ignore the law. But to reveal these sorts of things now will hurt the country. We haven't recovered from the Pentagon Papers. Senator Church's sideshow will damage what little trust people have left in their government."

Dillon understood Leigh's concern about the impact of the Pentagon Papers on how Americans viewed their leaders. The leaking of the documents had exposed the duplicity of Jack Kennedy and Lyndon Johnson's key advisers and how they had lied repeatedly about the state of the war in Vietnam.

"Perhaps they need to earn that trust," Dillon said.

"And what of overseas? You were a diplomat. What do you think the rest of the world will say? The Soviets will capitalize on it for their propaganda, notwithstanding that their regime is up to its neck in blood. The Chinese, too."

"We need to confront what was done in our name. That's more important."

"Not now. Some rocks aren't meant to be turned over. Some things should remain secret."

"I can't agree with you," Dillon said. "It needs to be out in the open. *Fiat justitia ruat cælum.* Let justice be done, though the heavens fall."

"I've always hated that saying," Leigh said. "It's too self-righteous for my taste. What's left after you tear everything down in the name of what you've decided is justice? Have you thought about that? You destroy trust. Reputations. You pave the way for the demagogues and the opportunists."

"We don't need to tear everything down. We do need an accounting. I believe shameful things were done, Leigh, and the way to keep them from happening again is to expose them to the light of day."

Leigh shook his head. "I hope you think this through. People need something to believe in. You know I never cared much for the Kennedy brothers, but dragging them through the muck now only blackens their reputation and accomplishes nothing. Do you want that?"

"We have to take the good with the bad," Dillon said. "And haven't we learned by now what happens when the people in power don't think they're accountable? Palmer Knox has been gone nearly ten years now—who in the government lifted a finger to stop what was going on? I hate what they did in our name. It was a betrayal of what this country should stand for. Finally, there's a reckoning, and it's long past due."

* * *

The American military presence in South Vietnam might have been dramatically reduced in scope, but there were some continuing reminders of the war. Dillon spotted the headline, below the fold, in the *Charlottesville Daily Progress*: RADICAL ARRESTED IN BOMBING CASE. He quickly scanned the article. The FBI had arrested Evan Bauer, a member of the Weather Underground sought for his role in a series of bombings of federal buildings in the early 1970s. Federal agents had hunted him down in New Mexico, where he had been hiding. A grainy photo showed Evan being escorted into the courtroom before his arraignment. He had lost most of his hair and had compensated by growing a bushy beard, but Dillon recognized him as Jill's friend from the past.

According to the article, Evan had spent six years on the run from the authorities, living under the assumed name of James Scott. He had kept on the move, residing in California, Oregon, and then New Mexico where he found work as a carpenter in Albuquerque. Dillon was surprised; the idea of Evan Bauer on a construction site with a hammer or a power saw didn't fit the intense young academic he remembered from Washington. FBI sources suggested that one of Evan's former SDS comrades had tipped off the Bureau to his location.

Evan had a young child and a girlfriend, a woman named Ava Stein, who he had met in New Mexico. She claimed to have known nothing of Evan's past, but told the Associated Press that whatever actions he had undertaken would have been justified by the immorality of the war. "It's the government that has committed criminal acts," she said. "Bombing innocent people. War crimes around the world. Even if he did what they say, Evan was only trying to stop that madness, to stop the war machine."

Dillon wondered if the news had reached Jill. Evan's journey from ambitious junior faculty member to hardened radical had been a strange one. It was the radicalization that Leigh had warned against. If not for Vietnam, would Evan have become James Scott, Weatherman, bomber, and terrorist? Instead of facing prosecution in federal court, and a lengthy prison sentence if convicted, Evan Bauer would have been boring undergraduates with windy lectures and amusing them with his clumsy attempts to appear hip.

* * *

Leigh's condition began to deteriorate rapidly in early March. It became clear to Dillon that he was not going to recover. His mind was still sharp, and he hadn't given up, but there were more and more days when he didn't come downstairs. He also began to talk openly about his own death.

It was hard for Dillon to see Leigh trapped in bed, his body shrinking, his face drawn and haggard. How could that be? He had always thought of his uncle as indestructible. At least they had time to say goodbye, and Dillon was grateful for that.

"I've few regrets," Leigh told him in one of their more somber conversations. "You've been like a son to me, so I don't regret not having children of my own. There are times when I wish I had remarried, but it wasn't meant to be."

"The Randolphs haven't had much luck with the ladies these days," Dillon said, hoping to lighten the mood. "You're not the only one."

"I pray that changes for you," Leigh said. "You should find a good woman. She's out there. You have to be open to the possibility."

"I haven't closed the door. I guess I do better with casual."

"Casual won't cut it. Not for the long term."

"We agree on that."

Leigh grinned. "At least we agree on some things." He kept his eyes on Dillon for a long moment. "I take it you're still thinking about what to do with Palmer's documents."

"I am."

"Well, you should follow your conscience, Dillon. That's the way to have fewer regrets."

"But you hate the idea."

"I do," he said. "But your motives are righteous—you want to honor a friend's request and you want to help set things right. In the end, only you can decide what to do. I believe that you'll make a decision you can live with."

* * *

Christ Church's pews were three-quarters full for Leigh's funeral service. Dillon knew most of those gathered for the service. Leigh's contemporaries were easy to spot—gray hair, wrinkled faces, hunched over men who wore dark business suits, now too big for their diminished frames, and frail women wearing outfits that were once stylish. There was a large contingent from McFarlin, Randolph & Woods, led by Charlie Woods. The employees of the firm, and many of its long-term clients, had turned out to bid farewell to Leigh.

Leigh had died in his sleep in the bedroom at Far Ridge that overlooked the back garden. His nurse had found him in the morning, and left a message for Dillon at the Alderman Library, where he was searching the stacks for an obscure book on Dante. After he had reached Far Ridge, Dillon called Charlie Woods, and together they made arrangements for the funeral and burial.

Charlie and Molly Woods and their children joined Dillon in the front. Dillon looked around the church, at the familiar pews and the stained-glass scenes of saints. As a young boy bored by lengthy sermons, Dillon had studied those figures for what seemed like a thousand times. He realized that much of his life was connected to Christ Church—his baptism, confirmation, marriage, and the funerals of his mother, brother, father, and now, his uncle. He knew that when his time came, there wouldn't be as many people gathered to mourn him, but he quickly rejected the thought as maudlin.

The eulogy was surprisingly stirring; it was clear that Reverend Stevens knew Leigh well enough to capture the essence of the man. He took as his text a passage from 2 Timothy: *For I am now ready to be offered, and the time of my departure is at hand. I have fought a good fight, I have finished my course, I have kept the faith.* Stevens talked about the good fights in Leigh's life, both public and private, and how he kept the faith until the very end.

As Dillon sat listening to the eulogy, his eyes closed, he thought about how much he had loved his uncle. Leigh had been a constant presence in his life—first, in helping to raise him and then as an adviser and friend. It was a hard loss. Dillon had been lonely before, but this seemed different. And it was.

Leigh had always counseled Dillon not to dwell on past failures and regrets. John Custis embraced the same philosophy. Randolphs always looked to the future. Now, in midlife, at the age of forty-six, Dillon wondered about the wisdom of that approach, about the limitations of an unexamined life. He hadn't handled the break-up of his marriage well, and the consequences included rarely seeing his thirteen-year-old daughter. He had shied away from lasting romantic relationships, worried that he would make the mistakes he had with Jill. And then there were his conflicted feelings about his time in Washington, and the unfulfilled obligation he had to Palmer. Why shouldn't he reexamine the past? Why shouldn't he think through the choices he had made, in the hopes of resolving what had remained unresolved.

He could make changes, he told himself. He would make changes.

* * *

A week after Leigh's funeral, Dillon took a spade from the garden shed and made his way to the sloping hill to the north of Far Ridge. He climbed the hill, keeping an eye for landmarks. He remembered that he had buried the canister with Palmer's papers under a large pine tree just past a rock outcropping.

It took him fifteen minutes to reach the spot. The cross that he had carved into the pine tree had faded, but it was still there. He stabbed at the ground in the place where he thought the canister would be. He encountered some resistance below the surface and thought he heard a metallic sound. He quickly began digging, tossing the dirt to the side. The spade hit something hard. Within minutes he had uncovered the canister.

He shook the dirt from the outside of the canister and carefully opened it. Inside, the bundle was intact—Palmer's documents were there, undisturbed from the day he had buried them, protected by having been wrapped in wax paper.

Dillon took a deep breath. He had struggled with what to do and had decided that following his conscience—as Leigh had recommended—meant providing the documents to the Church Committee. He couldn't live with himself if he stayed silent. He would not act impulsively, but he would not miss his chance. He owed that to Palmer, and to himself.

FORTY-FIVE

Washington, D.C.
Spring 1975

Dillon began therapy with Dr. Richard Jacobs, a graduate of the C.G. Jung Institute, at his offices near DuPont Circle. Dr. Jacobs was an affable man in his mid-sixties with a graying goatee and wire-rim glasses. He had a wry sense of humor, and Dillon had liked him from the start.

Every Wednesday afternoon, Dillon would drive from Charlottesville to Georgetown. He scheduled his appointment with Dr. Jacobs for an hour on Thursday morning. On Friday, Dillon would return to Far Ridge. He had decided to keep that schedule until he began teaching again in the fall.

Dr. Jacobs didn't say much during their initial sessions. In the beginning, he had asked Dillon what had brought him to seek psychotherapy and then had encouraged him to talk about whatever was on his mind. Dillon found it easier to unburden himself than he had expected. He told Dr. Jacobs about Leigh's death, and how it had made him think about the course of his life.

He found himself talking about the losses in his life. Leigh, his father, Wash, his mother, and the two women he had loved, Jill and Christa. In his weekly sessions, Dillon realized that he had never properly grieved over what he had lost. He had bottled up his feelings, his anger, and his pain. One afternoon, a few weeks into his therapy, he found himself crying, tears streaming down his face. Dr. Jacobs handed him a box of tissues.

"I hardly ever cry," Dillon said.

"But now you do," Jacobs said. "It is quite natural."

Dr. Jacobs encouraged Dillon to record any dreams when he awoke in the morning. Dillon discovered that the more he wrote down, the more he remembered, and the more likely he was to dream again. It was almost as if he had turned on a switch in his psyche, and his inner life had begun to surface when he slept.

His dreams were often a jumble of conflicting images. In one, Clay Blackburn, wearing his dress uniform, looked on as Dillon dug up the canister holding Palmer Knox's documents. In another, Jill and Sandy walked past him on a Georgetown street, ignoring him even as he called their names.

The therapy sessions often left him drained, but he believed that he was making progress, better understanding his emotional state, and how it had influenced some of his decisions in the past. By exploring what had been hidden territory, he hoped there would be insights that would help him not only to better navigate his daily life but also to face challenges in the future.

Meeting with Dr. Jacobs also convinced Dillon that he shouldn't wait to resolve the situation with Palmer's confession. It seemed the right moment, with the establishment of the Church Committee. He felt little fear about the consequences. Dillon had no desire to ever return to government service, so he didn't worry about damaging his career prospects. There was no reason to hesitate, or so he told himself.

* * *

It only took two phone calls before Dillon was able to connect with one of the lawyers for the Church Committee, a young staffer named Lamont Fox. Dillon explained that he had some information he wanted to share about illegal activity by the CIA in the early 1960s. When Fox pressed him for specifics, Dillon suggested they meet for a face-to-face discussion at the bar of the Willard Hotel.

Fox showed up twenty minutes late for their appointment. He wore a blue blazer, but no tie. His unruly reddish-blond hair spilled over his collar. Before the meeting, Dillon had called around to learn more about Fox. He had been a field organizer for the McGovern campaign in 1972 and had practiced public interest law before being recruited for the staff of the Church Committee. Lamont Fox was one of the new breed Democrats—he would have little use for the Democratic Party of John Custis and Leigh Randolph, a party forged during the New Deal and built on loyalty, local patronage, and mildly progressive politics.

Dillon began by explaining his background, his time at State, and how he had been in Washington during the Kennedy years. He had placed the envelope with Palmer's confession and the other documents on the marble top of the bar.

"I have something that might be of interest to your committee," he said, touching the envelope. "It's an account by a CIA officer of his involvement in various assassination schemes in the early sixties. Cuba and Vietnam. He called it his confession. There are some Agency documents that appear to back up his story."

"This officer." Fox paused. "Would he be willing to testify about this?"

"I should have been clearer. He's no longer alive. His name was Palmer Knox. He wrote what he called his confession shortly before his death in 1966. We were friends, and he made me the executor of his will." Dillon hesitated. "Palmer wanted his account to surface when it might do some good."

"And this account came into your possession in 1966?"

Dillon nodded. "You should also know that Palmer took his own life. He was never the same after he came back from Vietnam."

"Will it be possible to verify any of this?"

"Palmer was vague about dates and times, and most of the men involved are identified only by code names."

Fox frowned. "Not much to go on," he said. "We may be able to match up some of what he says with the information we already have." He paused. "And why have you waited nearly ten years to come forward?" Dillon didn't care for Fox's disapproving tone.

"And who was I supposed to approach? Your committee didn't exist. I tried through back channels to see if anyone in the State Department or White House would listen. No luck. So I filed the documents away. I figured that the day might come when they could be of use."

"You've waited for quite some time. The crimes of the intelligence agencies didn't end in 1966. Already, we've learned more about what the CIA was doing in Vietnam. Operation Phoenix. Targeted killing. They were throwing suspected Viet Cong out of helicopters. Torturing civilians. Barbaric actions." He looked over at Dillon. "Who spoke up? Who tried to stop it? No one. It's shameful. I'm not trying to assign blame, Mr. Randolph."

"But you are."

Fox shrugged. "Perhaps I am. You could have gone to the newspapers."

"I didn't. I always thought it was a matter best resolved within the proper channels."

"Proper channels?" Fox made a face. "Well, you have to live with your own conscience. The cost of your silence."

"I could have burned the documents years ago," Dillon said. "I didn't. I felt an obligation to Palmer. Now I want to fulfill it."

"How about an obligation to your country? To history? When this all comes out, there will be significant changes. We're going to clip the wings of the CIA and the FBI. Any of the agencies that are operating outside the law. What we've found so far is enough to turn your stomach. Assassination plots. Bribery. Illicit arms sales. Domestic wrongdoing. Opening mail without a warrant. The same for tapping phones. We're going to make sure that this never happens again."

"Good luck," Dillon said.

"What does that mean? You don't think that we can?"

"I applaud what you're doing. I hope that you can make progress on reforms. Checks and balances. More oversight. But I also know a bit about how power works. No one sets out to break the law or to commit crimes. They're given a mission, and they want to succeed. They want to please their boss. They discover they have to cut corners to do so. They rationalize that if they have to break the rules, it's for their country.

They won't let the perfect be the enemy of the good. They'll do whatever they have to in order to deliver results. And they're rewarded for that."

Fox stood up, shaking his head. "I hope that the day never comes when I'm as cynical as you. With all due respect."

"With all due respect, I hope that day never comes, too," Dillon said. "But I'm a realist, not a cynic."

Dillon stood up and handed the envelope to Fox.

"I'm turning this over to you," he said. "Do with it what you will. I'm willing to testify before the committee as to how the documents came into my possession if that's deemed necessary."

Fox took the envelope. "We'll review the material," he said. "If we have any questions, we'll call." He paused. "We're going to get to the bottom of what was going on, and when we do, we'll make sure that the world knows what we've learned. All of it."

FORTY-SIX

Washington, D.C.
Spring 1975

Lamont Fox did not contact Dillon in the weeks that followed. There were no phone calls from the Church Committee staff summoning Dillon to testify. When the public hearings began, he understood why he had been ignored—there was no shortage of evidence of CIA wrongdoing or of witnesses willing to tell their stories in front of the television cameras. In comparison, all Dillon could offer was a second-hand confirmation of what Palmer Knox had confided to him. Leigh had been correct—Palmer's confession lost its power when its author wasn't there to back up its claims.

Dillon found the revelations about the Phoenix Program particularly hard to take. CIA officials admitted sanctioning the killing of thousands of South Vietnamese suspected of being Viet Cong. The testimony validated what Palmer had told him about the excesses of the counterinsurgency program. Dillon saw it as a betrayal of the promise of the New Frontier. In his Inaugural Address, Jack Kennedy had outlined a foreign policy premised on American values of freedom and liberty. He signaled that he would move away from John Foster Dulles' dangerous policies of brinkmanship and massive retaliation and meet the challenge of Communism in Latin Africa, Africa, and Asia by winning the war of ideas. But that approach had been abandoned, cast aside in the name of expediency.

Dillon had been proud to serve in the State Department. There was honor in being a diplomat. There was honor in being a warrior. He didn't see how there was any honor in the Phoenix Program. Who could be proud of their involvement in it? He understood the argument that the ends—choking off support for the National Liberation Front—justified the means, but he rejected that as a form of sophistry. It reminded Dillon of the U.S. Army major who had told reporters that he had to destroy a Vietnamese village in order to save it. What did a campaign of targeted killings say to the local people about the values of the Americans and their ARVN allies?

He understood how it could have happened. The Kennedy brothers, impatient, reckless, surrounded by young men in a hurry, had been willing to turn a blind eye to the shortcuts. Dillon had been one of those young men, and he recognized the lure of the expedient. He realized that Alex Landauer had been correct—Dillon didn't have the stomach for it.

As painful as he found the testimony, Dillon thought the work of the Church Committee was necessary. Leigh had been wrong—hiding the sins of the past wouldn't allow for the necessary changes in policy and practice. The intelligence agencies needed to be reformed. Assassination shouldn't be a tool of American foreign policy. There had to be more Congressional oversight of the CIA and FBI. Who could deny that? Despite what he had told Lamont Fox, Dillon had hope that Congress would act decisively. He remembered what Winston Churchill once said, that he could always count on Americans to do the right thing after they'd tried everything else.

* * *

Dillon found that his sessions with Dr. Jacobs had a surprising, and unexpected effect—in part, prompted by the act of recording his dreams and talking about them, he felt drawn to begin writing verse again, to tell the story of what he had experienced during his time in Washington. Dillon purchased a slim notebook and began jotting down phrases and images. It had been years since he had felt such a strong urge to write—he had channeled his creative energies to translating the poetry of others.

In one sense, it was very simple. He had something to say and no longer felt blocked. When he looked back on his time in Main State, it was with a mixture of pride and shame. He believed that he and his colleagues in the Bureau and in Far Eastern Affairs had advocated sound policies, ones that could have meant a better future for the people of Vietnam. Despite the best of intentions, they had failed. Whether Dillon liked it or not, he had indeed been part of what Evan Bauer had called the war machine.

Dillon found himself quickly filling up his notebook. One memory would trigger another. The early days of the New Frontier, the palpable excitement and sense of near-limitless possibilities. The visits to Saigon, and the aftermath of the ambush on the road to Dong Xoai. His professional life in Washington, the bureaucratic fashioning of policy, so removed from reality. The March on the Pentagon and the faces of the alienated young protesters. And then there was the disarray of his personal life, a reflection of the chaos of those times.

There was a line that came to him one late afternoon on a long, meandering walk where he found himself on the steps of the Lincoln Memorial. He thought about Clay Blackburn, buried in Arlington National Cemetery across the Potomac: *Arlington's ghosts appear at dark*. He decided to begin with that line, and let the poem flow from there.

* * *

Vietnam's long civil war ended quickly. In the early spring, the North Vietnamese Army launched its final offensive, capturing the cities of Hue and Da Nang by the end of March. Some elements of the South Vietnamese Army fought bravely at Xuan Loc, but without American air support and resupply, cut off by a Congress tired of the war, the NVA quickly closed in on Saigon. Dillon watched with dismay the images of panicked Americans and Vietnamese fighting to board the helicopters leaving from the U.S. Embassy, of anarchy in the streets of Saigon, of crews on aircraft carriers pushing the arriving Chinooks off the deck into the South China Sea to make room for more aircraft.

After the conclusion of Operation Frequent Wind, the evacuation of Americans from the besieged capital, President Ford conceded that the war was over, and talked about closing a chapter in the American experience, about closing ranks, about avoiding recrimination about the past. Dillon wondered how easy that was going to be. The scars were deep and lasting.

Two days later, Dillon received a call from Clay Blackburn's sister Grace. She asked if she could drop by Far Ridge. "There's something of Clay's that he left for you," she said. "I'm a bit embarrassed because we only just found it."

Grace looked like her brother, with piercing blue eyes and high cheekbones. Dillon guessed that she was in her early thirties. They sat down in the living room with cups of coffee. "Clay told me that you didn't remember me from your graduation," she said. "I was a little girl, then. I remember you. The poet. That's what Clay called you."

She explained that she had returned to Charlottesville to help her mother tidy up the family home before they put it on the market. Grace found some boxes in the basement that had belonged to Clay. At the bottom of one box was an envelope. Clay had attached a note to it, saying that if anything ever happened to him, he wanted Dillon to have it.

"I'm sorry," she said. "My mother couldn't bear to go through his stuff after he died. It's been sitting in the basement all this time."

"I understand," he said.

He took the envelope from her and undid the clasp. Inside, there was a stack of photographs. He looked at the top picture—it was of him and Clay at the Caravelle Hotel, a photo taken by Isabel Lavalle. He showed it to Grace. "This was taken in Saigon in the winter of '64," he said. "It was my third and last visit to Vietnam."

"Clay looks so young," she said. "So do you."

"It seems like a million years ago."

"There are times when I can't believe he's gone," she said, tears welling in her eyes. "We begged him not to go back to Vietnam. I knew his luck would run out someday. The week that we lost him, I had a nightmare. In my dream, Clay was lying on a stone bier with his eyes closed and his hands clasped together over his chest. It reminded me of a storybook about the Knights Templar that Clay loved as a young boy. When I looked closer, there was blood on his hands, and I knew he had been wounded in the chest." She paused. "A day later there was an officer and a chaplain at our front door with the news that Clay had been killed. Later, I met one of Clay's men. He told me that my brother had been shot in the chest."

"'A dream itself is but a shadow.'"

"Where does that come from?"

"Shakespeare. Hamlet."

"You must know that Clay admired your family. Your older brother, the Marine captain. I think it was partly the reason Clay joined up. I wish he never had. He'd be here now. I know that's selfish, but I'd rather have a brother than a hero."

"I felt the same way when we lost Wash. It didn't seem right that a bunch of half-frozen peasants with machine guns could end his life. That didn't fit the script. But Clay told me the last time he was back that there were no heroes, just survivors. Some men were braver than others, but that everyone had their limits. The time to worry was when you weren't scared by incoming fire because that meant your adrenaline was all used up. Or you no longer cared."

Grace put her coffee cup down on the side table and sighed. "You know I'm a nurse at Walter Reed. The last few weeks have been very hard for the guys, the veterans. They're angry, and I can't blame them. They've been asking what was the point of all the fighting and dying if we were going to bug out? Why go in there in the first place? Some of them ask what will happen to the South Vietnamese. The ones who fought against the Communists."

Dillon shook his head. "The losers in a civil war pay a high price. After our Revolution was over, we didn't exactly treat the Tories with kid gloves. That's why so many went to Canada. It will be rough for the Vietnamese who helped us."

She frowned. "Why did we bother if we weren't going to fight to win? It certainly wasn't worth Clay's life. When we buried him at Arlington, there were crosses as far as you can see. All those young men, sacrificed for what?"

"I'm sorry about Clay," he said. "I regret whatever part I played in encouraging us to stay."

"I don't blame you because you were in the government, Dillon," she said. "I blame the people at the top. The President, the men around him."

"I was part of the system," he said, shaking his head. "I wrote the memos and the briefing papers for the men in the room with the President. And when I realized what we were doing was a terrible mistake, I didn't speak up. Not forcefully enough and not often enough. If I could go back, I'd change that. I only wish that I could."

FORTY-SEVEN

Washington, D.C.
Spring 1976

Dillon made sporadic progress on what slowly was evolving into a long poem about Vietnam. He had given it a fitting title, *District of Columbia*. It was Washington, after all, where policy was shaped, where decisions were made, where the powerful decided the fate of the powerless.

He wrote in stops and starts, and there were long stretches where he didn't work on the poem at all. He had learned to wait for the urge to write. He had to be in the right mood, and there were days and weeks where he couldn't bring himself to sit down with his notebook and typewriter.

In early March, he was distracted from his work by a segment he saw on the nightly news. A federal prosecutor in New Mexico had announced a plea bargain in the case against Evan Bauer. The felony charges had been dropped, and Evan had pled guilty to two misdemeanors involving identity fraud. Sources close to the prosecutor conceded that the government could not prove Evan's complicity in the Weather Underground bombing in question because crucial evidence had been obtained through illegal wiretaps. With credit for the time Evan had served, the judge set him free.

Evan had been interviewed briefly after the announcement. Dillon leaned forward and gave his full attention to the screen. "I want to teach again," Evan told the camera. "I believe that it represents a better avenue for social change. For the moment, at least." When he was asked whether he felt any remorse or regret, he raised his eyebrows. "Have you asked Robert McNamara or Dean Rusk or William Westmoreland whether they regret their crimes?"

The reporter repeated the question, and Evan stared at him. "I don't regret having resisted an immoral war. I'm sorry that people here might have been hurt, but I won't apologize for trying to stop American imperialism." He raised a fist. "Power to the people."

Dillon switched off the television set, disgusted, unwilling to watch any longer. Evan might imagine that he was some sort of revolutionary hero, but Dillon saw him as a misguided zealot with delusions of grandeur. The Weather Underground hadn't shortened the war by a single day—if anything its campaign of violence had prolonged the conflict by convincing Americans that Richard Nixon was right about the radical nature of the antiwar movement. Dillon thought of Yeats' line—*The best lack all conviction, while the worst are full of passionate intensity.* That was Evan Bauer, full of that passionate intensity, gripped by a twisted ideology, one that inevitably led to men with guns taking matters into their own hands.

* * *

The Church Committee issued its final report during the last week of April. Dillon procured a copy of it during one of his trips to Washington. He had followed the revelations of the Committee over the past year, as it documented wrongdoing by the intelligence agencies during every Administration from Roosevelt through Nixon. What they had uncovered was as astounding as it was disturbing. Coups engineered by the CIA in Iran and Guatemala during the Eisenhower years. The assassination plots during the Kennedy years. And domestic spying during the Johnson and Nixon Administrations with federal agents infiltrating the civil rights and antiwar movements.

He skimmed through the first several volumes of the report. It made for disquieting reading, to see the details of plots for assassinations and coups spelled out in black-and-white. Dillon wondered what the men named in the report thought of being exposed publicly. No doubt they had believed that their secrets would be kept. Now the world knew.

Later that afternoon, he went for a long walk. He suspected most Americans would read the newspaper accounts about the Committee's work, conclude that some bad things had happened in the past, and go on with their lives. He wondered how Leigh would have reacted to the extent of wrongdoing uncovered. It was more than Dillon had imagined, more prevalent, more institutionalized. The officials involved had been quick to resort to covert action, to violence, to achieve their ends. He was reminded of the old saw that over time the police began to resemble the criminals they were meant to watch over. Is that what had happened? Had American intelligence agencies started to mimic the tactics of the KGB? And where would that end?

Dillon recognized that there were times when clandestine operations were necessary. But employing assassination as a tool of foreign policy was beyond the pale, on both moral and practical grounds. Who knew what the consequences might be? Had the Cubans responded to the plots against Castro by guiding Lee Harvey Oswald to the sixth floor of the Texas School Book Depository? Or had the Mafia, recruited for the Cuban misadventures, settled its old score against the Kennedys? Or the nearly unthinkable—had rogue CIA officers, embittered over the Bay of Pigs, engineered the assassination?

Then there was the question of the domestic spying by the FBI and CIA, spying at a scale not seen since the Palmer Raids and the Red Scare just after the First World War. Federal agencies had repeatedly violated the civil rights of those opposing the government's policies. With what Dillon knew now, he was sure that the break-in at Far Ridge hadn't been an isolated operation, but one of many.

He didn't know whether the reforms advocated by the Church Committee would ever be adopted. Better Congressional oversight. The involvement of special courts. A tighter rein over the intelligence agencies. He was hopeful. At the same time, what mattered most to Dillon was that he had kept faith with Palmer Knox, however belatedly. He had done what he could.

* * *

Eleven months after the last helicopters had lifted off the roof of the U.S. Embassy in Saigon, Dillon was contacted by a State Department official by the name of Bowers. They spoke by phone, as Dillon was spending the week in Charlottesville.

"Hong Kong has asked for some guidance," Bowers explained. "There's a refugee from Vietnam claiming to know you. Says he was stationed in Washington in the sixties as an attaché and that you'll vouch for him. Name of Huy Dinh Dao. All he has to back up his story is an expired diplomatic passport."

"I can vouch for him," Dillon said. "I knew Dao in Washington when he was with the South Vietnamese Embassy. He was anti-Communist, a Diem supporter. I believe that he had a daughter going to school here. Wellesley. I remember that he didn't want her to return to Saigon."

"That matches what he has told us," Bowers said. "We were curious as to why he didn't get out when the going was good, in April of last year. He says he couldn't get to Saigon. We have some questions. How did he avoid the re-education camps? He doesn't have a convincing story about how he got from Saigon to Da Nang, and then onto a fishing boat. He was picked up in the South China Sea by a freighter. The boat was about to sink."

"What's your concern?"

"As you can imagine, we don't want the Reds infiltrating their people into the refugee flow."

"He's no Red. He's a Catholic, and I believe that his family came south after the Viet Minh took over the North. He's a nationalist. A patriot."

"You were aware that his brother is a North Vietnamese general?"

"Dao told me about him, years ago. Is that a surprise? It was a civil war, after all. Family members on different sides. They were estranged. But Dao's a resourceful man, and he may have leveraged family ties to get out." Dillon didn't say anything more. He assumed that Dao's brother had somehow assisted in his escape.

"So you don't believe that Dao could be under North Vietnamese control? Sent to spy on the other refugees?"

"Not the man I knew," Dillon said. "I don't think he would agree to that. I would be shocked if that was the case."

"So you think we should grant him refugee status?"

"If it were my decision to make, I would."

Bowers thanked him. "He certainly can't return to Vietnam, now," he said. "From all we can gather, conditions in the South are deplorable. We believe the North Vietnamese may have liquidated thousands of those who helped us, and put even more into the camps for brainwashing. Hundreds of thousands. Our diplomatic sources say that it's even worse in Cambodia with the Khmer Rouge. Mass killings. They're targeting the upper classes and the educated for liquidation. The same pattern you see whenever the Communists take over, but raised to a new extreme."

"If you could get a message to Dao, I'd appreciate it," Dillon said. "Let him know that if there's anything I can do, he should let me know. If he needs sponsorship. Or help for his daughter."

"That's quite generous. I'll pass it along to Hong Kong."

"It's the least I can do," Dillon said. "If our roles were reversed, I have no doubt that Dao would do the same for me. No doubt."

FORTY-EIGHT

Washington, D.C.
December 1980

Dillon regretted having agreed to the book launch party, but his publisher had pointed out that for a book of poetry entitled *District of Columbia*, it was only fitting that they hold the event in Washington. Dillon couldn't argue with that logic.

He had mailed invitations to his friends in Washington, and to the remaining members of the Group of Five. Jan Nowak wrote back that he would be overseas, traveling, but sent his best wishes. Grayson Talbott also sent regrets that he couldn't make it. Alex Landauer didn't respond to the invitation. Dillon figured that he harbored resentments from the past. They hadn't parted on the best of terms.

He also extended an invitation to Adriana Donati, a new faculty member at Emory & Henry where he had taught his poetry seminar the past two semesters. He had been curious about what it might be like to teach at a small liberal arts school. He found it a nice change of pace from teaching at Georgetown. The students were serious and welcoming, and the campus—tucked away in southwest Virginia—was a comfortable place.

He had been attracted to Adriana from the very first time that they met, to her dark Italian good looks and keen intelligence. They shared an interest in Dante, and he enjoyed her wry sense of humor about matters small and large. Dillon wasn't sure what she had thought of him, and he had been careful not to show too much interest. He didn't expect her to come to the book party, and he told her that when he handed her the invitation.

She shook her head. "I wouldn't miss it for the world, Dillon. I have a girlfriend in Washington I owe a visit, so I'll stop by your party on Friday and then stay for the weekend."

The party was held at the Mayflower Hotel in a small meeting room. As Dillon moved around the room, greeting his guests, he found himself scanning the small crowd, looking for Adriana. He was pleased when she arrived, and he immediately went over to welcome her. She wore an elegant black dress and had pinned her dark hair up, giving her a classic look.

"I'm delighted that you could make it," he said.

"I said I'd be here. I'm a woman of my word."

She stayed by his side as he introduced her to his Washington friends, and she proved quite adept at small talk. The room was filling up, and the waitresses busied themselves offering glasses of white wine and sparkling water and an assortment of hors d'oeuvres to the guests. Dillon and Adriana were left alone for a moment, and he found Adriana studying him carefully, a puzzled look on her face.

"You're not completely comfortable here, are you?" she asked.

"No, I'm not. But what makes you say that?"

"I've been watching. You're different here. Not like you are at school. I can see it in your face. And it shows in your posture. You're very stiff."

"Washington's not been a particularly happy place for me."

She grinned. "I've read the poem, Dillon, so I know that." She looked around at the small crowd. "I'll bet that I'm one of the few who has. Isn't that always the case at book parties?"

"Ouch," he said. "A blow to my vanity. But you're right."

"It's a shame, because it's quite marvelous, your poem."

"Thanks," he said. "Coming from you, that's quite a compliment. It counts more than the praise I'll hear tonight from people who've just glanced at the book jacket."

Lily Taylor, one of the publicists from the publishing house, took Dillon by the arm and guided him to a lectern at the front of the room. She tapped her wine glass lightly with a spoon, and the room quieted. Lily explained that Dillon would read from *District of Columbia* and sign copies of the book afterward.

"I wanted to thank you all for coming," Dillon began. "It's been almost twenty years since my last book party. I'm a different person, a different poet, and it's a different country. That's what *District of Columbia* is about. What has happened in those two decades." He put his reading glasses on and smiled. "And I didn't need these twenty years ago." He opened his copy of the book and began to read.

> *Arlington's ghosts appear at dark*
> *They float o'er white crosses and granite slabs*
> *Pleased with the grisly harvest beneath*
> *Generals, privates, a president and his brother, congregate*
> *A different kind of body count*
> *A silent rebuke to the mighty*
>
> *Across the Potomac, voices and fists are raised*
> *Hey, Hey, LBJ. How many kids did you kill today?*
> *What price victory? What price peace?*
> *Hell, no we won't go*
> *Ho Ho Ho Chi Minh, NLF is gonna win*
> *And the killing fields await*
>
> *Now there are only ghosts and echoes*
> *Who remains to tell the tale?*
> *Not the boat people, lost at sea*
> *Not the re-educated, lost in the camps*
> *Not the whiz kids, nor New Frontiersmen*
> *Guilty silence rules the District of Columbia*

When he looked up from the page, there was a long silence. Then someone in the back began clapping, and there was polite applause.

"This was a difficult poem to write," Dillon said. "I started and stopped several times over the past ten years. It meant dredging up some painful memories. I finally did get it down on paper. Now, if you'll indulge me for a few minutes more, I'll read the last stanza, because I'd like to end on a more hopeful note."

He found the bookmark at the end of the volume and turned to it.

> *This gentle man, carved in granite*
> *Face creased with lines of pain*

He gazes across a chastened city
A people reckoning the cost of war
Time for truth, time for tears
Time for atonement, heartfelt and clear

He heard a few people sigh, and he closed the book, blinking back tears. Then there was applause again, louder this time. Dillon stepped away from the lectern.

To his surprise, the first person who came up to him was Alex Landauer, who took him by the elbow and steered him to a corner of the room.

"I purchased a copy yesterday and read it," he said. "All of it. I wanted to come and tell you that. It spoke to me, Dillon. I didn't expect that. It was a very dark time, wasn't it? We learned the hard way about the limits of power."

"Did we?"

"I certainly did. I've thought a lot about it. How we got off track. What signs we missed. How we could have been so wrong. McNamara realized that the war was unwinnable in '67. They say he was crying at his desk, distraught over all of the killing. By November, he had announced his resignation. Then the job at the World Bank. A chance at redemption. In his mind, at least."

"And you?"

"I turned against the war shortly after," Alex said.

"Not that soon," Dillon said. "You gave me the party line the day after the March on the Pentagon. October '67. Don't you remember?"

"I remember. I didn't want to admit my doubts to you. Perhaps not to myself. I thought we were turning the corner. Then, Tet happened. It made me see things clearly. The generals had assured us that we were close to victory. They were either lying to us or deluded. Or perhaps both. That was the straw that broke the camel's back for me. I recognized the ends couldn't be justified by the means. That's when I began speaking out against the war. The folly of it. After I returned to Cambridge." He paused. "I've been consulting with Carter's people at Defense, you know. When Reagan and his cowboys take over in January, that will come to an end."

"I owe you an apology," Dillon said. "I know that you didn't call the FBI about the documents Palmer left me. I'm sorry that I accused you of that."

"No hard feelings. To tell you the truth, I did consider calling them. I decided not to because I didn't think you would take the risk in the end. You're not the type to do something that foolish."

"I did do something," Dillon said. "I gave Palmer's papers to the Church Committee. I regret that I waited so long before I did something with them."

"I don't believe in regrets. Never have." Alex offered his hand, and Dillon shook it. "I've got to go. Catch the shuttle to Boston."

Dillon watched as Alex made his way toward the exit and wondered how much he had changed. If he didn't have any regrets, did Alex at least recognize his complicity in the mistakes of Vietnam? Was he more likely to question his own assumptions? Less confident that he had the answers? Perhaps, like Robert McNamara, Alex had learned some lessons. Perhaps the day would come when he would feel a greater remorse over his past.

Dillon heard his name being called and turned to find an elderly Asian man standing near him, a copy of *District of Columbia* in his hands. He recognized him immediately—it was Huy Dinh Dao. Dao's hair had turned white, and his face creased with wrinkles. He was dressed in a dark suit and wore wire-framed glasses.

Dao bowed slightly and smiled. "Dillon Randolph. It has been many years."

"I'm honored that you would come."

Five years ago, after Dao had reached the United States, he and Dillon had exchanged several letters. Dao had lived in Southern California for a few years, and then had moved to Roslyn where he had opened a Vietnamese restaurant. He had invited Dillon to the restaurant opening, but Dillon had been traveling and couldn't make it—he had sent a floral arrangement and a note of congratulations, instead.

"I read about this book party in the newspaper. I didn't want to miss the chance to see you, and thank you. I can't stay long." Dao looked around the room. "I have responsibilities. To the restaurant."

"I see. Thank you for coming."

"I have read your poem. It brought back many memories for me of my time in Washington. It helped me understand better what happened." Dao handed the slim volume to Dillon. "Will you please sign it for me?"

After he had signed the title page, Dillon gave the book back to Dao. "I thought of our conversations over lunch many times," he said. "You saw the future more clearly than I. What would happen."

"I take no comfort in being correct," Dao said. "Losing the war has been a tragedy for my country. What the Communists have done since. I have wondered if there could have been a different resolution. A neutral country? A coalition government?" He shook his head slowly. "I know that is a dream. It could never have happened. There was only one destiny possible for us."

"I have to agree reluctantly," Dillon said. "I wish there had been a different ending."

"I have never properly thanked you," Dao said. "For vouching for me after I left my country."

"There is no need to thank me. You would have done the same for me if you were in my place."

Dao pressed a business card into Dillon's hands. "I have happy news to report. My daughter, Linh, do you remember her?"

Dillon nodded.

"She graduated from Georgetown," Dao said. "The Law School. Now, Linh will be working for the State Department."

"Congratulations," Dillon said. "I'm happy for you and your daughter."

Dao gave him another slight bow, shook his hand, and left.

Adriana came over to him. "You have very nice friends," she said. "They think the world of you, you know. Can't say that I'm surprised." She took a step closer, and he caught the scent of her Chanel perfume. "So what do you have planned for the weekend?"

"I'm going to drive to Charlottesville tonight," he explained. "Spend the weekend there."

"You really don't want to stay here any longer than necessary, do you?"

Dillon nodded. He didn't care for the memories that being in Washington surfaced, nor for the changes in the city, the recently-constructed steel and glass buildings, the congested roads, the traffic. He felt like a stranger.

"I've never been to Charlottesville," she said.

"It's home," he said. He paused, wondering if he should act on impulse, and then decided to ask her to join him. "If you're curious about what it's like, you're welcome to drive back with me. We have guests who stay with us all the time. We've got several spare bedrooms. We can drive to Emory on Sunday." He felt himself blushing. "Of course, I'm sure you have plans with your friend."

"How could I turn down that invitation?" she asked, her lips curved in a slight smile. "Sophie will understand."

"Our house, Far Ridge, is a bit of a white elephant. You'll see. Too many rooms. It's expensive to maintain, and I end up rattling around in it when I stay there, but I can't see my way to giving it up."

"You are attached to it," she said.

"It's home."

"I'd like to see your Far Ridge," she said. "I can collect my overnight bag from my friend's place, and we can leave whenever you'd like."

* * *

They talked at length, quietly, during the drive from Washington to Charlottesville. He knew a fair amount about her academic career, but little about her life story. Adriana had come to the United States for her doctorate in linguistics at Columbia. She had always wanted to live in New York City.

She had been engaged to a fellow graduate student, a friendship that had become a romance. "At one point, I was living in Italy, and he was living in New York," she said, tilting her head to look at Dillon. "He met someone else, an undergraduate. A cliché, I know, the adoring younger woman. Samuel wanted to be looked up to, I think. It didn't come as a great surprise. We had our issues."

Dillon told her briefly about his marriage and his on-and-off-again relationship with his daughter. "Sandy just started at UCLA. I try to stay in touch, but it's difficult. Her mother doesn't encourage contact. Not how I'd like it, but I've had to accept it. When Sandy is older, I hope that she'll be willing to reengage."

"And you did not remarry?"

"It's been twelve years since the divorce. I've had a few little romances. Nothing serious. I wasn't looking to get married. That narrows the field. I was seeing someone last year, but it ended. Mutually."

"And have you been lonely?"

"There were times when I was. But I had my work, and I would come to Charlottesville for the holidays and weekends. I have some wonderful friends here. People I grew up with."

When they arrived at Far Ridge, there were no lights on in the house, and its bulk loomed above them in the dark. A cool breeze from the south swept through the nearby oak trees. Dillon fumbled with the keys at the front door, and once he had opened it, he was able to hit the switches for the front foyer and living room lights.

"Quite impressive," she said. "A beautiful old house."

"I've always loved it," he said.

They were startled by the sound of the grandfather clock chiming on the hour—it was eleven o'clock.

"Sorry," Dillon said. "One of the cleaning women must have wound it up." He paused. "Shall I make us some tea? And a fire?"

He went into the living room and quickly moved some of the wood stacked nearby into the fireplace. With a rolled-up copy of the *Daily Progress* for kindling, he started a fire. Dillon made some tea, and they sat on the couch together, sipping from their mugs, enjoying the warmth of the fire. He was careful not to move too close to her or to signal romantic interest. He wanted to make love to her, but he held back. If his advance proved unwelcome, it would jeopardize their friendship. She seemed attracted to him, but did she want him as her lover? He could wait. That was one of the advantages of experience; there was no need to force the issue.

"It's been a long day," she said.

"I'll show you upstairs to your bedroom. There's a bathroom nearby, and there should be clean towels and washcloths if you want to take a shower or bath." He stood up and began to move toward the foyer where he had deposited her suitcase

She stopped him with a touch on his arm. "There's no need for us to play games, Dillon," she said. "I'd rather keep you company in your bed than sleep alone. Would you like that?"

"You know that I would," he said. "You are so beautiful. Luminously so."

He leaned in and kissed her softly on the lips. She kissed him in return, pressing her lips against his.

"I've wanted to kiss you all night," he said.

"*Il bacio sta all'amore come il lampo al tuono,*" she said. She unpinned her hair, letting it fall to her shoulders. "The kiss is to love, as lightning is to thunder."

* * *

Dillon woke at first light. He shifted in bed and glimpsed Adriana's raven-colored hair spilling over the pillow next to him. He studied her for a moment, listening to her rhythmic breathing, marveling at the beauty of her exposed shoulder.

She shifted around, her arms moving, but her eyes remained shut. Dillon kissed her on the shoulder, lightly, and when she stirred, he kissed the nape of her neck.

"That's a nice way to wake up," she said, her voice husky with sleep.

"Good morning," he said. "Shall I make us some coffee?"

She rolled over and faced him, a smile on her face. "I can think of some things we could do first."

"I like that idea very much."

They made love again, looking into each other's eyes. There was no awkwardness between them. Afterward, they lay together in the bed holding hands, legs touching.

"I have read your other poems," she said. "I was curious about you, Dillon Randolph, from the start. The first one, *Cedar Creek*, the poem about the Civil War, was quite different. Your connection to the past, to the past of your family."

"That was my poem of memory," he said.

"And *The Island City*?"

"Love lost."

"Yes. It made me want to know you better. And I might not have accepted the ride from you if I hadn't learned about you from the poems, about the way you see the world."

"Last night has changed things," he said. "I'd like to keep seeing you. I hate the idea of letting you out of my sight."

"There's little danger of that," she said. "It's a very small campus."

"And you? How do you feel?"

"Yes, Dillon, I want this to be more than a fling. I'm willing to take the risk."

"The risk?" He was puzzled.

"The risk that you might break my heart."

"No less a risk for me," he said. "No less. But a risk well worth taking."

EPILOGUE

Washington, D.C.
December 1989

They left Far Ridge on Friday morning and made the drive to Washington in a misty rain. The traffic heading east was light, and Dillon and Adriana took turns behind the wheel. He had made reservations at the Hays-Adams Hotel for them to stay the weekend. They would have dinner with Jan Nowak at his apartment that night and the next day visit the National Mall and the Vietnam War Memorial and its stark long stone wall.

Dillon had never been to the Wall and walked its length. He had passed by on Constitution Avenue a few times since its dedication seven years earlier, but he hadn't stopped and joined the throngs of visitors drawn to the dark granite memorial.

Jan had expressed surprise when the topic came up as they were relaxing with drinks after dinner. He was on his second glass of wine. Jan's hair had thinned, and he had packed on twenty pounds since gaining tenure at American University. Other than some pudginess in his cheeks, he carried his weight well.

"You've never been to the Wall?" he asked. "Not even once? It's quite something, Dillon. Very powerful in its own way as a symbol."

Dillon shook his head. "Since I sold my Georgetown place, I haven't come back to the city very often. I guess I wasn't ready for it. Too many bad memories. Some guilt, if I'm honest. I feel that I should have done more. Said more. When I resigned from State, I should have gone public with my opposition to the escalation of the war."

Jan nodded. "I understand. Who doesn't have regrets? The first time I went to the Wall, I looked for the name of a high school buddy. Raul Martinez. Happy-go-lucky kid. He was killed at Khe Sanh in '68. When I found his name, it hit me hard, seeing it carved in stone. It made it real, again."

"I'm glad that Dillon has decided to go, now," Adriana said. "I've encouraged him."

"But why now, if I can ask?" Jan asked, directing the question to Dillon.

Dillon glanced over at Adriana before he answered. "It seemed the right time. We were there the night the Berlin Wall came down. I'd never experienced anything like it. It's hard to put into words. But it resolved some things for me. About what all of us in the Foreign Service were doing there, about whether we had done the right things."

"That night was amazing," Adriana said. "The young people dancing and singing, and chipping away at the concrete, smashing it with hammers and chisels. They were so happy. Exhilarated. Liberated. And then the next few days all the East Berliners wandering around the Ku'damm, peering into those sidewalk display cases, marveling at all the luxury goods, the jewelry and shoes and frocks. And the West Berliners greeting them as long-lost family."

They had been vacationing in England when Dillon had seen the BBC footage of the demonstrations in East Berlin, and suggested to Adriana that they fly to Berlin. He had not been back to Germany in nearly thirty years.

That historic night, they had hitched a ride from the Savoy Hotel in Charlottenburg to the center of the city with a young American journalist from the *Christian Science Monitor* and his colleague, a British photographer. It had been a wild scene after the East Germans opened the border crossings and had, for all intents and purposes, conceded that they could no longer keep their people imprisoned.

The visit to Berlin had stirred memories for Dillon, some of them surprisingly vivid. For the first time in years, he had thought about Christa, and it spurred him to wonder what it might have been like if he had stayed and they had made a life together. The visit also reminded him of the swift, inexorable, passage of time, how the days and weeks slipped by, and before long years had flown by, leaving himself, as Dante wrote, "in the middle of his journey, in a dark wood." Writing *District of Columbia* had helped him cope with some of his conflicting feelings about his involvement in the war, but he still struggled with flashes of anger and remorse.

"After Berlin, I realized that I had been avoiding *our* Wall," Dillon told Jan. "Visiting it is a way of closing the circle for me."

"The sixties are ancient history, now," Jan said. He ran his hand through his thinning hair. "Many of my students were toddlers during Vietnam. I try to give them some context. What we were thinking at the time. Otherwise, we look like we were blind, deaf, and dumb. And we weren't. Momentarily blinded, perhaps." He turned to Adriana. "Dillon and I were in the process of leaving the government when Johnson moved toward a full-scale escalation of the war. Sending American combat troops. That doesn't absolve us completely from what happened, although I believe that if President Kennedy had lived, he would never have allowed us to plunge into the quicksand."

"I don't know," Dillon said. "Jack Kennedy saw it as a noble cause. We all did. Part of the struggle against Communism. In the beginning, we believed we were on the side of the angels."

"And the antiwar protesters thought we were devils. I do point out to my students that once Nixon Vietnamized the war and stopped drafting so many young Americans, the rallies and marches and teach-ins stopped. Then, Watergate, and Congress cut off the money for the South Vietnamese military." Jan took a sip of his wine. "Of course, our leaving didn't end the bloodletting. It got worse after. More innocents died in Southeast Asia at the hands of Communists after we left than during the war. So much for the peace-lovers in Hanoi. More than a million South Vietnamese herded into re-education camps or New Economic Zones. Hundreds of thousands of boat people. Cambodia, a nightmare. The killing fields of the Khmer Rouge."

"What do they say when you tell them this?" Adriana asked. "Your students?"

"They're silent. They don't know what to say. I understand. Last week President Bush and Mikhail Gorbachev more or less announced the end of the Cold War when they met in the Mediterranean. My students can't appreciate the existential nature of the conflict. They don't know what it was like during the Cuban Missile Crisis when we wondered if the world was going to end in a day or two. Or the showdown in Berlin. That's the context. But who wants to look back? The kids I teach certainly don't."

"And your regrets?" Adriana asked.

"Regrets?" Jan shrugged. "Could it have ended differently? Success, like the British in Malaya? Or if Diem had stayed in power? Had we avoided sending Americans into combat? Who knows? It's unlikely but possible. We were so full of ourselves. So certain we could bend the arc of history."

"So there is a point to telling the story to your students," Dillon said. "If we don't look back, will we repeat the mistakes? Let's say Gorbachev is on the level, and the Cold War is ending. We'll be the one superpower left standing. The winner. Won't we be tempted to throw our weight around? Thinking that we can decide the future for others?"

"Let's worry about that once we've reached agreement with the Russians," Jan said. "Keep the nuclear genie in the bottle with the lid tightly screwed on. That's what we need, now. A chance to integrate the East into Europe. Moscow, too."

Dillon shook his head. "It's a cliché, but power corrupts. Good intentions aren't enough. Isn't the road to hell paved with them?"

Jan laughed. "I'm not sure about the road to hell, but the road to Washington certainly isn't. You need lots of campaign contributions for that."

* * *

In the morning, they had a light breakfast, and Dillon and Adriana read the newspapers over their cups of coffee. The *Washington Post* carried several stories about the ongoing political turmoil in Eastern Europe.

They walked to the Mall with umbrellas they had borrowed from the hotel. It was a chilly, gray day, and Lafayette Park was deserted as they passed by. Their route took them around the Ellipse, the White House to their right, the Washington Monument to the left. There were only a few tourists about—a function of the weather and the time of the year. They made their way toward the Lincoln Memorial, walking at a brisk pace with Constitution Avenue to their right.

There was a sign posted at the entrance to the Vietnam Memorial, warning that the pathway ahead could be slippery. Dillon was surprised by the Wall. The photos he had seen didn't reflect its relatively small scale. He had expected something more monumental. The polished black granite that made up the Wall was etched with thousands of names. There were a few flowers, letters, placards, and other memorials left at the foot of the Wall. Dillon took Adriana's hand, and they walked slowly down the deserted pathway.

Adriana hung back as Dillon moved closer. The names were arranged by the date of death. It didn't take long for him to find the name he was searching for, etched in the black granite: CLAYTON BLACKBURN. He touched the name, his fingertips running over the letters. He remembered the last time he and Clay had met, in Washington, and how his friend had thought that the tide might be turning. He had been wrong.

Every name etched in the stone represented a discrete tragedy. There were missing names—the survivors whose lives had been forever altered, the walking wounded in mind and body. Palmer Knox and the others like him. And then there were the Vietnamese, the hundreds of thousands if not millions who had died in the long war, and those who had perished in the aftermath, in the brutal prison camps of the victors or in the waters of the South China Sea. To say nothing of the killing fields of Cambodia.

"Are you glad that we came?" Adriana asked.

"I am. It helps to close a chapter in my life. I keep thinking about what Jan said last night. I have more regrets than he does, I imagine. It was more theoretical for him. He never went over there. I was closer to it. Perhaps because of Palmer Knox. Clay. Dao. The people I knew whose lives were devastated by the war. In the end, it comes down to the personal. What has touched you."

"*La storia si ripete*," she said. "It has been the same throughout history. Men fighting for their country or for a cause. It's the human condition.

The only question you must answer is whether you fought for the right reasons, for the good cause."

"In Berlin, I felt that I had," he said. "Vietnam is different. We were so arrogant. Noble intentions, or at least I thought so at the time. But did we open Pandora's Box? That's what my uncle always thought."

Adriana pointed over at the Lincoln Memorial. "Can we go there?" she asked. "You've told me you like to stop there."

They left the pathway behind, and passed the sculpture of the Three Soldiers, solid bronze figures staring forlornly into the near distance. The rain had let up, and it felt slightly warmer. As they approached the Lincoln Memorial, Dillon remembered how it had looked on the Saturday of the March on the Pentagon, the tidal pool ringed by demonstrators, the platform for speakers constructed on the steps, the banners and signs, the sense of growing frustration and anger.

Now, a group of Girl Scouts in their green uniforms clustered on the steps, facing their parents who were taking photos. They smiled and laughed, mugging for the cameras. Dillon imagined that they might be from out-of-town, on a field trip to Washington, excited to be in the capital and visiting the famous monuments they had read about in history class.

He found tears welling in his eyes as they took in the scene. "They're the future," he said. "They can start over, leave the past behind where it belongs. No need to be burdened by our mistakes. And then, anything will be possible. As long as they have hope, and faith. That's all they need."

"You are a decent man, Dillon Randolph," Adriana said. "It's why I love you." She took his hand in hers. "Let's go home tonight, *amore mio*. To Far Ridge."

"Are you sure? We can always stay the night and visit the museums in the morning like we planned. We don't get here that often."

"No, Dillon. Tonight, if you wouldn't mind."

He thought about the drive ahead of them, how the suburbs would give way to the Virginia countryside, the fields and fences and strips of woodland, how they would encounter valleys and then foothills as they got closer to Charlottesville.

When they reached Far Ridge, he would take a moment to stand on the back porch and take in the night sky, the stars shining brightly overhead—no city glare to dim them—and the familiar eastern white pines and red cedars on the hill to the north. When they went to bed, would his sleep be troubled? Would their visit, and all the memories it stirred, surface in his sleep. Who would appear? Clay. Jill. Palmer Knox. Dao. Leigh. John Custis. What would he dream? Or would the night pass without incident, dreamless?

He wondered if they would get frost in the morning. Perhaps even snow flurries. He would like that, the ridge to their north covered, the trees frosted in white. It would truly feel like home.

AUTHOR'S NOTE

Those of us who write historical fiction sometimes face questions about the accuracy of our descriptions of the past. How much is true? How much invented? I've always felt an obligation to hew closely to the historical facts in my novels, to tell stories that don't distort, to illuminate the truth of the past as best I can.

While *District of Columbia* is a work of imagination, I've tried to stick to the historical record. I think the novel fairly reflects the concerns and controversies of the time, including the debate in Washington over Vietnam policy. The Pentagon Papers demonstrated that our leaders repeatedly deceived the American people about the progress of the war, and the prospects for success. I think *District of Columbia* accurately captures that dynamic.

What of the wrongdoing by our intelligence agencies during the 1960s and 1970s? Again, I've kept to the public record. The Church Committee exposed the sordid details of the CIA assassination plots targeting Fidel Castro and others, and the widespread abuse by the FBI with its surveillance programs targeting civil rights leaders and antiwar protesters.

Some of the history of our involvement in Vietnam remains contested. Had Jack Kennedy lived, would he have chosen the path of escalation? He had resisted sending combat troops to Vietnam, although there were some 16,000 military advisers in the country by the end of 1963. Would he have accepted the advice of his National Security Advisor, McGeorge Bundy, the Joint Chiefs, and the American commanders on the ground in Vietnam that only the intervention of U.S. troops could avert defeat? Would he have felt compelled to act, partly in guilt over American complicity in the overthrow of the Diem regime?

What is incontestable, however, is the tragic nature of our involvement. It was a poorly chosen battlefield in the struggle against totalitarianism. The mistake began with Jack Kennedy's initial decision to prop up the Diem regime and was compounded by Lyndon Johnson's escalation of the war. Extending the conflict cost the lives of millions in Indochina, before and after the American exit in 1975.

* * *

The literature on the Vietnam War is voluminous (and growing). I turned to contemporary accounts whenever possible.

In describing the attack on the road to Dong Xoai, I drew heavily on Associated Press correspondent Malcolm W. Browne's account of a similar ambush in *The New Face of War*. For life in Saigon for American civilians, *Station Hospital Saigon: A Navy Nurse in Vietnam, 1963-1964* by Bobbi Hovis proved helpful.

Among the many books I consulted on the Washington scene in the early 1960s, *A Thousand Days*, historian Arthur Schlesinger Jr.'s wonderful firsthand account of the Kennedy years provided insights from an insider on the decision-making process in the White House. I also found helpful Roger Hilsman's *To Move a Nation: The Politics of Foreign Policy in the Administration of John F. Kennedy*, Thomas J. Schoenbaum's *Waging Peace & War; Dean Rusk in the Truman, Kennedy and Johnson Years*, and *The War Council: McGeorge Bundy, the NSC, and Vietnam* by Andrew Preston.

Norman Mailer's *The Armies of the Night: History as a Novel, the Novel as History* and *Miami and the Siege of Chicago: An Informal History of the Republican and Democratic Conventions of 1968* offered a colorful picture of the antiwar movement; Mark Rudd's *Underground: My Life with SDS and the Weathermen* illuminated the dark corners of that movement.

This novel was not the easiest to write. I want to thank Glenn Speer and Julie Flanders for their encouragement during my creative struggles, and Colin Macdonald and Tony and Clayton Flanders for their insights as advance readers.

Any errors of historical fact or flaws in interpretation are mine alone.

And as always, my gratitude for the support, understanding, and patience of my family.

ABOUT THE AUTHOR

Jefferson Flanders has been a sportswriter, columnist, editor, and publishing executive. He is the author of the First Trumpet trilogy, set in the early years of the Cold War, and of *An Interlude in Berlin*.

www.ingramcontent.com/pod-product-compliance
Lightning Source LLC
Chambersburg PA
CBHW020511260626
47156CB00006B/1962